AN ENDLESS CORNISH SUMMER

For Rose, every day is a gift. She narrowly survived a life-threatening illness and owes everything to her anonymous bone marrow donor. Determined to thank him, Rose follows a trail of clues that lead her to the little Cornish fishing village of Falford.

But things become complicated when Rose is drawn into local life, getting involved in the legendary Falford Regatta, and meeting the handsome Morvah brothers — one of whom might just be the man she's looking for. But which one?

Can Rose find the answer she's searching for, or will she lose her heart before the summer is over?

PHILLIPA ASHLEY

◆

AN ENDLESS CORNISH SUMMER

Complete and Unabridged

CHARNWOOD
Leicester

First published in Great Britain in 2021 by AVON
A divison of HarperCollins*Publishers* Ltd
London

First Charnwood Edition
published 2022
by arrangement with
HarperCollins*Publishers* Ltd
London

*A catalogue record for this book is available
from the British Library.*

ISBN 978–1–4448–4794–9

Published by
Ulverscroft Limited
Anstey, Leicestershire

Printed and bound in Great Britain by
TJ Books Ltd., Padstow, Cornwall

This book is printed on acid-free paper

For the Cambridge COG UK team
With thanks

Prologue

'OK, love?' Rose's gran waved through the window of the isolation ward. Granny Marge hadn't moved from her post outside for the past two hours.

She wasn't able to enter the sterile room where Rose was lying in bed. At seventy-nine years old, and not in the best of health herself, Marge had often remarked that she should have been the one lying in the hospital bed. Yet it was Rose who was vulnerable.

Rose's mother Stella would be back in a moment — maybe. She'd come over from California on a rare visit to see her daughter before the transplant. She'd gone for a coffee — another one. Rose knew she couldn't cope and needed an excuse.

Rose understood that it was hard to deal with someone being so ill, especially your own daughter, even if you'd grown apart over the years. Rose's mother had been on the threshold of a glittering career as a TV producer when she'd become pregnant with Rose after a one-night stand. Her father had been an actor, apparently, and Stella hadn't even had time to tell him about Rose before he'd been killed in a motorcycle accident, after a night of drinking.

Stella had come back to the UK to have Rose, but returned to America when she'd been offered a dream job on a long-running series. Rose had stayed in the UK, and her mother had provided for her financially, coming home when she could.

It was Granny Marge who had taken on much of the responsibility for bringing Rose up. Stella had wanted

1

her to go to school in an English village and have the stability that staying with her grandmother could bring. Rose had missed her mum, but she'd enjoyed being at school in England and had been excited to get a place at Cambridge to study archaeology, which had made her gran almost burst with pride. Rose's late grandfather had been a librarian and was very keen on history. Sadly, he had passed away when Rose was still at nursery school but one of her few recollections of him was being taken to a castle by the sea. They'd arrived by boat, she recalled, but the rest of her memory of him was hazy. Her grandad had sailed them there and Rose had later discovered it had been St Mawes Castle in Cornwall. He'd loved to sail in his spare time but had died before he could teach Rose.

Granny Marge spoke of him often and fanned the flames of Rose's own passion for the past, especially ancient worlds. It helped that there were books everywhere in the cottage, spilling out of bookcases, piled up by beds and stacked by sofas like literary Jenga blocks.

Eventually, Rose had studied A-level history at the local high school, and, encouraged by her gran, had applied to read archaeology at Cambridge. To her amazement, she'd got a place. She'd never forget the day she walked into the college hall, dressed in a black gown and carrying her mortar board. She'd half-expected to find Professor Dumbledore waiting at the High Table to welcome her and the other students. In reality, it was a woman about her mother's age with green hair and a Geordie accent.

Rose resolved to make the most of her opportunity and one day, perhaps, stand in front of a new intake of freshers herself, ready to teach them the wonders of archaeology.

The thought of those happy — naive — times brought back bittersweet memories. She'd no idea, then, of the storm waiting beyond the horizon. It was several years later before she'd begun to feel ill and more until she got a final diagnosis.

At first, she'd expected them to tell her they knew exactly what was wrong with her and how to treat it, but it had taken months to diagnose her condition as aplastic anaemia.

'That doesn't sound so awful,' her gran had said, sitting by her side. 'Lots of people are anaemic. You can sort that out, can't you?'

The consultant's brief, kind smile had given Rose the answer even before she'd explained. Besides, Rose had been on Dr Google too many times not to realise what her symptoms could mean . . . what the worst-case scenario was.

'Aplastic anaemia isn't the same as other types, I'm afraid,' the consultant had told her gently. 'It means your bone marrow isn't making any of the blood cells your body needs to function healthily, which is why you're feeling so tired and light-headed.'

'Does that explain the bruises and headaches?'

'Yes, it does.'

Rose remembered her gran's hand tightening around her own, hurting her fingers as the consultant went on to explain that she would need a bone marrow transplant — also called a stem cell transplant — or her condition would deteriorate and that without one, the outcome wouldn't be good. Rose knew what that meant. She could — would — die without a transplant.

'I can donate my stem cells!' her mother had said

3

when the news had been broken via phone call.

'You're too old, Mum,' Rose had explained. 'I don't have any close relatives so I'll probably have to hope there's a match on a global register.'

Her gran had managed to contact several second cousins and anyone of the right age in the village, while Rose's best friend Maddie had organised a campaign to get all her student friends to be tested. No one proved a match, so Rose had no choice but to hope for someone from the bone marrow donation register. She'd tried to be positive and not let her grandmother know how worried she was, but she knew that her gran wasn't fooled and that the worry must be bad for her own health.

Even though she'd tried to stay optimistic, those long weeks between going on the register and waiting to hear if a donor was suitable were an exquisite form of torture. Her whole life was on hold. With her studies paused, there was nothing to do but wait, while the weeks ran out as slowly and surely as sand in an hourglass. Then came the moment she was told that a match had been found — and quicker than Rose had ever dreamed. She'd wept with relief at the news but had immediately been overwhelmed with the weight of expectation. Granny Marge and Maddie had been in tears and her mother had been jubilant, but Rose knew it was only the start of a long process with no guarantee that the outcome would be a success.

For the past few weeks, she'd had conditioning therapy to remove her existing blood stem cells, so that the donor's cells could be added to her blood as soon as possible and start to rebuild her immune system. The treatment had ended the day before and she'd been in isolation in her own hospital ward since

4

then, to protect her from infection and prepare her for her stem cell transplant. It was hard to know if the sick and weak feeling was from fear and excitement, or side effects of the chemotherapy drugs used to destroy her stem cells.

Granny Marge waved again and mouthed 'I love you'. Rose recalled the conversation they'd had the previous day. Her mother had been flying over from LA at the time, but Rose wouldn't have wanted to have the conversation with her mum anyway.

'What if it doesn't work?' she'd said to her grandmother.

'It will. Your donor match was excellent. Your consultant said so.'

'But what if it doesn't? What if . . .'

'No 'what ifs'. It *will* work and you will get better.' Granny Marge's blue eyes had twinkled. 'I intend to see you finish that PhD and be a professor. You'll be on *Time Team* with that Baldrick bloke next.'

'Gran, they don't make *Time Team* any more.'

'Well, whatever. You can be on something with that nice Neil whatshisname. The Scottish one with the lovely hair.'

'I'd rather be on TV with Alice Roberts,' Rose said, amused at her gran's description of Neil Oliver. 'But I'd settle for just getting my PhD one day and *any* job in archaeology.'

Her grandmother had smiled and patted her hand. 'You will *never* have to just settle for anything, my love. You're a star.'

Smiling back, Rose had accepted a kiss on the forehead and a hug, knowing that it would be the last physical contact she would be able to have for quite a while. She'd be in isolation for weeks after the transplant while her immune system rebuilt itself, with the aid of the donor's stem cells.

She closed her eyes, imagining what he must be like. Tall or short? He was British, she knew that, and most donors tended to be fit, healthy and under thirty. Fit young men made the best donors and Rose had absolutely no quarrel with that.

She hardly dared dream that she could resume her PhD. Her brain was like cotton wool these days. It used to be sharp and adored learning; she had loved studying for her degree in archaeology, and her master's but she'd had to give that up when she became ill. Lately, she'd barely had the energy to open a book, let alone take in complex ideas. The headaches hadn't helped either.

It was almost impossible to remember what normal life was — or that it would ever come again. She had to cling on to it, not let it slip away, give up hope . . .

The nurse came in, dressed from head to toe in full PPE. She smiled with her eyes and her voice was matter-of-fact, but kind. There was no hint that Rose's life was about to be saved.

'Well, Rose. It's time for your very special cocktail,' she said in a cheerful voice. 'Are you ready?'

'As I'll ever be.'

'Good . . .' The nurse looked at her. 'But it's OK, you know, to feel apprehensive as well as excited. It's a big moment.'

'Yes, I know.'

'So, do you have any more questions before we start the procedure?'

Of course she did, but they were the same ones she'd asked before, and had answered by the consultants. The same ones that she turned over in her head

6

a hundred times, never really being satisfied with the answers. Her fate was as unknowable as an object lying buried in the earth. No one could tell her the answer to her biggest question: would she live or die?

'No, I don't think so,' she replied. 'I think I'd just rather get it over with.'

The nurse's eyes crinkled. 'OK. Then, let's get the show on the road.'

Rose smiled and tried not to worry about the way her pulse rate had shot up as the nurse connected up the bag to her central line.

Let's get this show on the road. Should there not be fanfares? A circus parade? Party poppers and fizz spraying high into the air?

Instead, there was only the whirr and beep of monitors, and the occasional comment from the nurse, explaining what she was doing.

It didn't hurt at all. The nurse simply connected a fresh plastic bag to the drip stand next to her bed.

Just a bag. A plastic bag of orangey-red liquid that reminded her of the tomato soup sometimes served by the college.

It could have anything in it.

Rose stared at it, fascinated. A bag of life.

She giggled.

'What's amused you?' the nurse asked, with only the briefest glance while she concentrated on adjusting the tubes connecting Rose's central line to the stem cells bag.

'That.' Rose nodded at the life-saving fluid. 'It's a bag of life, rather than a bag *for* life. Like you get in Tesco's when your old one's worn out.'

The nurse's eyebrows met in confusion and she hesitated before nodding and laughing. 'Oh, yes. I see what you mean.'

Yet Rose knew she didn't really. She could have no idea of what that bag meant, no matter how many patients she'd connected up before, how many she'd helped, or how much training she'd had in patient care.

No one could know unless they'd been through it themselves.

The nurse finished setting up the drip, constantly asking if Rose was OK, staying with her to talk a while longer to make sure Rose understood what to expect during her isolation over the coming weeks and the treatment she'd have to counter the effects of the transplant.

Then, she left. Rose looked around her. There was no one at the window. Even though a chance for life was literally flowing into her veins, she had a sense of being utterly alone in the world. There was only her now.

Then, suddenly, Granny Marge was back at the window, waving, her arm around Rose's mother, whose face was streaked with mascara. Her mother blew her a kiss and Rose lifted a hand to blow one back but felt too weak. She really wanted to sleep . . . She'd had none the night before.

She watched the bag drip, drip, drip the precious gift into her veins, and felt a surge of hope and fear that almost made her shout out. Today was the start of her new life and if she survived, she vowed to make the most of every moment.

1

Four years later, early March

'Rose, honey . . .'

Rose glanced up. Her mother was standing by the armchair with a china cup and saucer.

'Here's your tea.' She wrinkled her nose while handing it over. 'It's that Yorkshire stuff you can stand a spoon in. I couldn't find anything else.'

'Gran wouldn't have anything else,' Rose said. 'She loved a good strong cuppa.'

'I brought some herbal with me just in case,' her mother said, sipping a brew that Granny Marge would have described as 'cats' pee'.

The thought brought a smile to Rose's face; one of the few that she'd enjoyed over the past few weeks since her grandmother had passed away. Even now, with her mother by her side, the clock on the mantelpiece seemed to tick more loudly than it had before, emphasising the emptiness of the space. Rose drank her tea, while her mother answered a phone call.

★ ★ ★

Knitting still lay on the workbox; a pile of Mills and Boon paperbacks were piled by the armchair, with her grandmother's tablet on top of them.

Rose didn't think she would ever get used to her grandmother not being in that chair, even though it had been two weeks since they'd laid Granny Marge to rest.

Her mother had flown over for the funeral and stayed at the cottage since.

'Sorry about that,' Rose's mother said as she finished her call. 'It was one of the executive producers. I hate to say this, but I can't stay here forever. I'm going to have to get back to work.'

Although Stella Vernon's American accent had become more pronounced over the years, the East Anglian popped out from time to time, especially when she was agitated or upset.

'It's fine,' Rose said mechanically. 'I'll be OK.'

Her mother patted her hand before surveying the sitting room. 'At least your gran left you the cottage so you won't be homeless. It must be worth quite a bit, even though it's not actually in the city. I heard Cambridge house prices have rocketed.'

'I wouldn't know. I haven't been checking the property pages lately.'

'You'll stay here, then, not get a little flat in town?'

'I couldn't afford a dog kennel in town,' Rose said, with an eye-roll. 'The cottage isn't worth as much as you think, and besides, I love it here.'

'But surely you'd like to live in the middle of the action?' Her mother wrinkled her nose and pulled her cashmere wrap tighter. 'Especially in the winter. It's freezing here!'

'It's still only March, Mum. You know how bitter the wind is in the Fens this time of year.'

'I've gone soft, being out in LA. Surely you don't cycle to college every day?'

'I can take the car if it's really bad but cycling to work helped me get fit after the transplant and I actually enjoy it. There's nowhere to park in Cambridge these days anyway.'

'Nowhere to park your car? Not even for a lecturer?' Her mother laughed. 'You are quaint, Rose.'

Quaint?

Before Rose could protest that riding a bike was not considered eccentric in Cambridge and that she was at the very bottom of the academic food chain, her mother had embraced her. 'I'm truly sorry we lost Mum. I loved her even though we were never that close, and I can never thank her enough for taking you on.'

The unexpected display of emotion made Rose's own tears spill over again and she held her mother tightly.

'I'll try to get back over here more often in future, honey,' she said. 'I promise. I might even get a job back in the UK. These few weeks have made me miss it — even the weather.'

The words brought a smile to Rose's lips as she popped into the kitchen for some kitchen roll to wipe her eyes. When she returned, her mum was turning the pages of a paperback book that Marge had been reading the morning she'd died.

'I'm glad Mum didn't have a long illness,' she said, with a break in her voice. 'Easier on your gran but hard on you. Such a shock.'

Rose had thought this many times, but always came to the same conclusion. Her grandmother had died from a massive heart attack while working in her garden. Rose had found her when she'd come home from college to fetch a notebook. She shuddered at the memory of her grandmother on the cold ground though the paramedics had said it would have been almost instant.

'She wouldn't have had it any other way...' Rose said. 'She was clearing leaves from around the crocuses, her favourites...the first bright jewels that said spring was on its way.'

'She loved that garden...Will you get a gardener in or do you have time to do it on all your holidays?' Stella moved on swiftly, obviously keen to avoid dwelling on gloomy topics.

'I have plenty to do in the 'holidays',' Rose said patiently. 'And I might not need a gardener because I'm thinking of renting out the cottage.'

'Renting it? I thought you said you weren't moving into town?'

'I'm not, but I've seen a summer project I like the look of. It comes with a small grant and it would enable me to help run an archaeological project in conjunction with another university during the vacation.' She smiled. 'It's a new dig at a really interesting site and it's right up my street.'

'I think that sounds like a cool idea. Give you a change of scene and a chance to meet new people,' Stella said, by which she probably meant new *men*. 'Where is this dig?'

'In Cornwall,' Rose said. 'Down on the Lizard. It's a great chance to do some *research* and learn more about the site,' she added, squashing any idea her mother might have about her meeting someone on the dig.

'Cornwall? How romantic and wild. How very Poldark.'

'I doubt he'll still be there...' Rose said. 'But I did think I might learn to sail. I always liked the idea. That is, *if* I can get the grant. I haven't even applied yet. I haven't had the heart since Gran died.'

12

'I understand that, honey,' her mother said briskly, 'but you must move on. The most important thing is you getting away from this cottage and Cambridge. It'll do you the world of good. Let's face it, this whole place can be claustrophobic. I know you love it here and you've felt safe while you've been recovering but it's time you spread your wings.' Stella smiled. 'Even if it is only to Cornwall . . . you know, your grandad loved Cornwall. He used to sail there when he was younger.'

'I remember. Sort of. He took me out on a friend's boat once but Gran didn't come.'

'She didn't like sailing with him. She was always too seasick.'

Rose pictured herself at the helm of a yacht, cutting through the waves. It seemed glamorous and exhilarating and so very far from the flat Fenlands of the cottage.

'I think you should go,' Stella added firmly.

'Well, I still haven't even got the grant yet and I'd need to find tenants to rent this place. I want to help someone who can't afford accommodation in the city. Maybe some nurses or junior doctors.'

Stella waved a hand dismissively. 'You'll have a stampede! When do you have to start this new project?'

'I'd have to go down in May and stay until the start of the new term in late September.'

'Go for it,' her mother said, then went quiet, examining her polished nails. 'While we're on the subject of new starts and Grandma, there's something I've been meaning to tell you since she died.'

'What?' Rose jumped on the comment and goose bumps prickled her skin. She'd heard that tone before.

13

It was edged with guilt and reminded her of times her mother had had to break the news her visit home would be delayed or even cancelled. Rose had learned to live with the disappointment, but it still stung from time to time.

'Your gran gave me a letter for you.'

Rose's cup trembled in the saucer. 'A letter? What?'

'She gave it to me at Christmas when I flew over. She told me she wanted me to keep it and give it to you if 'something happened to her'. I told her not to be so silly, of course, but I was a bit worried about her.'

'You never told me you were worried.' Rose spoke slowly, reeling that her grandmother had left the letter in the hands of her mum, not Rose directly.

'No, because she asked me not to and I respected her wishes.' Stella's voice rose in frustration, but she tempered it. 'I was going to hand it over before the funeral, but we were both feeling so raw after Mum died, so I thought I'd wait until a calmer moment and well, this feels like it.'

She got up and retrieved a leather tote bag from under the coffee table. From inside, she produced a pale blue envelope, the kind that no one sent now but which Rose recognised instantly as her grandmother's favourite stationery.

'I took it back to the States with me in case you found it and I've kept it in my bag ever since. It's a bit shabby now.' She handed over the slightly dog-eared envelope to Rose.

'I still don't understand why she didn't give it to me herself . . .'

'Because she didn't want to worry you. I've no idea what's in it. You can read it now or wait until I'm gone.'

Rose held the letter, choked with emotion. She had to be alone to read it. 'Do you mind if I wait a little while?'

'Of course not. I have a Zoom chat with a producer planned anyway and I need to prepare,' she said. 'I'll give you some space.'

Stella left the room with a squeeze of Rose's arm. Rose was still shocked that her mum had kept the letter a secret, but it was typical of her gran not to want to worry her. She wondered what it contained, and how she'd cope with reading the contents while her emotions were all over the place.

Yet the voice of her gran was in her ear, telling her to be brave.

She made another, much stronger cup of tea and took it into the little sunroom that overlooked the cottage garden. Already she knew she had to read the message right there and then. No point putting it off: her experience with her illness had taught her that it was best to seize the moment.

After taking the letter from the envelope, she unfolded the two sheets of paper and read her gran's neat hand:

Dearest Rose,

If you're reading this then I'll probably be gone — unless your mum hasn't been able to keep it a secret, of course. That wouldn't surprise me. Please don't grieve too much for me. I've had a long and joyful life and that's been largely because of you. I know you don't really remember your grandad, but he'd have been so proud of you.

It has been the biggest joy of my life to see you recover from your illness and go on to achieve

15

your dream of being an archaeologist. I know it's what you always longed for. My, I spent so many nights reading all those *Horrible Histories* books to you and trying to stop you from digging up other people's gardens to find buried treasure.

Rose smiled through her tears.

The day I sat in the audience in the Senate House to watch you get your PhD was the proudest of my life. To call my granddaughter 'Dr Vernon', and see you bursting with happiness, will live with me to the end of my days.

Of course, we've had some dark times too. Rose, only now can I tell you how worried I was about you, and how my whole existence would have meant nothing if you hadn't received your transplant. I would have jumped off a cliff in a heartbeat to save you. I know your mum would have too — in fact, she told me. Even if she wasn't able to let you know how worried she was, I promise you it was true.

I also know that you've wanted to contact your donor for a long time, to thank him for the gift he gave you. I didn't think it was a good idea at the time and I was worried it might tempt fate. That will sound silly now you're well, but I was scared it was too soon and that things could still go wrong. I was also worried that if you didn't hear back, you'd be hurt and disappointed.

Well, lately, I've changed my mind and I think you should contact him. Time has passed and you're ready to move on now.

So I say you should go for it. Write to him and

see if he'll meet with you. Thank him from me, whoever he is and shake his hand. Thank him for saving your life — and making mine worth living.

   All my love,
Gran
XX

★ ★ ★

It took Rose a good hour before she was ready to face her mother after reading the letter — half an hour of tears and the same again wandering in the garden, composing herself. The crocuses were past their best and the daffodils were blooming as the cycle of the year moved on. Soon there would be tulips and then the hawthorn would burst out in May . . . Time marched on and Gran was right: it was time to seize the moment.

Rose went inside, hearing muffled conversation from above in the spare room where her mother was having her Zoom meeting. She'd already decided she wouldn't show the letter to her mum, but she might tell her a little about it — but perhaps not the part about contacting her donor.

Her mother might not understand or try to interfere or dissuade her and Rose wanted to make her own mind up without any influence.

Without further ado, before she could chicken out, she marched into the sitting room and opened the bureau. In one of the wooden pigeonholes, she found the remaining few sheets of blue writing paper, and took them into the sunroom, where the spring sun had warmed the room. Outside, the tête-à-tête daffodils her gran had planted nodded their heads in the breeze. A more fanciful person than Rose might have imagined they were telling her to go ahead: that the time was now right.

She picked up her pen and began to write.

2

Two months later, Falford, Cornwall

The mermaid was hanging around the boatyard again.

Finn had seen her standing next to the slipway, looking back at the open door of the shed where he'd been working until a few minutes before. It was still quiet in Falford and the main tourist season had yet to start so he could hardly fail to notice her.

She had her back to him, looking out across the water. Finn had spotted her when he went out to fetch a plank of larch from the planing machine. He walked a little way down the yard, sensing she was transfixed by the view over the estuary. Who wouldn't be, when the water sparkled in the gentle breeze and the gulls scudded across the surface on this fresh May morning?

The breeze tossed her hair across her face and she held it back from her face and turned to look straight at him.

He fought the impulse to walk down to the slipway and speak to her, ask her why she'd been looking back at the boatshed for the past three days at various times of the day. He felt drawn to her, but wasn't it the mermaid who was supposed to do the singing? Wasn't it Finn and his brother who were meant to hear her, and follow her and her song into the estuary and out to sea? Shouldn't she be sitting on a rock and combing her yellow hair or something? Her blonde locks certainly looked long enough for a mermaid.

19

He tore his gaze away from her, telling himself not to be so fanciful.

Another young woman waved at Finn; one with her hair in a ponytail and a cherry-print apron over her dungarees. Bo, who worked at the boatyard café, mimed a coffee-drinking sign.

Finn smiled and gave her the thumbs up before striding back to the planing machine, and heaving the larch plank over his shoulder. It was heavy but he could manage it on his own — he didn't want Joey to help him, just in case he saw the mermaid too.

The client was expecting the gaff rigged cutter to be ready by the autumn, but if Joey had his way, it would be next Christmas. The vessel was a major commission for Morvah Marine and doing an outstanding job on it would enhance the reputation of the business further, but Joey seemed far too busy dating half the women in Cornwall to focus on the build.

Morvah Marine was part of Falford Boatyard, which was also home to a charter company that hired out bareboats and skippered craft, and a hire centre for kayaks, paddleboards and smaller motor boats, and various long-term moorings, winter lay-up and overhauls. Both residents and visitors also kept their own craft at the pontoons and some even lived on them all year round.

It was a bustling hub of the community and Finn loved his work, despite the constant struggle to keep it going. They needed at least one major project on the go, like the cutter, to keep them in business. Few clients had the cash to spend on a traditional wooden boat that might cost as much as a small property, and so it was vital that Morvah Marine kept its reputation by doing an outstanding job on each commission.

20

They needed all the smaller jobs too — repairs and refits — and they prided themselves on treating those with equal care. The livelihoods of half a dozen crafts-people and apprentices depended on the business thriving.

This sobering thought reminded Finn that his own mind should be on his work too, and not on the blonde stranger. She was probably one of Joey's fans, or more likely, an offended ex who'd come to give him a mouthful after being left in bed, with him making promises he'd never intended to keep. On cue, a snatch of raucous laughter carried outside the shed on the fresh May breeze and Joey emerged, grinning.

Joey met him just outside the door to the shed. 'Where've you been? Doesn't take that long to find a piece of wood, does it?'

Finn allowed Joey to take the plank from him and rest it by the hull of the boat.

Their mother, Dorinda, joined them, hands on hips. She pushed a lock of grey hair back under the bandana she used to keep it off her face. 'Is that strange woman round here again?'

Wiping his hands on a rag, Joey joined Finn by the truck. 'She's not that strange. Not what I've seen of her. She reminds me of a mermaid.'

Finn laughed in derision. If Joey or his mother knew he'd been indulging in fantasies of the same kind, they'd think he'd gone crazy.

Their mother walked a few yards towards the river, scanning the slipway for the stranger. 'You know what happened when the mermaid came calling, Joey.'

'No idea, but bet you're gonna tell me.'

'She lured away the young men to their deaths.'

'Thanks, Mother, that's cheerful.'

Finn stood by, privately agreeing with Joey, but refusing to side with him against their mother and cause further aggro.

'Joey,' she said with menacing sweetness. 'When we're at work, I'm not your mother, I'm your gaffer, and that boat won't get finished if you stand here mooning after strange girls.'

'Firstly. I'm not mooning — whatever the hell that is. Second it was Finn who was watching her. I saw him trying to get a better look.'

'I wasn't watching her,' Finn muttered. 'She was watching us — or watching the shed.'

Their mother peered out. 'Well, she's not here now and if she turns up again, I'll go out and ask her what she wants. This is a working environment.'

'Maybe she wants a boat?' Joey said, with a smirk. 'Built by my own fair hands.' He held up his hands, grimy with oil.

'Then she'll have a very long wait if you intend to spend half your time swanning around.'

Whistling, Joey wandered back into the shed with no real sense of urgency. Their mother followed him, taking a call on her phone while gesturing to one of the boatbuilding apprentices at the same time.

With a sigh, Finn returned to the planing machine, which was kept outside under a tarp so they could work in the fresh air. He had a lot of sympathy for Dorinda. She'd had a hard life, having to take over the management of the boatyard when her own mother had died when Dorinda was in her early twenties, leaving her and her father Billy to run the whole set-up. Not only had she taken over the financial and admin side of Morvah Marine, she'd also learned to paint boats from Billy.

Finn's parents had never married and Dorinda rarely mentioned their own father, considering him 'an irrelevance' in their lives. Finn barely remembered him. He'd left a week before Finn's fourth birthday when Joey was still in nappies. The only legacy he'd been endowed with, according to his mum, was his dad's dark looks.

When Billy Morvah had retired, Dorinda had taken over Morvah Marine and weathered the storms to keep it a reasonably thriving business that had provided careers for both her sons; a trade that Finn adored and that he knew Joey loved too, though perhaps slightly less obsessively. Joey didn't quite have Finn's feeling of duty towards the management of the business. Finn was keen to share the burden and learn the admin side for himself, even though it was his least favourite part of the job.

Grandad Billy had passed away a few years ago and everything now fell on the shoulders of Finn and Dorinda. Their grandad used to love to pop in and do some work when he could, and he'd been sailing his own dinghy in the calm waters of the estuary when he'd suffered a massive stroke. The Morvahs were devastated but they also agreed that it was what Billy would have chosen.

These days, their mum had no time to work on painting the boats, and the management of the yard was eating into Finn's own time as a craftsman too. As well as the three family members, Morvah Marine usually had another two or three self-employed craftspeople working on various projects.

Finn tried to return to his work but his mind was pulled back to the mermaid time and again. He was desperate to know why she was so fascinated by the yard.

It had to be something to do with Joey, something that his brother was keen to hide. Joey attracted women like a magnet attracted iron filings and had a sure-fire technique for impressing them. With his surf dude looks — not that he surfed — he'd take them out on his boat on a mellow evening, drop anchor at a secluded cove and usually not return until dawn.

It worked every time and for a while Joey would be grinning like a Cheshire cat and out every night — until he grew bored. Over the spring, two different exes had already rocked up at the boatyard and told him what they'd thought of him, and Finn didn't blame them.

A chilly breeze brought goose bumps out on his bare arms. He had no right to judge Joey. Finn had secrets of his own that he wouldn't want anyone to find out — especially not his younger brother.

3

Had the dark-haired brother seen her?

Rose kept her eyes glued on the estuary as she crossed the slipway and rejoined the coastal path towards Falford village. She wondered if she'd turned away too quickly. Perhaps she should have smiled rather than hastily pulling her eyes away like she was guilty of a crime.

She'd found it impossible not to stare at him. How could she not? He was tall, with collar-length hair that was almost black. He wore a dark blue hoodie and cargo trousers, and even at this distance, she was sure he was frowning.

She'd seen another young guy, too, on her two other visits to the boatyard; fairer, hunky but more — dare she use the phrase? — 'boy band'. Yes, that was it. The blond one was almost *too* handsome. She smiled at herself. She was making a lot of assumptions about these men, although admittedly, she did know their names now, and a little bit about them. Finn and Joey Morvah. She'd looked them up on the Morvah Marine website and knew that they were partners in the yard run by their mother Dorinda.

The coastal path in this part of south-west Cornwall wound its way around the creeks of the Falford estuary like a child's squiggle. It had rained overnight and the path was muddy in parts and bordered by trees, ferns and bluebells. Rose was glad she'd decided on Doc Martens to go with her midi sundress and denim jacket. With an umbrella in her backpack, no

25

one could say she wasn't prepared for anything.

She lingered at a point in the path where the trees parted and there was a pocket of sand that you could almost call a beach. It was barely big enough for more than two families, but there were none anyway, on this May morning. Tucked into a small promontory that jutted into the sea, the spot gave her a good view back at the yacht club and the Morvah boatyard.

She could make out Joey in his bright red T-shirt and Finn, stretching his arms high into the air as if he'd been too long bending over a boat.

Until now, she'd been careful to approach from different ways or observe the yard from the Ferryman pub on the opposite side of the creek. The previous day, she'd found a table on the terrace of the thatched inn, and ordered a coffee, so she could get a better look at the boatyard from a safe distance. It was a good place to watch all the comings and goings, and while she'd enjoyed her cappuccino, Joey had spoken to a young woman in a leather jacket. Rose had seen her throw her head back and laugh. He obviously knew her well and the way she batted him on the arm showed they were very good friends, possibly more.

Dorinda had emerged shortly afterwards and the mood had turned less sunny. Joey's 'friend' had left after throwing up her arms in frustration — or anger. A little while later, she'd stormed into the pub as Rose was walking out. She was still visibly angry and Rose had overheard one of the bar staff asking her: 'What's up, Sophie, as if I couldn't guess?'

However, it was only today that Rose had dared to venture much closer to Morvah Marine itself. The sounds had been loud and intriguing: the whine of an industrial machine, hammering and banging that almost drowned out the clanking of sails against the masts and the cries of seagulls. She'd taken a risk, getting so near, and she'd paid the price. Finn had seen her today and he'd definitely seemed disturbed by her presence.

She would have to be more careful. Although she had no intention of doing it, she wondered what she would say if she did march up to the Morvah brothers, ready to confess.

'Hello, I'm Rose. You don't know me, but I think one of you saved my life?'

It sounded *weird* — deranged even, and Rose wouldn't blame anyone for thinking she was odd at best, a dangerous stalker at worst.

Over the past few days, Rose had wondered many times if she should have come at all, but the fact remained that she was still very excited about the chance to research the dig location and the many other ancient sites in the area. That was reason enough to be here. Life had taught her to grab every chance and so she had — if she found out who her donor was too, then that would be a bonus. A *huge* bonus.

For now, her focus had to be on finding a place to live. She couldn't live at the Haven guest house forever although she planned to stay for at least the rest of the week while she looked for more permanent accommodation in Falford.

Picking her way along the shore, she eventually found the creekside footpath again. It wasn't shaded by trees so she could see the estuary clearly and watch the oystercatchers pecking at the mudflats with their orange beaks. The scene struck her as familiar, even though she'd never been there before.

Was this the spot?

27

Rose found a low flat rock to sit on and pulled a hardback out of her backpack.

A Guide to Ancient Sites of Penwith.

The well-thumbed guidebook fell open to the pages where she kept the greetings card from her donor. Even with careful handling, it was becoming a little worn from being looked at so often — just like her gran's letter to her.

She had sent the letter to her donor via the donor charity the same day she'd read Granny Marge's letter and received the card in response a few weeks later. She hadn't been allowed to give her name, of course, and he hadn't given his in reply. Encouraged, she'd written again but he hadn't answered a second time. However, Rose's curiosity had been fired up and fanned further by her gran's suggestion that she find the man and thank him in person.

She held the card to check the watercolour scene on the front against the view over the creek.

'Hmm . . .' It could be . . .

The pub wasn't in exactly the right place, but the pink cottage with a thatched roof was there . . . and the artist, whom she'd googled many times, had been born in Falford. She was pretty sure he'd painted it while sitting somewhere nearby.

The sun came out, glinting on the shallow pools of water and its rays were hot on her back. She took off her jacket and felt the sun warm her shoulders, inhaled the smell of wild garlic and let the murmurings of waterfowl fill her ears. It was great to be alive — especially when you'd come so close to not being.

★   ★   ★

'You look done in,' Katie, the landlady of the Haven B&B, said before sitting Rose down in the conservatory with a large pot of tea and two cream scones.

Katie's comment and kindly manner reminded her of Granny Marge. She was also right. Rose had been knackered after her walk to the boatyard. In the end, she'd decided to take a 'circular route' back to the guest house and had become lost. Her phone said she'd walked over six miles and by the time she got back, she was hot, stung by nettles and thirsty. Cycling the flat Cambridge fenland was no match for the ups and downs of the Cornish coast.

After devouring the cream tea, she went up to her room intending to have a quick bath before coming down for the evening meal. However, the exertion, and probably the emotional toll, had drained her and she'd been too tired for dinner and fallen asleep. She woke at dawn, lying on top of her bed, still wrapped in the fluffy robe from the shower, a towel under her head.

That morning she sat in the window seat of her room with a pot of coffee, examining the handwriting again. It was neat, but sloped backwards. It hadn't been dashed off. It was a man's handwriting — well, the transplant centre had been able to reveal that much. 'Men make better donors,' Rose had explained to Maddie.

'Glad they're useful for something,' Maddie had joked.

Smiling, Rose read the words again, reflecting on the efforts she'd made to find her donor's identity despite him not replying to her second letter.

Glad you're feeling better.

Good luck in the future,
Wishing you a fair wind and calm seas.

No name, of course. That wasn't allowed but the card was her first clue. It could have come from anywhere, of course, but she was sure it had been sent by someone with connections to Falford. The sailing allusion had led her to google marinas and boatyards in Falford and she was off, lit by the flame of curiosity. After all, in her job as an archaeologist, she was used to research, digging deeper and never letting go until she found what she was looking for.

It had taken a few days trawling the Internet, using a myriad of search terms, before she'd struck gold. It was a comment on a local Cornish newspaper article about a drive for bone marrow donors in the area around Falford. Rose had squealed with delight. A colleague had poked his head around her door and asked if she was OK, and she'd had to make up some guff about finding an academic paper she'd been searching for.

The comment, from 'Anonymous' sounded angry and upset, and bemoaned the fact that only a few people had responded to the appeal for donors and that going on the register was a 'no-brainer' that could result in someone's life being saved. It implied that the young locals were 'snowflakes' — a word Rose detested. Rose suspected the writer of the comment might have lost someone recently, or be waiting for a transplant. Whatever the circumstances, they were very distressed.

Rose's heart went out to them, and she hoped their situation had had a good outcome. Although it was by no means certain or even likely.

The comment did give her the glimmer of light she was seeking, however.

She now knew that there had been a campaign to recruit donors in the Falford area, and that some people had come forward. It also made sense that her donor lived locally. Her great-great-grandparents had come from Cornwall, so it wasn't so improbable that a match was found there. She probably had a genetic connection. She'd had a lot of time to wonder, to research while she was ill, and it was well documented that most Cornish people would probably have married partners local to their place of birth in those days. Many local people could probably trace their ancestry back nine hundred years or even longer.

However, Rose wouldn't have even thought of Cornwall or made the connection to her ancestors until she'd received the greetings card with its picture of the Falford estuary. On the rear was a line saying.
Falford Creek at high tide
From an original by Nash Santo.
Armed with more information, she'd done more googling that had led her to a few more tantalising clues that the treasure she was seeking was waiting for her in Falford. She'd unearthed another newspaper story showing Nash with 'the Morvah family' at an exhibition. There were pictures on Facebook from the Falford Regatta, where they seemed to be part of the organising committee or at least heavily involved.

In one photo, Dorinda was handing over a trophy to a man in oilskins and it was clear the family were key members of the community. Finally, she'd come across a sad piece of news: an obituary in an online news site saying that Nash had died around five years ago.

31

By now, Rose had spent so long searching for these people, inhabiting the place they lived, imagining them going about their daily lives, staring at their faces, that she felt she knew them. Discovering that one of them had died felt personal — like the few occasions when she'd had to deal with the deaths of other people she knew who were waiting for transplants or whose treatment hadn't worked. People she hadn't even met or people whom she'd only gotten to know via an online forum.

Poor Nash was gone, but the nugget of gold he'd left behind — the clue to her donor's identity — was safely preserved now and could lead her to the man who'd saved her. While she couldn't be one hundred per cent certain it was one of the Morvah brothers, instinct told her it was.

It was true that Granny Marge had urged her to find the man who'd saved her just when she'd been thinking of applying for the Cornish grant. But how was Rose to know that her donor came from Cornwall too — and only half an hour's drive from the dig site?

Surely it was fate? Surely, she was *meant* to track him down and thank him?

Rose laughed at herself. She needed to get real. Fate was merely the way people justified doing things they wanted to but probably shouldn't.

In reality, confronting her donor was a step too far for her and most of all, the tone of the card hadn't indicated he wanted any further contact with her. On the other hand, that didn't mean he actively *didn't* . . .

She told herself she was here legitimately anyway, for her work, so surely, just finding him and *seeing* him wasn't a crime — was it?

4

After Katie had presented her with a full cooked breakfast, Rose decided to explore the part of the village on the opposite side of the water to the boatyard. She could have wandered up the creek to the little footbridge along the valley but the passenger ferry saved a mile-long walk and anyway, looked much more fun.

Even on the short journey across the water, it was cool and she had to wrap her scarf around her neck. She'd put her hair up in a twist to stop it blowing wildly. When your hair had fallen out and you didn't know if it would ever grow back again, you tended not to take it for granted.

Since her transplant, she'd barely visited a hairdresser apart from for a treatment and the very tiniest trim. Her hair had also grown back a couple of shades lighter than before. It had been mousy but had come back to a blonde that her mother had said it had been like when she was three. Rose hadn't been sure whether this was a good thing or not. She didn't want to come across as Goldilocks. She might have cut it into something 'manageable' or 'practical' before her illness, but not now. She gloried in it, leaving it loose and flowing whenever she could. Like letting her hair grow wild, she was ready for an adventure — to take a risk.

The other two people on the boat were clearly hikers, middle-aged and clad in sturdy boots. Rose sat facing forward, and as she climbed out of the ferry, the boatman gave her his hand to make sure she didn't slip.

33

The houses on the other side might only be a hundred yards across the water, but they had a different character and looked much older. The boatyard bank had mostly Victorian houses such as the guest house and the yacht club, which had been rebuilt and added to over the past century.

In contrast, the granite and whitewashed cottages of the older part of the village must date back many centuries, Rose thought. She wondered if any fishermen or boatmen could still afford to live here but thought it was unlikely, given the number of discreet holiday-let plaques displayed outside front doors bedecked with roses and flower tubs.

A man with pink shorts and dreadlocks was unbolting the door of the Ferryman Inn and said a good morning as she walked up the steps by the pub. Briefly, Rose thought of asking him about finding a place to stay. Maybe he even had a room to rent, but then she noticed the sign for 'luxury waterside accommodation' and thought the rooms would be way out of her budget for the summer.

Her salary as a junior academic was OK-ish and she didn't have a mortgage on the cottage Granny Marge had left her. Plus her mum had helped her out with inheritance tax and so Rose knew she was very fortunate. She'd managed to find two junior doctors to stay at the cottage at a token rent, and in return for keeping the garden neat and tidy. However, any waterfront property in Falford was likely to go for hundreds a night in the summer.

Of course, it would have helped if she'd known she was coming to Cornwall months before but that wasn't how life worked and she'd only learned that her grant application had finally been successful two weeks previously. Since then, she'd been caught up in the whirl of term end, looking after her students as their exams approached and marking.

Funny that she'd only finished her own PhD a few years before, even though she was a decade older than some of the PhD students. They must think she was an old fogey at thirty-two.

She smiled then stopped in the lane above the pub, suddenly unsure of what to do and where to go next — struck again by the realisation that she had no unequivocal idea of what she was actually doing in Falford.

A few yards down the lane, she came across a row of whitewashed cottages with knobbly walls and thatched roofs. In addition to the Creek Stores, which sold groceries and supplies, there was an expensive-looking gallery, and — rather randomly — a shop with a driftwood sign above the bow window that declared:

Cornish Magick

Its bow-fronted window was crammed with crystals, healing stones and a mishmash of folklore bits 'n' bobs that Maddie would have called 'tat'. Imagining her friend turning up her nose, Rose decided to reserve her opinion until she'd had a better look. She was strictly scientific herself, but her illness had also made her far more tolerant and understanding of other people's ways of getting through tough situations and life in general.

She couldn't resist walking under the thatched porch where a display of dreamcatchers brushed her face as they wafted in the breeze off the estuary. A bell dinged as she entered, but there was no one behind the small cash desk, which had a bead curtain separating it from who knew where. Rose was in no hurry

35

and tried to luxuriate in the fact she had some time, now that the whirlwind of term was over. She allowed herself to browse the jewellery with its semi-precious stones, inhale the scent of joss sticks and candles and look at the rocks and minerals, all neatly arranged in glass cases or on shelves.

'Mornin'. Can I help you?'

A shop assistant appeared at her side. She had close-cropped hair, glossy and jet black, and several piercings in her lips and nose. Rose had three studs in her ears but was seriously impressed at the display of metalwork.

'No, um, I'm just mooching about,' Rose said with a friendly smile. 'If that's OK?'

The assistant shrugged. 'Mooch away. If you want to know anything just ask.'

Rose picked up a piece of grey stone with sparkling purple crystals inside it, as the assistant went to tidy a display of joss sticks. The stone was beautiful and made her smile at a memory of a time long gone. She'd dated a geology student for a while before she'd become too ill to carry on with her course. She'd tripped over a piece of rock in his room and then found a piece of coprolite — dinosaur poo — in the bottom of his bed when she'd woken up in the morning.

'That one's my favourite,' the assistant said, coming over to Rose's side again. 'It's an amethyst crystal geode.'

'It's very beautiful.' Cradling it in her hands, Rose examined the stone more closely. Its grey 'shell' had been sliced in half to reveal a miniature 'cave' of crystals that twinkled with purple fire. There was a little card next to it saying things like 'rebalance your chakras', 'millions have benefited from the soothing and calming effects of crystals' and 'discover the secret powers of crystals that the ancients have known for millennia'.

When the card started extolling the 'stone's healing powers', Rose thought they were pushing it, yet she was still transfixed by its beauty. She voiced her thoughts out loud. 'Do you think these actually do anything? I mean like curing ailments?'

The assistant shrugged. ''Bout as much use as a chocolate teapot in my opinion but they look pretty and some people get comfort out of them, like most of the stuff in here, so who am I to judge?'

'You run a folklore shop and you don't believe in the supernatural?' Rose said it with a smile in her voice.

'Nope. Don't think there's anything in any of it but I don't judge others. If you want a pisky charm or a magic stone, be my guest.'

Rose laughed and carried on browsing before returning to the geode. It was thirteen pounds, but she was sorely tempted. It would brighten up her temporary 'home' — when she managed to find it. A little knot of panic in her stomach reminded her she had to find somewhere soon because she couldn't afford to stay at the Haven guest house much longer, no matter how comfortable it was. The Haven was lovely and her mum had treated her to a week there, but Rose was well aware she couldn't stay there all summer.

Deciding that she couldn't resist the geode, she took it to the till where the assistant's eyes widened in surprise.

'You're havin' it, then? Good choice. It's a real beauty.'

'Do you sell lots of crystals?' Rose asked, tapping the machine with her card.

'In the summer the shop used to do a roaring trade, especially around the solstice when the hippies came to dance around the stones,' she said, her tone upbeat.

'You mean the Nineteen Maidens?' Rose said, intrigued.

'Yeah and there's also the Merry Maidens, Carn Euny, Men-an-Tol.' The assistant gave Rose a penetrating look. 'Why? Are you into all that too?'

'As a matter of fact, I am.'

'That's fine. Like I say, I never judge. Always happy for a chat about it and always ready to be converted. I sell a lot of stuff to people trying to convert me.' She grinned. 'Or I used to do.' Her grin faded. 'We're not as busy as we'd like to be. We don't get the coach parties so much lately and this place isn't as well-known as it was.' Rose felt a little sorry for the woman if her business was in the doldrums. 'Well, I'm definitely into ancient lumps of rock. I'm an archaeologist.'

'Oh. Right.' The assistant looked as if she'd seen it all before. 'Are you here doing some research, then?'

'You could say that,' Rose replied, with a clear conscience. 'I got a grant to study some of the sites in the far west over the summer. I'll be working on the dig by Arthur's Pool.'

'I heard about that.' Her eyes sparked with interest. 'What are you hoping to find? Treasure? King Arthur's bones?' the woman said, referring to the legend that the pool was the final resting place of King Arthur and his sword, Excalibur.

Rose laughed. 'I wish. Sadly, I doubt we'll find any bones, but the students have already uncovered some Iron Age artefacts. Some pottery, a small brooch and some grindstones. There was a settlement on that site that's not been excavated before.'

'Oh.' The assistant was clearly expecting skeletons and hoards of gold coins. 'Nice work if you can get it. I'm Oriel Stannard by the way. Oriel with an 'O' not an 'A'. I'm not the Little bloody Mermaid.'

Rose burst out laughing and shook Oriel's hand. 'Rose Vernon.'

Oriel frowned hard at her. 'Are you a professor or something?'

Rose snorted. 'In my dreams. Only a doctor, but not a 'doctor' doctor. If you chop your finger off, I'd be no help and I only use the doctor bit for academic purposes. I'm staying at the Haven B&B.'

Oriel did an 'oh'. 'Very nice. Very pricey too.'

'Yes . . .' Rose wondered if Oriel thought she was minted. It was almost a hundred quid a night, and she'd be the size of an elephant on all the cooked breakfasts that it seemed rude to refuse. 'Actually, I'm looking for some accommodation for the summer. A holiday caravan on a farm, or a little flat would be fine. You don't know of anything here in the village or close by, do you?'

Oriel snorted. 'Good luck with getting a caravan or anything in this village for the whole summer. Most of the places are either second homes or they'll have been fully booked months ago and you'll need a mortgage to rent them.'

Rose sighed. 'I'd a nasty feeling that might be the case. I should have planned better in advance, but I didn't know I was getting the grant until just over two weeks ago.'

Oriel cocked her head on one side, sizing Rose up. 'You know . . . what you need is a short-term let,' she said. 'Something that can't be let out to emmets.'

'I *am* an emmet,' Rose said, loving the idea of the

39

Old English word for an ant, which she'd heard used before. It summed up the scurrying of millions of people — of which she was one — to the south-west every summer.

'Not really, if you're planning on livin' and workin' here.' Oriel smirked. 'Not that I judge.'

'For a few months I do.'

'In that case . . . and you're not looking for something posh, I might be able to help.'

A few minutes later, Oriel drew back a bead curtain and gestured for Rose to follow her up a dark, twisty staircase. At the top was a tiny landing with only one door off it.

'In here.' Oriel paused outside the door, which was scuffed and in dire need of a lick of paint. 'I know it needs a bit of a clear-out and a good spring-clean, but I can do that.'

Wondering what she'd let herself in for, Rose braced herself for ravens flying out of the room or a skeleton falling on top of her, Indiana Jones style.

'You go first,' Oriel said.

Rose turned the handle on the door and pushed it open. She had to adjust to the gloom. The room was in deep shadow, mainly because the flowery brown curtains at the window were drawn — almost, because they didn't meet in the middle, allowing a shaft of light to penetrate the dimness. The floorboards creaked under her feet and dust motes whirled in the shaft of light. The room smelled musty with a sweet and sickly undertone.

Words — nice ones — were impossible to come by. It was hard to imagine spending the summer here, living and working in this dingy room.

Oriel's face fell. 'Totally mingin', isn't it? I knew it.'

40

'I wouldn't say that.' Rose tried to be upbeat. 'Although it *is* a bit of a time capsule.'

'Hold on.' Rose blinked as Oriel ripped open the curtains, shedding light on the room, which might not have been the best idea.

The décor hadn't been upgraded since the Eighties. The Seventies curtains with their orange swirling flowers contrasted with wallpaper with faded red and grey slashes that must have been the height of fashion in 1982. Cardboard boxes, plastic crates and bulging bags for life were stacked in front of two doors and on the dining table and sofa. Safeway? Since when had that been a supermarket? And Woolworths? Rose mainly remembered that shop for the pick 'n' mix counters that her granny had loved.

On the other hand, she was intrigued by the doors leading off one wall and an interesting little cupboard in the corner.

'It's been vacant for ages. No one wants to live here these days. Not in a hole like this.'

Rose presumed Oriel meant the flat not Falford Creek, which was idyllic . . . or at least idyllic to an emmet. 'Don't you live in the village?' she said to be sure.

'No way! I live with my girlfriend in a new-build apartment in Trecarne. It's only a mile away but it's civilisation compared to here. No disrespect, but I'd hate to live above the shop and there's not room for two in here.'

Rose glanced around her. The room wasn't huge but it would surely seem a lot more spacious with some of the boxes, buckets and paraphernalia cleared out. She was warming to it a tiny bit.

'There's a single bedroom behind that old vacuum

41

cleaner and a poky shower room — the door's behind that old display rack.'

Oriel weaved between some boxes and shifted the stand away from one of the doors. 'Bedroom's in here but I'll have to clean it out first. Don't think anyone's been inside for years. Could be a bit of wildlife in there for all I know.'

Rose was beginning to slightly regret her enthusiasm to view the flat. Helping to declutter the room was one thing, but the idea of spiders and mice nesting in her bedroom — and untold horrors in the shower room — was another matter entirely.

'I'm surprised you haven't done it up and let it out before,' she said. 'To someone else,' she added.

'Yeah, well. Maybe we should. This place is meant for someone working in the area but we've had no one interested for years so it's been used as a store-room. Auntie Lynne has kind of stepped back from the business since she met Nige — her boyfriend — and leaves it all to me. She can't sell it or holiday let it, otherwise she might be keener.'

'Auntie Lynne? I thought you owned the shop?'

'No way, although I may as well. My auntie used to enjoy working in here with me but like I say, she's been distracted lately . . . She seems to have lost interest since her boyfriend came on the scene last spring.' She almost spat out the word 'boyfriend', by which Rose guessed she didn't approve of him.

'I just run it and work in it, apart from having some help on my day off in the summer season.' She sighed. 'To be honest, though, up here is probably in a worse state than I'd realised. I'll understand if you're not interested.'

Rose hesitated, wondering how long it would take

42

Oriel to make the place habitable and knowing she'd probably have to muck in herself as her stand-in land-lady would be busy in the shop.

'*If* I moved in, where would you store the stock?'

'In the storeroom downstairs.' Oriel's tone was more upbeat at the sniff of a possible tenant. 'All the stuff up here is years old and it's needed clearing out for ages. Most of it was accumulated by my auntie — she used to buy so much rubbish — but I can help you get rid of it, so don't worry about that. If you take it, that is. I'd enjoy some company in the shop and I can let you have it really cheap,' she said, hopefully. 'The letting income would be very welcome.'

Even at the price Oriel named, which was very tempting, Rose still wasn't sure. She thought she could hear squeaking from behind the bedroom door.

'I'm likely to be out most of the day,' Rose said warily, worried she could be sucked into being Oriel's assistant when she was supposed to be getting on with her work. 'I've promised my boss I'll do a lecture series for my students and write a paper about my research.'

'I know you'll be busy,' Oriel said, looking down-cast. 'I know it's probably not what you're used to but the view's great.' She climbed over a box to the window and tugged the curtains so hard the ring fell off one end of the pole. The room was filled with sun-light, illuminating the shabby furnishings and clashing covers and endless stuff.

Oriel rubbed a patch on the window with the sleeve of her kaftan. 'Worth a hundred grand, that view, my auntie says, *if* she could ever sell the place to someone from upcountry.'

Rose wanted to help Oriel out but she was finding it hard to see past all the rubbish in the flat. It was very small and God knows what lay behind the doors. Feeling guilty that she might have to turn the flat down, Rose picked her way over to the window. Oriel squashed into a corner so that Rose could stand next to her.

Her breath caught in her throat.

Through the panes, with their years of grime and seagull crap, the estuary stretched out before her, glittering in the sunlight. She could see over the thatched roofs of the cottages and the roof of the Ferryman, to the yachts in the marina, and the ferry itself, currently making its way from the yacht club jetty to the quay at the end of the village.

And there, almost directly opposite the window, was the boatyard, where a sailing dinghy was hauled up the slipway by a tractor. She was so close, she could even make out the words 'Morvah Marine' on the back of Finn's polo shirt and see the sun glinting on Joey's Aviators.

Her heart was beating faster than it really ought to be, but she couldn't suppress a thrill at living so close to the Morvahs.

'Do you want it, then?' Oriel asked, sounding less than hopeful.

'Oh, yes,' Rose said, almost breathless with suppressed excitement. 'Yes, please. It's absolutely perfect.'

5

That evening, Rose video-called Maddie with the news. Her friend had a G&T in her hand and was in her study. She'd worked very hard to get a partnership in a solicitor's practice in London, where she now lived with her husband, Geraint.

'Good news! I've found somewhere to live,' Rose said. 'It's a flat above the local pixie shop. It's a bit old-fashioned but the view is to die for.'

'Above a *pixie* shop?' Maddie said. 'Are you sure that's wise?'

Rose laughed. *Is that wise?* had become Maddie's mantra as far as Rose was concerned. 'I don't know but it was available, it's cheap and the landlady is lovely. It's actually a folklore gift shop called Cornish Magick.'

'Cornish Magick? You're kidding me!'

'Nope. It sells crystals and joss sticks and yes, pixie charms. That kind of stuff,' Rose said, hearing the chug of the ferry approaching her side of the river. 'The woman who runs it — Oriel — doesn't believe in magic herself. She suggested I take the flat and she's great fun and it has an amazing view. I've been lucky to find a place to rent in such a touristy spot during the holiday season.' Rose felt she was over-egging the pudding, but she wanted to be as upbeat as possible to forestall any warnings from Maddie.

'Well, I'm happy you found somewhere so um . . . quaint to live in, but won't you miss civilisation?' By which Maddie actually meant: would Rose

45

be lonely? Maddie had been gutted when she hadn't been a bone marrow match for Rose and had only stopped saying 'I'm sorry' when the stranger's transplant had worked.

'I'm missing you but not Cambridge yet. It's beautiful here.'

Maddie snorted. 'It must still feel like a holiday. Just you wait until you're longing for a nice cocktail or a drink by the river.'

Rose smiled to herself. 'You know, Maddie, we have a river here . . . and there are even cocktails at the pub. In fact, I'll send you a photo at the weekend when I've moved in. You can also visit me if you don't mind sleeping on a sofa.'

'I'd love to come and the sofa is fine. I'll check my diary but do send loads of pictures in the meantime. I want to see and know everything.' Maddie broke off to look at her phone and she rolled her eyes. 'Oh no. I'm sorry, I have to go out. One of my regulars is in a spot of bother at the police station — again. Speak soon and I promise I'll come down as soon as I can find a few days spare.'

'I'll look forward to it.'

'Good luck with your bones,' Maddie said, already out of her office chair.

'I'm here for the stones. I don't do bones.'

'Byeeee!' Blowing a kiss, Maddie cut her off.

Rose sat back on the bed with a sigh. She loved Maddie but she wasn't quite sure she took Rose's job seriously. Maddie had celebrated with Rose at her PhD ceremony, joining Rose and her grandmother and a couple of other friends in the pub. Her mother hadn't been able to get away from work because she was shooting a series in the Rockies.

46

Rose did wonder if Maddie regarded archaeology as a bit of a jolly, and not a 'proper job'. After all, Rose would never be called upon to dash off to the local nick and prevent some young man or woman from getting into even more trouble than they already were — or being unjustly accused of something they hadn't even done.

Rose hadn't minded not having a large family at her PhD ceremony, like some of the other students. She had her friends and was simply overjoyed she was alive but now she'd been given a second chance, she also wanted to live it to the max. She wanted to pursue her passion, expand her knowledge, enjoy a successful career, meet someone who made her laugh, and have lots of great sex with him — hopefully have a family if it was possible. Was all of that too much to ask?

None of it would have even been possible to contemplate without the donor.

Once again, she wondered why he hadn't responded to her second letter or asked to get in touch. Their minimal communication so far had been carried out through the donor charity so she didn't have an email address or phone number, just the card and her research. This wasn't very promising, and yet . . . perhaps he might change his mind if he actually met her? It was a dangerous yet intoxicating idea.

* * *

With a rising feeling of excitement, Rose drove off to the dig site the next morning. She'd already been once to introduce herself and had been struck by the stunning location. It was located a few hundred yards from the romantically named King Arthur's Pool, slap bang in the middle of the Lizard. The moorland site was wildly beautiful with sweeping views and the distant sea visible on three sides. On a misty day, you probably wouldn't be able to see more than a few yards but today it was glorious, with blue skies and skylarks twittering overhead.

After leaving her car at the entrance to a field, which a farmer had allowed them to use, she tramped the mile or so across agricultural land to the moorland. She soon realised that she'd have to get fitter if she wanted to do all this walking to remote sites and work at the dig all summer.

The dig area itself was roped off and there were a couple of open-sided tents to protect the finds plus a portaloo. Half a dozen students were kneeling down, scraping away at neat trenches. Rose breathed in, enjoying the scent of the freshly turned earth and the sight of people doing what they loved. She stayed for a while, hearing about the site and looking at some of the recent finds.

Maddie might laugh at her, but she felt the location was incredibly atmospheric, imagining the ancient people who had built the stones. She relished the sun on her back, the wind in her hair and skylarks twittering overhead. From time to time she'd hear the distant whirr of helicopters from the naval base, but that was practically the only modern sound. She'd been sceptical about such things at one time, but personally, she felt that having a new lease of life had heightened her senses: colours, scents, sounds all seemed more intense than they were before.

Feeling positive about her new job, she returned to the B&B, and resisted the urge to cross the estuary to see if she could spot Joey and Finn. In a little place like Falford, she was bound to meet them face to face at some point, a thought that sent alternate thrills of excitement and apprehension through her.

There was no rush to reveal herself. She needed to approach her task like a dig; prepare, be patient, unearth the truth with the same delicate care she'd unearth a fragile piece of pottery or jewellery.

After all, she had the rest of the summer . . . Her pulse picked up. She had to admit, now reality had hit, she was way more nervous than she'd thought about revealing who she was.

★   ★   ★

The next day, Rose returned from the dig and went to visit Oriel at the flat. She found Cornish Magick closed but the side entrance was open. Her nose twitched at the pungent scent of patchouli oil and she could hear Oriel singing along to the radio. When she entered the flat, Rose found her standing on a step stool, wearing pink Marigolds and flicking a feather duster at the light fitting.

Rose looked around, her eyes widening. 'Wow! Is this the same place?'

All the clutter was gone, and the room looked twice as large. The kitchenette surfaces were full of cleaning products.

'I've been dusting the cobwebs off the light fitting.'

'Have you done all of this?' Rose noted the scrubbed floorboards, which now had a dhurrie rug. There was also a brand-new sofa. 'I didn't expect new stuff.'

'Auntie Lynne and Nige did most of it while I worked in the shop. Nige works for a builders' and he said the furniture had to meet the latest fire regs so he went to Truro and got a new one. I was surprised he was so helpful to be honest.'

'Why?'

'Because he's not normally so obliging and that worries me,' she said. 'Anyway,' she added briskly, as if she'd thought better of elaborating on Nigel's motives. 'It's a sofa bed,' Oriel added, 'in case you want an overnight guest.'

'Thanks. It's fantastic. I can have my friend Maddie to stay,' Rose said, imagining Maddie's face when she saw the flat.

'You really like it, then?'

'I can hardly believe the transformation! Thank you and please thank your auntie and her boyfriend too. Now, what else can I do to help finish it off?'

'I haven't had time to tackle the loo yet. You could do that.'

'Show me where the bleach is and I'll get to work.'

The bathroom wasn't as bad as feared and an hour later, it was respectable. 'I always wanted an avocado-coloured bath,' Rose said, as she and Oriel took mugs of coffee to the door to survey their handiwork. 'And I didn't have the heart to throw out the loo roll fairy.'

Oriel giggled as they looked at the pink crocheted cover placed over a loo roll on the windowsill.

'It'll look cosy with some nice tea lights. I'll bring some of the sandalwood ones up from the shop,' Oriel said. 'And some camomile room spray for the sofa and lavender bags for your cupboards.'

'Lovely,' Rose replied, wondering if her nose could take any more floral scents. Surrounded by them every day, Oriel must hardly notice them now.

An hour later, the flat was finally habitable. Oriel had popped downstairs to gather in the smellies while

Rose gave the inside of the windows a final once-over with the spray. At seven p.m. the sun was still bright though the shadows were lengthening and the creek was shady. The tide was low and she could see people crossing the narrow channel via the ford. There were already drinkers sitting at the pub tables of the Ferryman enjoying a pint in the evening sun.

Two more nights and she'd actually be living here.

'Here you go!' Oriel arrived on a waft of perfume and placed a box on the little dining table. Rose stifled a sneeze but also felt a pull of gratitude. She had a home and a new friend in Falford and she'd been here less than a week. All in all, it was a good start.

'Whoops!'

Oriel knocked over Rose's bag and a small plastic box fell out. Packets and bottles of pills and tablets spilled out of it.

'Sorry! Wow, you've got more medication in here than our village pharmacy,' Oriel commented, picking up the bottles.

'I like to be prepared,' Rose said, groaning inwardly as she picked up a bottle that had rolled to the window.

'You can say that again,' Oriel said, replacing the packets in the carton. Rose held her breath, wondering if her new landlady would dig any deeper about her array of meds. However, Oriel seemed more excited about the clean windows.

'Blimey, you really can see through there now. Lynne got the window cleaner to do the outside while you were out at the dig, but you've done a great job on the inside. You can spy on the whole village from here. Look, there's the yacht club, and further down the estuary, that's Finn's place, Curlew Studio — it's the white triangle-shaped roof over the boathouse. Finn keeps his boat on the jetty outside.'

Rose kept her reply casual. 'Finn?'

'Finn's one of the Morvah sons who works at the boatshed.'

'He must have a lovely view from his house.'

'Well, it's only a small place. Auntie Lynne calls it a pigeon loft.' Oriel laughed. 'I've been in once and it's all right if you like living right on the water, I s'pose. It used to belong to the artist who owned the gallery but he passed away a few years ago.' Oriel sighed. 'Lovely man. He was only forty-four when he died. He had some rare type of cancer.'

'That's awful . . .' said Rose, suppressing a shudder at how young the artist was and at being reminded of her own brush with death. 'How sad . . .' She knew that she would never shake off that fear, the kind that took hold of the pit of your stomach and induced a momentary panic. It would be with her for the rest of her life, but at least she did have a life, unlike the poor artist . . . and now her donor might be living in his studio.

'Are you OK?' Oriel asked. 'You look a bit worried.'

'Yes. I was just thinking of this artist. What a shame he died so young.' She did think it was awful, but she was also intrigued about the artist. If Finn now lived in the guy's studio, then it made it far more likely that he was her donor.

'Was he anyone I might have heard of?' Rose's gaze drifted to the white gable end of the studio, with its small balcony, imagining Finn in there now, oblivious to what he'd done for her and her family.

'I doubt it cos he wasn't famous even though I thought he was brilliant. He was called Nash Santo,' Oriel said. 'His dad was Portuguese, but his mum was from St Austell.'

'Oh. OK. I must look up his work,' Rose said, feeling guilty that she already had a file on Nash on her laptop.

'You won't find much. Nash didn't like the Internet. He wanted people to look at his paintings in the flesh.' Oriel smirked. 'Some of them were *of* flesh. Some really beautiful ones of nude men, if you're into that sort of thing. They used to have some of his pictures in the gallery next door but the rest were given away when he died.'

Rose smiled. Even Nash couldn't hide away from Google. She decided she'd pop into the gallery just in case they had any more of his work, though male nudes didn't really fit with the tranquil — and rather bland — waterside scene on her card.

'Anyway, that's the sailing trust centre, almost where the creek opens out into the main estuary,' Oriel said pointing to a low-roofed hut on the opposite bank, largely obscured by masts. 'Ah — that looks like Finn tying up there now.'

Rose had no idea how Oriel could tell.

'That's *Siren*, his yacht . . . the Bermuda rigged sloop. He made it himself,' Oriel said, sounding impressed. 'He must be off to the sailing centre. He and his brother, Joey, teach kids and novices to sail there.'

'Mm . . .' Rose strained her eyes trying to make out the boat amid all the others around the sailing trust.

'And that's the north side of the Falford estuary in the distance,' Oriel said indicating the line of greenery blending into a hazy sky.

'It's so beautiful . . .' Rose said, still transfixed by the scene before her, particularly the activity at Morvah

Marine and the sailing trust. 'It's hard to tear your eyes away, isn't it?'

'Oh, look, there's Finn's brother, Joey, with Sophie Crean,' Oriel said with disgust. 'He's taking her out in his own boat. I thought it was all over between them.'

They watched Joey take a picnic basket from a young woman before helping her climb aboard a yacht. She was the same woman Rose had seen arguing with Joey a few days previously.

Oriel snorted. 'I think we can guess they're off for more than a pork pie.'

Rose had to laugh. 'Do you know Sophie well, then?'

'Sophie's Naomi's cousin. Naomi's my girlfriend.' Oriel rolled her eyes. 'You'd never know they shared any genes though. Naomi is lovely and would never say a bad word about anyone, but Sophie is toxic. She's horrible to Naomi so we try to avoid each other. Have you got any brothers or sisters?'

'No. Just me, though I suppose Maddie is like a sister.' Rose smiled.

'Close, are you?'

'Yes, I guess we are. We met in our first week at uni. We have our moments, but she's always been there for me when I need her,' Rose said, thinking of her friend.

'Best kind of mate. I hope Sophie's boat capsizes, preferably with her in it,' Oriel said then smirked. 'Not really and anyway, I'm sure she'd love it just to be rescued by Joey.'

Rose burst out laughing. 'Would you like a glass of wine?' she asked, impulsively. 'I picked up a bottle from a vineyard on my way back from the dig site.'

'Thanks, but I should be getting home to Naomi. She's made vegan pizza.'

'Oh, OK.' Rose tried to hide her disappointment. She rather fancied a good gossip and Oriel was fun company. However, she did obviously have a life of her own . . . and Rose was a newcomer.

'Tell you what though, would you like to come to the yacht club party on Saturday night to celebrate you moving in? Naomi's on the late shift so she won't mind. She's a paramedic,' Oriel added, visibly puffing with pride.

'Sounds great. I'd love to.'

Oriel's lips twitched with a sly smile. 'I think you'll enjoy it.'

Rose was even more intrigued and the butterflies started up again. 'Is it a private party?'

'They like to call it a members' social event, but anyone can join for a few quid. They need to get people in all year round spending money, so they do a locals' social rate. You can be my guest.'

'Will it be busy?'

'Not this early in the season. The yachties tend to turn up in the school holidays. They have it in the downstairs room not the posh restaurant at the top so it's more local from around the estuary and inland villages. They sometimes have a band and always a happy hour. The brewery sponsors it, so the drinks are cheap. It'll be your chance to meet everyone.'

'Everyone?'

'Anyone worth meeting.' Oriel screwed up her nose. 'And a few who you'll want to avoid.'

'Anyone in particular?' Rose asked lightly.

Oriel pulled a face. 'Sophie, I expect. I should let you make up your own mind but . . . her mum runs the village stores. Don't tell her anything private.'

Rose mimed zipping her lips.

'Other than that, there's a few sailing types from the village. A couple of guys from the paddleboard hire centre, Bo Grayson from the boatyard café — oh and the Morvahs of course.'

Goose bumps popped on Rose's arms. 'Oh?'

'Their mum can be a bit scary. She's overprotective of the boys, according to Auntie Lynne, but I doubt very much she'll turn up. Finn and Joey will probably go. They usually do.' Oriel smirked again. 'Joey is hard to miss.'

'Really? In what way?' Rose asked, trying to keep the rampant curiosity out of her voice.

'Most of the straight women roundabouts think he's hot . . . and I suppose he's handsome, if you like that sort of thing.' Oriel wrinkled her nose. 'I doubt he'd be *your* type though and don't take this the wrong way, but you're not his.'

Rose's interest was piqued even more. 'Am I not?'

'You're too, I dunno, low-key, not really glamorous enough for him, and he likes women who are impressed by him. You wouldn't fall for all that charm and the muscles.'

Rose felt that she was being given a backhanded compliment. 'I'm glad you think so,' she said, catching sight of herself in the mirror over the hearth. Her hair was frizzy in the humid air, coming down from its bun, and her face was flushed and devoid of any make-up. She was wearing a pair of faded dungarees that Maddie said made her look like a children's TV presenter from the 1970s.

No, she was definitely not Joey Morvah's type, which was probably a very good thing in the circumstances. The very last thing she needed was a crush on the man who might have saved her life. That would be the worst kind of cliché — rescuer syndrome — and sure to end in a broken heart.

'Of course,' Oriel said. 'You might already have someone . . . only you haven't mentioned anyone yet and you've come to live down here on your own . . .' Oriel gave her a piercing look. 'Or you're gay?'

Rose smiled. 'No, I don't have anyone and I'm not gay. I was too busy finishing my PhD and after that, settling into my job at the university. I was lucky to get it and I daren't have any more distractions.'

It was true she'd been too busy recovering and getting her career back on track since her transplant.

She hadn't had a serious boyfriend since the geologist. She'd thought she was in love with him, but he'd been unable to deal with her illness and Rose didn't blame him, even though the split had felt like salt had been rubbed into the wound of her problems.

'I'd have thought there were plenty of single men at a university,' Oriel said.

'Plenty of men, yes, but most of them are in relationships by now or more interested in old stones than women,' Rose said. 'They probably think I'm more interested in old stones than them and in most cases, it would be true.'

She laughed and Oriel laughed too, but actually, Rose's heart was heavy. Love was on her wish list, not top of it but an important part of the long life she hoped to live to the full.

Oriel nodded. 'Anyway, I don't think you'll like Joey. Since he split up with his girlfriend, Lauren, last year, he's dated a string of women, but he never stays with any of them. I don't know what went wrong there but he hasn't been the same since.'

'Really?'

57

'She went to London. Got a better job in a hospital. She was a doctor . . .' Oriel said. 'They sold their flat and Joey moved back into the boatyard annexe. He's gone totally the opposite way. Naomi's mum says Dorinda worries about him, bringing different women back every week.'

'Every week?'

'Well, every few months. Sometimes he has two on the go at once. One caused a scene at the boatyard a month back. Screaming in the yard and throwing things at Joey.'

While Rose didn't want to prejudge, she also didn't think she'd like Joey much. He sounded thoughtless at best; a user of women at worst — could this be the man who'd been generous enough to save her life? Of course he could, she reminded herself. You didn't have to be a saint yourself to do a good deed. Why had she even expected that? For all she knew, her donor might have been a really nasty piece of work in every other way. He might not have expected ever to be called on to donate, and done it most reluctantly and yet . . . the card hadn't seemed to come from someone callous and unfeeling.

From the little she'd heard, it sounded as if Joey was still suffering from the fallout from his split. Perhaps Oriel had exaggerated his romantic exploits.

In fact, the more Oriel had warned her about Joey, the more desperate Rose was to meet the guy and make her own judgement, but she didn't want to give Oriel — or anyone — the slightest hint of exactly how keen she was.

'Do you sail?' she asked. Rose hadn't got Oriel down as the yachtie type but didn't like to say so. 'Or is that a stupid question?'

'I can a bit but it's such a faff. I'd rather get about in my dad's motorboat. It's not very big and it's a bit old but it gets me where I want to.' Oriel grinned. 'You can use it if you like, under my supervision until you get used to it, of course.'

'Um, that's very kind of you,' Rose said, thinking that any kind of experience of the local waters was a good start. 'I should warn you though, I've never handled a boat of any kind in my life.'

'I'll show you. It'll save you hours of trying to drive round these lanes, dodging emmets and scraping your car. It's easy.'

Rose didn't think it looked easy at all, and would greatly prefer to take her chances on the road rather than dodging the hazards of yachts, fishing boats, rowing dinghies, paddleboarders and everything else that puttered and sailed past the village jetty. She had visions of turning the tiller an inch the wrong way or a second too late and mowing down a family in a rowing boat or ploughing into the passenger ferry. However, she had to begin somewhere, and it might be far better to get to know the hazards of the estuary before she decided on anything more ambitious like sailing.

Oriel must have noticed her doubtful expression. 'Don't look so scared. It's much easier than learning to drive a car.'

Rose managed an optimistic smile, while praying she would acquire some hitherto magic power and some sea legs. The yacht club was tantalisingly close and offered the potential of a huge reward: the chance to meet the Morvah brothers.

'Tell you what, we'll go to the yacht club party in the boat,' Oriel said blithely. 'And you can have your first driving lesson.'

6

Rose moved her few possessions from the guest house and into Cornish Magick on the Friday. Maddie had promised to collect a few more things from the cottage in Cambridge and bring them down when she visited. It was mizzling — the perfect description for the mix of mist and drizzle that clung to every surface — but she headed to the dig site anyway and spent a few hours working in the trenches alongside the students. They unearthed a few fragments of pottery but nothing exciting, yet she still enjoyed it. It was a joy simply to be able to do her job.

In the afternoon, she returned to the flat to write up her report but kept getting distracted by her new surroundings, especially as the sun had chased away the clouds and revealed the village in all its glory. The sunlit creek and chocolate-box scene demanded to be captured. She didn't think it would ever grow old.

She pushed back the frame, and leaned out, holding her phone to get the best view. She scrolled through the pictures, ready to press the edit button to lighten them up or add a filter. It took less than thirty seconds to realise that no magic light wand or filter improved the scene. The natural light, sparkling on the water, the purple wisteria on the white cottage, the rich greens and earthy russet of the mudflats left by the retreating tide. None of it needed enhancing, but the sun had just come out fully.

She pushed the window to its limit, keen to get more of the yacht club with its marina full of masts into the shot. With one hand on the sill, she leaned as far as she dared, angling her phone when it suddenly slipped.

'Arghh!'

'Hey!' she heard from below. A man looked up from the lane right beneath her. It was Finn Morvah, and judging by his furrowed brow, he was less than impressed.

'Sorry!' Rose called. 'I hope that didn't hit you.'

'No. You've been lucky,' he said, stepping back a little into the lane, presumably to get a better look at whoever had almost put a dent in his skull.

'I think you're the lucky one,' she said, trying to sound apologetic but keep things light. 'It could have hurt you. It just slipped out of my hand while I was trying to take a photo of the — um — boats in the marina.' She lowered her voice, realising that a few people had stopped to see what the drama was about.

Finn held up the phone. 'I meant you were lucky because I caught it. It slid down the thatch on the shop porch.'

'Oh, thank you! I'll come down and get it.'

Rose hurried down the twisty staircase as fast as she could, wondering if Finn thought she'd been trying to take a photo of him.

Slightly breathless, she put a cheery smile on her face when she reached where he was waiting outside in the lane.

If she'd hoped to catch her breath, the sight of him up close was no help whatsoever. He had to be six feet four at least, with a tanned face and dark wavy hair brushing his shoulders. Wherever his genes had originated from, they were pretty extraordinary.

Gathering herself, she nodded at the sloping

thatched porch of the shop and her still-open window. 'Well done on catching it. You should play for the village cricket team.'

'I do — but it's the first catch I haven't dropped since the start of last season.' He smiled and Rose was filled with relief. 'Maybe you should make sure it's working before you get too excited?'

'Hmm. Yes.' She took it from him. There didn't seem any damage to the case. She pushed the button and it flickered into life. 'It seems OK.'

Dark brown eyes scrutinised her. 'I hope you got a good photo.'

She detected more than a hint of amusement in his voice. 'I'll take a look when I get back upstairs.' She wiggled the phone at him. 'I was trying to get in as much of the estuary and marina as possible, to show a friend how fantastic it is.'

He glanced up again. 'A room with a view,' he said carefully.

'It's perfect. I mean, it's ideal for what I need. Lucky for me that it was available.'

'I expect Oriel is pleased too. I think she's been hoping to get a tenant for ages and the rent will come in handy,' Finn said. 'Will you be working in the shop?'

'I'm happy to help out from time to time.' Did he know why she was here? Or at least one of the reasons she'd told Oriel she was here? Which wasn't a lie — simply not the whole truth. 'Though I'm no expert on crystals and healing stones.'

He smiled wryly. 'I'm sure you and Oriel will get on very well.' He seemed to catch something out of the corner of his eye and nodded at a fishing boat passing by, before returning his attention to Rose. 'Well, I'm glad I saved your phone,' he said.

Now she'd got him, Rose didn't want to let him go, even if she felt she was keeping a fish wriggling on a hook.

'I'm actually an archaeologist,' she blurted out. 'So, although I'm interested in folk myths and legend, it's from an academic point of view.'

'So, you're down here to *work*?' He sounded incredulous.

'Oh, yes. I've got a small research grant to study some of the ancient sites over the summer, on the Lizard and in the far west. There's a dig up on the moors near King Arthur's Pool. So, that's why I'm here,' she added then wished she hadn't because it sounded as if she was trying too hard.

Her work also didn't quite explain why she'd chosen a literal backwater in Falford Creek when she could have stayed somewhere more central to the sites she was interested in, such as Falmouth where she might well have found some university accommodation close to the students and her temporary colleagues. Then again, even if he did know where all the locations were, he'd probably just think she didn't know the area.

'Sounds like an interesting job,' he said, and Rose believed he meant it. 'I'm sorry to say I don't know anything about those old sites, but I am aware there are dozens of them dotted about. Have you got a car to get around?'

'Yes. I left it in a reserved space on the village car park, though Oriel seems to think I'd be better off learning to drive a boat.'

He nodded enthusiastically. 'Good idea. It'll save you hours, especially when the holiday season ramps up. Who'd choose to be stuck on the road behind queues of tourists when you could be out on the water?' He lifted his hand and turned towards the estuary where a man was in the main inlet, chugging out towards the open mouth of the sea in his boat. 'A boat gives you freedom . . .'

'I'm beginning to realise that. Um. Do you work around boats?' She hoped she didn't sound as guilty as she felt.

'Yep. At the boatyard opposite.' His smile belied his keen scrutiny of her. 'I think you might have seen me the other day when you were walking past the yard.'

Rose's pulse quickened. He definitely had noticed her spying on the yard. 'Oh yes. I think I must have, but I hadn't made the connection.'

'I'm Finn,' he said. 'Finn Morvah. Our family owns Morvah Marine.' He held out his hand.

Rose took it. It was a brief contact, firm and warm, yet she couldn't help the tingle of excitement his touch sent through her. She'd wondered for a long time how it would feel to meet the person who might have given her life back — now she'd shaken his hand. Possibly.

She'd also wondered if she'd know instantly, by some instinct, even though that was medically impossible and totally fanciful.

'I'm Rose Vernon,' she said, letting go of his hand suddenly as if it was a hot coal.

He gave a wry smile. 'I know.'

She exhaled in surprise. 'How?' Then she laughed. 'Oh, I see. Oriel has already told you.'

'A newcomer moves into a tiny place like Falford? News travels fast. I didn't know you were an archaeologist though. That hadn't reached me yet.'

She laughed. He'd admitted he knew her name. She'd lied about not knowing his. This was going to

64

be much harder than she'd even imagined. As for any instinctive recognition that he was her donor . . . She had to admit she'd felt nothing other than — undeniably — she fancied him. A lot.

'Well, I must be going,' he said. 'Unless . . . you wanted to get a quick coffee? Or a cold drink? I'd like to hear more about the dig.'

'Really?' Rose was amazed at being asked and slightly worried she'd let something slip that gave her secret away, but still she answered, 'I'm sure I can spare time for a coffee.'

'OK. The pub does coffees on the terrace.'

They walked the hundred yards down to the pub, ordered coffee and a Coke for Finn before finding a seat in the afternoon sun. There were a few obvious tourists outside, taking pictures with expensive-looking cameras or selfies with their phones. They were oohing and aahing about the view and Rose overheard one say: 'Wouldn't mind living here, must be Paradise.'

Finn exchanged a wry smile with Rose. He mouthed 'Paradise?' and she smiled back. She was pleased that already she wasn't considered a tourist.

'It is incredibly beautiful here,' Rose said when the tourist was out of earshot. 'You can hardly blame people for thinking it.'

'True, but it's not Paradise.'

'I know. I suppose if you live and work here all the time, you have a different perspective.'

'Yup. Nowhere is perfect, least of all Falford . . .' He smiled. 'But I wouldn't be anywhere else.' His gaze travelled to the boatshed on the far side of the estuary. Rose thought he also glanced at his watch and wondered if he felt guilty about taking time off work.

'I'm sure you're busy working on that big boat,' she said.

His eyebrows met in surprise. 'How do you know about that?'

'I noticed it through the doors. It's impossible not to,' she said, desperately trying to explain away her interest in the yard. 'I didn't know what type of boat it was.'

'She's a gaff rigged cutter. We're building her for a client. Or should be.' He grimaced, and Rose was now certain he felt guilty about being away from work.

Somehow, she hadn't really expected Finn to refer to the boat in female terms. It seemed like the stuff of centuries before. Yet he dropped in the feminine pronouns naturally enough. Rose wondered why boats were called 'she'. Who had decided it?

'Will I be seeing you on the water soon?' he said.

'I hope so, but I need a driving lesson from Oriel first.'

'I'm sure you'll be fine. Oriel knows this estuary like the back of her hand. She's a good sailor, even if she does insist on sticking to the motorised variety.'

'I'm pleased to hear it,' Rose said. She was warming to Finn even more. She'd half-expected him to laugh when she'd said she was going to learn to drive the boat. Yet he hadn't, and the passion for his surroundings was clear.

She'd only been here how long . . . ? And she'd already discovered that Finn and Falford were full of surprises. She wondered whether he'd react to her secret in the same positive way if he knew about it. Maybe he'd be delighted, rather than freaked out, but she wasn't ready to take that risk.

They chatted about her work, although Rose

66

wondered if he'd simply used that as an excuse to invite her for coffee. Finn told her that his grandfather had taken him and Joey to King Arthur's Pool when they were young boys and that they'd both believed that Excalibur really had been thrown into the water. Rose found it fascinating to talk to local people and hear how legends were handed down over the centuries.

They also talked about the boatshed and the estuary for a while, with Finn pointing out some of the features along the bank. He didn't mention his own home, which was clearly visible from the pub, but Rose hadn't expected him to. She was still recovering from being invited to coffee, and guessed that it was an impulsive suggestion, possibly one that had surprised him as much as her.

The landlord appeared at the table and nodded at their empty cups and glasses. 'Get you anything else?' he said.

'Not for me. I have to be going,' Finn said, turning to Rose.

'I ought to do some work too,' Rose said, and the landlord left.

'Yes . . . maybe I might see you on Saturday?' Rose blurted out.

'Saturday?'

'Oriel invited me to a party at the yacht club. I thought, as you and your family like sailing, you might be going?'

Finn hesitated. Rose feared she'd put him on the spot. 'I hadn't really made any plans yet but maybe I will see you.' He smiled.

'I won't keep you from your work any longer,' Rose said lightly.

'Hmm. Good idea, but I've a got a more important

67

job first. I have to pick the kids up from school.'

Rose covered her shock with a smile. 'Oh. Oh, I s-see,' she stuttered. 'You had better go. Thanks for saving my . . . phone.'

'You're welcome. See you around, I hope?'

With that, Finn was gone.

Kids. She hadn't expected that. She'd blithely assumed her donor would be young, male — and single? It was as if she'd been blinkered. Of course, he might have a partner and a family.

A family . . . that thought was like a stab to the heart. It was regret. Her treatment prior to her transplant meant that she was unlikely to be able to have children without a lot of help, if at all. It also made her think carefully about whether she should ever reveal who she was to her donor. Blundering into the life of the person who'd chosen to help her was one thing, intruding into his family was quite another. It made Rose more determined than ever to tread very carefully around the Morvahs — and she certainly wouldn't hold her breath for the yacht club party as far as Finn was concerned.

7

After having a drink with Rose and doing the school run, Finn picked up little Ivy and Ethan and went back to work at the yard. It was past seven p.m. by the time he left, walking along the estuary path to Curlew Studio. Still, he found himself unable to get Falford's newest resident out of his mind. The 'mermaid' who had turned out to be very far from a disappointment in real life.

Finn had been fascinated by her and eager to know more about her. If he hadn't had to pick up the children, he could easily have stayed at the pub for hours talking to her — looking at her. Hmm. Maybe it was a good thing he'd needed to leave, or he might never have gone back to work at all.

And why oh why hadn't he sounded more enthusiastic about the yacht club party? His hesitation was only because Rose's request had taken him by surprise. He'd actually decided not to bother with it, not being in the most sociable of moods these days.

However, if Rose was going, he might change his mind.

The thought of getting to know her better brought a glow of pleasure and put him in good spirits while he found a bottle of beer from the studio fridge and took his 'dinner' out of a paper bag. The yard's apprentice boat painter, Gurdeep, had brought mountains of home-made snacks into the yard for her birthday. There had been so much food that everyone had taken a large bag of samosas, bhajis and pakoras home. Finn

69

carried the snacks outside with a beer. The breeze was cool and the deck in shadow, but sailing and working outside had made him hardy.

He'd bought Curlew Studio from Nash Santo six years previously. It was one long room, converted from the eaves of a rather elaborate boathouse that had once belonged to a grand house higher up the bank of the estuary.

With its position, in walking distance of Morvah Marine, yet out of sight of it — and with its own sheltered mooring too — it was perfect. However, whenever Finn thought of his good fortune in getting the studio, it was always tinged with regret that it had come about as a result of Nash's terrible luck.

Finn had known Nash since he'd first come to Falford and had his wooden dinghy repaired by Morvah Marine. He was an excellent sailor and soon joined both Finn and Joey crewing for them in races and regattas, or simply for pleasure; however, Finn had grown closer to him than Joey. Finn was always interested in other artists and craftspeople. Added to which, Nash had brought a fresh dimension to Falford life, with his experience of sailing and working in exotic locations.

It had been a huge shock to discover just how ill Nash was, and a deep source of sadness when Finn had found out he was dying.

Nash's offer to sell him the studio had come as a complete surprise, although it was typical of the man's pragmatism and kindness. Nash knew Finn was desperate to move out of the annexe of the family home at Morvah Marine. Nash had had a partner before he'd moved to the studio, some young guy who was in the fire service, but it had all ended acrimoniously. Finn

70

never knew exactly why. Nash had been single since, he'd told Finn, and while he had many friends, he'd no close living relatives apart from a cousin. Once she knew Nash was ill, she'd been trying to badger him into selling the studio to her.

'She'll strip every ounce of character from the place, paint it fifty shades of grey and flog it at a ludicrous price as a holiday home,' Nash had told Finn when they'd shared a beer on the tiny deck overlooking the river. 'I want someone who works here to have it, someone who lives and breathes Falford.' He'd smiled. 'Mind you, you'll curse me when I'm gone. You'll always be bumping your head on the beams.'

Finn stood on the deck now, looking over the water. He'd never cursed Nash, no matter how many times he'd bumped his head on the beams supporting the roof. He was, he thought, incredibly lucky to own — along with the bank, of course — Curlew Studio.

The walls still held a number of Nash's paintings. One was a large oil painting of a male nude, left by Nash specifically to Finn. Finn left it exactly where it was, on the gable end above the kitchen table. He didn't have a problem with it — unlike his mother who'd said it was 'a bit full-on to look at over your fish and chips'.

The remaining originals, along with the copyright to produce prints, had been sold to fund a scholarship at the art college in Falmouth. It comforted Finn that Nash lived on in the fabric of Finn's home, and in the creativity of many young artists.

Finn's good fortune had also enabled Joey to move back into the annexe at the boatyard. It had been added for their grandfather and had its own entrance leading into an open-plan kitchen diner and separate bedroom. It gave Joey some independence, yet was still far too much under the eye of his mother for Joey's liking. In this, Finn couldn't blame him.

'Thank you, mate,' Finn said aloud, raising his beer to Nash.

After watching Cornish Magick and the comings and goings at the pub for a while, Finn finished his beer. With no sign of Rose, and no time to take out *Siren*, he made himself busy with the accounts for the business, sitting with the laptop and another beer until it grew dark and lights twinkled along the estuary and coastline.

The gaff rig cutter was worth a six-figure sum to the yard but they were behind schedule. The client, a retired IT entrepreneur, had moved back to Cornwall the previous year and was planning on taking her around the Bay of Biscay and into the Med in the autumn. He'd made it clear to Finn and Dorinda that he wanted no expense spared on her construction or fit-out. Quality was everything, which was why he'd chosen Morvah Marine. He was paying them by the hour, which was a thing to be prized in itself. More than a few boatbuilders had been left seriously out of pocket by agreeing to a price and then finding the work dragged on far beyond the budget.

So Finn was well aware of the responsibility, and spent a while sketching out a new schedule of work to ensure they got back on track.

After working late, he was back at the boatshed by seven on Saturday morning, looking forward to losing himself in the physical and creative part of his job, rather than the admin. Joey sauntered in at eight, which was early for him on a weekend, and immediately went to fetch the morning coffees and bacon butties from Bo's Café.

Finn joined Joey.

'Are you going to the yacht club tonight?' Joey asked.

'Maybe.'

Joey gave him a 'WTF' look.

'OK. Yeah. Probably.'

'Good. You need to get out more. Who knows, you might spot a mermaid . . .'

'How do you know I haven't already?' Finn said, unable to resist.

'Hey, what's that supposed to mean?' Joey's desperation to hear more was almost funny. 'Have you spoken to her?'

'Might have. I picked up her mobile. She'd dropped it outside Cornish Magick.' Finn decided not to tell Joey that he'd also had a drink with Rose, although gossip could already have reached him, of course.

'You picked up her mobile? Wow.' He laughed. 'Actually, I'd heard she'd moved in up there. Well, well, you're a dark horse, as usual. So, is she coming to the yacht club tonight?'

'I'm not one hundred per cent sure.' Well, it wasn't a lie.

'You mean you didn't ask her?'

'It was the first time I've ever met her so no, Joey, I did not ask her on a date.'

'More fool you. You'll have to hope she turns up anyway.'

'I'll leave that to you. I've more important things on my mind.'

Ignoring Joey's scornful snort but unable to keep a grin from his face, Finn returned to the boatshed. There *was* no way he would have asked a strange

73

woman on a date after five minutes' acquaintance, even if he had been fascinated by her. Yet despite what he'd implied to Joey, he was very much hoping Rose made an appearance at the yacht club later so he could get to know her a whole lot better.

8

Rose had spent Friday night in the Magick flat, tossing and turning. That wasn't only down to the bed needing a new mattress, but largely because she'd spent hours running over her conversation with Finn.

She'd allowed herself to imagine that her quest for her donor would be exciting and romantic, but it was already proving complicated. She found Finn very attractive, but she reminded herself she hadn't come to fall for the first handsome man who came in her path — and that her primary purpose was work. She was also feeling embarrassed in case he'd misconstrued her comment about the party as some kind of pick-up line.

'Arghh . . .' Rose said, sorting out her bag ready for the day ahead.

Her sleepless night at least meant she was up super early to visit some of the more remote sites that were associated with myths and legends. She drove through rainy mist for over an hour to reach the high moorlands where the first site — a holed stone with the lovely name of Men-an-Tol — was situated. Rose thought the 'mizzle' only added to the atmosphere of peace and solitude. At this time of day, she was the only person parked in a lay-by at the roadside and the only one yomping over the heathland to the doughnut-shaped granite ring that was about the size of a cartwheel.

Her research found that the stone was associated with curative and magical powers — Oriel had mentioned many of her customers were keen on it and that was probably why. It had been said to do everything from curing rickets and back pain, to helping 'barren' women get pregnant and bringing farmers a bumper harvest.

You were supposed to pass through the stone to get the most benefit and while Rose thought she might just about squeeze through it, she didn't want to end up stuck and having to call the fire service to rescue her. She had visions of Naomi turning up in her ambulance . . . no, Rose decided just to peer through the hole rather than risk becoming a local legend herself.

After taking lots of photos and treating herself to lunch in a local café, she drove back to Falford to write up her morning's field trip. As the crow flew, it wasn't that far, but on the narrow lanes that wound up and down river valleys, it took her well over an hour. While she wouldn't have been able to sail to the sites, Oriel and Finn's advice to use a boat for most travel made more sense by the minute.

She went upstairs and made a cup of tea before taking a mug down to Oriel. It felt good to enter the shop through the bead curtain rather than the door; somehow it made Rose feel like one of Falford's own. Oriel was busy fixing a poster to the wall behind the till. It was an advert for the Falford Regatta, the same event, she assumed, she'd seen online when she'd been hunting down the Morvahs.

Oriel turned around and smiled at the sight of the mug.

'Oh, lovely. I've had a busy day,' she said, taking the mug. 'There was a minibus of Americans in the village on a Daphne du Maurier tour. I sold two geodes, masses of candles, and even a pisky charm!'

'Great. Glad you've been busy. Is that a regatta poster?'

'Oh yes. It's not until August but we like to advertise it early. It's the highlight of the Falford year.'

It was said with a wry grin, so Rose wasn't sure if Oriel was joking or not.

'What happens at the regatta?' she asked.

'It's one big party on and around the water. There's a sailing regatta, swimming races, a sandcastle competition . . . but the best bit is the fancy-dress water pageant.'

'That sounds exciting.'

'It is. We all decorate our boats and the winner gets a prize, but it's the glory that matters. Bloody Nigel won last year but I have plans this time.' Oriel tapped the side of her nose.

'Sounds mysterious . . .' Rose said, with a smile.

'It is and maybe you could join in if you fancied it?'

'Um .....' Rose spluttered, surprised and unsure if she wanted to be so involved.

'I'll let you know more when we've finalised our plans so you can decide,' Oriel said with a mysterious smile. 'So, how did you get on, today?' she said.

'Good. I found Men-an-Tol.' Rose was relieved to be back on more familiar ground.

'Did you climb through the hole?' Oriel said.

'I didn't dare in case I got stuck.'

'Coward. The magic won't work unless you do.'

'What makes you think I need it?'

'All those pills,' Oriel said and eyed Rose. 'They're not for nothing, are they?'

Taken aback, Rose decided on some honesty — of a kind. She wasn't yet ready for long explanations and the inevitable questions. 'No. I had a bit of a problem with my blood but it's under control now. I still need to take the meds but otherwise I'm fine.' She smiled. 'Now, what about this party? Is there a dress code?'

'As long as you wear some kind of clothes and don't walk in naked, anything goes but don't forget we'll be taking the boat so maybe ditch the six-inch stilettos.'

'That's OK,' Rose said with a grin. 'I don't own any.'

At seven o'clock that evening, Rose had her first driving lesson. 'Best you try now before you've had a few glasses of wine,' Oriel said as they stood on the pub quay.

Rose had worn her smart jeans — her only pair — and a floaty top that was a favourite for drinks and parties, and slung her denim jacket over the top. She'd bought a pair of silver dangly earrings with turquoise stones from Cornish Magick and a toe ring that looked pretty with her leather sandals. Oriel had given her a bottle of glittery plum nail varnish, which wasn't Rose's colour but she loved it anyway.

The boat was a small motorboat with a canvas cover over the wheel, which was folded down. As Rose stepped into it from the pub jetty, it wobbled alarmingly. She pushed a strand of hair back into her twisted bun. She'd assumed it would be breezy on the water, even though the inlet was narrow, and the wind was blowing straight up from the main estuary.

'This isn't a Morvah boat, is it?'

Oriel snorted in derision. 'You're joking! This is a fibreglass hull. The Morvahs wouldn't be seen dead with something like this. They make fancy wooden heritage yachts and dinghies. They cost a bomb and there's not many people can afford them now, but they seem to do all right out of it. They do repairs as

78

well, of course.'

With Rose at the helm, Oriel crouched on the quay and started to explain how the engine, throttle and tiller worked. 'It's easy,' she said. 'And very quiet this evening. All you have to do is make for the yacht club jetty and avoid running into any other boats.'

The terraces were quite busy with drinkers and diners, much to Rose's alarm as she hadn't expected to have an audience. A few were watching their departure.

Ignoring them, Oriel climbed in, untied the rope, started the engine and they were off.

Rose made it to the other side without any mishaps even though she was 'driving like a snail' according to Oriel, who took the tiller to guide them to a mooring at the club jetty. Minutes later, they were walking past masts and all manner of shiny craft into the small function room on the ground floor. She imagined being at the helm of one of them and smiled at herself. Maybe starting with something a bit smaller was a better idea.

Three sets of French doors opened onto a small terrace where people had spilled out with their drinks.

Despite her misgivings, Rose had been unable to rein in her curiosity to meet Joey Morvah — and to see Finn again. Her stomach churned.

'Oh shit. Sophie's here. Hold on.' Oriel put a hand on her arm. 'Let's get a drink and go outside.'

With a glass of wine and half a lager for Oriel, they walked onto the terrace. Most of the people they passed smiled and nodded at Oriel and, Rose noted, cast the odd curious glance in her direction. After introducing Rose to the commodore of the yacht club and chatting to a couple of people, Oriel took Rose out to the terrace where around a dozen people were chatting and drinking. She pointed out the homes and boats of various people who lived in the communities on either side of the estuary. They'd been outside about ten minutes when Oriel grimaced.

'Sophie's coming over. It'll be to find out everything she can about you so don't tell her anything.'

Rose wasn't sure whether to be amused or alarmed. Surely Sophie couldn't be as horrible as Oriel painted her.

Sophie made a beeline for them. She was sipping a flute of fizz. Her hair was beautifully cut, and blow-dried into a bob. Rose knew her own had turned frizzy the moment she'd stepped out of the flat and the breeze on the water had probably made her look like a scarecrow.

'Evening. You must be Rose?'

'News travels fast,' Oriel shot back. 'This is Sophie,' she said in a resigned tone, as if she was introducing Rose to a yappy chihuahua.

'Hi,' Rose said in a friendly tone, unable to think of any other reply that wouldn't stoke the fires between Oriel and Sophie.

Sophie smiled. 'Heard you're going to be staying in Falford over the summer.'

'Rose is living above my shop,' Oriel said.

'Your shop?' Sophie's eyebrows formed an impressive arch high up her forehead. 'I thought it was your auntie's place?'

'I run the shop and I invited Rose to stay there,' Oriel said.

'Really? I thought you had to live and work in Cornwall to use that flat...' Sophie said silkily. 'Doesn't it have a local occupancy clause?'

Rose opened her mouth to speak for herself, but Oriel was battling for her. 'Rose is living here. She's doing her research.'

'I'm not sure that ticks all the boxes.'

'And she's helping me out in the shop.' Oriel threw a triumphant glare at Sophie.

'Am I?' Rose blurted out. 'I mean, of course, I'm *very* happy to help out when required,' she added as a suspicious gleam lit up Sophie's eyes. She would never drop Oriel in it.

'With her specialist knowledge of our field, Rose is perfect,' Oriel said.

Specialist knowledge? Of joss sticks and crystals? Rose knew more about boats . . . but she was determined to be loyal to her new landlady.

'Oh look, Joey just arrived. This is going to be interesting.' Oriel scanned the terrace. 'I wonder where Finn is?'

'Oh?' Rose turned briefly and saw Joey on the terrace, chatting. He was . . . Rose could only think of one word:

Beautiful.

However fanciful, he reminded her of a classical statue of an archangel, though she sensed he'd be rightly horrified at the very idea. It was the strong regular features, the wavy honey blond hair. He was several inches over six feet, and his job had given him a body that was muscular and honed in a natural way.

Rose couldn't take her eyes off him, loving the way the sinews and muscle flexed in his arms. He laughed and the two women talking to him were as transfixed as she was. No wonder Oriel, immune to Joey's charms, had warned her.

Rose was disappointed not to see Finn too, but

81

hoped he'd be along later. Meanwhile meeting Joey was going to be more than interesting. In fact, it had sent shivers of anticipation through her, and her fingers were slippery around her glass. She was about to come face to face with the man who might possibly have given her life itself.

Oriel waved at him.

Sophie pursed her lips and the gleam in her eye turned to annoyance. 'I'll leave you to it,' she said. 'Nice to meet you, Rose.'

Before Rose could say the same, Sophie had marched off towards the party room. She passed Joey without even looking at him.

Joey might have said something, but Rose wasn't sure.

'Here we go,' Oriel said, rolling her eyes as Joey made his way over, exchanging words and smiles with a couple of younger men on the way. Anticipation made Rose's pulse quicken.

'Evenin', ladies. Enjoying the party?' Joey said in a soft Cornish accent, which to Rose, used to so many BBC-type accents, seemed exotic. The blue of his eyes was cornflower.

'This is my new tenant,' Oriel said proudly. 'Rose.'

Joey had a gleam in his eye. 'Watch yourself or Oriel will be checking what time you come home and what visitors you have.'

'I'll be keeping an eye on some of them, don't you worry,' Oriel said.

Joey raised an eyebrow. 'Has Rose got anything to worry about, then?'

Wondering if Oriel was referring to Joey as a potential visitor, Rose laughed. 'I don't know but I'm glad Oriel's looking out for me.'

'Where's Finn?' Oriel asked.

'Skippering in the Roseland sailing race,' Joey said. Oriel pulled a face. 'That sounds exciting.'

'You know Finn. Never could resist being in charge'

'Is that in his own boat?' Rose asked, crestfallen to find that Finn wouldn't be at the party at all.

'No, it's for a friend,' Joey said. 'We often crew and skipper for other boats in races. He was asked to step in at the last minute because he knows the boat well.' He smiled. 'We both do. We built it.'

'Oh, I see,' Rose said, reminded of what a close-knit community Falford was, and feeling very much an outsider.

'So, what's led you to the bright lights of Falford, Rose?' Joey asked.

'Rose is an authority in our field. She's an archae-ologist,' Oriel declared.

'Wow. I thought you were an expert in fairies for a minute. Like Oriel here,' Joey said, smiling.

'I don't believe in all that crap about elves and pisk-ies Joey, as you well know.'

Even though Joey had a gleam in his eye and Oriel was well used to him, Rose was a bit annoyed with him for winding up her new friend. Sensing an air of tension, she tried to pour oil on troubled waters. 'Actually, I don't believe in the supernatural either. What Oriel probably means is that I'm interested in myths and legends, particularly those surrounding ancient sites. Actually, your brother told me that you'd once been to King Arthur's Pool.'

Joey and Oriel stared at her.

'You've already spoken to Finn?' he said.

'Well, we had a chat,' she said, realising that Joey and Oriel had been taken by surprise. 'He rescued my

83

phone yesterday. I, er, dropped it out of the window of the flat. By accident,' she added, already deciding to leave out the part about the pub drinks. 'But he was in a rush to pick his kids up from school.'

'His kids?' Joey burst out.

'He hasn't got any kids,' Oriel said.

'Not that I know about,' Joey shot back with a grin. 'He would have meant Rob Brewster's pair, Ethan and Ivy. Rob's a single dad and he had to rush off on a lifeboat shout so Finn offered to collect them. They came to the office while they waited for their dad to come back.'

'Oh, I see . . .'

Oriel raised an eyebrow. 'I could have told you that,' she said sharply.

'Sorry, I didn't think to mention it.' She smiled, but both Joey and Oriel were clearly churning over the fact she'd already met Finn.

'Look, your glasses are almost empty. Would you both like another one?' Rose asked. 'What are you having?'

'I'll come to the bar with you,' Joey offered. 'Help you carry the drinks.'

'Thank you but I'm sure they can give me a tray,' Rose said sweetly. 'And I'm used to carrying masses of pints back from the college bar.'

Joey seemed a little taken aback but let her go. However, while she was waiting to be served, he turned up.

Instead of making a joke as she expected, his expression was serious. 'Look, I'm not sure what Oriel has said about me, but wouldn't it be better to make up your own mind?' His eyes held hers. 'I'm quite sure you will anyway.'

'You're right. I never make judgements without

examining the evidence thoroughly,' she said. 'And for now, all I want to do is relax and get to know some new people. So shall we call a truce?' She smiled. 'For one night, anyway?'

Those blue eyes glinted. 'Why do we need a truce? I didn't even know there'd been a battle yet.'

'I was making a pre-emptive strike,' she said, amused and alarmed at the way he'd managed to draw her into a conversation she'd been determined not to have. She broke off to take the tray of drinks. 'Now, shall we go back to the others?'

'We'd better. Tongues will wag otherwise.'

'Why? You're only helping me with the drinks.'

'Exactly, but plenty around here will want to make more of it.'

'Then, we won't let them.' Rose took the tray, leaving him trailing in her wake, yet alarmingly, also wanting him to follow her. In some ways, he'd lived up to Oriel's description, but she was still a long way from making up her mind.

She was desperate to know if Joey could have been the donor. Should she have steered the conversation in the direction of the past? Or simply ask Oriel if she knew if Joey had been on the register? When he'd given the stem cells he'd have had to spend a day in hospital, and attend screening and appointments. However, that really *would* sound weird.

When they were back from the bar, Oriel was telling Joey about one of the customers she'd had to deal with, but the talk soon turned to some of the boat-handling mishaps in the estuary, most of which seemed to involve overconfident local skippers. Rose suspected the stories had been related to 'newcomers' many times before. Still, she found herself laughing

85

and relaxing as the evening flew by. The band started up, the buzz grew and more people arrived, spilling out onto the terrace and enjoying the evening sun sinking over the estuary.

Briefly, Joey left them and Rose spotted him talking to Sophie Crean again. When he came back, Oriel said something to him that Rose didn't hear. She enjoyed hearing Joey's gossipy tales about the sailing scene and how he and Finn had been taught to sail and work by their late grandfather. Their mother, Dorinda, sounded a formidable woman.

When Oriel whispered that they had to leave or be caught out by the falling tide, the stars were visible in the navy sky and Rose was genuinely disappointed. Oriel steered the boat home in the inky twilight before true night descended. Rose was quiet, preoccupied with trying to examine her feelings towards Joey as objectively as she could. She couldn't deny that Joey was gorgeous, charming and sexy. She wanted to know so much more about him, ask him everything — and most of all, find out if he was the one who'd saved her life.

9

It was midweek before Rose had any more contact with either of the Morvah brothers.

She'd spent the morning indoors hunched over the laptop, working on an academic paper, and was desperate for a walk, so headed out to blow the cobwebs away. As May drew to a close, the natural world was at its most beautiful. Bluebells shone in the shaded areas, and the trees and water were alive with birds, all competing to outdo each other. A family of ducklings pootled around in the shallows as Rose approached the sailing centre at the end of the creek where it opened out to the sea.

In the calm waters outside the centre, she saw Joey with a bunch of primary school children. They looked to be just under ten and were clambering out of their boats after a sailing session. Rose watched as Joey supervised the return of the boats to the shore and saw the kids safely into the care of the sailing centre manager.

Spotting Rose, Joey came over. She had to admit that he rocked the shorty wetsuit and buoyancy aid he was wearing.

'Hello,' he said when Rose met him on the shingle shoreline. 'Fancy a lesson?'

She laughed. He'd handed her the perfect opportunity to say she wanted to learn, but she felt suddenly nervous. 'Um. I don't know . . . I've always loved the idea of it, but not the falling in.'

'You won't fall in,' he said. 'Or not very often.' He

grinned. 'And if you do, I'll make sure you know exactly how to get back in the boat safely. That's the idea of proper lessons.'

Rose wasn't too sure about the idea of falling in being part of the process. 'It looks exciting. My grandad took me out once but I was so little, I wasn't allowed to sail the boat!'

'Yet, it must have stuck in your mind. Trust me, it's a hundred times more exciting when you're at the helm yourself. Once you've had a go you'll never look back. Now's your chance — you're in the best place in the world to learn to sail.'

She laughed again, swept along by his enthusiasm.

'And I might add, with the best person in the world to teach you.'

She let out a playful gasp of amazement at his cheek — and charm.

'You think you could teach me. Some of these little ones look scarily confident — and competent.'

'Yeah . . . I like seeing the kids gain their confidence. Even if they decide sailing's not for them, I've helped them see that they can at least try.'

'I know how you feel. I love teaching . . . It's a great privilege to be able to do it, if that doesn't sound corny.'

'Why would it be corny? Not everyone can do it.' He winced. 'Joking aside, I'm not saying I'm great at it,' he added. 'Though I'm sure you are.'

'I doubt it, but if we both enjoy it so much, that has to be a good start,' Rose said, then added, 'OK, I would like a lesson. But I'll pay.'

'There's no need for that.'

'We'll need to use the equipment here and the boats.'

'I've a better idea. Look, I've almost finished up here. Want to grab a coffee afterwards and I'll tell you about it?'

Rose couldn't resist the opportunity to get to know Joey better. 'OK, that'd be great.'

★ ★ ★

Joey made drinks in the sailing centre kitchen and brought them to a bench outside. He'd changed from the wetsuit into shorts and a hoodie but was still barefoot. He looked so comfortable and in his element.

Joey asked her how she was settling into village life and after a remark about the shop and the gallery next door, Rose took the chance to ask him more about the artist who had illustrated her card. There was always the chance, she thought, that it might trigger him into giving her a clue that he'd sent it.

'Did you know Nash Santo?' she asked, as casually as she could.

Joey frowned in confusion. 'Course I did. Why?'

'Just wondering. Oriel was talking about him the other day and I, um, saw a print of his in the gallery next to the shop.'

'Oh Nash — he was a nice guy. Finn thought a lot of him. I wouldn't say he looked on him as a father figure, but they were close. Nash liked Finn — as a friend — and sold him the studio.'

'Really? It looks a quirky kind of place. I can, um, see it from the flat,' she added quickly.

'Yeah, it's nice. Finn can keep himself to himself there.' Joey smirked. 'As for his pictures, I preferred the sailing stuff and the estuary views to some of his others.' He smiled. 'Finn likes them though. Guess that kind of thing is more in his line.'

Rose presumed Joey was referring to the nudes. She didn't dare go any further with her slightly random line of discussion. They were supposed to be talking about sailing. A woman waved at Joey from near a rack of wetsuits. Joey waved back.

'You know, at the risk of living up to your low expectations of me, maybe we could continue this conversation another time?'

'Yes . . .'

'You might find me surprisingly good company.' He grinned. 'Would you like a look around the boatyard this weekend?'

'The yard?'

'Yes. I know, it's not very exciting. I just thought you might enjoy getting a closer look at what we do all day. If you want to learn about sailing, it might be a good idea to learn about boats. I can show you *Spindrift* — my boat — too.'

'Sounds fascinating but aren't you busy?' She tried to sound amused, but was cringing too at the idea of going out on Joey's yacht, after Oriel's hints that it was his dating technique, and yet . . . she really would like a glimpse into a side of their lives that was such an intrinsic part of them. You could say boatbuilding was in their DNA and that was of massive interest to her — now that their DNA was literally part of her.

'Always, but we are allowed visitors, you know. Who knows, you might even commission a boat afterwards.'

She laughed. 'I need to learn to sail first . . .'

'We can arrange something over a coffee at Bo's after too, if you've time?'

Oh, how deftly he'd moved from a quick tour of the business on to coffee. However, Rose couldn't resist and, after all, it was only to talk about her lessons . . . and she might find out the answer to her bigger question too. The idea sent a rush of adrenaline through her.

'Sure. Why not?'

'Great.' His eyes flicked back to the woman in oilskins who was now standing at the door to the sailing centre. 'Sorry. I need to speak to Tonia about my next session. I'll message to arrange a time. Do I have your number?'

'I don't think so,' said Rose, but half a minute later, he certainly did. With a wave, he jogged along the shingle, leaving her trying to work out who exactly had manipulated whom during their conversation.

On balance, she suspected Joey's motivation was simpler than hers.

10

It was Saturday afternoon when Finn next had chance to take *Siren* from Curlew the short distance up the creek to the boatyard.

Joey was aboard his own boat, *Spindrift*, but seeing Finn approach, he climbed out and helped him tie up alongside the boatyard jetty.

'Have you brought her in to fix that auto helm?' Joey asked, climbing aboard.

'Yes. It's an intermittent problem, so I'd like to see if I can sort it before I have to splash out on a replacement.'

'Intermittent fault? Worst bloody kind. Want a hand?'

'Yeah. Thanks.' Finn was a little taken aback to find Joey in such a cordial mood, before reminding himself that he shouldn't be. He and Joey had always, by and large, got on and they were still close. If he was honest, it was only since Lauren and Joey had split that they'd grown apart.

The little niggles and competitive spats that were part and parcel of their relationship — of any relationship between siblings, Finn supposed — had blown up into bigger rows or simmered between them at a low level. Joey had been hurt badly when Lauren had left and worrying that he'd had a hand in the split only made Finn more upset that their relationship was not as good as it could have been.

As the afternoon wore on, he was able to relax a little as they worked together, absorbed in the job, or talking about boats: their own and other people's, ones they'd like to own one day.

It had been too long since they'd spent time like this together — messing about on the boats for pure pleasure — and it reminded him of the bond they'd once had. Or still had. Perhaps it hadn't entirely been severed yet.

Finn found a couple of beers in the fridge and brought them up on deck.

They stood for a moment, enjoying the contrast of cold beer and the hot early June sun on their faces.

'Thanks for the help,' Finn said.

'You're welcome.' Joey tilted his beer to his lips and wiped his mouth. They drank their beers but Finn's eyes were drawn to the opposite side of the water, where the afternoon sun glinted off the upper windows of Cornish Magick.

Joey must have noticed, given his next words.

'By the way, I've invited Oriel's new lodger to take a look around the boatyard tomorrow.'

'You mean Rose?'

'Yes. She came to the yacht club party and she wants to learn to sail. I suggested she have a look at *Spindrift* and the yard at the same time. I thought I'd warn you.'

The hairs on the back of Finn's neck stood on end. He might have known Joey was brewing something.

'Why would you need to warn me?'

'I didn't want you to be surprised when she turned up.'

Finn shrugged. 'It's fine with me.' He'd wondered if Rose had gone to the party, but hadn't wanted to ask Joey. Now he had his answer. Rose obviously hadn't told Joey that she'd had a coffee at the pub with Finn, either. Why would she? It was only a coffee.

'When's the first date?' he said, as jokily as he could manage. 'Is it on land or water?'

'Neither. I haven't asked her on a proper date.'

'But you will.'

'I don't know. I'd like to,' Joey said.

'For all you know, she might have some bloke at home,' Finn said. 'A partner — or a husband.'

'I doubt it.' Joey scrutinised him. 'Look. Do you know something I don't?'

'If you mean about Rose, no.'

'If she has, well he's not here to see us, is he?' Joey replied.

Finn shrugged, on the verge of saying, 'You wouldn't have liked it if some guy had taken Lauren from you behind your back,' but he realised in time that that would have been the worst thing he could possibly say. Incendiary even.

He drank his beer then shrugged. 'It's nothing to do with me.'

Instead of a sarcastic reply, he found a hand on his arm. 'Hey, bro.'

He glanced up. 'What?'

'If it's a sore point . . . if you're interested in Rose, then I won't stand in your way. She did mention you'd already met . . .'

Finn's guts twisted, but he laughed. There was no way he was going to let Joey think he'd also been taken with Rose or interfere in his brother's love life. 'It's none of my business but I don't think romance is on her mind.'

'Are you trying to say she's out of my league?'

'I don't think she's interested in a relationship. She seems dedicated to her work to me.'

94

'Maybe, but I can always try to help her see there's more to life than a pile of old stones and a pisky shop.' Joey grinned.

'She won't hang around, you know.'

'Since when has that been a bad thing?' Joey asked.

'You're not immune to getting burned.'

'Is this a warning about Lauren again? That's ancient history.' He laughed. 'See what I did there?'

'I didn't hear you laughing at the time. I seem to recall you were really upset. You've not been the same since — sowing your wild oats.'

Joey's reply was full of scorn. 'Sowing my wild oats? I'm thirty-two, not fifty-two. I don't want to be tied down with a load of kids.'

'You did want that once.'

Joey's eyes glinted with anger. 'Maybe I was wrong. Maybe Lauren deciding she could do better was the best thing that could have happened.'

Finn thanked his stars that no one, not even Joey, could see inside his heart and find it racked with guilt about Lauren. She'd told Joey that she wanted to spread her wings and that staying in the village was stifling her. She'd taken a job in a London hospital to further her career and live 'a bigger life'. Finn desperately wanted to believe that that was one hundred per cent the reason.

'She never said she could do better,' Finn said. 'She left because of her career. Don't make yourself a martyr.'

'What do you know about it?' Joey said coldly.

'OK. I don't want to fight. I'm sorry I even made a comment. Think what you want. Do what you want. You will, whatever I say.' Finn decided to take his empty bottle below. He needed to get out of his brother's way before he said something they'd both regret.

Joey's anger ballooned. 'I'm a grown-up despite what you may think and Rose definitely doesn't need a protector. You don't need to act like a knight in shining armour looking out for her virtue. She knows her own mind, if you haven't noticed.'

Finn had noticed. It was all he thought about lately: and not only Rose's mind.

'Do you know what she's looking for from this relationship? Does she know what you're looking for? Do you?'

'Oh for . . .' Joey almost swore. He stared at Finn. 'It's you who needs to look at what he wants. Because from my point of view, it seems like you want Rose for yourself and you just won't admit it.'

'Don't be ridiculous. I hardly know her. Neither of us does.'

'And I've been trying to put that right. Christ, Finn, you sound like you're scared of her.'

'That's so stupid I won't even reply.' Turning his back on Joey, Finn went below. He heard Joey thump along the deck and climb onto the jetty then walk away.

He took the bottles below, emptied the rubbish from the bin, cleaned the head — otherwise known as the toilet — and gathered up the sleeping bags he kept on board to take to the marina laundry. God, he must be angry if he'd resorted to shit jobs like that.

Despite every effort, he couldn't dislodge Rose Vernon from his mind, like a nail that wouldn't be prised out of a hull. She stuck in his thoughts, and not only because he was so drawn to her physically. She

96

was guarded, and she was interested in Joey — and perhaps in Finn himself — yet he was sure she wasn't looking for romance.

11

On a Sunday morning Rose had expected Morvah Marine to be deserted so was taken aback to find Finn outside, manhandling a piece of wood from a pile outside the door. The plank still appeared to have the bark on the edges and she watched him manoeuvre it towards a machine tucked under a tarpaulin, presumably to protect it from the rain.

She slowed her step, waiting for him to become aware of her presence and if she was brutally honest, she was enjoying the view. He was wearing jeans that were faded and ripped from actual hard use, rather than in a fashion factory, and a black T-shirt. The way his arm muscles tautened and relaxed as he shifted the heavy wood to the machine . . . she loved it. The wood seemed to slip. He gained purchase of it again but not before swearing softly.

The moment he laid it on the bench by the machine, he caught sight of her.

'Morning,' she said.

Finn looked startled and was breathing hard. 'Morning,' he said, but frowned.

'I — um — came to look around.' She was reluctant to say she'd had a direct invitation from Joey. She wondered where Joey was.

'Oh, yeah. Joey did mention it.'

'If it's a bad time, I can come back another day.'

Finn shook his head. 'No. Joey went up to the office. I'm sure he'll be down in a minute. Come on in.' His smile was warm. 'Be careful. It's a bit of a mess.'

Rose stepped into the shed, her eyes taking a moment to adjust to the shadow. There was a light on, but it was no match for the bright sun outside.

The smell assailed her. It almost blocked out every other sense. She knew it was wood because every spare space was filled with planks and offcuts. There were pieces tucked behind the door, long lengths balanced on metal racks suspended from the ceiling. Piles of it — all still with the bark on — had also been laid outside under tarpaulins and corrugated sheets.

'Wow! That smell.'

'Smell?'

'Of wood.'

'Oh, yeah.' He nodded but said no more. She realised he'd been surrounded by it so long he didn't even notice it, but it was like a perfume to her.

As her eyes adjusted, she saw what was making the shed so dark: the boat was on scaffolding and seemed huge close up. It looked recognisably like a finished vessel, but from the trestles and machinery around it, she could see it was a work in progress.

Finn also emerged from the shadows and stood before her eyes, hands on hips, gazing up at the deck way above his head.

'This is it: our latest project.' There was unmistakeable pride in his voice.

Her lips parted. She'd never been so close to a boat in such a confined space and what struck her was how much of it — its keel, she supposed — was below the water.

'Beautiful, isn't she?' He was still gazing at the boat.

'Very.' Still awestruck, she stared up at the boat too.

'What did you say she is again?'

'A gaff rig cutter.'

'OK . . . and that means?'

'A gaff is a four-sided sail. The cutter just means it has more than one fore sail.'

'There's a lot of wood. I mean, obviously because you make wooden boats, but I hadn't expected quite so much of it to be stored on the site. I saw piles of it outside.'

'We leave the timber to season outside under tarpaulins. Some of it's been here for years. We could use green wood but seasoned makes a sturdier boat.'

'Green?'

'Unseasoned wood. Some boatbuilders use it but we prefer to wait. See the piece I just put on the planing machine? I know which tree that came from on the Tresize Estate. I chose it.'

'Wow. I'd no idea you actually got the wood from so close by, let alone picked the tree.'

'It's important to us that we know the provenance of the wood. Important to the clients too. Some of them, anyway.'

In her head, Rose couldn't help wondering what type of client had the cash to keep a team of craftspeople working.

'Boats aren't just boats,' Finn said. 'Wooden boats are more like a living thing.' He rested his hand on the hull, spreading his fingers. They were strong and dusty and there were healed scars. Boatbuilding must be a hazardous business.

She'd noticed boats and sailing had a whole language of their own: maybe they didn't want her to understand it, a secret code between them . . . She wanted to collect the words and write them down in a book. Then again, archaeology had its own language. Didn't any activity, be it hairdressing or soldiering?

100

'Here's your man,' Finn said, as Joey clattered down the metal steps from the office. 'I'll get back to my work, then.'

However, Joey had only just reached Rose when a female voice bellowed from the top of the steps.

'Joey!'

Joey's eyes flickered with annoyance. 'Sorry. I won't be a sec,' he said. 'I just need to see what Mum wants.'

Rose was amused by Adonis having to see what his mother wanted, but he'd barely moved when Dorinda herself trotted down the metal steps and joined him and Rose. 'Oh, hello . . .' she said, clearly taken aback to have a visitor in her domain. Unlike Finn, Joey clearly hadn't warned his mother she was coming.

Keen blue eyes — like Joey's — swept over Rose and her summer dress and Converse. Clad in dungarees and work boots, Dorinda was taller than Rose by a few inches. Her hair, gold shot through with grey, was held back by a spotted bandana tied in a bow. Rose immediately saw who Joey took after, at least in looks. Dorinda was a striking woman in every way.

'I didn't realise we had a visitor,' she said pleasantly enough.

'This is Rose,' Joey said. 'I invited her to see where we hang out.'

'Hello, Rose. You must be the girl who's moved above Cornish Magick.'

Rose had ceased to see herself as a 'girl' when she went to university, but she decided not to ruffle Dorinda's feathers by pointing it out.

'I'm Dorinda,' she said. 'I've heard a lot about you.'

'Not from me,' Joey shot back, rolling his eyes.

'All good, I hope?' Rose tried to keep things friendly.

'You're an archaeologist, aren't you?' Dorinda said,

pointedly avoiding the question.

'Yes, I'm here to study some of the ancient stone circles in the area. I'm also working on a dig down at King Arthur's Pool with Penryn University.'

'Sounds fascinating,' Dorinda said, then turned to Joey. 'Joey, have you finished the renovation on the Choudhurys' dinghy because I've had Mrs C on the phone. The family are coming down for the weekend and they'd like you deliver the boat to their mooring.'

'It's all in hand,' Joey said. 'Just chill out.'

Dorinda let out a snort of disgust. 'Chill? As if I have time to 'chill'.'

He kissed her cheek. 'I know but what I meant was, don't worry. I'd already planned to take it down there. Mind you, I'll need a lift back . . .' His voice lifted hopefully. 'Maybe Rose can pick me up if she's going past this week? It's on the way out of the village.'

'I'm sure she's got enough to do with her work without changing her plans to ferry you about,' Dorinda said turning to Rose with a sigh. 'I do apologise for my youngest son. He can be very presumptuous.'

'Well . . .'

'I thought you'd be working at the dig this week? I can call you when you're on your way home and wait at the top of the drive for you.'

'That shouldn't be a problem,' Rose said, feeling awkward at being caught in between this power tussle between mother and son.

Dorinda rolled her eyes. 'You've put Rose on the spot now. If it inconveniences you, you must tell him.'

'It'll be fine,' Rose said. 'If I change my plans, or I'm delayed, then I'll text you.' She directed this at Joey.

With an eyebrow lift to Rose that seemed to express

amused frustration, but could also have concealed genuine anger, Dorinda left.

Out of the corner of her eye, Rose caught a glance from Finn.

Joey ushered Rose towards the open door. 'Sorry about that,' he said. 'Mums eh? What can you do? Look, there's going to be a racket around when Finn starts planing so shall we go down the boatyard café for a brew?'

'Sounds good but can you afford to take a break?' Rose was tempted to add 'Will your mum let you?' but didn't dare.

'Not really, but that won't stop me. She'll still be here when I get back.'

'*She?*'

'The boat. The cutter we're building.' Joey began walking in the direction of the slipway.

'Oh, I see.' Rose had thought he meant Dorinda.

'A project like this can't be rushed.' He grinned. 'Not when Finn's in charge. He's a tree hugger, you know.'

Rose wasn't sure how to react. She was amused but also liked Finn. She felt she was being subtly manoeuvred into joining Team Joey and she wasn't sure she liked it.

'He certainly seems passionate about making sure the boat has the right provenance.'

'You can say that again.'

'But isn't that why your customers are attracted to your work? Because of all the attention to detail, the heritage and the fact that you guys care so much?'

'Yeah . . . sure they are and I care too. I'm not knocking Finn; he knows what he's doing and he really believes in the craft, and all the authenticity and, and,

and . . .' He smiled. 'I just wish he wouldn't take life so seriously all the time. He looks like he's carrying the world on his shoulders since he got more involved in helping Mum run this place.'

'It's not the same thing but I love getting out on digs and to ancient sites. I enjoy teaching the students, but all the admin and departmental politics grinds me down.'

'You mean you don't spend your whole time digging up gold coins and skeletons of kings and queens?'

'I wish!' Rose said then smiled. 'That's not my thing, but no, I do spend a lot of my time in a dusty library, office or boring faculty meeting.'

'You could have fooled me.' He gave her the look, blue eyes shining with amusement. 'I don't mean to be sexist, but you don't look like an archaeologist.'

'Mornin', Joey!'

Before Rose could respond, a young woman hailed them as they approached a wooden café kiosk beside the slipway. Rose recognised her from one of her earlier forays to the yard.

'Mornin', Bo,' Joey replied.

They were clearly on very familiar terms. Joey mentioned that Rose was staying in the area for her work and Bo made polite conversation while she made a cappuccino for Joey and a fruit tea for Rose.

'Bacon butty too?' Bo called above the hiss of the coffee machine.

'Not today. Have to watch my weight.'

Bo looked him up and down. 'Doesn't bother you usually,' she said archly.

'I've turned over a new leaf,' he said and Rose noticed the slight compression of Bo's lips before she laughed and said, 'That'll be the day. I know you'll be back for the usual soon enough.'

Sophie, Bo . . . Rose wondered if it were true that Joey had left a trail of broken hearts around the local area, like crumbs left by Hansel and Gretel. She was following them . . . but she knew what she was doing, didn't she?

They took their drinks to a small paved area behind the kiosk that bordered the estuary. The two tables were occupied so they sat on the wall with their feet dangling above the water. Moorhens and coots dabbled around in the water. In the distance, Rose could hear the high-pitched drone of machinery, presumably from the boatyard. Once again, she was aware that Joey was chatting to her while his family worked. She didn't want to keep him too long, but she was compelled to know more about him.

He drank his coffee, seemingly content to sit and contemplate the scene for a few moments.

Rose spoke first: 'So, what does an archaeologist look like, then?'

'Weedy, beardy and weird,' he shot back.

That might account for half of Rose's colleagues but she didn't say so. 'A high proportion are women, actually.'

Joey smiled. 'I was joking.'

'Oh, really?'

'OK. Not really.'

She laughed. 'It's an accurate description of some, but by no means all. As I said, quite a few of us are women. None of us had beards when I last looked and most are surprisingly ordinary.'

'You're not.'

Rose's reply dried in her throat but she recovered after a sip of tea. 'Oh, I am. I promise you. Boringly

105

so.'

'No. There's something . . . extraordinary about you.'

I could say the same about you, thought Rose, finding it impossible to tear her eyes from that handsome face. 'Come off it.'

'No. I think you're very unusual. Different in a good way.'

'I'm just a novelty here, that's all, and I don't blame people if they think what I do is a bit weird.' She laughed. 'I promise you that by Cambridge standards, I'm distinctly average. And, anyway, I thought we were here to arrange a sailing lesson?'

'If you're not busy. I thought we could go somewhere once I've delivered the Choudhurys' dinghy to its mooring after work one day this week. Then afterwards we could go for a sail. How does Tuesday or Wednesday evening sound?'

She smiled. 'Blimey. You seem to have it all worked out.'

'Well, to be fair, the tide's right midweek for taking the dinghy back in the early evening so I would have sailed it back then anyway.' He had a glint in his eye.

'Oh. OK.' She shook her head in amusement. 'I can probably do Wednesday after work. Why not?' she said, trying to sound casual, while her beating heart told her she felt anything but casual at the prospect of finding out more about Joey. 'Had you got anywhere in mind?'

'I could suggest a couple of waterside pubs for a drink and a bite to eat. The Ferryman's a great local but that's a mixed blessing. It's *too* local and we might feel like we're living in a goldfish bowl,' he said. 'I'd got somewhere a bit . . . different in mind. Somewhere we can combine with your sailing lesson. If that's OK with you?'

Rose was too intrigued to refuse. 'OK. I'll trust your judgement on where.'

'Great. I'll make a booking then, shall I? Wherever it is, it'll be an easy sail.'

'It'll have to be! I thought I'd be taking out one of the little dinghies from the sailing centre, not in charge of a proper boat.'

'The principle's the same,' Joey said. 'And you will need to get some experience on your own, but I thought it would be more exciting to go out on *Spindrift* for your first time.'

'Sounds good. I'll look forward to it.' She drained her coffee. 'I think we'd both better get back to work now. I need to finish a paper on Iron Age burial rituals.'

'You do know how to live,' said Joey with a chuckle, before getting to his feet and collecting their mugs. 'I'll take these back to Bo.'

'Thanks. See you Wednesday, then.'

They went their separate ways. Rose taking the long route over the footbridge to the village car park, and Joey towards the boatshed.

Even as she drove out of Falford, Rose's mind wasn't on ancient fogous and Iron Age settlements, but on the intriguing new developments surrounding Joey. He'd already lived up to one of Oriel's dire warnings, but Rose felt perfectly safe. After all she was pre-warned and certain that she could resist his charms even if his reputation might be well earned. Sophie and Joey clearly had history and there had been something in the look and undercurrent of tension between him and Bo that had put her on the alert.

Plus, he'd deftly steered her into accepting his offer

and she suspected it could be very easy to get in deeper with Joey. She longed to know if he was her man, but she didn't want to let her guard down and reveal her own secret until — and if — she was ready.

12

'Finn?'

Finn kept the hammer in his hands and didn't turn round. It had been inevitable that this moment would come and he braced himself for it. He'd convinced himself he didn't care and yet . . .

Joey appeared at his side. 'I thought I should tell you that I'm taking Rose out for a sail tonight.'

'Why are you telling me?'

'I thought you should know. I don't want you to find out from someone else after the event, so to speak.'

Finn's stomach knotted but finally he met Joey's eyes. 'She's been here five minutes and you're acting as if I was about to propose or something. Go out and enjoy your date but spare me the gory details. Keep it private for a change.'

'For a change?'

'Don't go showing her off like a trophy. I don't think Rose would take kindly to it. If you want my advice.'

'I don't, but thanks for the tip. I know how to handle her.'

'Handle her? She'll have you for breakfast, bro. Trust me.'

'I thought she'd only been here five minutes? You already seem to think you know her so well?'

'Just my opinion, Joey. I shouldn't have offered it. Have a nice evening.' He clouted the nail with the hammer, blocking out the sound of Joey's muttering. Joey left or at least Finn thought he'd gone. Finn kept tapping away, refusing to even risk a single glance to check. Eventually, he paused and felt he was alone.

After work, Finn walked back to his studio. Thunderclouds were gathering over the open sea and the shipping forecast wasn't great, but that wasn't why he decided to stay in. For once in his life, he chose to open his laptop instead of heading out to sea. He typed the words into Google.

Dr Rose Vernon
Archaeologist

He didn't know what he was searching for or why he was even looking again. Like the young man drawn to the mermaid, he simply couldn't stop himself from wanting to know more about her.

13

Rose turned her car into the track that led to the Choudhurys' waterside home. She'd messaged Joey to say she was leaving the dig and heading back to Falford and allowed plenty of time, but found herself back earlier. He'd texted to say he was running a little late. It seemed pointless to wait at the top of the track so she drove further down.

The track led gently through overhanging trees but every so often a shimmer of water would appear through the canopy. The track went on for almost a quarter of a mile before Rose saw the house come into view.

She parked on a neat gravelled area by the garages and followed a wide path that was the obvious route to the water's edge. Joey had told her the occupants weren't arriving until the weekend so she felt safe that no one would see her. She was secretly excited to see how the other half lived. She guessed the house, which was a white Victorian double-fronted property, must be worth several million.

Once she'd rounded the corner of the house, she stood on the terrace, beyond which a strip of lawn stretched the width of the house and led down to the water itself. There was a jetty at the bottom, which she presumed was the private mooring. A small motorboat was already tied up, along with a grey rigid inflatable boat. The Choudhurys were clearly a three-boat household, not forgetting that this was their holiday home.

She wandered down, doing up her jacket as the breeze blew in from the estuary. The house was situated at the very end of the creek where it opened out into the main inlet and the contrast with the sheltered waters of Falford was obvious. Wavelets rippled the surface and some were topped with whitecaps. Yachts sailed past, their spinnakers billowing while fishing boats bobbed up and down making their way out to sea.

She didn't know what she was looking out for, only that the sailing dinghy probably wouldn't be that big, and it would be sailing or motoring from the inland end of the creek, which was out of view.

She sat on the stone wall that held back the lawn from the jetty, and kicked off her sandals, waiting for Joey. She had wondered if hanging around for him here looked a bit desperate but it was far more fun to watch him sail up than waiting by her car.

Twenty minutes and a few false alarms after she'd arrived, the Choudhurys' boat motored up with Joey at the helm.

He called her to the jetty and showed her how to secure it to the mooring posts. Some of the knots looked incredibly complicated but Rose had already had practice with Oriel's boat.

'I can see you've done this before,' he said. 'I'm impressed.'

'No, you're not. You're just flattering me,' she said, laughing.

'I'm not and as you're already so good at tying up, I'll expect you to be ready for something more advanced when we get to my boat.'

Rose protested but Joey's grin told her he was — she hoped — joking. She had to admit that she had been thinking how lovely it would be to sail off into the June evening with him, stop at some waterside pub, or moor in a tiny creek and have a glass of wine . . .

Then she realised that she was buying into the fantasy. Perhaps he wanted her to be desperate to be taken out on the boat. Other women had been . . . and according to Oriel's dire warnings, look what had happened to them.

Rose thought of the Maidens turned to stone for dancing on the Sabbath. Just because she might sail off with Joey, didn't mean anything had to happen. Women were allowed to enjoy sleeping with attractive young men without falling for them hook, line and sinker and certainly without being turned into stone.

She was still chuckling to herself as they walked up the track to her car. 'Are you going to tell me where we're going by the way?'

'Turn left out of the end of the track. I'll give you directions as we go along.'

Rose knew he wanted to surprise her. Once again, Joey was leading her in the direction of his choosing — literally — and this time she was happy to oblige.

Their destination wasn't quite what Rose had expected either. After negotiating many lanes snaking around different creeks, Joey directed her down a rutted track with a faded sign at the entrance that she didn't have time to read. Shortly afterwards, he told her to turn into a yard.

In seconds, the sea opened up before them, in all its glory. The early evening sun shimmered on the water. Joey got out and motioned for Rose to follow him to what could only be described as a shack. It had peeling wooden walls and a corrugated tin roof and a wooden deck on stilts above the water. The deck held a solitary table and she could just make out a few fading words stencilled on the walls of the shack: *Falford Seafood and Oysters.*

A man emerged from the door, a tea towel in his hands. He was built like a front row rugby player and his grin was broad when he saw them.

'Evening, Joey.' He nodded at Rose. 'Hello.'

'Evening, Kev. This is Rose.'

'Table for two?' Kev asked with a strong East End accent.

'Do you think you can squeeze us in?' Joey asked.

Kev sucked in a breath. 'I'll see what I can do.'

'Kev ran a seafood restaurant in Grenada for a while before he opened up a place in London and then he decided to pack it in and retire here.'

Kev's belly laugh resonated through the decking. 'Who said I retired? I'm busier than ever.'

'Is this an actual restaurant?' Rose asked him.

'Not really. Call it my front porch. I supply to restaurants all over the UK but I only open up for my buddies.'

Telling them the 'menu' was on the board outside the shack, Kev went inside leaving Joey and Rose alone.

'If I'm meant to be impressed, I am,' she said.

'I wasn't trying to impress you.'

She shook her head, laughing at his innocent expression.

'OK. I *was* hoping you'd love this place,' he said, a little sheepishly. 'But as we drove up here, I had cold feet about the idea. It's hardly some posh joint, is it? And it's just occurred to me you must dine out in some really grand places.'

'Some grand and very *dusty* places and even then,

it's almost always for work. It's not relaxing sitting next to some antiquated don intent on making you feel like you're a fresher while asking you to pass the port.'

Joey grimaced. 'Jeez. I couldn't handle that. It must feel like being on *University Challenge* all the time. Not that I watch it. You can probably tell.'

'I don't watch it much either and I promise you, I don't want 'grand'. I just want relaxing and simple. This is perfect,' she said, realising as she said it that Joey had — accidentally or very deliberately — delivered just that. The perfect location.

'I also took a chance you like seafood,' he said, nodding at the board by the door into the shack.

'Good job I'm not veggie, eh? I do like seafood. In fact, I think I'll try the Falford oysters.'

'Wow. I thought you'd go for the lobster salad.'

'I love oysters, not that I get them as often as I'd like.'

Kev reappeared. 'Can I get you two some drinks?'

'I'm driving,' Rose said.

'I shouldn't worry about that.'

'Joey!' Rose was shocked.

'You're not driving *home*.' He pointed to the small yacht tied up by the quay. 'But we are sailing, so I'd just have the one glass.'

'You keep your boat here?'

'I may live at the yard but let's just say that I like a bit of privacy at least some of the time. I'll give you a lift back to your car tomorrow.'

It was such a beautiful evening, how could she resist sailing up the estuary as the sun set?

Kev served the oysters, fresh as anything on a bed of ice with lemon wedges, along with a bottle of wine that was on the house because he wasn't licensed.

Joey tried an oyster and grimaced, making Rose laugh. She loved the tang of them, the true taste of the sea and the chilled Spanish white wine was the perfect complement. Afterwards, he brought a half lobster salad for Joey and a fresh crab salad for Rose, with a bowl of crusty sourdough from his wife's bakery. As they ate the main courses, water lapped the deck. The tables were in shadow and Rose pulled her jacket around her.

'What made you want to be an archaeologist?' Joey asked.

'I've always been a geek.' She laughed. 'I loved books about the Vikings rather than ponies. I would beg my gran to take me to castles and one day when I was around six . . .' Rose almost blushed. 'She found me digging up her garden pretending to find treasure. Eventually, after a lot of digging, a lot of never finding any treasure but enjoying it all anyway, I got the job at the college a couple of years ago. I kind of drifted after I'd left university, I started my PhD and then I just . . . lay around, not doing much,' Rose said, skating over her life-threatening episode with a laugh. She'd suppressed the part where she really *had* lain around for years, trying to finish her studies around her increasing fatigue and growing terror of never being able to finish it at all. Then the long weeks when she'd been put on the register for a bone marrow transplant and the waiting.

'I can't imagine you lying around not doing much.' Joey picked up the bottle and topped up her glass.

'Not too much.' She laughed. 'I may not be driving but it's going straight to my head.'

'OK. I'll take the rest home. I can't have too much

either as I'm responsible for getting us and *Spindrift* back to Falford in one piece.'

'I'm glad to hear it,' Rose said. 'So, what made you become a boatbuilder?'

He shrugged. 'Can't imagine ever doing anything else. I've lived and breathed boats since I can remember. Mum took over the boatyard from her father. My grandfather, Billy — he only passed away the year before last.'

'I'm sorry. My grandma died earlier this year. They have quite an influence, don't they?'

'I'm sorry for your loss,' Joey said kindly. 'And you're right. My grandad taught Mum everything about boats. It's a pretty unusual field for a woman to work in. She runs the place now, rather than doing a lot of heavy stuff, but she knows exactly what everyone else should be doing and she still does a lot of the painting. Our apprentice, Gurdeep — who you might have seen the other day — Mum is her mentor. She's kind of taken on the role that Grandad did for her.'

'It's such a different life to mine.'

'Then tell me about your life. We were interrupted by you telling me you didn't want me to try to get you drunk.'

Rose laughed out loud and out of the corner of her eye, she caught Kev watching them with a wry smile. How many women had Joey brought to the shack? The love shack, she thought with a suppressed giggle. How many women had Kev seen come and go? He probably now thought she was one of them . . . Her consolation was that she also wanted something from Joey and he wasn't aware of it.

Joey, who was asking her about herself, and seeming to really listen, making jokes about his ignorance

117

of archaeology. He seemed perfect, handsome, funny, and altruistic enough to — potentially — save someone's life, but modest enough not to want to make a thing of it.

What was below the surface? The big, important part . . . the hull? She wondered if it was Lauren who might have inspired or encouraged him to donate. Rose also puzzled over why she'd left him at all? Was it really because she wanted a career in London — or had Joey driven her out of his life?

After their meal, Kev cleared away and had a few words before they went to the jetty. Rose helped Joey untie and they set off. Once away from the jetty, he turned off the engine and showed her how to hoist the sails and keep the boat steady. It was worse than learning to drive, she thought; so many different things to consider at once. She really thought it would have been better to have had some lessons in a tiny dinghy first — but nowhere near as much fun.

There was exhilaration in the way the boat heeled over, powered by the wind, with no artificial sound of the engine, just the slap of the waves against the hull. She took the wheel and he showed her the safe route back around the headland and onto a stretch of open sea.

'We can't rush. The sea's our mistress,' he said.

Skirting the coastline, they passed fishing boats and gleaming motor yachts, all heading for the haven of the estuary or into the port of Falmouth further up the coast. Gulls shrieked overhead. Joey left her with the wheel while he went below to find her an old waterproof coat from the cabin as even the gentle breeze made her shiver and the spray flew over the bow.

He handed her the coat and took the wheel again, seeming lost in his thoughts.

'You're quiet,' he said.

She laughed. 'I could say the same about you.'

'I expect you've heard a few things about me?'

'No. OK. A few things but the reality hasn't lived up to the hype, apart from taking me out on your boat.'

'Wow. I do have a reputation, then.' He sounded quite proud. 'What exactly did she tell you?'

'Oriel mentioned you like to take people — dates — for a sail. When you asked me to drive you to the restaurant earlier, I was wrong-footed.'

'In that case, I've been very predictable. I must try harder.'

'Only in that way. Not in others. Let's just say I've really enjoyed the evening. It's been fascinating.'

'Good. I knew you'd make your own mind up about me. What else has Oriel told you?'

'Not much . . .' Rose had to lie. She would not reveal that she'd listened to any more of Oriel's gossip.

'That's a miracle. Did she tell you about Lauren?'

'She did mention you were together once but I don't know any details and I don't need to. It's *your* business, Joey.'

There was an edge to his voice that was both bitter and longing. 'If Oriel mentioned her then you must know that we were close and that we split up.'

The way Joey spoke left Rose wondering if Oriel was right and Lauren and Joey hadn't split up by mutual consent. He could still be in love with his ex . . .which made her even keener to make sure that learning to sail was her only interest in Joey — apart, of course, from her hidden agenda.

'Yes, she did say something like that.'

119

'Jesus, this place is so bloody claustrophobic. I should get away from it!'

'You don't mean that: your boat, the business, the estuary. You love it.'

'Yeah, but there are other estuaries and a boat can move.'

Rose remembered what Oriel had said about Lauren leaving for the sake of her career. Had she wanted Joey to go with her? Had it been impossible for them to make it work or had she simply not wanted it to?

'It's not that easy to change your whole life when you have everything invested in a small place,' Rose said gently.

'Ah, but you're describing Finn, not me. Falford water flows through his veins. He'd never leave.'

Rose smiled. 'You sound very sure.'

'He's my brother and while we may not always agree —' Joey gave a wry laugh '—I do know him. He's loyal and he has a sense of responsibility that I don't always get but hey, say what you like about Finn, he's definitely one of the good guys.'

Intrigued by what exactly Joey meant, Rose pushed him further. 'Are you?'

Joey turned his blue gaze on her, and she could see why so many women might have fallen for him. 'You mean you haven't decided yet?' he said slowly.

"Good' can mean a lot of different things, not all of which are necessarily appealing. I'm still making my mind up.'

'I'm really very boring but I couldn't commit to the yard forever the way Finn has. I need to get my own place away from the family home for a start, then perhaps I wouldn't have to take all my dates out on my boat.'

120

He sighed in frustration, but Rose allowed herself a smile and then shivered. She might have Finn's blood running through her own veins.

Rose pictured Dorinda with her binoculars trained on the estuary, and Finn watching from his balcony. No wonder Joey felt trapped.

'What about you? Would you change what you do — working for a university — to do something else? Be someone else?'

'Maybe one day, but for now, I feel I've only just got started in my career. It's not only my career either. Archaeology may not sound as exciting as sailing, but I love it. I love the stones, the tombs, the digs and teaching. It's what I always wanted to do.'

'If it's your passion, then why change?' He didn't make the 'passion' sound boring. 'So you've been studying or working for the uni your whole life?' He looked puzzled. Rose was aware of the gap in her life story and wondered if he'd pick up on it although few people who weren't in her line of work would think to question the arcane ways of academia.

'I took a while to finish my first degree and my PhD before I got the job as a lecturer,' she said.

'Did you go travelling? I'd like to do more of it. Sail round the world . . .'

'You could say I went on a journey.'

He mistook her ironic comment. 'Did it involve a man?'

'One guy in particular.' Rose thought of her geologist. 'We were definitely on different paths.'

'That sums up Lauren and me. Different paths, but I can't blame her for being ambitious. She was a doctor, though I bet Oriel's already told you that. She was offered a promotion in London.'

Rose stayed silent and Joey suddenly announced, 'There's the mouth of the Falford estuary.'

'So soon?' Rose exclaimed. The past hour had flown by.

'Yes. So soon.' He watched as she steered the yacht through the mouth of Falford Creek, occasionally offering advice on what to aim for and giving her a tutorial on the meaning of various cardinal buoys and what they were there to warn against, like reefs and sandbanks.

The wind dropped and they turned on the engine, as the boat puttered through the glassy waters. At any moment, Rose still half-expected him to slow the engine and steer the yacht into some secluded bay. He'd lower the anchor, muscles cording in his arms, and turn to her with *that* look.

Rose shivered again. How did she feel? She'd only known him a short while, but she also knew she'd be out of her mind not to want to sleep with Joey Morvah, and yet, she held back. Was it because she felt she was with him under false pretences? A part of her felt that no matter how expertly he might be trying to 'manage' her, she was the one using him . . .

'There's the boatyard pontoon,' he said.

'Oh . . .' She'd been so focused on examining her motives, waiting for Joey to make a move and rehearsing her response that she hadn't noticed they were just off the boatyard jetty.

'I could have dropped you at the village public quay, but we'd be right in the sightline of the pub and I thought this was slightly more discreet.' He grinned. 'Mum's out.'

She laughed. 'Yes, good idea. Thanks.'

Rose helped him tie up before they stood together

in the twilight. She was still carrying her slip-on Vans.

'Goodnight then,' she said, a little relieved they were home and that nothing had happened that she might regret. 'I've had a really lovely time. Not dull at all. Thank you.'

'Me too.' She felt it was safe to stand on tiptoes and kiss his cheek. Then, somehow she got it wrong or Joey moved his head unexpectedly and her lips brushed the edge of his.

'Sorry,' she said, pulling away, her cheeks burning.

He raised his eyebrows. 'Don't be.'

'It was an accident,' she said hastily. 'Must have been the wine,' she said lightly.

'I hope not.' He lifted one of her hands in his before letting it go. 'Goodnight, Rose. See you tomorrow.' He nodded at Cornish Magick across the water. 'You'll definitely see *me*.'

'I can hardly fail to.' Her brittle laugh echoed across the water. 'Thanks again for a lovely evening and the meal,' she said hastily before walking away.

A glance behind showed Joey on deck, with ropes in his hands.

She didn't look his way again. She slipped on her pumps and hurried on along the front of the boat-house, past the café and to the footbridge at the very top of the creek. Insects buzzed in the air and the sky turned indigo. The memory of his warm lips against hers lingered while she made her way along the creek to the footbridge, grateful for the cool air on her cheeks and the cover of trees to hide her embarrassment.

It had been so long since she'd spent an evening with an attractive man — any man — but even so, she shouldn't have even allowed herself to get into such an intimate situation with Joey: the romantic setting, the wine, the exhilaration of the sail.

And yet — even during the 'accidental kiss', no fireworks had gone off for her and she had to admit, perhaps he'd felt the same. If Joey had really wanted to, he surely would have returned it with some enthusiasm — and perhaps he'd have even suggested they take things further. The more she thought about it, the more relieved she was that Joey hadn't responded.

It was a sobering thought for Rose as she let herself into a dark and silent Cornish Magick and drew the curtains. Lights twinkled in the main house and the ground floor of the annexe opposite, but Rose turned away from the Morvahs' house quickly. She was no closer to discovering which brother was her donor and after her embarrassing slip-up this evening, she wasn't sure how far she dared go in finding out. She felt she was already past the point of no return with the Morvahs and in far too deep to reveal her secret even if she decided to.

14

Dawn broke, breezy and bright, so Finn was on the water early. He only had time for a short sail, but *Siren* had been idle too long. To be one of the first craft on the estuary was a joy to him, and at times, there was only him and the seabirds pecking on the banks or soaring overhead. The lively conditions challenged him and went some way to blowing away the cobwebs.

After spotting *Spindrift* returning the previous evening with Joey and Rose on deck, Finn reminded himself he needed to let go of any stake in their relationship, whatever that amounted to.

Tying up at Morvah Marine alongside Joey's boat, he felt fresher and more determined to mind his own business and move on from both Lauren and Rose. He even found himself whistling, so instead of heading straight to the sheds, he dropped by the café where Bo had just opened up and was stacking fresh cups by the espresso machine. He may as well make his good mood last as long as possible.

As expected, Bo's cheery smile lifted his spirits further. She was into Fifties-style swing dancing and today wore a fitted blue dress that looked great on her.

'The usual?' she said, emerging from the counter with a chalkboard. She crouched down and wrote something on the board in flowing script, her ponytail bobbing about as she added to the menu.

'Thanks,' he said, admiring her smile and ability to multi-task and look so good at eight a.m. He and Bo had been on a date a few years back, just to make sure they were better off as friends. They were and nothing had gone beyond a kiss, which according to Bo, had felt 'like kissing a cousin'.

He smiled at the memory of her comment, but Bo stood up, put her hands on her hips and gave him a hard stare. 'You look in a good mood. I don't need to ask why. I saw you were out early.'

'It was great out there.'

'Hmm. I bet.' She raised an eyebrow. 'Flat white coming up.'

While she made the drink, Finn spotted Joey striding out of the annexe. Something about his walk made Finn's hackles rise. For a moment, he half-expected to see Rose slip out of the wide door, but she didn't.

He was paranoid. What happened to moving on?

'Here you go.'

'Oh. Thanks, Bo.'

She handed it over but instead of taking it to the yard, he lingered. He couldn't bear to go just yet and hear Joey talking about his date with Rose.

'You OK?' she asked.

'Yes.'

'Good vibes not lasted long?'

He laughed. 'Busy day ahead. We're behind with the gaff rig cutter and the client doesn't have endless patience.'

'You work too hard.'

He rolled his eyes. 'You sound like Mum.'

'I hope not! I'm not that much older than you, but if I do, then she's right. You should get out of the house more and I don't mean sailing that boat alone.'

This was met with genuine amusement. Bo was great even if she was always trying to match-make him and he did enjoy female company. He'd love a lot more of it. He had been on a couple of dates since his last serious relationship had ended. He'd shared a house for a year with a girl called Rowena who he'd met at college, but it had fizzled out and eventually they'd agreed to go their separate ways. That was over three years ago now and he hadn't had a serious relationship since.

It had been disappointing when they'd split up, but he'd known they were going nowhere and that it was the right thing. Since then he'd been on a handful of dates, one arranged by friends at the sailing trust, a couple from an Internet site. None had lasted beyond the third meet-up.

'I'm too busy. I'm married to my boat — boats — and it wouldn't be fair on any woman,' he joked.

'Rubbish . . . unless there's someone you have in mind that I don't know about?' She leaned on the counter.

'No, there isn't but you'll be the first to know, I swear.' He finished his coffee and handed her the cup. 'Great coffee.'

'By which you mean 'mind your own business, Bo'?'

'No, I meant you make great coffee.' He smiled warmly. 'I appreciate the fact someone cares. Honest.'

'Don't let anything come between you and Joey.'

Finn's laughter hid how uncomfortable he was feeling. Bo had clearly noticed the air of tension between him and his brother. 'We've always been competitive.'

'Over sailing, yes. I've seen you when you're racing each other, but you know I don't mean that kind of competition. You can tell me to mind my own business all you like but I care about you both. Call it sisterly love.'

'I wish I had had a sister sometimes, rather than a brother.'

'You don't mean it!'

'No, I don't and you're right. Things have been difficult recently. Keeping the yard afloat is a lot of pressure and I don't blame Joey for not wanting to shoulder the burden.'

'And then there's Lauren . . .'

Finn winced inwardly. 'Yes, the split hit him hard. He's not got over it.'

'He must miss her. Dorinda too. She liked Lauren a lot. We *all* did.' Bo's knowing look made Finn wonder if she knew that he'd also 'liked Lauren a lot'.

'Mum was upset when she left so suddenly but mainly because she'd hurt Joey. And she was closer to you than Lauren.'

Bo nodded. 'Your mum has a lot on her plate. I just provide a friendly ear. I can see that some people are intimidated by her, but she's a strong woman and she adores her boys.'

'Ouch. That makes me feel about five years old.'

'Probably how she still sees you both!'

Bo made Finn laugh out loud and her honesty was refreshing, even if it had dragged him out of his comfort zone.

She rolled her eyes. 'Get to work and crack the whip over Joey. He was down here with another of his entourage just the other day.'

Entourage? Was that how Bo had seen Rose?

He left, unable to shake the thought. By now, all of Finn's post-sail Zen had vanished, but he had to start work, so he steeled himself, fixed a blank expression on his face and headed for the shed. Yet he still couldn't banish Rose from his mind.

His Google searches on her last night had been both fascinating and frustrating. The upside was he now knew a lot more . . . about Iron Age settlements, stone circles and burial barrows, which wasn't saying much, but only about Rose the academic, not about Rose the person.

One thing that had struck him was that she looked far better in person than in some of her work photos. By 'better', he meant healthier and — what was that phrase his grandad used to use — 'bonnier'? Finn thought she'd seemed pale and almost frail in some of the pictures, but she'd seemed blooming to him, and now the Cornish sun was tingeing her cheeks a pale gold.

He couldn't deny that she intrigued him as a person and that he felt a powerful physical pull to her. He sucked in a breath. The mermaid . . . yeah. Mermaids didn't spend part of their lives digging up old vases and writing about 'grave goods'.

Another thing that puzzled him was that many of the sites she was interested in and had written about in the past weren't that close to Falford. Then again, the local university wasn't that far and he had seen a joint paper she'd written in collaboration with another academic, a professor. Had that woman suggested she stay around the area?

Short of asking her why she'd chosen to base herself there, he wouldn't find out. Maybe Joey knew.

That thought left a nasty taste in his mouth. Joey probably knew everything there was to know about Rose by now. There was nothing Finn could do — or should do. If Rose and Joey got together, then it was fate and he was determined not to do anything to stop them.

'Morning. Not like you to be late,' Joey said as Finn walked into the shed.

Finn refused to rise to the bait. 'I thought I'd stop for a coffee at Bo's. I saw you sail past Curlew last night.'

Joey's eyebrows lifted. 'Don't say you were spying on us?'

'If you think that, there's no hope,' said Finn gruffly. 'I was doing the books for the yard. I was only making conversation.'

'Sure you were. For your information, I brought Rose straight back here from Kev's and she walked home to the pisky shop. I need to give her a lift to the Seafood Shack to get her car later this morning.'

Finn didn't look up. 'Like I said, it's none of my business.'

With that, they set to work but Finn could not shake Bo's comment about him 'liking Lauren a lot', or Joey's animosity towards him. Disturbing thoughts stirred in his mind. Had Joey somehow got it into his mind that Finn might have been partly responsible for Lauren leaving Falford?

And worse, was Joey trying to get his own back by dating Rose because he knew how strongly Finn was attracted to her?

15

Rose had woken early. She hadn't slept terribly well, reliving her awkward moment with Joey and knowing she had to prepare for a meeting with Professor Ziegler.

She hadn't actually met the professor in person yet, and she was a little nervous, only having shared a brief phone conversation and lots of emails. The eminent academic had sounded quite abrupt on the phone and was very highly regarded in the archaeology world, so Rose felt rather like she was an undergraduate meeting a tutor for the first time.

First, however, she needed to get a lift from Joey to pick up her car. In the cold light of day, she wished she didn't have to go over to the boatyard to ask him, even though he'd insisted on taking her. She might have walked, even though it looked several miles along the shore path — but it was pouring down with rain. Maybe she could call a taxi, if Falford had such a thing in a place where most people travelled by water — or a water taxi, but that would cost far too much.

As she went downstairs to the back door, she heard Oriel on the phone in the shop. Her voice grew louder and sounded angry so Rose decided to leave without saying 'good morning', but suddenly the bead curtain swept back and Rose came face to face with Oriel.

'Oh, it's you!' Oriel's face was red.

'Yes . . . but I was just going out, so I won't disturb you.'

'I'd like to go out and never come back!'

131

'I'm sorry . . . I heard you on the phone and it sounded heated so I didn't want to disturb you.'

'It's OK.' Rose followed Oriel into the shop where she plonked herself on the stool behind the counter and rested her chin on her hands.

'How was your evening with Joey?'

'OK . . . It was good.'

'Did he take you out in his boat?'

'Yes — to be honest, it was meant to be a sailing lesson.'

'A sailing lesson!' Oriel rolled her eyes.

'Well . . . I really did sail the boat.'

'OK. If you say so.'

'I do. Or rather, I helped under his supervision. We drove to Kev's for dinner and then we sailed home. I'd have thought you'd know about it by now. We moored at the boatyard last night and most of Falford Creek must have seen us. I need a lift to get my car and he told me to go over to the boatyard but really, I don't want to disturb him.'

'Why not? It's his fault your car's at Kev's.'

'True but you know . . . I'd rather be independent.'

Oriel looked at her hard. Maybe she was wondering why Rose was so keen not to rely on Joey after they'd been out on a 'date'. 'I can take you up to Kev's in the boat if you really want me to.'

'Oh. Aren't you busy?'

'Yeah, but not busy enough according to Auntie Lynne. Know-it-all Nige has been talking to some mate down the cricket club and reckons I should be 'more proactive in developing opportunities'. He says I should develop 'an online sales portal'.' Oriel let out a groan. 'I'd already suggested to Auntie Lynne last year that we get a web business up and running but

132

Nigel told her it wouldn't work. Now he's an Internet sales guru!'

'An online store sounds like a brilliant idea.'

'I think so, but I don't want any interference from him. I can't stand him. Auntie Lynne and I got on before he came along and we were doing OK. She's all right, really. She's my dad's sister, not that I see much of him or Mum. They moved to Scotland a few years ago but I wanted to stay here. Auntie Lynne suggested I run the shop and I had so many plans until Nigel came along.'

'How long ago was that?'

'About eighteen months. Auntie Lynne was lonely, I suppose, so I can't begrudge her having a bloke but he's such a bully. I never thought she'd let a man walk all over her because in other ways, she's quite bossy.'

'Do you think she'd become desperate?' Rose asked.

'Yes. She'd been on her own for years since she split from my uncle. She met Nigel at the cricket club. Auntie Lynne does the teas,' Oriel explained. 'He moved in with her after a couple of months and now he's got her under his thumb and persuaded her I'm useless. He's a gold-digger. I'm sure he's after her house and that he'd love to sell this place and spend the proceeds. I'm worried she'll marry him and then he'll run off with all her savings!'

Rose had no answer to the gold-digging theory, but she didn't like the sound of Nige at all. 'You should discuss the shop with your auntie and tell her you're willing to look for new ways to get customers in, but you want the freedom to run the online sales your way because you know your clientele better than Nigel,' Rose said, dismayed at Oriel's downbeat mood. Rose didn't really know what she was talking about, having never run a shop, but she hated to see Oriel feeling bullied.

'I wish I could sound as confident as you. I need to write some sort of plan to show her I can deal with it all myself without Nige interfering.'

'You can,' Rose said. 'Why don't we sit down over a glass of wine one evening and have a bit of a brainstorm?'

'Great idea. Tell you what, I'll ask Naomi along too.' Oriel looked outside. 'Oh God. It's pissing down. We'll be drenched if we take the boat. Can you wait?'

'Not really,' Rose said. 'I'm meant to be meeting a colleague at the uni.'

'Hmm. Well, there's no buses and I doubt the taxi will be available so it'll have to be Joey.'

'It's no problem. I really don't mind a bit of rain and he did offer,' said Rose.

With an umbrella and her waterproof jacket, she trudged over the footbridge and along the shore to the boatyard.

Dorinda and a younger woman were leaning over a rowing dinghy by the door and there was a strong smell of varnish and paint.

Dorinda became aware of Rose lingering and came over. 'Can I help you?' she said, pleasantly enough.

'I'm here to meet Joey,' she said, feeling about fifteen, knocking on the door of a boyfriend's parents' house.

'Oh, yes. He did mention he was going to give you a lift to Kev's. Did you have a good dinner?'

'It was delicious, thanks. He's a great cook.'

'He is . . . but I'm sorry Joey's not here. I'm afraid he's been called away to an emergency. He's had to go and help bring a yacht back from up the coast.'

'Oh, I hope everything will be OK.'

'I'm sure it will but they need someone with experience with that type of boat. We sailing folk help each other out, you see . . .' Dorinda said. 'That's no use to you. I expect you still need a lift back to Kev's place. I can run you there if you really want?'

Dorinda sounded less than enthused about having to give her a lift, and Rose didn't blame her. 'No. I wouldn't dream of taking you away from your work. I'll get a taxi.'

'You might have a wait. There's only one who comes out here and he might still be out on the school runs.'

'It's not a problem. I can wait until later. I'll call my colleague and tell her I'll be late.'

'If you're sure.'

'Totally.'

Rose could tell Dorinda was relieved not to have to leave her work and Rose certainly didn't want to be beholden to her.

Wishing she'd called a taxi in the first place, Rose wandered away from the shed, and stood by the slipway, messaging the professor and hoping to sound apologetic but in control. Luckily the rain had eased off. She hadn't finished her message when Finn called to her.

'Rose!' he shouted as he jogged over. 'Mum mentioned you'd been round. I'll take you to get your car.'

'Oh. No. I mean it's very kind of you, but I've caused enough disruption already.'

'No, you haven't. I need to go to the woodyard and chandlery at Penryn at some point, so it might as well be now.'

'OK. I'd appreciate it. I would like to make the meeting on time.' She put her phone away.

135

He showed her to his car, a small pick-up truck parked next to the house behind the yard.

Finn set off, whizzing along the twisty lanes far faster than she had. 'Joey did have to go to the yacht recovery. He's skippered that boat before in races and he knows it best. He wouldn't have gone if it hadn't been urgent. Just in case you were wondering,' he added.

'I wasn't,' she said firmly, then smiled. 'I think helping out with a stranded boat is a bit more important than giving me a lift.' She kept it as light as she could.

He smiled back. 'I only said it because some people don't always find Joey's reasons for not being at the yard that convincing.'

'You mean some women?' Rose said lightly. 'If it was an excuse, it still wouldn't matter. I only came over because he insisted on taking me back to my car. The return journey from the Seafood Shack wasn't what I'd been expecting.'

'It's none of my business,' Finn said, and the rest of the short journey was spent in silence, with Finn driving along like the car was on rails.

He was so like Joey, she thought, but like his brother's negative image, and she didn't mean that in any bad way, only that they reminded her of twins in height, physique and profile: light and dark. However, Finn was older and it showed in more lines on his face, perhaps it was the responsibility of the business that had aged him more than Joey.

The pick-up made light work of the unmade track to the Seafood Shack, unlike her car, which had rattled her bones. Still, it was with relief that she saw the faded sign announcing they were at Kev's.

'Here we are.' He turned the wheel.

136

'Jesus!'

He slammed the brakes on.

Rose let out a cry too, as the truck's wheels locked and gravel flew up.

Then there was silence. The grille and cab of a huge white refrigerated lorry was inches from the bonnet of the truck, totally blocking access to the site.

Finn swore softly. 'Are you OK?' he asked. 'I'm sorry about that. I'd no idea a truck would be there. He shouldn't be there, but I shouldn't have been so casual about turning in.'

'I'm fine,' Rose said, still a little breathless from the sudden tightening of the seat belts. 'Are you all right?'

'Yeah. It's a wonder the air bags didn't go off. We'd better go and ask Kev to get the driver to move it before even worse happens.'

They squeezed down the space between a hedge and the side of the truck, Rose first. This morning was turning into one of those when everything goes wrong, but she could still make her meeting, especially as Finn had shaved ten minutes off the journey.

'I'll go in and see Kev,' Finn said but then Rose heard him swear.

'What's the matter?'

Emerging from the space, she put her hand over her mouth. The back of the truck was a few feet from her car. Or what *had* been her car because the bonnet was crumpled like a milk carton; the bumper was hanging off and there were orange and red shards all over the ground from its smashed lights.

Kev ran down the steps from the shack.

'Bloody new driver. Wasn't paying attention. He's in the office now, dealing with his boss and the insurance. He's admitted liability.'

'Oh God.'

The rain was being driven in off the estuary and despite her waterproof, Rose was getting soaked. It was almost impossible to imagine she'd sat in the sun, drinking wine and eating oysters with Joey the night before.

Today had gone from bad to worse and even worse. Despite her vow not to sweat the small stuff, Rose's spirits had dropped like a stone. She'd have to tell the professor she wouldn't be able to make the meeting after all.

'After you've phoned the insurance company, I'll take you to Falmouth,' Finn offered.

'No. No you can't do that. I could be a while.'

'The woodyard isn't that far from Penryn Uni campus. I'll see them and do a few more errands. I'll be a couple of hours at least. Is that enough for you to see your colleague?'

'Plenty but I can't keep putting you out. Anyway, the tow truck will be here in half an hour and I need to wait for it.'

'I'll sort that,' said Kev sheepishly. 'I'll get them out straightaway and make sure they look after you as a priority. The garage is only in the next village, where Oriel and Naomi live.'

'Your insurance will send a courtesy car, won't they?' Finn said.

'I hope so but . . .' Rose tried to be positive even though she was horrified by the look of her car. It looked like a write-off.

'Why not salvage something from this mess?' Finn said, adding, deadpan, 'After all, things can't get any worse.'

'You think?' she said then relented. 'Let me exchange

details with the truck driver and phone the insurance people. If you're sure you can hang around, then I'd appreciate a lift.'

Twenty minutes later, they were finally on their way again. Rose was assured that it was OK for Kev to wait with her car, although she still felt uneasy at leaving it. There was nothing more she could do and she decided to try and do as Finn suggested and make the best of the day.

'This sounds like an important meeting?' Finn said, driving smoothly along the lanes but still faster than Rose would have liked.

'I'm trying not to make too big a deal of it, but it could be,' she said, alarmed at the Cornish hedges inches from the pick-up's windows. 'But I'll admit I'm nervous. Professor Ziegler, the head of the university archaeology department, is brilliant and has a bit of a reputation for being . . . quite exacting, if you know what I mean. I'd love to work with her though. I'm hoping she'll help me apply for a grant from the Antiquities Society for a joint project between my department and hers.'

'I'm sure you'll be fine,' Finn said with a reassuring smile. Rose wished she shared his confidence. 'What will you do with your grant?' he added to her surprise, as she hadn't thought he'd be that interested.

'Well . . . it's not a huge amount but it could make a big difference to our work. We could use it to explore more of the dig site at King Arthur's Pool or another site . . . but more important than that, we could share our work and all the exciting finds with the local community. I'm sure people would love to know more about the amazing history in their own back garden and this grant would enable us to set up

139

an exhibition or tour it round local communities and schools.'

'Sounds like a great idea. I'm sure the professor will agree when she hears how much it means to you.'

'I hope so. I'd love to share what we're finding with the people who actually live here. We might even be able to find a job for a local student if we can get the grant.'

'You care about your students.'

'Yes. I was one myself. I want to help them as much as I can.'

'My friend, Nash, funded an art scholarship at Penryn Uni, with the proceeds of his estate.'

'Oriel mentioned an artist used to live in the studio. I hadn't realised he'd done that.'

'It's not named after him, but the money came from him. He was a very modest man who shunned the limelight, which is probably why he wasn't better known.'

The card, the *card*. She wanted to blurt out and ask him. Did you send it? Are you the one? If she did, he'd — rightly — be horrified. She had stalked him and Joey. She didn't dare risk it. She didn't want to destroy the friendship that seemed to be developing between them.

With no further hold-ups they made it to the Penryn campus. 'Shall I collect you from here at midday?'

'Yes, that would be great. I'll grab a coffee if I'm early.'

'OK. See you later.'

★ ★ ★

140

Rose's meeting with Professor Ziegler went well and was promising, without any promises actually being made. The professor was brisk, wasting no words, but she seemed enthusiastic and supportive of Rose's ideas for getting their research out to the community. There was also better news about her car. The local garage had messaged to say her own car could be repaired, and meantime a courtesy vehicle would be delivered to the Falford Creek village car park the following morning so at least she would be independent again.

When Finn collected her, the back of the truck was full of wood and tins.

'How did it go?' he asked driving away at a more leisurely pace than the one they'd arrived in.

'OK. I think. Let's say I'm keeping my fingers crossed.'

Rose told him a bit more about the project and the dig, trying not to go into too much detail about Iron Age artefacts, although he seemed interested and asked a lot of questions, some of them about the ancient craftspeople who must have made them. That made sense, as he clearly loved working with his hands himself. Soon they were out in the open countryside and nearing 'home'. He suggested they stop for lunch, and they pulled into a quaint thatched café in the centre of a village where they grabbed a fresh crab sandwich and sat outside in the sunshine.

'This is delicious,' Rose said.

'It's been here donkey's years. Mum used to bring us both quite often at the weekends when we were little. We'd call in for ice creams or pasties after we'd been to cricket practice or shopping in Falmouth.'

He sounded nostalgic and Rose found herself

141

wishing they could stay longer.

'It's a lovely little place. I can see why you kept coming back.'

He gazed over the village green, a wistful look in his eye. 'Did you know there's a stone circle near here?'

'I don't quite have my bearings? Which one?'

'The Maidens . . . Nine or something. I can't remember the exact name. Not my field.'

'The Nineteen Maidens? Oh, of course. I haven't seen them yet.'

'It's about a mile on from here. There's a Celtic cross at the side of the road and a little track leads to it, apparently. I've never actually seen it though. You know when you live in a place, it's one of those things you always pass by and never make an effort to visit. Mind you, ancient history wasn't on my radar much before now.'

'Oh, you must! I'll definitely come back now.'

Finn looked at her. 'Why wait? Come on, let's go and take a look.'

'Oh, no. I didn't mean for you to take me now,' she said.

'I want to see it, now you've told me about your dig.'

'Aren't you supposed to be working?'

'Yes. Aren't you?'

She laughed. 'This is work for me.'

He smiled. 'I can spare the time. Come on.'

Shortly afterwards they stopped in a small lay-by and got out. There was no grand sign indicating an important historical site was so close but that was the same for many of the ancient places throughout Britain. In one way it was sad but in another, Rose found it exciting that you had to search for them, find out

142

they even existed and that they lay undiscovered by most people.

'I think it's along this footpath,' he said, helping Rose over a high granite stile.

'I've read a lot about the place,' she said, almost tripping over a bramble in her haste to reach the site. It was exciting to see somewhere new and she had to admit, even more exciting to share it with Finn, who lived here and yet had never been to see it himself. The ground rose steadily and the ridge of the low hill came into view.

They walked onto the top and the stones appeared, as if by magic, Rose thought, and she smiled at the thought of the people who must visit Cornish Magick after seeing the stones. They were positioned in an almost-perfect circle, with a much larger stone at the centre, angled like a javelin in the earth.

Rose was stopped in her tracks. 'Wow. What a view!'

All around was a three-sixty panorama of the landscape. On one side, moorland and on the other rolling fields gently descending to the sea. Underneath, a small stand of oak trees and bluebells swayed in the breeze.

Finn walked into the centre of the circle, turning slowly. 'I can only see twelve.'

'There were nineteen stones once and if you look carefully you can see indentations in the ground from where they must have been. It's thought the others were moved or broken up for building materials over the centuries.'

'But why maidens?' he asked. 'I've heard of a few more with names like that but never bothered to ask why before.'

'Ah, the maidens . . .' She was amused. 'It seems to

have been a popular idea in Christian legend to claim places like these were once young women turned to stone for doing something wrong.'

'What? For enjoying themselves?' He sounded incredulous.

'Oh yes. The Merry Maidens is the best known. They committed the sin of dancing on the Sabbath too.'

'Wow. A heinous crime. Dancing on a Sunday.'

'Yes. Terrible thing to do.' She laughed. 'I expect parents and the church thought it was a good way of keeping their daughters in line.'

'I hope it didn't work.'

'Me too.' Rose laughed. 'It's a good story for the tourists.'

'So, why are they really here?' Finn asked.

'Hmm. I could write a whole book about that and several people have.' She walked towards the quartz stone, admiring its smoothness. 'Well, it's widely agreed that a lot of stone circles like this one are Bronze Age. That's around 2500 to 800 BC,' she added, hoping she wasn't patronising him. 'We're not really sure why they were built but this one, for example, is probably linked to the moon and sun.'

'How can you tell? I mean, it's amazing to think that people moved huge pieces of rock without any equipment but there seems to be no clue why.'

'We know how old it is roughly from the type of pots and jewellery found round here. The number nineteen is linked to the moon's cycle, which is why you get a lot of circles with that number of stones.'

'But there would have been twenty-one,' Finn said. 'If you count these two that aren't in the circle.'

She joined him by a paler, flatter stone. 'That's

because it's different. Special. It's made of quartz for a start. It's supposed to symbolise the feminine and marks the position of the rising moon at the summer solstice.'

'OK . . .' His gaze settled on the other prominent chunk of granite thrusting up to the sky in the centre of the circle. 'What about that one?'

Even though she'd discussed and written about circles like this a hundred times without the slightest embarrassment, she found herself blushing. 'It's er — possibly meant to be phallic.'

His eyes widened. 'In that case, I'd like to have seen a Bronze Age bloke.'

'I wouldn't.' She hesitated a moment, gathering herself. 'Um. So, you have the coming together of the masculine and the feminine, you see . . .'

They were several yards apart, in a moment of stillness and quiet. Rose was conscious of herself breathing and the blood pulsing in her veins. It was hot in the afternoon sun, with spring sliding into summer, and she pushed her hair out of her eyes.

'I can hardly miss it,' Finn said with a wry smile.

With the light behind him, standing in the circle, he looked so imposing and handsome, Rose felt a magnetic pull of attraction to him. It was a completely different sensation to the one she experienced with Joey; this was a physical kick, a tightening of her limbs. She realised she loved looking at Joey, at his face — like a beautiful piece of art — but her reaction to Finn was far earthier.

Could it be a subconscious reaction to the situation, being alone in this place and talking about, well — sex? Was there an ancient magic at work? Or was it because of an actual connection with Finn?

145

'*I could hardly miss you.*'

The words — seeming to come from his direction — were no more than a whisper on the breeze. She blinked, wondering if she'd misheard them or even imagined them in the heat and strangeness of the moment. His back was turned but she hadn't noticed him move. She'd been too wrapped up in her own thoughts. The moment pulled her back years to when she was ill in hospital, with a fever, high on a cocktail of drugs. She'd heard things that hadn't been said then, too. This was different. She was completely present, with a virtual stranger who she found incredibly sexy.

She laughed out loud at her own foolishness. There was no magic, just good old sexual desire and it was completely impossible that she could guess whether Finn or Joey was her donor.

'Of course, there is another theory as to why that stone leans like it does,' she said, deciding to pretend she hadn't heard him. Was he even aware of the effect he was having on her?

He turned back to her and joined her by the big stone. 'Oh really? What's that?'

'Well, some say it was on its side at one time a couple of hundred years ago, but a bunch of drunken lads moved it into that position, to make the circle more . . . interesting, they fuelled the theory it was a symbol of — well, what we discussed.'

He laid his hand on it and chuckled. 'That sounds more like most of the Cornishmen I know.'

His phone rang, the modern ring tone jarring in the ancient place.

'Sorry. I'm amazed anyone can reach me out here.' He pulled the phone from his pocket and his amusement faded. After reading the message or text, he was serious again.

'I'd better get you back. I'm sure you've a lot to do.'

Which meant he'd a lot to do, she thought, wondering why the clouds had descended on his sunny mood. However, it had been his idea to visit the stone circle. 'You've already gone way beyond the call of duty in ferrying me about,' she said.

'It wasn't a duty. I've enjoyed it,' he said quickly. 'I'm sorry it has to end but Joey's back and I'm needed at the boatyard.'

With that, they walked swiftly back to the pick-up and drove the few miles to the yard. Rose was on the phone much of the way, talking to her insurance company, and she was glad of something to occupy her as Finn had reverted to his more taciturn self. She didn't go inside the boathouse but instead, hurried to the flat, crossing the river via the footbridge.

Rose was left alone, wondering if her moment of magic with Finn was only a figment of her imagination or if she might, literally, share the same blood as him and her body had sensed it . . . his too, and that's why he'd suggested they visit the circle together. No matter how much her rational side deemed it to be impossible, she couldn't chase the idea from her mind.

16

'You were a long while at the woodyard,' Joey said to Finn the moment he walked back into the Morvah boatshed.

'How did the rescue go?' Finn shot back, ignoring the comment.

'It was OK. Everyone's back in one piece thanks to my supreme skills.' Joey laughed.

'I'm glad to hear it . . . Why did they ask you to go? Wasn't there anyone closer who could have helped?'

Although Finn had told Rose there was a good reason that Joey was called to help, he had wondered whether Joey was the only skipper available or if he'd put himself forward to avoid helping Rose.

'Maybe because I'm the best at handling that type of craft. I hardly had a choice, did I? Luckily, you were able to come to the rescue, eh? You took your time though. Hours in fact. Where *have* you been, Finn?'

A clatter of boots on metal steps alerted them to Dorinda coming to join them.

'The frozen fish lorry ran into Rose's car and she needed to get to an important meeting at the university. That's where I've been.'

Dorinda swept down on them.

'Finn. You're back. How's Rose's car? Kev phoned me to say what had happened. Thank goodness no one was hurt.'

'Yeah. She's fine and we made it to her meeting. Luckily, her car can be repaired too.'

'Mum never said Rose had had an accident. Lucky

you were around to play knight in shining armour,' Joey murmured.

'Rose doesn't need a knight,' Finn said.

'I offered to take her to Kev's,' Dorinda cut in. 'But she wouldn't have it.'

'She knew you were busy, Mum, and didn't want to put you to the trouble,' Finn said, frustrated and annoyed by Joey's insinuations that he'd tried to keep Rose to himself. 'She didn't want to put anyone to the trouble, but she could hardly help it when Joey left her without transport.'

Joey snorted. 'So, it's my fault the truck ran into her car?'

'No, but you have to admit she wasn't expecting to leave it at Kev's.'

'I hate to be predictable,' Joey said. 'Did she actually complain to you about me while you were enjoying a trip to Falmouth?'

'No, she didn't. She was in her meeting for most of the time and I was busy.'

'We're *all* busy,' his mother said pointedly. 'So, can we possibly focus on building boats for a while? I've been trying to speak to the bank about a loan for that new machine and I've had the client on the phone while you were both out about this gaff rig cutter. He wants a firm date for completion and an estimate of the costs to finish it.'

Joey rolled his eyes and turned his attention to the cutter.

'I'll put together a plan of exactly what still needs to be finished and work out a realistic timeframe. It'll get done,' Finn said, putting his hand on his mother's arm. She looked exhausted, and behind the bluster, she must be weighed down by the burden. 'Why don't you leave that to me while you go and deal with the bank?'

Joey gave her a kiss on the cheek.

'Oh, go on with you,' she said, but a smile burst out on her face and lit up her eyes. Once again, Finn thought of how much his mum had had to deal with after their dad left and more recently, when Grandad Billy had died. Only recently, when he'd started to share some of the burden, had he realised what a remarkable woman his mother truly was. 'I'll be checking up on you later.'

'I'll look forward to it,' Finn said. 'Don't forget the cricket match on Sunday. You need the day off and you know you enjoy it.'

'Me? Waste an afternoon watching a bunch of blokes hitting a ball and sinking pints? I did enough of that when you were young.'

'And we're very grateful for it.' Finn was reminded of his lunch with Rose, at the little tea shop the family used to visit. He put his arm around his mother. 'You know you love it, really.'

'I might put in an appearance.' There was a twinkle in Dorinda's eye as she said it. 'Bo asked me if I'd help with some of the costumes for her dance club's regatta boat.'

'Sounds like a good idea. I'll give you a lift.'

Relieved to see his mother in slightly better spirits, Finn went back to work. He spoke to Joey, deciding to involve him in the plan to get it finished. Peace broke out, in their working lives at least, though Finn thought the tensions simmering around Rose wouldn't be so easily quelled.

17

'How was your meeting?' Oriel said in greeting when Rose got back to Cornish Magick at around four o'clock.

'OK . . . once I finally made it. The shellfish lorry squashed my car in Kev's yard.' Now that was something she wouldn't be saying in Cambridge . . .

'Oh my God. Is it driveable?'

'Not at the moment. The garage in your village towed it away and said it can be repaired, but it'll be a few days. There's a courtesy car arriving tomorrow.'

'What a pain in the bum for you. How did you get to Falmouth, then?'

'Finn was going to the woodyard so he gave me a lift.'

'Finn?' Oriel frowned in confusion. 'I thought Joey was taking you back to your car?'

'He was called away to an emergency yacht rescue. Apparently, he was the best skipper available because he was familiar with that particular boat.'

'Hmm.' Oriel frowned again. 'Was he?'

Rose wasn't sure what Oriel was implying, unless it was that the emergency had been an excuse not to take her. Rose couldn't believe Joey would have let her down, but that tiny element of doubt nagged at her. Then again, if he hadn't been called away, she wouldn't have got to know Finn a little better.

'It all worked out in the end. I saw my colleague and Finn was going out to Penryn anyway.' She smiled. 'On the way home we passed a sign for the Nineteen

151

Maidens, so we made a quick detour to see it.' Keen to distract Oriel, Rose glided over the fact that they'd had lunch and that Finn had actually invited her to see the circle.

'You mean the one with the big stone like a penis?'

Rose laughed. 'That's the one, though I'm not sure the stone was always standing up at that angle.'

'Naomi says it's phallocentric.' Oriel curled her lip. 'Bet that was the idea when some hairy caveman built it?'

'Maybe.' Rose couldn't help chuckling at Oriel's disgusted face. 'Not many people know about it. It's way off the beaten track.'

'Auntie Lynne found me reading about it in one of the guides in the shop when I was a teenager. She took all the copies off the shelves and told me off. Anyone would think we live in Victorian times now.' Oriel rolled her eyes. 'She almost passed out when I told her I was gay and moving in with Naomi but she's accepted it now.'

'Good for you.' Rose liked Oriel even more.

'Well, I love Naomi and I want everyone to know,' she declared.

'Could you channel some of that assertiveness and make them listen to your ideas more?' Rose asked.

'It's different. I enjoy working here and I'd like to make it more successful, but it isn't mine, you know? I feel I'm totally dependent on what my auntie has to say. She was easier to talk to before Nige came along, but now she defers to him on everything.'

'That's annoying.'

'He's still going on about getting the Internet business up and running too.' Oriel looked around her and sighed. 'We've had no one in since lunchtime.

I think he'd like Auntie Lynne to sell the shop and flat and try to get planning permission for it to be a holiday home.'

'I thought you said the council would never allow it.'

'Nige knows people at the cricket club who are in planning. Nothing would surprise me.'

'They're very strict on conflicts of interest,' Rose said.

'Maybe where you come from. I don't feel so confident here. We need more customers. We've got a coach tour planned for next Saturday. It's a local literary society. We need more like that.'

'Is it another du Maurier society?'

'Yeah. We keep some of her books in here . . .' Oriel smirked. 'The tours are run by an old guy called Mr Simpson and I wish we could get more of them. He's a bit of a rogue but the tourists love him. He tells people that the shop is featured in several of her novels. It was a fisherman's cottage then and it does sound exactly like the descriptions in the books, but no one knows for sure. Some of them ask me if she visited the shop.' Oriel smirked. 'Not even Auntie Lynne remembers that far back, and I don't like to say that the tour guide has made it up.'

'That doesn't matter. Look at all the legends linked to places in Cornwall. No one can prove them, but they still draw people to visit. Like the Merry Maidens, and the Mermaid of Zennor. It's the romance and mysterious aspect that appeals.' Rose smiled. 'You don't have to believe in any of it to enjoy the magic. I wouldn't be here if there were no legends, would I? However interesting these places are in an archaeological sense, it's our imaginations that bring

153

them to life.'

'True. People buy crystals and herbal stuff because it makes them feel better, even though I know there's no science behind it,' Oriel said, cheering up again.

Rose was transported back to her moment of magic with Finn. Previously, she'd thought she'd become immune to any romantic notions about sites, but it wasn't true. It had been incredibly powerful and atmospheric, for whatever reason.

'Anyway, back to your day with Finn! Did you see any piskies dancing around or spriggans?' Oriel said with a mischievous smile.

'Not this time.' Piskies were supposed to live around stone circles and other ancient sites and featured in a lot of Cornish tales. 'As for a spriggan, I don't think I've come across one yet?'

'You don't want to,' Oriel said. 'They're evil little buggers. The woman from the post office said her great-grandad saw one hanging round the Nineteen Maidens on a midsummer evening. He was on his way back from working in a tin mine with some mates.'

'Wow.' Rose thought it sounded like something from a period drama.

'They'd probably been on the ale though.'

Rose burst out laughing. 'It's funny how a lot of these sightings seem to happen after the pubs have closed.'

Oriel rolled her eyes. 'Talking of which, are you coming to the cricket match on Sunday afternoon?'

'Um. What cricket match?'

'What cricket match?' Oriel sounded scandalised. 'Falford Creek versus The Lizards. It's an annual grudge match. Everyone goes!'

'Oh, sorry I hadn't realised.' She smiled, thinking

of how important such events were in a small community like Falford. 'Yes, I'll come, though I know nothing about cricket.'

'I'm doing the scoring and Naomi's on first aid duty. You can meet her.'

'In that case, count me in.'

'Great, I'll give you a lift. Finn and Joey will be playing for Falford.'

'Oh. I heard Finn mention cricket practice, but he didn't say anything about a match.'

'I help with the scoring and Auntie Lynne does the teas.' Oriel wrinkled her nose. 'Bloody Nige will be there too. He's an umpire.'

'That sounds right up his street.'

'You're telling me. He'll be in his element, enforcing nit-shit rules and ordering people about. He's power mad.'

Rose laughed out loud.

The shop bell dinged. 'Customers. Looks like the Druids,' Oriel mouthed. Rose took her cue to go upstairs, vowing to stop daydreaming about magic and actually do some real work.

18

Rose's interest in cricket might be minimal but she was looking forward to meeting more of the Falford villagers and even, in a strange way, to finally meeting Nige face to face. If all else failed, she had the idea that she could find a quiet spot and pretend to do some research while keeping an eye on the Morvahs.

Rose's car was already fixed and she wondered if Finn or Kev had put a word in for her with the garage to get it mended double quick. The mechanics seemed to have done a decent job so she took it out for a run and met Oriel and Naomi at the cricket club.

Naomi wasn't what Rose had expected. She'd pictured a tall, broad-shouldered young woman capable of lifting drunken rugby players into an ambulance single-handed. Naomi was more elf than giant, with delicate features, piercing hazel eyes and the lithe physique of a marathon runner. She carried a large bag with a green cross on it, presumably full of first aid kit.

'I've heard loads about you,' Naomi said. 'Oriel never shuts up about you.'

'I do!' Oriel protested, blushing.

Naomi laughed. 'I'm winding you up. See you later. I hope you've got plenty of water and sunscreen. We don't want too many of this lot flaking out in this heat.' She eyed the crowd of largely middle-aged men with a worried look. The pavilion's outside bar was already busy. 'Some of them look like they need to lay off the pork pies and pints!'

With a kiss for Oriel, Naomi headed for a gazebo designated the first aid post. Oriel took Rose into the scoring hut, which was elevated and had a good view of the field. Hundreds of people arrived, the players distinct in their whites, although white was a loose definition of shades varying from toothpaste to beige. They were also a mix of all ages, shapes and sizes from late teens to late middle age.

A young guy with a doleful expression like a basset hound turned up to do the first session of scoring so Oriel was free. Leaving her companion to set up ready for the match, she dragged Rose over to the pavilion where a tall woman in her fifties was wafting herself with a red fan. She had tightly permed blonde hair and was wearing emerald green cropped trousers and a floral top.

'That's Auntie Lynne. Come on, let's meet her while Nige isn't here.'

Rose determined to be positive and polite, no matter what Oriel had told her.

'Auntie Lynne. This is Rose who's renting the flat.'

Lynne loomed over Rose, fanning herself furiously. 'Pleased to meet you. I hope everything's OK with the flat?'

'I'm fine, thank you. It's good of you to rent it to me. Oriel's made a great job of clearing it up.'

'Hmm. She did work hard. Is there enough room for your fossils?'

'Erm . . .'

Oriel exchanged a glance with Rose. 'Rose is an archaeologist not a palaeontologist, Auntie Lynne. I did tell you.'

'Oh, yes. Of course. Well, I'm glad you're happy . . . Oh, look, there's my partner, Nigel. He's been dying to meet you. He loves history. He knows all the answers on *University Challenge.*'

'That's more than I do,' said Rose, steeling herself.

'Oh dear. Really?' Auntie Lynne looked genuinely shocked at Rose's ignorance but then brightened up. 'Look, here he is. He can tell you all about it.'

A man Rose presumed to be Nige sauntered up, a pint in one hand. He was wearing an umpire's coat and a panama and . . . was that an actual pipe poking out of the pocket of his coat? His face had a ruddy complexion, which Rose suspected made him look far older than he was. All in all, there was an air of the pre-wartime gentleman's club about him. Rose could picture him in a leather armchair, puffing away and demanding another brandy from a white-coated waiter.

'Nige! This is Rose, who's rented the flat above the shop.'

With a head-to-toe assessment, Nige sized Rose up like she was a sheep at a show. 'So, you're the lady archaeologist? Oriel never shuts up about you.'

'Oh, really?' Rose said through gritted teeth, wondering what a lady archaeologist looked like. Should she have worn a crinoline and a safari hat with a face veil? 'Yes I'm —'

'Interesting field.' He cut her off before she could even say hello. '*If* you've got the time and leisure to pursue that kind of activity of course. I take an interest myself. I'm not a professional, naturally, but I've read a *lot* about the subject.'

'Really?' Rose said again through a forced smile.

'Oh yes. In fact, only the other day I was reading about the Pyramids. You do know the theory they were built by extra-terrestrials?'

Rose almost choked but managed to turn her astonishment into a cough.

Nige smirked. 'I know what you're thinking,' he said, before Rose had uttered a word. 'But I'm totally convinced by the alien construction theory. Successive governments have covered up the evidence, of course, so that people don't panic.'

'Er . . . I have heard that theory, y-es,' Rose replied when she'd regained her powers of speech. 'B-but it's not a theory widely supported by the majority of expert Egyptologists . . .'

Nige snorted. 'Now come on, my dear. Ancient people couldn't possibly have had the technology to build structures like that on their own. It's obvious they had extra-terrestrial help.'

'Yes, but it's *extremely* unlikely . . .' Rose said, desperate not to be rude to Nige, but only because she didn't want to offend Lynne and make the situation worse for Oriel.

'The experts are wrong. I can recommend some Facebook groups where you'll find all the information you need,' Nige said, squashing all resistance like a giant steamroller. 'Let me have your email and I'll send you some links. I think you'll be impressed.'

'Er. Thanks,' Rose said, wondering how she could escape without swearing. She certainly wasn't going to give Nige her email.

'Nige amazes me every day. He says he's a polymath,' Lynne said, gazing up at him in awe.

'That's one word for him,' Oriel muttered.

'Oh! Isn't that man from the scoring hut waving at you, Oriel?' Rose said, keen to escape.

'Oh, yes! I have to go.'

'Don't you bollocks up the score, young Oriel!'

Nigel shouted after her.

Oriel turned her head and shot a glare of pure evil at him.

'I should be going too,' said Rose sweetly, while feeling evil herself towards Nigel. He had that effect. 'I'm sure you can't wait to get out on the field.'

Without waiting for an answer, she scurried off, still wondering if she should have explained to Nige that every expert on the Pyramids could have shown him all the evidence that the Egyptians could and did build them, without any help from ET, Mr Spock or Darth Vader. However, sometimes it was better just to nod politely and make a discreet exit.

She walked over to the boundary line and found a shady spot under a tree.

She was used to people telling her things about archaeology. She always tried to be kind, and anyway, anyone who thought they knew the definitive truth about ancient sites was deluded. She'd be the first to admit that she certainly didn't but that was the point of studying, to look deeper at the evidence and come to your best conclusion — or your best guess — and be willing to change your mind when there were new discoveries.

She remembered how scared she'd been when she realised her doctors were also, when you got down to it, making their best guess about how to save her life.

'Are you OK?' Rose blinked back tears and found Oriel at her side.

'You had your eyes closed,' Oriel said.

'Oh, yes, I'm fine. I was taking some time out. To be honest, I might have dozed off.' She pushed herself upright reminding herself that everything had turned out better than she could ever have hoped and that she was extremely lucky. 'Aren't you supposed to be scoring?'

'Pre-match drinks break. Hadn't you noticed?'

'You mean they haven't even started yet?'

'They tossed the coin and Falford are in first.'

'Oh, I see.' Rose saw two huddles in the middle of the field. 'I really must have been daydreaming.'

'You know what I mean about Bloody Nige now?'

'Yes. I can see exactly what you mean.'

'Thought so,' said Oriel with satisfaction. 'Oh God, here he is.'

Rose looked up as Nige took his place some way behind the bowler, legs apart, a smug smile on his face. Two figures in whites and helmets emerged from the pavilion, striding towards the wicket. The taller of the two swung his bat overhead.

'Looks like Finn's opening the batting,' said Oriel, popping a strawberry into her mouth.

Rose had a flicker of the same hot, breathless feeling that had seized her at the stone circle. Maybe she could develop a passion for cricket after all.

In the end, her interest hadn't lasted more than ten minutes when Finn was given out by Nige for some inexplicable reason that drew a man nearby to swear loudly and complain it was 'never LBW — it was going down the leg side by a mile and bloody Nige needs to go to Specsavers.'

Judging by the language she'd heard from a group of Falford supporters, Rose guessed that many people agreed Finn had been unjustly dismissed. He seemed to think so too, trudging off the field, swishing his bat in obvious disgust. He caught sight of Rose and she thought he'd mouthed something. She managed a sympathetic shrug as he climbed the steps of the wooden pavilion, to a pat on the back from Joey. Not having seen him since their sailing 'date', and the awkward 'kiss', she was wondering how he'd react to her.

As for the game itself, Rose's interest waned further, especially when Naomi wandered up and informed her that Joey was a bowler and wouldn't be taking the field for a while.

The afternoon drew on, with groans and applause from the crowd becoming more raucous by the minute. The bar had a constant queue of people, which might have had something to do with the buzz growing. Several people were dozing in deckchairs near to Rose, as bees buzzed over the grass.

Rose collected a cool drink from the outside bar and passed Dorinda and Bo sitting side by side in deckchairs outside the pavilion. They were laughing together and, bizarrely, seemed to be sewing. Rose could hardly believe her eyes. She didn't want to intrude but they'd already marked her interest, and Bo called out 'Hello'.

Rose joined them. 'You look busy,' she said, seeing the fabric spread over Bo's lap and the sewing box by Dorinda's deckchair.

'We have to pass the time somehow,' Bo said. 'The cricket bores me to tears, but I offered to help with the teas.'

'I've had enough of blokes running around fields to last me a lifetime,' Dorinda said, rolling her eyes.

'Oh yes, Finn told me you used to take him and Joey to cricket matches.'

'Did he?' Dorinda's eyes widened.

'We drove past the Thatched Tea Shop on our way back from Falmouth,' Rose said, wondering why she felt reluctant to admit she and Finn had had lunch there. 'He said you often used to visit after the matches.'

'We did, yes. That seems a long time ago . . .' Dorinda sounded wistful, a word that Rose would never have associated with her.

'Can I ask what you're sewing?' Rose said, eager to move the conversation on.

Bo held up a spotty skirt. 'They're our costumes for the Falford Regatta. I'm adding a few extra sequins. Our boat — well, it's one of the guys' from the dancing club — is going to be transformed into Bo's Fifties Diner.'

Dorinda laughed. 'If we ever get the costumes ready.' She held up a floral headscarf, of the kind Rose had seen her wearing in the workshop.

'It sounds amazing,' Rose said, meaning she was amazed that Dorinda was into dressing up in full skirts and twirling around to rock and roll.

'I wouldn't expect too much,' Bo said and Dorinda smiled quietly. It was clear the two women had a close bond despite the age difference.

Bo glanced behind Rose. 'No rest for the wicked. It's tea and I offered to help in the kitchen.'

'I'll give you a hand,' Dorinda said.

A moment later, everyone trooped off the field and Oriel, freed from the scoring box, ran up to Rose. 'Want to come inside the pavilion for a drink and some food?' she asked.

'Isn't that just for the players?'

'No one cares. I'm a member and I'm inviting you.' She smirked. 'Joey and Finn are in there.' Then she sighed. 'And bloody Nige.'

This was a mixed blessing, if ever there was one,

but Rose couldn't possibly resist. 'OK.'

The pavilion veranda was packed by men in whites, laughing and talking loudly about the match. Oriel wrinkled her nose at the smell of beer and Deep Heat. 'Yuk,' she said, trying to avoid contact with any of the players as she ushered Rose inside.

Despite the invitation, Rose felt like an intruder, but Oriel showed her to the tea table and grabbed two glasses of elderflower cordial. Auntie Lynne was there, unpeeling the cling film from a platter of sandwiches in the window of the large serving hatch, while barking orders to several other middle-aged women and Kev from the Seafood Shack. Having met Lynne, and seeing that she was clearly in charge of the catering effort, Rose wasn't quite sure why she held Nige in such high esteem. Once again, she thought that Lynne must have been very lonely to have become involved with him.

Dorinda brought out another platter and added it to the trestle tables arranged down one wall of the pavilion. They already groaned with sandwiches cut into triangles, sausage rolls, slices of quiche and platters of cake. Yet Lynne, her helpers and Kev were still bringing out even more food, trying to find space on the tables. There were plates of fresh prawns, around a bowl of lemon mayo, and others piled high with hunks of buttered brown bread.

People descended on them instantly like a swarm of wasps and the noise levels grew louder.

Rose wondered how anyone could possibly run, bat or bowl after eating such a feast, though she supposed that the cricket probably came second to the tea — or rather, the beer — and the socialising.

Several of the Falford players and opponents had

164

glasses in their hand although Finn and Joey were sipping from bottles of water and Coke. Finn looked relaxed, and seemed to have accepted being dismissed by Nigel.

Joey immediately came over to Rose, while Finn nodded and smiled at her, but stayed with his team mates. She had a feeling he was purposely keeping his distance.

'Hi, Rose. Glad you could make it,' Joey said as he reached her.

'Me too. Oriel invited me.'

'I didn't know you were a cricket fan.'

'To be honest, I'm not but I'm enjoying it all the same.'

'Not nodded off yet, then?'

'Um . . .'

Joey laughed. 'I'll take that as a yes.'

'It's not you, it's me,' Rose said then realised how that sounded. 'I've been up late working on a paper and it was hot and . . .' God, she sounded decrepit but there was no way of explaining to Joey why she wasn't quite at her fittest, even now.

He just kept looking at her, a smile on his lips and those blue eyes twinkling, letting her dig a deeper and deeper hole that certainly wasn't leading to any kind of treasure.

'You're winding me up. Again,' she said eventually.

'I didn't mean to. Actually I came over to see if you'd like another sailing lesson?'

'On your boat?'

'I was thinking we could go back to basics at the sailing centre this time.'

Rose hesitated.

'I had a great time on *Spindrift*, but in all honesty,

it would be better for you if you learned to sail single-handed first. That's how Finn and I started and it makes the best sailors — safer and more competent — in the end. I can give you some individual lessons at the sailing centre when you have time.'

'That sounds like a good idea,' Rose said, carefully, filled with a mixture of embarrassment but also relief. 'I've been thinking the same myself, but do you have time to teach me? I'm more than happy to join a regular class.'

'Whatever suits you best,' Joey said. 'We can still go out on *Spindrift*. I really did like having you aboard and you can get more experience of a bigger boat. It's good to have someone who really seems to like the actual sailing and wants to be hands-on, not just sit there with a glass of wine and watch me . . .'

'It was fun,' Rose said, remembering the wind in her hair and the boat cutting through the water. 'Exhilarating.'

'Yes, and it's great to have someone to talk to who's not from Falford. Someone with fresh ideas who isn't set in the ways of this bloody place. A new friend . . .'

Rose might have been imagining the slight emphasis on the word 'friend' but she wasn't going to let the opportunity pass to set things right between them.

'It's always good to get a fresh perspective on life. That's one reason I wanted to come here to work . . . to have new experiences. Look, Joey, I'd love to carry on with my lessons and sail with you again but on one condition: I'll book myself onto a beginners' sailing course as my part of the bargain.'

'Great.' His grin was broad. 'And I'll expect you to take charge of *Spindrift* the next time we go out on her.'

Rose laughed.

'I'm glad we've got that straight,' Rose said, noticing Finn watching them from afar. He'd been sitting outside the pavilion with the rest of the team earlier. He still hadn't made any effort to come over during the interval and she wasn't going to push things.

'Joey!' the team captain called to him. 'Come on, tea's over. Get ready.'

'I'm coming!' His voice was laced with frustration. 'I'll call you to arrange a time for our next outing on *Spindrift*? OK?'

'Yes,' Rose said. 'Yes, why not?'

She watched him march towards the crease, hoping she'd done the right thing in agreeing to another sailing trip but finding it impossible to resist another chance to dig deeper and find out more about him.

19

Oriel was outside, peering into the shop window when Rose returned from the dig site on Monday afternoon.

'Rose! Hello. I've done a new window display. What d'you think?'

Rose took a closer look at the display, which seemed to show a mini stone circle and lots of yellow and sun faces. 'That looks great. I love the henge and the sundial.'

'Yay! You noticed. Well, the summer solstice will soon be here so I arranged some of the crystals into a circle like a mini stone henge. We had a couple of new books in and I found all the sun-themed bits and pieces I could.'

'It's gorgeous. I'd definitely come in.'

'I'm going to do a King-Arthur-themed window when the solstice has gone. I've been inspired by your dig.'

'I doubt we'd find anything to do with King Arthur, but it's a great idea.'

They went back inside. Oriel poured Rose a cold drink and they chatted in the shop.

'So, how did you enjoy the cricket match? And what about Know-it-all Nige? Was he as bad as you expected?'

'Um . . . actually, he was probably worse.'

Oriel banged the counter in triumph. 'See, I knew I wasn't making a fuss. What the hell does Auntie Lynne see in him? No, don't answer that.'

'I can't but . . . I'm convinced that she must have

been desperate for the company. That's understandable but she seems a — um — very capable woman. I don't know why she thinks she needs him.'

'She was capable. She is — but he's browbeaten her . . .' All Oriel's pride in her window display had evaporated. 'I overheard him telling her she should get this place valued. By one of his estate agent friends, naturally.'

'I thought it wasn't worth much?'

'Even with the local occupancy clause on the flat, it would still fetch several hundred thousand. I wish she'd realise what a prat he is and dump him. She doesn't need him. If I could get more customers and show my auntie I don't need him telling me how to do my job, it would be a start.'

Rose thought so too, but didn't want to be part of any plan to actively split up Nigel and Lynne. On the other hand, Oriel shouldn't have to put up with Nigel's trying to take away her livelihood. Rose wondered if he was interested in Lynne's money rather than simply being a total prat.

'I could have died when he said that aliens had built the Pyramids,' Oriel went on. 'I'd like to see him beamed up by the Martians. Mind you they'd probably beam him straight back down once he started telling them how they could triple their warp speed or something,' Oriel said, then continued imitating Nige's smug and ponderous voice: 'Of course, if I were you, I'd take a look at the gasket head on that spaceship. Mind you, what do you expect with that model of warp core? You can't beat the old V12 nuclear thruster . . . Drone, drone, drone . . . I can see them fighting each other over who gets to zap him down to Earth before their brains shrivelled . . . Honestly, I swear if he met Mr Spock, he'd outdo him too!'

Rose was laughing out loud as Oriel regaled her with more stories about Nigel. She was a real character and a natural comedian . . . and an idea formed in her mind. If it worked, it might go a little way to solving Oriel's problems with the shop and Nigel.

'Oriel, have you thought about persuading Mr Simpson to run a folklore tour in conjunction with Cornish Magick? He could take people around the sites and bring them here to the shop afterwards?'

Oriel's eyes widened. 'That is not a bad idea although . . .' She grimaced. 'He might know a lot about Daphne du Maurier but I don't think he knows anything about the ancient sites.' Her eyes lit up suddenly. 'You could do it though. If Mr Simpson advertised it and organised the transport and took the money as usual, you could lead the actual tour. You know where the sites are, and all the stories. It could start and end here at the shop and we could all take a cut and bring in extra custom.'

'Me? I didn't mean me,' Rose replied, in horror. 'I've never run a holiday tour in my life.'

'You give lectures, though?'

'I'm there to teach the students. I'm not trying to entertain them . . . although there is an element of entertainment because I'm trying to engage them and inspire them. I don't want them nodding off in my lectures . . . though it has happened when they've been up all night partying. I hope it wasn't totally my fault,' Rose added with a grin.

'No way. They were probably still off their faces. I love listening to your stories about the sites round here.'

Rose warmed to Oriel even more but refused to

accept she was anything more than a reasonably decent lecturer.

'Don't people like you go on telly?' Oriel said. 'Auntie Lynne went on a cruise last year. They had some guy off *Time Team* and a famous gardener.' Oriel rolled her eyes. 'Nige said he could have done a better job but he's an idiot. He'd have bored people senseless within five minutes. You'd be brilliant.'

Rose had been put on the spot and was struggling. She wanted to help Oriel, and show Know-it-all Nige where to shove his bullying and interference. Damn. She'd even suggested the idea of Oriel persuading Mr Simpson to run the extra tours but she couldn't turn into a tour overnight, especially if it meant making stuff up to entertain people and besides . . .

'I'd love to help but . . .' An idea popped into her head.. 'I know someone who'd be much better at it than me. Someone who'd be a natural.'

Oriel looked puzzled. 'Who do you mean? Tell me! If you could even just plan a folklore tour and I can get them to do it, it would be brilliant.'

'You could do it,' Rose said.

Oriel's mouth opened in astonishment. 'Me?' She snorted. 'I love the legends but I don't know enough about all those sites. I'd be hopeless.'

'I could help you. You're very knowledgeable about your stock and you're definitely entertaining and engaging. You sold *me* a geode.'

'Yeah but — telling people who are paying . . . What if I get a Nige?'

'You'll handle them easily. I've seen you deal with customers. You're funny, you're sharp and you have local knowledge. Much better than an outsider like me.'

171

'I'd have to say what I thought, on these tours. If I got a Nige-type, I'd have to put him right if he started talking bullshit.'

'Quite right,' Rose said, already wondering what the tourist groups would be letting themselves in for. Oriel would certainly be memorable. 'I can give you some techniques on dealing with hecklers if you like?'

'Do people dare to heckle in lectures?'

'Well, not exactly heckle and obviously I'm there to encourage them to ask questions but sometimes, you do get a student who's out to cause trouble.' She thought of her terrifying first lecture, when she had to rush to the loo to be sick beforehand. There was an exam going on in the same building, and one of the senior examiners had told her off for being out of the exam room. He'd thought she was an undergraduate.

How far she'd come, she thought, thinking of how she took the lectures in her stride now and enjoyed teaching. Her transplant had made that possible. Her donor had made it possible. She owed it to Oriel to help her achieve what she wanted — and actually that applied to herself too. She made a note to call in at the sailing centre before it closed.

'You can do this,' Rose said firmly, referring to herself as much as Oriel. 'Speak to Mr Simpson to see if it's feasible and let's do a practice tour together and then you can take over. Cornish Magick has the potential to be a big success and what's more, we'll show Nige we don't need him and his bullying.'

20

Finn hadn't seen Rose — properly — for a week since their day in Falmouth. They'd barely exchanged more than a nod at the cricket match because he'd been keeping his distance so as not to get in Joey's way. He'd been too busy working on the boat and to be fair, Joey had put in the hours too. They were making progress, thanks to the new plan, and if there were no unexpected problems, they should make the September deadline.

With this in mind, he met up with the boatyard manager to discuss the launch. The date wasn't set in stone yet, but plans had to be made now. With coffees from Bo's they held their 'meeting' outside in the June sunshine, and were finishing up when the manager nodded down the estuary.

'Isn't that the woman who's moved into Cornish Magick?'

Finn looked closer at the Laser dinghy, which was tacking towards them. It was definitely Rose at the helm, in her buoyancy aid. She was part of a flotilla of half a dozen beginners.

'She's doing well,' the manager said.

'Very well,' Finn echoed, impressed at the way Rose turned the boat downwind away from him, becoming just another sail among many. She'd never mentioned she was having lessons . . . unless . . . Was Joey involved in her decision?

'I'll email you with the details about the launch, then, mate,' the manager said, throwing his coffee cup in a bin.

'Yeah. Thanks . . . see ya.'

Finn watched Rose for a few seconds more until she disappeared from view completely. Surely it was no coincidence that Joey had taken her sailing and now she was learning herself? Joey hadn't said anything about it, but why would he? It was nothing to do with Finn. He resolved to tear his mind away from her and concentrate on his work.

A couple of hours later, Rose herself approached him when he'd gone to Bo's to get brunch butties for the team. All hopes he had of trying not to be attracted to her vanished. She looked glowing and happy, and Finn wasn't sure if that was a result of the sailing or something to do with Joey.

'Hello!' she said, brightly. 'I came over to grab a sandwich and some cakes from Bo's to take to the dig. The students have been working hard and I wanted to treat them.' She laughed. 'Who am I kidding? I'll probably eat the cakes myself. I'm starving.'

Because of her sailing . . . Finn thought . . . 'I saw you earlier,' he blurted out. 'Having a sailing lesson.'

'Oh, did you? I'd hoped it was too early for anyone to notice! It's my third lesson this week and they let us sail up here.'

'You were doing really well,' Finn said.

'Was I? I was too busy hoping I didn't capsize to notice anyone watching.'

'I didn't know you wanted to learn,' he said.

'I didn't either, or rather I didn't until . . .' She hesitated. 'Until I was sure I'd got the research grant and knew I was coming here. I'd vaguely fancied it, but Joey said I should have some lessons and so I took the plunge. Not the literal plunge, I hope. We haven't

174

done a capsize drill yet.'

'You'll be fine. You're a natural.'

'Thanks, but I *really* don't think so.'

Finn was tongue-tied but he didn't want her to leave.

'Um — talking of Joey, is he around?'

Finn's heart sank. 'He's in the shed.'

'Of course, he is. I'm sure he's very busy only . . . he sent me a message about taking *Spindrift* out . . .'

Having not heard a word from Joey about Rose, Finn had half-hoped they weren't taking things any further. Those hopes were now crushed.

'Want me to call him down here?' Finn scraped up a smile. 'He's been at work since seven. I'm sure he'd like an excuse for a break.'

'Thanks, I'd rather not disturb him. I had to come this way so I thought I might see him at Bo's.'

'Come on, I'll take you up there. He won't want to have missed you.'

With a tentative 'OK, but only for a moment,' Rose joined Finn. When they reached the shed, Joey was at the wood stack and spotted them.

'Hello, Rose!'

'Here he is. I'll leave you to it,' Finn said, turning to leave, but not before he spotted something in Rose's eyes. She was ultra-polite but there was a definite coolness when Joey kissed her on the cheek.

'I've been meaning to call you,' Joey said.

'Don't worry, it's no problem. We've both been incredibly busy.'

'I thought you might have been. Finn's had my nose to the grindstone.'

'And I'm going back to it,' Finn said. 'See you, Rose.'

175

Finn went back to the woodpile by the entrance to the boatshed but found it impossible not to hear snatches of their conversation. Finn could have walked away and yet he didn't.

'So, how did this morning's lesson go?'

'OK, I think. I didn't run aground or capsize.' Rose laughed, sounding far more relaxed than she'd been when she'd spoken to Finn about her sailing efforts. 'I think I'm getting the hang of it more. I was better than when you came out with me the other evening.'

'You'll soon be entering the regatta. They have a novice class.'

'I don't think so! But the tips you gave me about getting into the right position in the boat were really helpful when I went single-handed and I tried to relax.'

'You only need some confidence. So, are you ready to handle a proper boat?'

Rose gasped but sounded amused by Joey's teasing. 'I already *have* handled a proper boat, but if you've time to take me, you know I can't resist a chance to sail *Spindrift* again.'

'What about . . .'

A loud bang startled Finn. He swore under his breath and heard Gurdeep apologising for dropping a bag of tools on the floor.

Maybe it distracted Joey and Rose too, because Finn could no longer hear their voices clearly. He went back inside and engaged in some banter with the others about apprentices being butterfingers, but inside he was eaten up by what he'd heard. It was wrong to be jealous, but he couldn't help it. Joey and Rose obviously got on like a house on fire and Finn found it hard that they were sharing a passion for his beloved sailing. Still, he had to master his feelings.

Joey had lost one love of his life and if he was going to be happy with Rose, Finn had to find a way of living with that fact, no matter how much it hurt.

21

Late June brought hot sunshine to Falford and a marked influx of visitors. A few of them found their way into Cornish Magick, but Oriel was still keen to get even more of them inside and spending cash.

The village car park was full by ten most mornings and it seemed to take longer each day to reach the dig site, with queues on every narrow corner while nervous drivers tried — and often failed — to reverse so they could let other vehicles past. Her half-hour journey had almost doubled some days and she would probably have been better off living closer to it rather than in Falford itself, despite its other major temptations . . .

She'd made increasing use of the water for her local journeys, zipping up and down the estuaries and creeks to the local pubs. She'd had two more sailing lessons at the centre and one scary moment where she'd almost capsized but managed to right the boat just in time. She was looking forward to her next outing on *Spindrift*, but until the night before, both she and Joey had been too busy to fix a time — or the tide and weather had been wrong.

The other thing she was determined to do was make time to help Oriel, although she half-wished she hadn't been so bullish about turning Cornish Magick into the folklore tourism capital of Cornwall.

However, she was determined to be positive for Oriel's sake and suggested they have a trial run for the first tour. The plan was to visit Arthur's Pool near the dig site and then head off to some more ancient sites in the far west. It would be a long day but they were all up for it.

They all piled into Naomi's camper van, a turquoise affair with a bay window and three seats across the front. It reminded Rose of the Mystery Machine from *Scooby-Doo*, which seemed appropriate as they were off to investigate spooky myths and legends . . . words she would never dared have voiced to her colleagues at the university but which made her grin like an idiot. While she had a feeling it was going to take quite a while to get all the way from Falford to the moor, it was also going to be a lot of fun.

Accustomed to driving an ambulance at breakneck speed around south Cornwall, Naomi had the van trundling along at a surprising pace. She told Rose it was a Brazilian import with a modern engine but even so they almost had to shout above the road noise and the sound of twigs snapping against the windows in the narrower lanes.

Naomi entertained them with some of the more light-hearted tales from her job and soon they climbed higher up towards the moor.

'This would be a long day out for your tour party,' Rose said.

'They won't mind. They like to think they're getting their money's worth and there's a lovely pub in one of the villages they could have lunch at,' Oriel explained.

'My cousin runs it,' Naomi said, turning the huge steering wheel to make a left onto a moorland road. 'It's supposed to be haunted. They'll love that.'

Rose let Oriel lead the way to the dig site. The pool was a little further on from the site itself in a hollow at the top of the hill. Rose knew a little about it, but wanted Oriel to be in charge. She was looking forward to acting the part of a 'tourist' and hearing Oriel's take on it. She was buzzing with anticipation as they walked higher onto the moor and its calm surface came into view, reflecting the sky and clouds.

'See, told you. It's so mysterious . . .' Oriel stood at the side of the pool, eyes shaded.

Naomi joined them after locking the van. 'It is a bit creepy . . .'

The others followed Oriel down to the edge of the pool. Not even a light breeze ruffled the surface and a couple of swans floated serenely past.

'I love Cornwall,' Rose said with a sigh. 'This is beautiful.'

Naomi sat on the grass overlooking the water, and the others joined her, drinking from their water flasks. 'This place gives me goose bumps,' Naomi said again.

'Funny you should say that. There was supposed to be a girl who was murdered here. They called her Dozy Mary though there's the same story told about a lake on Bodmin Moor.'

'Nice.' Naomi pulled a face.

'Poor Mary,' Rose murmured. 'Can you tell us a bit more?'

'You must already know all about it,' Oriel said, then sighed. 'I'm nervous even with you and Naomi here so how will I manage a group of strangers?'

'Actually, I don't know much about Mary. I've only read snippets on the Internet, never heard the real story behind it,' Rose said. 'And I'd love to hear it from someone who actually lives and breathes Cornwall.'

Oriel turned to gaze over the pool. 'I always thought it was so sad. When I was little it made me cry. It's such a tragic tale.' She turned to Naomi and Rose, a wistful look on her face. 'And yet, it looks so peaceful, doesn't it? With the ponies grazing and the skylarks singing, no one would think that there was anything sinister about the tranquil waters of this moorland pool. And yet, it's a place of bloody murder and some say, it's the last resting place of King Arthur himself . . .'

Rose hid her delight as Oriel got into her stride, her Cornish burr deepening as she relished telling the story of poor Mary, a local girl who was reputedly murdered and thrown into the pool. It was a gruesome tale but Oriel obviously loved talking about this place and knew a lot about it.

'Some folk thought that the pool was bottomless and that's why King Arthur commanded Sir Bedivere to throw Excalibur into it. Twice, the faithful knight tried to throw the shining sword into the water and twice, he hadn't the heart to let such a treasure sink beneath the murky water. But on the third time, he finally let go of it and an arm appeared from the pool, caught Excalibur and pulled it down.'

'Wow . . .' Rose said, in awe at the transformation in Oriel.

'Is it true?' Naomi asked. 'Even a *bit* true?' she added hopefully.

'Well, no one can prove that Arthur *didn't* find his last resting place here on the moors. As for the lake, it retains its mystery but during the Great Drought back in 1976 . . .' Oriel paused and addressed Naomi and Rose with an eye-roll. 'The oldies will remember that.'

She continued: 'The pool dried out completely, revealing the lakebed, but despite a thorough search, no trace of the magic sword could be found . . .'

'Ohhh,' Naomi said in awe.

Rose found she had goose bumps on her arms, just like Naomi. No matter how improbable the story — mainly because King Arthur had almost certainly never existed — the idea of finding any sword in the lake was thrilling.

'I loved tales about Arthur when I was little,' she said, thinking back to sitting with Granny Marge on the sofa, being read to from a big book of myths and legends. It was stories like this that had fuelled her obsession with ancient sites when she'd been small. Even though she could read herself, she loved listening to her granny bringing them to life.

'It must look so atmospheric up here when the mist comes down,' she said. 'I can imagine the Lady of the Lake reaching up to catch the sword.'

'Was I OK, then?' Oriel said. 'Not over the top?'

Naomi hugged her. 'I loved it.'

'Me too,' Rose said. 'You're a natural at this.'

'Only because this is one of my favourite places.'

'You can learn about the other ones,' Rose said. 'And if you forget anything, just make it up! At least you don't have to write papers on it that will be ripped apart by other academics.'

'Do they do that?'

'It's called peer review,' Rose said. 'And it's the way we make sure that academic research has been carried out properly but sometimes,' she sighed, 'it can feel like being thrown into the arena with the lions!'

They went for a walk but as the sun climbed higher, everyone was hot so they sat in the shade of a tree and ate their picnic. It turned out that Naomi liked to unwind from her stressful job by baking so there was home-made sourdough, pasties and a chocolate brownie each.

Rose thought it was all very *Bake Off* and that she'd need to walk back to Falford to balance out all the calories. There were no loos nearby so it was a trip off the path and through a rocky hollow to the tallest clump of bracken they could find. An unfortunate consequence of being an archaeologist, Rose thought, picking her way back through bracken as tall as she was.

'Oh!' she said, as she caught her foot on a rock and stumbled. Automatically she put her hands out to stop herself and landed face down in the bracken. Immediately she felt a sharp stab in her hand and swore.

The soft earth had cushioned her fall and nothing felt broken, but there was blood all over her hand. When she looked down, she saw a piece of rusty barbed wire lying in the bracken. Blood trickled down from her thumb and she cursed. Why did that have to happen now in the middle of nowhere, when they were having such a good time?

Holding her injured hand high, she made it back to Naomi and Oriel.

'Oh my God, look at your hand!' Oriel cried in horror.

'I fell over and cut it on some wire.'

Naomi took charge immediately. 'Sit down there and keep your hand up.'

She ran to the camper van and fetched a first aid kit, going into action, cleaning and disinfecting the cut while Rose tried not to wince.

'I don't think you'll need stitches . . .' she said, putting a dressing on it and bandaging it up. 'Are you OK? You look a bit pale.'

Rose nodded. She felt a little bit light-headed, if the

truth were known. 'I'm OK,' she said, desperate not to make a fuss.

'Water, please, Oriel,' Naomi ordered.

Rose sipped from the fresh bottle handed to her by Oriel. 'I'm already feeling better. It's a bit hot here, that's all, and I feel such a prat. I never saw the rock in all that bracken.'

'Don't worry,' Naomi said kindly. 'Have you had a tetanus lately?'

'Yes. I'm up to date.'

'OK, then I won't make you go to hospital. Are you really feeling better? Is there anything I should know?'

'No, I'm fine, only . . . this probably isn't relevant, but I want to tell you anyway.' She shot an apologetic glance at Oriel. 'I should have told you ages ago.' Her pulse picked up. It shouldn't be a big thing to share, but it felt like it. Her instincts told her now was the moment, that she was among friends and it would be such a weight off her mind.

Oriel's eyes widened.

'I've wanted to tell you this since you offered me the flat, Oriel, but there never seemed a good time and some people can have a strange reaction. I don't want anyone feeling sorry for me or worrying about me.'

'Oh God, don't tell me you have something terminal?'

'Oh no, don't worry about that although . . .' She took a deep breath. 'I *was* very ill a few years ago. I had something called aplastic anaemia, which is life-threatening, but I was very lucky to get a stem cell transplant which — so far — has meant I can enjoy a completely normal life.'

It was odd, she felt the need to put in the caveat:

184

'so far'. It was the verbal equivalent of crossing her fingers or touching wood. She didn't think she'd ever be able to say she was 'cured' even though she was as close as it was possible to be.

'All those tablets . . . I knew something was wrong.'

'It's not. Not now, for which I'm so grateful to my doctors and the donor. The tablets were prophylactic antibiotics. I take them as a precaution.'

'To help reduce the risk of infections developing,' Naomi explained to Oriel.

'Exactly. The other stuff is bog-standard. Paracetamol, travel sickness pills, some vitamins.'

'I put my big foot in it. Sorry,' Oriel said.

'Don't worry. I didn't mind . . . this stuff has been weighing on me and I wanted to share but I would really like it kept between us. I don't want anyone feeling sorry for me, or looking at me in a different way. There's only so many questions and long-winded explanations I can handle.' She smiled.

'I won't say anything,' Naomi reassured her. 'And neither will Oriel, will you?'

'My lips are sealed. So this transplant thing was a total success?'

'Yes, I'm very lucky. Not all transplants go as well so I count myself doubly fortunate. I can basically get on with my life as normal.' *Almost like normal*, Rose thought, reflecting on the long-term effects of some of her treatment including the fact she might not be able to have children. She moved on, refusing to dwell on the bad things. 'How amazing is that?' Rose felt a shiver, of relief and joy — and fear — as she always did when she was forced or allowed herself to dwell on the past. It was normal to be anxious, to have emotional moments, but she'd learned to let them out bit

185

by bit . . . so she could control them, like a drip feed. The sudden reminder, the questions, were almost overwhelming her.

Oriel was still in awe, clearly, and not about to let Rose off the hook. 'So, does that mean you have their DNA in you? I saw a TV thriller where the murderer got away with the crime for years because he'd had a bone marrow transplant,' she added, sounding excited.

'Yes. Yes, I do have their DNA inside me. If you did a blood test, you'd think we were exactly the same person but if you did a cheek swab then you'd be able to tell the difference.'

Naomi shot Oriel a warning glance. 'Oriel, this is a big thing for Rose. We shouldn't interrogate her like this.'

Rose silently thanked Naomi, although Oriel wasn't ready to let go yet.

'So, your donor — they're not related at all?'

'I suppose because we're a match, there is a slim chance of some distant connection. Then again, it might just be a lucky roll of the genetic dice.'

'Oh, then your donor *might* be related to you!'

'Well, most people in England whose families have been here for many generations are likely to be related,' Rose said, being vague, and not actually lying. 'If your family have been here for hundreds of years, you're almost certainly related to Richard III.' Rose laughed, keen to move the conversation away from her. 'You see, Danny Dyer is nothing special.'

'Really? I'm royal?' Oriel squealed. 'I hope so!'

Thrown off the scent, Oriel bombarded Rose with questions about how she might be related to royalty and Rose did her best to explain, even though it wasn't really her field.

She had absolutely no reason to suspect the Morvahs were any kind of *close* relation, but what if they were very distant cousins or something?

It was a ridiculous idea. She laughed at herself, standing around the pool with Oriel, buzzing with excitement, and Naomi, her hand resting protectively on Oriel's back.

'You don't even know if they're a man or woman?' Oriel said, treading into dodgier territory. 'You might have a serial killer's DNA in you!'

Naomi burst out laughing. 'That's reassuring for Rose.'

'Don't worry. They aren't a serial killer,' Rose said firmly, skating over the question of her donor's gender. 'Although I'm not sure I'd have said no, whoever it was.' She had wondered about this herself until the card had arrived and she'd narrowed the donors down to the Morvahs. 'You wouldn't believe how desperate I'd become, even though I tried to stay positive for my family's sake.'

Naomi smiled, as if she understood the instinct to cling on to life. She must have seen it so many times.

'You will keep all this to yourselves?' Rose said, half-wishing she hadn't 'confessed' after all.

Oriel went serious. 'I won't tell anyone. I swear.'

'She won't,' Naomi said firmly, and Oriel laughed.

'But imagine if they *were* Cornish and you happened to be here working. You might pass them in the street, or be in the same pub as them, and never even know.'

Naomi laughed. 'That would be a pretty massive coincidence,' she said. 'As Rose said, the donor could come from anywhere in the world.'

Rose smiled weakly, thinking that she'd chosen to

live in Falford itself precisely because her donor lived there. She could have found somewhere closer to the dig site if she'd really wanted to.

'OK?' Naomi asked. 'You've more colour in your face and your pulse is normal now.'

Rose glanced at her hand, neatly bandaged, then smiled. 'I'm fine,' she said, taking a sip from the water bottle.

'Ready to head back to the van?' Naomi asked Rose.

'We don't have to go home; I don't want to spoil the day.'

'I've got an idea that'll cheer us all up, and if you still feel fine, we can go on to the other sites.'

Naomi turned off the road a short way to a 'greasy spoon' café called Nora's Nibbles. The roadside van looked like it had been craned straight from a motorway roadworks, and had a couple of mismatched chairs and tables outside. Nora greeted her warmly and it turned out she was used to serving tired and hungry ambulance staff. There were free mugs of tea, a steaming Cornish brew with sugar, served with even more brownies, which Naomi insisted were medicinal. Rose perked up and forgot the throbbing in her hand.

They then headed off to Men-an-Tol and the Merry Maidens, and with a bit of encouragement, Oriel soon got into her stride with the stories associated with the sites. She said nothing more about Rose's medical situation, although Rose was convinced she was like a coiled spring, dying to ask more.

It was early evening when Naomi dropped her off at the flat. As she waved off Oriel and Naomi from the window, Rose saw Finn was tying up his boat at Curlew Studio in the light glinting on the water. She was glad she didn't have binoculars or she'd have been tempted to reach for them.

You might pass them in the street, or be in the same pub as them, and never even know . . .

Oriel's words came back to her, along with a painful dose of conscience.

She'd been forced — or rather, decided — to be economical with the truth as far as knowing who the donor was.

She wanted to tell the brothers, but she didn't want them to find out elsewhere. It had to be in her control, on her terms when the time was right.

22

Rose arrived at Morvah Marine for her sailing lesson, expecting to find Joey waiting at the pontoon next to *Spindrift* as arranged. It was a breezy but clear evening, showing off the estuary at its most beautiful, with the light mellowing. Rose thought Falford looked as if it had been gilded by a supernatural hand.

To her surprise, when she arrived, there was no sign of him. No sign of life at all on *Spindrift* so she checked her phone for messages. He'd be there soon . . . but after almost half an hour, he still hadn't turned up and Rose was beginning to wonder what might have delayed him. She ought to call him just to make sure they were still going out. But before she'd had a chance to, Finn walked down the jetty towards her.

'Hi,' he said, a little hesitantly. 'Are you OK?'

'Yes. Fine. I was kind of expecting Joey to be here. He's taking me out for a sail.'

'Tonight?' Finn asked, and Rose was surprised Joey hadn't told him.

'Yes, we arranged to meet here but he's a bit late. You don't know why, by any chance?'

'No . . .'

'No problem. We can do it another time.' Her phone pinged. 'Oh, this is probably him.'

Rose opened the message. 'Oh . . . no it's Maddie. Friend of mine. Nothing urgent.'

Finn's lips compressed. 'He must have a good reason not to be here.'

190

'I'm slightly worried . . .'

'Don't be. I'm sure it's nothing serious.'

'Probably another urgent rescue?' Rose said, half joking.

'Yeah. Maybe . . . I haven't heard that but he could be somewhere with no signal, of course,' Finn said.

'Probably.' Rose kept thinking there was such a thing as a radio and that Joey could have used it to call the boatyard.

'I'm sure we'll find out later. I'd better go home, then. As it's off.' She shoved her phone in her bag, a little annoyed — at herself for agreeing to a trip she didn't really want to go on and for falling for Joey's promises. She'd thought she was different.

She shivered in a sudden breeze. Rolling her eyes to hide her humiliation, she said, 'See you.'

'Rose. Hold on. Now you're here, it seems a shame not to make the most of such perfect sailing weather. I was going to take *Siren* out anyway, so do you want to come out with me . . .?' He shifted awkwardly. 'For a sail, I mean. I'd need to pop home for a few things, but it won't take five minutes.'

The offer robbed her of a reply for a second. The chance to see inside Nash's studio was irresistible . . . not to mention the bonus of Finn's company for the evening.

Finn took her hesitation for reluctance. 'I know it won't be the same.'

Rose's phone pinged with a message. 'It's Joey,' she said.

'Oh. There you are then.' Finn smiled. 'Is he on his way?'

She read the message. It didn't take long. 'No. He says he can't make it after all.'

Finn frowned. 'Is he OK?'

'He says so . . . but he can't come and he says he'll explain tomorrow.'

Finn seemed to struggle with a reply but then said, 'I'm sure he has a good reason. Meanwhile, my offer still stands. If you want to.'

Rose looked at the sea glittering in the early evening light and at Finn, looking even more irresistible. 'I do. I'd love to come out on *Siren*.'

He nodded. 'Then, let's waste no more time.''

It took two minutes to drive to the studio. Finn put some food into a bag and then vanished behind a partition that Rose presumed was his bedroom.

She waited in the living space, which was bathed in early evening sunlight, with a glimpse of the estuary sparkling beyond the French doors at the end.

A check of her phone showed no reply to her return message or even an indication that it had been read. She hoped Joey was OK. She felt guilty for going out with Finn, then dismissed her guilt. She'd been stood up, and that was all there was to it so she might as well make the best of the evening.

She didn't want to pry, but she couldn't help taking a look at the pictures on the walls. Were they all by Nash? A few were landscapes, but most were people and one struck her in particular.

It could hardly fail not to.

Rose stood in front of the male nude above the dining table.

Wow. Rose stared at it, reminded of the way she'd been 'admiring' the Morvah brothers. Some would say ogling, or at the very least, objectifying.

'Rose?'

She was startled. 'Oh, sorry, I was miles away.'

192

Finn was carrying the bag, now bulging with food and clothes. He didn't try to hide his smile.

'OK, I was looking at the painting.'

'I've lived with it for a long time so it's just part of the furniture.'

'It's very . . . striking.'

'Some people find it shocking.'

'I find it beautiful, but then, I've seen hundreds of nude males,' Rose said.

This comment was met with a slight raise of the eyebrows and an amused glint.

'What I meant to say was, I've seen hundreds of male nudes in art. Museums and galleries — and buildings — as part of my work.'

'I knew what you meant.'

Rose laughed. 'Phew. Glad we got that straight.'

'That painting is one of Nash's.' Finn gazed up at the painting, and Rose saw a brief flicker of sadness, but his reply was firm enough.

'I'm sorry he died so young.'

'I'm sorry too. I miss him and he was a good friend. He sold me the studio at a much lower price than he could have got. That was the kind of guy he was: generous.' He paused. 'He had a good soul. He deserved a longer and less troubled life, certainly not to die of cancer at forty-four,' Finn said. 'But life isn't fair, is it?'

'No.' Rose thought of her own ride on the roller coaster. Down to the bottom in the long weeks of waiting with failing health. Up to the top with the transplant, down again wondering if it would work and then the slow ascent, ratchet by ratchet . . . Was she at the top again? Would the ride level out? She suppressed a shiver. She hoped so, health wise.

He turned away. 'Have you seen some of his other work? He left me a few of his paintings and the others, as I mentioned, were sold to fund an art scholarship at Penryn University.'

Finn beckoned Rose towards some of the other artwork on the walls. She was still none the wiser who the painting was of, or if it had been intended as a gift for Finn originally, if anyone at all. She didn't know any other men with male nudes on their walls — or any women — come to think of it.

Then again, she didn't know anyone else who lived in an artist's studio. Finn was full of surprises.

'We'd better go. The wind's freshened so we can't be out too long, but it's going to be fun,' he said.

★ ★ ★

Siren was beautiful. She was longer than Joey's boat, and the sail arrangement seemed different to her untrained eye. Finn gave her a hand from the pontoon into the boat, just as Joey had. It was purely practical. Even so, his hand lingered in hers for a moment.

So what? He'd have given anyone new to that boat a hand, male or female, young or old.

It was a beautiful evening, with damselflies buzzing above the water and sun sparkles dazzling her. The sun was bright and still hot against her skin. If anything, it was warmer than the evening she'd sailed back from Kev's Seafood Shack.

Finn came up from below, with a sweater, waterproof jacket and trousers. Rose laughed. 'I hope we're not going to need those.'

'It's cool on the open sea and you'll notice it even more when we're sailing, but you'll know that . . .'

Finn trailed off, and Rose realised he was referring to her earlier trip with Joey. He handed her the navy sweater. 'If I were you, I'd put this on now. It's easier to take off layers if you're too hot than get chilled and add them. You might never warm back up.'

Rose nodded, though she was already a little warm. There were whitecaps out in the estuary though it was like a millpond in the creek. Fluffy clouds billowed on the horizon against a deep blue sky.

He handed her a buoyancy aid. 'Before we go, there's three things we need to worry about at sea . . .'

'Fire, flooding and falling in?'

'Sorry. I forgot you know the drill by now from your lessons.'

'Yes.' She smiled. 'Though I wouldn't really fancy experiencing any of them this evening.'

'Anything can go wrong at sea,' Finn replied, then smiled. 'It's how you react when it does that matters, but I don't expect any drama tonight. It's a great night for a sail.'

With that, he turned on the motor and the engine puttered into life. He jumped onto the pontoon and Rose helped him untie the lines.

She put his sweater on and donned her buoyancy aid. Moments later, they were easing away from the pontoon with Finn at the helm. They motored out of the narrow creek into the estuary, and he put the helm on auto while he hoisted the mainsail. He answered her questions about the boat, explaining it was a Bermuda rigged sloop, which just meant it had a triangular sail.

'We can turn this off now,' he said, cutting the motor.

The boat engine hadn't been loud, but the contrast

hit her just as it had when she'd sailed on *Spindrift*. The wind flapping in the sail, the creak of the mast, the plash of waves against the hull. The wind filled the sail and the boat changed direction so Rose moved across to sit on the other side of the deck, holding on as they cut through the water. Finn was clearly in his element, pointing out boats he liked, telling her about the characters who owned them, sharing stories of races and voyages.

'The wind funnels at the entrance to the bay,' he said, and Rose immediately felt the chill, almost as if Finn had flicked a switch.

She pulled the oilskin jacket over her legs, thankful she'd worn cropped jeans rather than a skirt, and for the loan of Finn's sweater. Soon, they were out in the Falford Bay, with the coastline of the Lizard on their left, heading south.

'Want to take the helm?'

Rose took over, and noticed immediately that out on the open sea the wind and swell was much stronger than on her short sail back from Kev's with Joey. It took a little getting used to. You obviously had a lot more space on the water, but you had to think about turning before you might in a car.

They were talking animatedly about nearby craft, and Rose tried to spot the difference between cutters and sloops and catboats. In the background, the radio chatter increased. Voices spoke in accented English — French, Dutch and others Rose couldn't make out. There was a lot of mention of the weather channel, but Finn didn't seem to be bothered, too intent on talking to Rose who'd asked him more about Nash.

'From what I hear, he was popular in the village,' she said.

'He was a generous man, kind and interesting. I think people felt a bit sorry for him too. He had no family and he'd split up with his partner years before.' Finn looked sad. 'He never really got over Ricardo leaving him. When he sold Curlew Studio to me, some people made assumptions. That's their business. I won't waste my time explaining myself to strangers and bigots.'

There was force in his voice and Rose wondered again about how close Finn and Nash had been.

'Even if you and Nash had been . . . more than friends — it's really none of my business,' Rose said.

Finn looked at her over the wheel and smiled. 'Rose. I'm not gay. If anything, Nash was more of a father figure to me though he'll be shouting at me from somewhere if he can hear me saying that.'

Despite the cold wind that was now buffeting the boat, she felt heat rise to her cheeks. 'I didn't think so. I'm sorry for prying.'

'I'm not offended by you asking.' His tone softened. 'Not at all and I'd rather we got that straight between us. I'm attracted to women.' He paused. 'Certain women.'

The boat tipped alarmingly and Rose stumbled against the wheel. 'Oh!'

Finn dashed to help her up, but she was already upright and in control again, just with a sore elbow where she'd banged her arm on a metal rail.

'Are you OK?' he asked.

'The wind's strong. I'm glad I added the layers.'

'Good. It's a shame the weather's gone downhill a bit.' His brow furrowed, and something — not fear but wariness — flickered in his eyes. 'I'll need to take some of the sails down.'

She tucked the coat tighter over her legs. A few moments later, the radio crackled and Finn turned up the volume. Dark clouds towered on the horizon. They seemed to be heading their way alarmingly fast. She caught enough of the forecast to hear force 7 gusting to 8 and a storm warning. Her stomach knotted and she felt very cold, so she donned the oilskin and fastened it up.

A call came through on the radio. Finn picked up the handset. 'I need to listen to this,' he said. 'I'll leave the automatic helm on to steer a course for now — so you don't have to worry about keeping her straight in this wind.'

While he answered the call, Rose tried to stand up to reach for her mug from the rack by the wheel, staggered and had to grab the rail. The coastline seemed a long way away, and the boat was bucking and rolling in whitecaps. She sat down again, trying to tell herself she felt fine, and she didn't feel sick, but it was too late now she'd focused on the movement of the boat.

She was also concerned about Finn's expression during his radio conversation. There was tension in his jaw.

'That was Mum calling me. I'm afraid we're going to have to cut our trip short. There's a storm heading in our direction and I don't want to run into it.'

★ ★ ★

A few minutes later, Rose could no longer pretend to herself that she didn't feel sick. Nor could she hide it from Finn who'd spotted her ashen face and sudden silence.

'I'm sorry about this. I did check the forecast,

198

obviously, but Mum radioed specifically in case we hadn't heard the emergency channel. This storm has changed course rapidly and it's going to be livelier than we expected.'

'Lively? What do you mean?'

'There's a series of squalls coming in. They're unpredictable at the best of times but they can make life tricky.' He smiled reassuringly. 'Don't worry, we'll be fine. I have a Plan B and a Plan C, but first I have to get the sails down or we won't be able to steer. I should have done it ten minutes ago.'

He pushed buttons on the console behind the wheel. Rose watched with a sinking feeling that didn't help her swishing stomach.

'The auto helm's stopped working. I don't know why but I can't worry about that now. You'll have to take over again.'

'Me? Yes — but . . .' Rose had been happy to be in charge when conditions were reasonable, but she didn't fancy steering now they'd gone so rapidly downhill.

'You'll be fine. Just do what you were doing before. Keep her steady and aim for that coast watch station on the cliffs and this side of that channel mark — the big green buoy. I have to drop the sails *now.*'

Without another word, he left her, and scurried around the decks to lower the sails with an urgency that worried Rose. She was sure he was holding back his own concerns and she didn't have to be a sailor to know that the seas had become much bigger and greyer within the past ten minutes.

The green buoy seemed even closer than before. Joey had said they marked reefs or sandbanks. What if they ran aground?

'Turn her to port!' Finn shouted, pulling down the mainsail.

Waves curled over, crashing back down and the boat lurched. Forcing herself to ignore her churning stomach, Rose focused on turning the boat away from the buoy. Her knuckles were white on the wheel and every second he was gone felt like an age.

Salt spray stung her face and rain drove against her back, driven by the gunmetal clouds marshalling close by. Thank goodness she'd put the oilskins on because there was hail mixed in with the rain. The sea was angry and the summer's evening had turned to an eerie twilight. Not only did she feel sick, she was also wet and cold and she had to admit, though she'd never say it to Finn, she was starting to feel quite scared.

The boat lurched and one of the sails didn't seem to be coming down.

'It's stuck!' Finn shouted. 'The halyard's jammed in the pulley at the top of the mast.'

'What does that mean?'

Finn climbed past her. 'I'll have to go up the mast and free it.'

Rose didn't like the sound of that, but things got even worse.

'I'll have to go up in the harness and cut the halyard.'

'That sounds dangerous.'

'It's not the most fun experience but . . .' He touched her arm briefly. 'I've done it before. I'll be careful and I always have the harness kit prepared just in case. Keep her steady. Just to warn you that the sail will come free and you'll need to help me with it. Stay here behind the wheel until I'm back down.'

Rose gripped the wheel as if her life depended on it and she was beginning to wonder if it actually did as Finn started tying elaborate knots around the mast and clipping them to a harness. All the while, the wind howled and the boat heeled over. She could only imagine what it would be like at the top of the mast, with the height and the rolls of the boat amplified. She almost threw up at the thought, but Finn was already pulling himself up.

Rose tried not to look. But if he fell, she'd be responsible for turning the boat around to try and get back to him. Her heart was in her mouth. The boat lurched and the mast swung from side to side like a pendulum. Now she was frozen with fear.

With a clatter, the sail fell onto the deck, the wind caught it and pulled it over the side and into the water. It was thrashing around, making a terrible racket to rival the wind. The boat was all over the place and Rose's heart pounded harder than it ever had in her life.

What if he fell? If the harness failed and he went into that churning sea — or crashed onto the deck. Her cry of fear was snatched away by the wind and the roar of the ocean.

23

A few seconds later, Finn was back on deck, unclipping himself. Rose heaved a massive sigh of relief but there was a new problem. The sail was flapping wildly in the wind.

Meanwhile, the auto helm flickered into life. 'I think it's working again. It's started steering a course,' she called to Finn as he freed himself from the harness.

'Thank God for that. Help me with this sail.'

Rose left the wheel, staggering on the rolling deck.

'Be careful!' She almost fell on top of him, but he helped her right herself and they managed to get the sail under control.

'It's secure now,' Finn said, looking at Rose. 'We'll be OK.'

Trembling with adrenaline and cold, Rose didn't feel OK. 'I didn't enjoy that.'

'I can't say I did either. No one goes aloft unless they have to but we're fine now.' He squeezed her hand. 'You're freezing.'

'At least I know I'm alive.'

'Sailing has a tendency to do that. Make you feel alive.' His reassuring smile was accompanied by a squeeze of her arm.

It was true. While she had been terrified and was still fearful and seasick, there had been something exhilarating about escaping the worst . . . She was filled with the urge to blurt out that it was the second time she'd had a brush with her mortality, but Finn was on the radio talking to someone about the con-

home in the dark in such rough seas.

'Until the storm has completely passed and the conditions are calmer. It's better that we get a night's rest and set off home in daylight back to Falford.'

'You mean we have to spend the night on the boat!'

'Yes, but Navas is a safe haven. It'll be like a mill-pond in the harbour.' Finn smiled at her over the wheel. 'You can get off for a break if you like and then come back and sleep on board.'

'Isn't there a hotel?' Rose felt stupid for asking, but she dreaded the idea of spending the night in these conditions. Or maybe they could be collected, she thought, but she didn't want to drag anyone out in this weather. It would be quite a long way by road. She didn't want to sound too much like a wimpish townie. First, they also had to make it safely into a harbour.

'No, but I promise you'll be fine once we're out of this swell and into calm waters. We'll be there in around half an hour. It'll go by quickly, I promise. If you feel too sick, please stay inside or go below. There's a bucket in the galley if you need it. And, Rose . . .' He seemed anguished. 'I'm so sorry the evening has ended like this. I hope it doesn't put you off sailing.'

'No,' she said, hiding the fact she'd give quite a lot to be on dry land. Never had she wanted time to fly by so quickly. To her eye, there wasn't an inch of shelter on the black cliffs of the Lizard. Half an hour sounded like a lifetime but eventually, Finn steered the boat closer to the shore.

'There's the entrance to the cove!' he said, pointing to two forbidding rocky headlands. She could see no entrance, or shelter in the black expanse of cliff but a minute later, a gap seemed to open up like magic. A

'Don't tell me you'd never done it before!'

'A couple of times when I've worked on other boats but never on *Siren*.' He grinned. 'You were brilliant, taking the helm in the conditions.'

'All I had to do was avoid running us aground on the rocks.'

'Believe me, that's not as easy as it sounds.'

Rose laughed. 'It wasn't! I had visions of you falling off and me having to call the coastguard.'

'There was no chance of that. Look. I think we should get off the boat for a little break and then go below and get warmed up.'

With her hood up, Rose stepped onto the steps that led up to the quay. 'Wow. My legs are still moving.'

Finn gave her his hand. 'You'll be fine in a few minutes.'

He helped her up to the quay and they walked around the harbour, stopping for shelter from the driving rain in a stone alcove, which must have once been used by fishermen, on just such a night as this. Navas cove was tucked into a small valley with a stream and a rough track leading steeply down to a cobbled slipway. There was no sign of human habitation apart from some ramshackle fishing huts, a rusty winch and a round, whitewashed hut on an outcrop above the harbour.

'What exactly was this place?' She had to raise her voice above the wind.

'Until a hundred years ago, it would have been a busy fishing cove for pilchards and crab. There's a hamlet about half a mile up the valley where the fishermen and their families would have lived but they're holiday cottages now. That round white shelter above the harbour is a huer's hut, from where the

ignore him when she'd been ill.

'Don't worry. I'll be fine on board.' She threw him the kind of smile she reserved for when she had to give her first lecture of the term. Confident, friendly and hiding the fact she was almost as nervous as her students.

'I'll radio the boatyard and let them know we've decided to seek shelter here at Navas.'

Rose wondered what had happened to Joey and what his reaction would be to her being stuck on Siren with Finn.

'Will your mother worry?' she asked.

'She'd have been far more worried if we'd tried to get home. I'll try and find out what exactly happened to Joey.'

'As long as you know he's OK, I'd rather you didn't push it,' Rose said.

Finn nodded, clearly understanding her reluctance to make a fuss. Joey could explain in his own good time.

She went backwards down the ladder into the saloon, followed by Finn. Having spent most of the voyage so far on deck, she hadn't had chance to see much of the interior. The smell was divine: a subtle scent of wood and varnish, nothing overpowering.

'This is beautiful,' she said. It truly was a perfect marriage of art and craftsmanship. An ancient art too, she thought, reminded of Viking ships buried in the mud. She guessed the same principles and skills applied to this boat, almost two thousand years later.

The saloon was next to a small galley and beyond that, a door led to the head and what she presumed was the cabin.

He put the kettle on the gas ring and found two

'It was a blow. We were very close, but Gran just keeled over in her garden among the bulbs. It was very quick, apparently, and it's how she'd have chosen it. No fuss, on a sunny morning.'

'Still, it must be hard for you. Still raw from her loss . . .'

'It is . . . I hadn't really thought about that. I'd say, if anything, it's made me want to look to the future even more than I did. Gran was always urging me to go for it.' A surge of emotion and excitement shot through her, knowing that Finn might be the one who was responsible for making that future possible. She could tell him right now. Ask him if it was him . . . but that would be an incredibly high-risk strategy. It could and probably would end in disaster. She felt they'd grown much closer after their experience. Why ruin it now?

'Grandad Billy thought a cup of tea solved a lot of things,' Finn said. 'I'm not so sure but it won't do you any harm. It was pretty hairy out there for a while. You were brilliant.'

She nodded and he pushed the biscuits towards her and said with mock sternness: 'Eat.'

Trying not to linger on what he was doing to her hormones and soothed by his soft Cornish burr, Rose nibbled at a Hobnob, finished it and then ate another. She found she was starving and when the hot tea was put in front of her in a tin mug, she ate a third. Slowly, her surroundings infused her with a sense of warmth, solidity and safety. Nothing to do with Finn, of course.

'Did you build and fit out the boat on your own?' she asked.

'Yes, with Joey's help.'

210

She ran her fingers along the smooth wood. 'It's beautiful.'

'Thanks.' His eyes filled with pleasure but then he rubbed his hand over his face as if he was embarrassed. 'We did all the woodwork on both our boats, but we had help with some of the painting and a few other jobs. We do get along some of the time . . . We used to get along all of the time.'

He got up, abruptly. 'Do you think you could manage something more substantial?'

'Yes, probably a good idea.' Rose was sure he regretted saying more about his relationship with Joey but didn't push it. 'As long as it's not a ten-course banquet.'

He laughed. 'OK, I'll keep the cordon bleu menu for another day.'

Cans of soup materialised from a locker and soon the tangy aroma of tomato filled the galley. He sliced up part of a sourdough loaf from the bread bin: 'a couple of days old, but ought to be edible toasted.'

'I could eat a horse to be honest.' Rose's mouth watered. An hour ago, she'd been sure she could never go near food again.

'No need for that quite yet. I keep a few supplies for emergencies.'

'Is there anything that smells better than toast?' she said when he plonked a plate of buttered slices in front of her.

'Not much.'

As the wind shrieked above them, they sat in the saloon, eating the steaming soup and bread.

Afterwards, Finn produced a bottle of malt from the locker and poured a dash into their coffees.

'Is this for emergencies too?' Rose asked.

He laughed. 'Call it medicinal. For both of us.'

The whisky was smooth as whisky went, not that Rose was an expert, and it warmed her inside, and relaxed her limbs. Impossible to believe an hour previously, but Rose was enjoying herself. This felt like the adventure she hadn't known she wanted — the kind of thing she'd dreamed of when she'd been lying in a hospital bed, wondering if 'normal' life would ever be hers. Or even a life at all.

'Penny for them?' Finn asked after she'd been quiet for a few moments.

'They're not worth it.' She laughed. 'I was thinking about my friend Maddie and what she'd make of me being here, on a boat that had to run from a storm.'

'I should think she'd wonder what idiot got you into this predicament.'

'God, no. She'd be so envious . . . and besides she's been in some predicaments herself. She's a criminal lawyer and you know what they say, when you sup with the devil, you need a long spoon.'

'I hadn't heard that, but I see what you mean.'

The food settled Rose's stomach and apart from being exhausted, she was none the worse for her ordeal. She'd used muscles she didn't think she had, and the tension had drained her. No matter how well she'd recovered, the past couple of hours on rough seas had taken it out of her. She mustn't let the whisky put her off her guard.

'Are you OK? You look better. I mean, you aren't so pale,' Finn said.

'No, really, I'll be fine. I just need to sleep, I think. Oh . . .' She suddenly remembered she didn't have her antibiotics, but it would be OK to take them the next day.

'Is everything OK?'

'Yes. Fine.'

Finn put the lights on as it was growing dark. The wind was still howling outside and every so often a wave would crash against the wall and the boat seemed to shudder a little.

'It sounds wild out there.'

'This harbour has withstood far worse storms than this and so has *Siren*. We're safe as houses,' he said. 'When you're ready, we'll get some shut-eye.'

When Finn had been swinging from the mast, Rose would have given all her worldly goods to be on dry land but now, she was happy to stay the night on the boat.

Although that did leave the question of the sleeping arrangements.

Reading her mind, Finn got up from the table. 'I'll clear away if you want to use the head before you go to bed. The cabin's through here.' He showed her the way and she joined him in the cosy space. 'It's not the Ritz, but it's comfortable enough.'

The two wooden bunks, a small double and a single, slotted perfectly in the bow of the boat. They both had mattresses on them and were as perfectly built as their maker.

The double already had a sleeping bag on it but Finn moved it across to the single.

'You don't have to move for me. I'll be fine on the single,' Rose said, thinking of that six-foot-four frame crammed into the smaller bunk.

'So will I. You have the double. I'll find another sleeping bag. I keep some spare bedding for emergencies,' he said. Not for 'guests' she noted, but for rare occasions. He obviously didn't share *Siren*

213

with many people . . . unless they shared the double with him, of course.

'I'll be fine,' Rose said again, noting that their heads would be feet away when they were both in bed. Her skin tingled at the thought of how close they would be all night.

From a locker with a brass handle under one of the bunks he pulled out another sleeping bag and pillow.

'I'll go and check everything's secure while you get ready.' He went up on deck to check all was in order while Rose went to the little 'head', which was only a pump action toilet and a minuscule shower. She had no clean clothes or toothbrush, but after a wash, she felt a little less salty. Creaks from above told her that Finn was on deck so she walked out of the shower room in her T-shirt and knickers, carrying the towel he'd found for her. She'd snuggle down in the sleeping bag and try to forget the storm raging outside — and the one within, with Finn's gorgeous self only inches away from her.

She walked straight into the cabin and caught her breath.

He was in the act of pulling his T-shirt over his head.

'I'm sorry. I didn't realise you were there.'

He turned, bare-chested. 'Me neither.'

'I thought you were on deck. I didn't mean to walk in, like this.'

She clutched the towel tighter. It wasn't as if either of them was naked so why did it feel like it? Was it because she couldn't tear her eyes away from his body?

'I'll leave,' she said quickly.

'No, don't! I mean, don't on my account. I'm just about to get into bed.'

She heard his breathing, felt her pulse beating. The

214

urge to touch him was almost overwhelming. She wanted to hold him and run her hands over his torso. It had been years since she'd done that to anyone. The need to touch him was urgent and powerful. She moved a few steps closer.

He didn't say a word. He didn't move away. She reached out her hand and rested her fingers on his stomach. The muscles tensed and tautened. She splayed her fingers around his navel, fascinated by the muscles, the warmth of his skin.

He reached for her and drew her closer. 'Rose,' he said.

She closed her eyes.

It had been years since she'd kissed a man. After so long, why did it have to be this man? This man who she was so powerfully attracted to? This man who she wanted to see naked, to touch every part of, to have deep inside her? Why not someone she didn't really care for or want so much?

She savoured every tiny movement of his mouth on hers, feeling his bare back under her fingers, his own calloused fingers sliding beneath her T-shirt, his hips pressed against hers.

'Rose.' Her name again, but without the warmth. He let go of her waist, shaking his head. 'I shouldn't have done that.'

Still dizzy from the kiss, she didn't quite understand him. 'Why not? It felt good to me.'

'It felt . . . good, but I'm not sure it was the best idea.'

'Not the best idea? I thought . . .' No, she knew. He'd responded, he held her, he leaned in for the kiss, his lips were as eager as hers, his hands exploring her body. What had changed in those precious, heady moments? 'Why wasn't it a good idea?'

'Because of . . .' He floundered, scrabbling for a reason. She knew he was. 'I just don't think the circumstances are right.'

She wanted to sink through the deck. She'd let herself be carried away. Christ, she must look desperate — that's how she'd felt, but she was only desperate to have sex with Finn. Not any man: just him.

'The *circumstances*?' She stepped back, keen to get away from him. 'Don't say anything. Please don't say another word. I'm embarrassed enough as it is.'

'Don't be. It's not — absolutely not that I don't find you attractive. You're gorgeous, but . . .'

Rose tried to smile and make light of it. 'Now, you're making it worse.'

'I mean it. I *really* like you but this won't work. It's late; you've had a hell of a day. We've both come through something intense and we have to be up at dawn — and . . . and . . . it's not the best time. I'm sorry I even got us into this situation. For me or you.'

She still didn't think they were good enough excuses; not for a man who claimed to find her 'very attractive'. She was angry with him and herself. She felt guilty that she'd agreed to come out because Joey had left her in the lurch, but mostly because she couldn't resist the opportunity to spend more time with Finn. Because it was Finn who lit her fire. Joey was merely a friend, but she'd fallen for Finn and acted on her feelings. She couldn't deny that to herself now, and it was excruciating that he obviously didn't feel the same way.

'I'm sorry I had the whisky,' she said tightly.

'It's nothing to do with the whisky. It's me. I should *never* have let this happen.' He sounded desolate. 'You'll realise that in the morning. I'm sorry.

216

Goodnight.'

He walked out of the cabin and closed the door. Where he went, she didn't know, but sometime later, she heard him creep past in the darkness and get into the bunk. She had her back to him, pretending to be asleep but she lay awake, staring at the moonlight that now and then peeped in through the porthole. She heard the waves breaking and, soon, Finn's regular breathing as he dozed off.

She tried not to move. She didn't want him to know she was losing sleep because of him. She wanted to pretend it had never happened but was too angry and hurt.

The kiss, Finn's sudden change of heart and the anguish in his eyes haunted her. She sifted through every moment, every possibility, trying to get to the real reason he'd backed away so sharply. Outside, the roar of the wind and sea grew louder and the boat rocked. The old harbour might protect them from the storm, but nothing could quell the tempest in her mind.

24

'Morning.'

Rose woke to the aroma of coffee and the sound of water slapping against the side of the boat. Finn stood by her bunk with a mug in his hand and morning stubble on his chin. He was fully dressed. She had just enough time to register how much she fancied him before last night's disaster flooded back.

She pushed herself up and rested against the hull, still surprised that she'd slept at all.

He handed her the mug. 'Thanks. Um. How long have you been up?'

'About half an hour.'

She realised that something was very different. Or rather, absent. 'I can't hear the wind or the waves.'

'Storm's passed. It's a fine, calm day. We'll be back at Falford by lunchtime.' He gave a crooked grin. 'I'm afraid it's Hobnobs for breakfast. There's not much else.'

'Anything will do,' she said, desperate to ignore the elephant in the room. What's more, Finn had been wrong. She didn't feel better this morning.

He made himself scarce while she went to the bath-room, washed and put her dirty clothes back on. After a quick breakfast, punctuated by a few comments about the weather, she cleared away the plates and mugs while Finn made ready to depart. The less she saw of him the better, she thought.

As they were about to leave, a local fisherman arrived and had a few words with Finn before they motored out of the cove and home. Rose had been in two minds about whether to let Oriel know she was spending the night on *Siren*, but thought better of it. The shop was shut on Sundays so she could easily get home without Oriel ever finding out she'd been away overnight.

As for anyone else in the village, that was out of her control. Finn said he'd radioed Morvah Marine and told his mother their plans to sit out the storm at Navas. Rose had no idea what had been said in return.

Halfway home she finally had a text from Joey.

**Gutted about last night.
I'll explain when you get back.**

The breeze was brisk but nothing like the previous evening, and she was glad to lose herself in the business of sailing and forget about her 'moment' with Finn.

By the time they entered into the mouth of the Falford estuary, she felt she'd learned a lot more, even if it had been a baptism of fire. It was late morning and the water was busy with all kinds of craft. Tino, the landlord, was serving drinks at the Ferryman when they finally tied up at the Morvah pontoon. Even if he'd taken her home to Curlew Studio, she'd have had to get a lift home and Finn needed to deal with the issue with the auto helm and repair the sail after the storm while they were in the boatyard.

There didn't seem much point worrying about gossip when every man and his dog had seen them arrive.

Which was ironic, given there was nothing to gossip about.

When they'd finished tying up, and they were walking off the pontoon onto the boatyard, Bo spotted them. She had a tray of pastries in her hands, and the aroma of croissants made Rose's stomach rumble. The Hobnobs seemed a very long time ago.

'Oh — hello, you two,' Bo said cheerily. 'Glad you're home safe. Heard you got caught in the storm last night.'

'Yes. We sheltered at Navas.' Finn was carrying a dry bag and a bin liner of rubbish on the pontoon.

'Bet that was an experience,' Bo said, directing her comment to Rose. She laughed, her ponytail swinging.

'You could say that.' Rose scraped up a wry grin. 'We were fine once we made the harbour but let's just say, I certainly wouldn't want to do it again.' She didn't look at Finn.

'It took everyone by surprise. The RNLI were out all night. It caught out Kev's brother. They had engine trouble and were almost blown onto the reef off Cadgwith. The lifeboat had to tow them back to Falmouth.'

'I think I had enough excitement without being rescued by the RNLI. Finn had to go up the mast to unjam the sail.'

Bo let out a whistle. 'Bloody hell, that would scare the crap out of me. Lucky you were with someone who knows what he's doing.' She smirked at Finn. 'Or thinks he does.'

Finn rolled his eyes. 'Thanks for the vote of confidence, Bo.'

She laughed and Rose sensed the empathy between them, as she had with Bo and Joey. She suddenly felt very much the outsider: a real fish out of water.

Bo seemed about to reply when Rose caught a flicker of something — surprise or wariness in her expression. It was followed a moment later by a huff of breath from Finn. A glance behind her showed Dorinda striding down to the jetty, like a galleon in full sail.

'I'll get back to work. I have to take these pastries to the kayak hire centre.' Shooting Rose a sympathetic glance, Bo scurried away to a hut with racks of plastic craft outside.

Rose heard Finn exhale as his mother bore down on them.

'You're back then.' She planted her hands on her hips, squarely blocking their route to the Morvah shed. 'All in one piece, I hope?'

'Good morning to you too, Mother,' Finn said curtly.

Dorinda shifted focus to Rose. 'I thought you were going out with Joey, not Finn?' she said. 'Or was I mistaken?'

'He was otherwise engaged,' Finn said.

'Really? He came back here about nine. I heard him.'

'We're back safe and sound. That's what matters,' Rose said as neutrally as she could.

Dorinda nodded and her expression softened. 'Of course it is and I'm very glad you're all OK.' She turned back to Finn. 'Client's been on the phone. I said you'd call him as soon as you got back.'

'OK, thanks for telling me. I'll be up at the shed shortly and I'll talk to him. *After* I phone the sailmaker about *Siren*, so you've no need to worry yourself any longer, Mum.' He turned to Rose, softening his tone but still to the point. 'I won't keep you from your

221

work either. I'm sorry about the extension to the trip. I hope it hasn't inconvenienced you.'

'Not at all. I can catch up later.'

Dorinda nodded and said, 'See you later.' Rose wondered if she was putting two and two together about Rose having agreed to go sailing with Joey and ending up spending a night aboard with Finn. It did look suspicious, Rose had to admit.

'Mum worries about me — and she'd have been worried about you too — and probably annoyed with Joey,' Finn said once Dorinda had left, seeming to have thought the same as Rose.

'It's OK, mothers do worry — or grandmothers in my case. Actually, Joey's texted me and he's fine. I'm sure I'll find out the answer to the mystery,' she said with a smile. 'Thanks for the sail, and for getting us — me — out of trouble.'

Finn frowned. 'I wish I . . .' His next words fell off a cliff, but he was gazing at Rose with the same longing — the same desire? — that had burned in his eyes when he'd pulled her into his arms last night.

'See you around, Finn.' She picked up her bag.

And yet she would try *not* to. She would henceforth try very hard not to see him, talk to him or even come within fifty feet of him.

25

Rose went home, showered and changed before heading off to the dig. Oriel had texted her to say she was glad Rose was home safely and Rose promised to tell her all about what had happened — some of it — when Oriel came into work on the Monday morning. She was ready to go out when she got a call from Joey to say he was outside the flat. Deciding she'd rather get the conversation over with, she let him in.

He saw her backpack on the table. 'I was just going to work,' she said.

'Is this not a good time?'

'I can spare five minutes.' She smiled but Joey looked anything but comfortable.

'I'm glad I caught you. I wanted to explain about last night. I'm gutted to have let you down, only I had a call from a friend. She needed me and I tried to get away but it was . . . complicated.'

'It's fine. It was only a sail. No big deal,' Rose said, a little taken aback that he seemed so worried.

'Sorry, that sounds feeble.' He pushed his hair back. 'OK. It was Sophie. You met her at the yacht club, remember?'

'I do, actually.' Rose also recalled the heated argument Sophie and Joey had been engaged in one of the first times she'd watched Morvah Marine.

'Sophie and me . . . We used to have a thing. It's been over for a while.'

'OK . . . Look, Joey. You don't have to explain yourself. I'm not annoyed with you.'

'Thanks . . .' He sat down on her sofa with sigh. 'I want to explain because you know sometimes people get the wrong idea about me. That I'm unreliable and . . . let people down but the truth is I couldn't leave Sophie.'

Rose sat down too, realising she was going to have to spare him more time than she'd anticipated. He needed to get whatever it was off his chest. 'Is she all right?' Rose asked.

'She is now, but yesterday evening she called me when I was on my way back from a client's to the boatshed. She sounded desperate and I thought I had plenty of time to see what was the matter and still make it back to take you out. She'd had bad news. Some bloke she'd been seeing . . . before me. They'd been engaged and split up. He had some problems . . . and he wanted to see her, but Sophie didn't want to see him. He'd been threatening to go round.'

'That sounds horrible. Poor Sophie. She must have been so worried.'

'She was, so I went over, intending to leave as soon as I could, but she begged me to stay. Her ex kept calling her.'

Rose wondered why Sophie didn't ask someone else for help, like her family or other friends, but she'd already worked out Sophie might want an excuse to see Joey.

'She didn't want to tell her family. They don't get on,' Joey said, as if he could read her train of thought and needed to explain.

'I see.' Life was complicated; people ended up in difficult situations. Rose knew that as well as anyone, having had to console and counsel students, homesick freshers and young people who'd split with boyfriends and girlfriends. She was sure Joey was genuine and Sophie must have been genuinely terrified.

'I didn't want to explain all of this in a text and I couldn't call you with Sophie there all the time. That's why I kept my message short. Sophie was with me and I didn't want to share it all with a . . . with someone she doesn't know.'

A stranger?

'I understand,' Rose said. 'Don't worry about it. I guessed it was something important.'

'It was.' He looked relieved.

'And how's Sophie now?'

'OK. Her ex's sister turned up at his and calmed him down. She's a counsellor and she's getting him some help. I don't think he'll bother Soph again.'

'That's good.' Rose treated him to a smile. 'Good job she had you to help too.'

'Yes, though I don't want to make a habit of it.' He sounded very relieved that Rose had taken his explanation so well. 'I hope you weren't too disappointed to miss out on our trip, though Finn stepped in, of course.'

'Yes, he did.' Rose tried not to give any clue as to how she felt about her night with Finn. Even the memory of it made her cringe with embarrassment in the cold light of day.

'Rough night though. I heard he had to climb up to free the sail. Lucky he took you to Navas to shelter instead of trying to run for home. He said you were brilliant, taking the helm when the auto packed in.'

'I was lucky and it's a good job Finn knows what he's doing or we might have been in trouble.'

Joey laughed. 'He's a regular knight in shining armour, my brother.'

'He is,' Rose said. 'Although I didn't need a knight. An expert sailor was more than good enough. And I learned a lot. I had to.'

'Of course not. I only mean . . . maybe we can try and go out sailing again sometime?' he offered. 'After the regatta?'

'That sounds great. Actually,' she said. 'My friend Maddie's coming soon. She'd love a sail and it would be fun to go out together. We could ask Oriel and Naomi too and Finn. Make a party of it?'

'A party? Yeah . . . yeah, sure. Let's do that. Sounds like fun.'

Looking a lot happier, Joey left. He had a genuine reason for letting her down, and she would have done the same in his situation. But if she'd learned anything from her adventure, it was that Finn not Joey was the one she'd choose to rely on in a storm.

★ ★ ★

After all the drama, it was a relief to spend the rest of her Sunday working at the site. She stayed until everyone else had left, hoping to exhaust her mind as well as her body. It wasn't difficult after the physical exertion of sailing and the dig, Rose fell asleep in her clothes and woke at seven with aches in places she didn't know she had.

Monday was a clear morning with the promise of a hot day ahead but first she faced a grilling from Oriel when she arrived to open the shop. She decided to get it over with, made them both a coffee and prepared to give Oriel her side of the story, i.e. the true one, rather than what Oriel might have heard on the grapevine.

Focusing on the drama of the storm seemed to

226

satisfy Oriel, who'd already heard from Naomi why Joey had been called to help her cousin, Sophie. Even so, it was a relief when Rose left the shop, feeling she really should concentrate on her primary purpose for being in Falford: her work.

Rose had another meeting at the university a few days later and had been up very early writing a report. With a rumbling stomach and an urgent need for caffeine, she decided to grab some brunch from Bo's before she headed off to King Arthur's Pool. With the sun blazing down, and the sea like glass, it was hard to believe the storm at the weekend had ever happened.

As she approached the café, Bo was fixing posters to the hut, encouraging people to register for the competitions at the Falford Regatta. Rose thought of Joey's joke that she take part in the beginner sailors' race.

The thought made her feel queasy, but she was looking forward to the event itself. Oriel still hadn't revealed any more about her own plans.

'Hiya,' she said, deciding to have something to eat and have a chat with Bo at the same time.

Bo smiled. 'Morning. Can I get you anything?'

'What's the special?'

'Brunch panini with local bacon and eggs,' Bo said.

'Sounds perfect.'

'What do you want to drink?'

'Americano, please.'

'To go?'

'No, I think I'll have a quick bite here before I get to work,' she said, thinking it would be much pleasanter than eating on the go. She could spare fifteen minutes. 'I need the energy for all that digging.'

'I bet. I'll be as fast as I can.' Bo popped a panini in

the toaster, then fired up the espresso machine. 'It's quiet just now but the lunchtime rush will start soon.' She raised her voice over the hiss of the machine. 'I have around fifteen minutes before they start coming out for the sandwiches and hot drinks.' Bo handed over the Americano in a vintage Cornishware mug. 'There you go.' She went back behind the counter and retrieved the panini.

'Thank you. That smells amazing.'

'You're welcome.' A boat motored up to the slipway, and it was clear it had a broken mast.

'Looks bad,' Rose said.

'Kev's brother's boat,' Bo said. 'The one the RNLI had to tow to Falmouth in the storm.'

Rose shuddered, thinking it could have been her and Finn. 'It was scary.'

'Of course. Still, no one better to be caught in a storm with than Finn.'

Rose laughed, wondering if Bo was now angling to find out how she felt about Finn. Rose sipped her coffee before replying.

'Yes, things could have been far worse. Spending the night at Navas was easier than trying to make it back to Falford.'

'Yes.' Bo gave a wry smile. 'Everyone's been caught out by the weather sometime. You can't really call yourself a sailor until you are.'

'No, I suppose not.' Rose paused. 'I do hope the gossip isn't too juicy?' she said lightly. She took a bite of the panini, which was still a little too hot for comfort.

'If it is, no one's shared any of it with me. Most of the people at the yard are only interested in boats and sailing. The rest are fully aware that I'm a friend of the Morvahs so they'd be unlikely to imply anything. And, it's really none of my business,' Bo added, evenly.

'Thanks,' Rose said. 'I wouldn't want to give people the wrong idea. Finn and I are just friends.'

Bo laughed. 'Same here.' She sat down on the other side of the bench. 'Finn's lovely. In fact, he's gorgeous, and we did have a few dates just to make sure we didn't want it to go any further, but it was like going out with my best mate.' She wrinkled her nose. 'You know what it's like with some men? You feel like you ought to fancy the pants off them but there's no connection between what you're seeing and the other stuff?'

'I know exactly what you mean,' Rose said, thinking of Joey. However, she still couldn't imagine not feeling 'the other stuff' for Finn and knew she wasn't being entirely honest with Bo. She and Finn might be friends, but that was mainly because he obviously wanted to keep it that way. 'They're an interesting family,' she said, with a smile, before risking another piece of the hot sandwich.

'You can say that. I know Joey has a reputation for being a bit of a lad but he's OK, really. They're both good guys and they're very close, not that you'd know it. They've been through a lot together.'

Rose abandoned the next bite of panini. 'Oh?'

'With their dad leaving when Joey was just a baby. Finn can hardly remember him. Dorinda and her mum and dad brought them up.'

'Dorinda's definitely an amazing woman.'

'She can come across as a bit scary . . .' Bo smiled. 'But she's had a tough life, running a yard in what's still, mostly, a male-dominated world. She'd die for those boys.'

'You've been friends a long time, then?'

'With Dorinda? She's been a big support since I opened this place and we've become mates. They're my best customers. I wouldn't like them to get hurt.'

For the first time, Rose sensed an edge to Bo's comment. A warning. She must know that Rose had spent time with both Joey and Finn. It must look as if she was playing them off against each other, when really Rose had only wanted to find out who was her donor, while not raising any suspicions about her quest.

Wasn't that equally bad? She was still using and deceiving Finn and Joey.

'They'd jump in the sea to save anyone, friend or stranger. Even an enemy. Not that they have any.'

Rose's pulse quickened. She wanted to ask Bo if she knew anything about the bone marrow donation. Instead she settled for something less obvious. 'I — I can see they're close. They're well liked in the community and they want to help people.'

'They're not saints. Of course not, especially Joey, but he's — had a rough time, with people he cared about.'

Rose was considering whether to ask what Bo meant when she saw a group of people approach and recognised them as workers from the yard. Finn was a little way behind them, talking on his phone. The sight of him made her heart beat a little faster.

Bo got up. 'Oh, it's Finn and some of the Morvah lot come for their brunch butties. I'd better get back to work.'

'Me too,' Rose said, wrapping her sandwich in its foil packet. 'I think I'll let this cool a bit and have it later.'

Bo turned for the kiosk but Finn spotted Rose. He

lifted his hand and Rose briefly waved before hurrying off, with a racing pulse and warmth in her face that had nothing to do with the hot food. If she'd hoped to quell her reaction to him by avoiding him, it hadn't worked. She was in danger of fancying him as much as ever and even more intrigued to know if he was her man.

26

For the rest of the day, Rose tried to concentrate on ancient mysteries rather than modern ones. They found some interesting pottery fragments and with the moors spread at her feet and the sea at a safe distance, she felt calmer.

She got back later in the day, and made a couple of drinks in her own flat before joining Oriel in the shop. 'Hello!' she called, backing through the bead curtain with a mug in each hand. 'I brought coffee . . .'

'Sodding sodding hell!' Oriel ripped up a leaflet and threw the pieces at Rose. The coffee wobbled in her hands. 'Oops! Sorry, I didn't mean to hit you.'

'I'm OK but why are you ripping up the leaflets?'

'Because we're doomed.'

'What?' Rose put the mugs by the till. 'What's Nige done now?'

'It's not Nige. It's Mr Simpson. He tripped over a rock at Frenchman's Creek and hurt himself so he's decided to cancel the latest du Maurier tour.'

'Poor man. Is he OK?' Rose fished a soggy scrap of paper from her mug.

'He's sprained his ankle and cut his face,' Oriel said. 'But he'll be OK.'

'Well, I'm glad he's not badly hurt but can't he get anyone else?'

'Not at short notice, but that's not the worst thing. He says it's a sign he should slow down and retire!'

'Oh no. That is a bummer.'

'I know. Why now — just when I'm getting sorted

out? I know he's pretty ancient. He must be well over sixty.'

Rose stifled a laugh; glad her mother couldn't hear. Rose hadn't even thought of her granny as 'ancient' and she'd been over eighty when she'd passed away. Then again, ancient to Rose meant at least a thousand years old. Her amusement evaporated as she realised the implications for Oriel. It was a setback, but hopefully wouldn't affect the folklore tours that Oriel was going to lead.

'I'm sorry to hear it. How many tour parties was he scheduled to bring to Falford?'

'Two a week and sometimes three in the peak season. They all spend money in here and the gallery and pub. It's bad for the whole community,' Oriel declared. 'But worse for the shop, when we're desperate anyway.'

Rose shared Oriel's disappointment, and scrabbled around for a positive spin. 'Has he actually cancelled the whole of the du Maurier tour schedule?'

'He's cancelled this week's. I don't know about the rest of them. Grr. After he phoned to deliver the bad news, he did send me an email saying he'd tried to get another tour guide to take over. Then just before you arrived, he's messaged me to say the woman who runs the other company is now pregnant with twins and can't take on any more work.'

'Arghh . . . There must be lots of people booked on the tours?'

'Oh yes. Literary types, pensioners, posers, Germans, Americans, du Maurier super-fans.' She bracketed the super-fans with her fingers. 'Some of them even dress up as Mrs Danvers or as pirates . . . but they bring in good money.'

Rose laughed at this. 'Then it's a terrible shame to let them down and waste the revenue.'

'It is, but I don't know what to do. I can't step in to lead the du Maurier tours. I don't know enough about her.' Oriel banged her mug so hard, the coffee slopped out over a pile of leaflets about reiki healing. 'Argh!'

Rose helped her mop up the mess with a tissue, her mind whirling. 'I agree this is a blow but we can't give up just yet. It won't affect your folklore tours, just makes it more important that they go well. Good job we have them up our sleeve!'

'I know but if they don't take off, I'll be really worried. Auntie Lynne even hinted she might sell up when I spoke to her last night if I can't get these extra tours off the ground and revenue coming in. That's Nige's influence.'

'We can't have that.' She had to be positive for Oriel, who was now her friend — and she hated the thought of Nige sneering in the background, rubbing his hands together at the idea of the perfect excuse to close down Cornish Magick. She thought on her feet. 'I know someone who might be able to help. Or at least someone who could.'

'Who?'

'A colleague at Penryn Uni. I'll ask him if he'll make enquiries in the English Lit department. See if any of the students know anything about du Maurier and need a bit of extra cash. Arts students usually do.'

Oriel wrinkled her nose. 'That'd be amazing but . . .' Her face fell. 'I'd have to ask Mr Simpson if it was OK and we'd have to do some kind of deal. This is just what Nige's been waiting for. Another excuse to persuade Auntie Lynne to shut the shop.'

'Would she really do that?'

'She used to say she'd never part with it but now I'm not so sure. It's been in Lynne's family for years. Lynne's mum — my gran — started it in the 1960s in the hippy era. I don't remember her but Lynne says she was ahead of her time. My own mum was never interested in taking it over, which is why Gran left it to Lynne.'

Rose was reminded of her Granny Marge again and how powerful an influence she'd been on Rose herself. 'Then you can't let her sell, if it means that much to the family.'

'Thanks, Rose. Um. I also have another favour to ask.'

Rose braced herself. 'That sounds ominous?'

'Not really. I was going to ask Auntie Lynne to mind the shop while I do my first folklore tour, but I heard her say she has a hospital appointment and I don't want to bother her so would you mind taking over, just for a few hours while I'm out?'

'I'll do my best but . . .' Rose started, alarmed at Oriel's enthusiasm.

'Yes!' Oriel punched the air. 'I feel so much better now. I'll call Mr Simpson now while you get in touch with this student. I won't give in!'

What had she let herself in for? Rose mused as she moved to let herself into the flat. On the other hand, Oriel had given her a great excuse to nudge Prof Ziegler about the progress of their potential new joint project. She might also be able to help some poor Arts student forced to live on Pot Noodle and baked beans. It wasn't all bad.

As Rose reached the beaded curtain, Oriel called to her, 'Oh, I almost forgot.'

'What?'

'I meant to tell you before, but we've decided on our theme for the water pageant at the regatta. We're doing Cornish myths and legends.'

'Oh — sounds great fun.'

'Yes, it'll help promote the shop — and the tours too.' Oriel beamed. 'You gave us the idea, actually, because we were struggling until we went to the dig site.'

'Glad I've been some use.'

'Naomi is King Arthur, I'm the lady of the lake and you're the Mermaid of Zennor.'

Rose let out a squeak of horror. 'Am I going deaf? Because for a moment there, I thought you said I was a mermaid?'

'Yes. It's a fancy-dress pageant. Naomi's done a design and we've started making the costumes. Didn't you realise we'd all be in costume?'

'I'd no idea we'd be taking it all that seriously.'

Oriel stared at her as if she was stark raving mad. 'Everyone in Falford joins in the regatta! It's the biggest day of the year. Evil Nige is turning his dinghy into an aircraft carrier and I'd rather jump off a cliff than let him and his cricket mates win the prize for best boat.'

Rose pictured herself in a shiny tail with glitter . . . 'But a mermaid.'

'You'll look amazing. You've already got the hair.' Oriel grinned. 'All you have to do is sit in the boat and wave at people. Oh, and the committee have put you down for judging the children's sandcastle competition too.'

'Why?'

'They thought you knew about castles. Never

mind, it'll be a laugh and it's a huge honour to be the judge. Every family in Falford enters it. Just don't pick those snotty Patel kids again. Their mum's an architect and she brings proper tools and a blueprint and everything.'

'Right . . .'

The shop bell dinged.

'Oh, must go. It's the Gweek Unicorn Appreciation Society. They're always good customers.'

★　★　★

Hours later, Rose was writing up a report on their latest finds at the stone circles and had accidentally typed 'unicorn shapes' instead of 'uniform shapes' when she decided she needed a break. She took the opportunity to call Professor Ziegler. To her relief, the prof was enthusiastic and said she'd ask around in the English department but was sure at least one student would be delighted to have the extra work. On the downside, the professor couldn't give Rose any update on the progress of the grant application for their joint project. Funds were tight — when were they not? — but she supported the basic premise and hoped the review committee would be sympathetic.

She returned a message from her mother then FaceTimed Maddie, who wasn't working for once. Maddie had had a bath and was sitting on the sofa in a robe with her hair in a towel. She 'casually' mentioned she had some leave she needed to take and that her husband, Geraint, would be working away. Rose took the hint.

'When are you planning on taking this leave?'

'It's flexible but Geraint has to go to Beijing for

work in a couple of weeks' time so I'll be at a loose end and I thought it might be a good time to come and see Falford — and you of course.'

'Of course.' Rose laughed. 'But . . .'

Maddie pounced on her hesitation like a cat. 'Is there a problem with me coming then? If it's awkward or you have plans . . .'

'No. I want to see you. I'd love to. I was going to invite you to the Falford Village Regatta, but that isn't until August and I don't think I can wait that long.'

'A regatta? Oh my God, that sounds delicious. I'm picturing lots of yachtie types braying over their champers on board their gin palaces.'

Rose suspected Maddie probably wasn't far off in her assessment, thinking of the hundreds of craft moored at marinas along the estuary. Finn had said ninety per cent of them never left their berths and some had never even sailed at all from the day they were delivered to their mooring. 'It's all a bit of fun. Oriel reckons it's totally non-serious and was started by the villagers to raise funds for the RNLI. I think it's more like a village fete, only on the water. There are sailing races, swimming and kayak races, a fancy-dress competition and sandcastle building . . .'

'A village fete on the water. I love it! I'll definitely come to that too. Will you be sailing?'

'I'm not joining in the races! I'm not up to that yet. Actually, I've been roped in to judge the sandcastle contest.'

Maddie shrieked in delight. 'Sandcastles? Why you?'

'Apparently as an archaeologist, I was deemed by the committee to know something about castles. Between us, I don't think they knew what to do with me, after Oriel had volunteered me.'

'You judging a sandcastle contest? Oh, I wouldn't miss this for the world.'

'You'll also get to meet Know-it-all Nige.'

'Is this the bullying old fart who makes your land-lady's life a misery?'

'That's Nige, yes.'

'I can't wait.' Maddie rubbed her hands together.

'There's something else too. I'm um — part of the water pageant.'

Maddie clapped her hands together, knocking a paperweight off the desk. 'Oh God, this gets better! What on earth does that mean?'

'Oriel and her partner are expecting me to be on their boat. It's decorated in a Cornish myths and leg-ends theme and I'm playing a mermaid.'

Maddie licked her lips in delight. 'A mermaid? I have to tell Geraint.'

'Calm down, Maddie. I had to say yes because I didn't want to offend Oriel. She's been very kind to me.'

'Yes, but an actual mermaid. Well, you don't need a wig, but you will need a tail. In fact, I'm going to treat you to a tail.'

'Maddie, no . . . we can make the costumes. In fact, I think that's the point.'

'No chance. I'm ordering you the best mermaid outfit ever. I have a client who runs a costume hire business.' Maddie's eyes gleamed wickedly. 'She owes me a favour. No more arguments. Leave it with me. We can talk more when I see you. I can't wait to meet all these quirky characters!'

With a weak smile, Rose closed the chat down. In one way, she couldn't wait for Maddie to square up against Nige and see for herself how gorgeous Falford was. On the other, the Morvahs would be under Maddie's scrutiny and Rose had never been good at fooling her best friend.

27

Finn slid a half a lager over the table to Joey. They were in a far corner of the Ferryman after a meeting to discuss the safety and marshalling arrangements for the regatta, which was just over four weeks away.

Finn had expected to endure some ribbing from the others at the boatyard about being caught out, but no one had said a word about his night with Rose, not even Joey, even though it had been almost a week.

To be fair, Joey had been to Brixham for a few nights to collect a yawl that needed restoring and they hadn't had much time to talk. Joey had put on the usual jokey front during the regatta meeting, but now he sat opposite Finn with a face like a slapped arse.

'What's up?' Finn asked him.

'Nothing's 'up'.'

'You look like the sky fell in.'

Joey laughed. 'Dunno what you're on about, bro.'

'Look. Is this anything to do with Rose? Because if it is, you should know that nothing happened between us.'

Joey laughed again. 'If you say so, though you know, the thing that puzzles me most is how you didn't see the forecast before you set off,' he added with a sly edge that made Finn's hackles rise.

'No one saw that squall coming. If you'd been out there, you'd have done the same as me. I might possibly have run for home if I'd been on my own but not with a novice on board. I wasn't going to put her in danger.'

'I just thought that the great Finn, who knows these waters better than anyone, might have decided to turn around sooner . . . I mean, I know it would have been a tricky judgement call but . . .' He grinned and tipped his glass to his mouth.

Finn was momentarily speechless. 'Are you trying to say I deliberately took her out so that I'd have to shelter up and spend the night with her? You know me better than that.'

'Do I? I thought I did.'

'It won't happen again. The field's clear for you.'

'What?' Joey frowned. 'And Rose has a say in this, does she?'

'Joey, read my lips. Nothing happened.'

'But you wanted it to, didn't you?'

Finn stared into his pint. Rose's body in the dim light of the cabin came back to him. Her soft breathing next to him in the darkness as the storm blew itself out. That kiss — yes, he'd wanted very much for something to happen after that. It had been a long and frustrating night.

'You can't even look at me.' With a smirk, Joey picked up his keys.

'I would never do that; I didn't because . . .' Finn was now almost certain that Joey felt more for Rose than physical attraction, but didn't want to admit he'd fallen for her.

The sailing lessons, as Finn had suspected, were merely an excuse to get closer to her. Joey must care for her or he wouldn't be so angry with Finn at spending the night with her. The problem was that Finn could no longer be sure exactly what his brother felt. They'd grown apart since Lauren had left. Life had seemed simple once; Joey loved Lauren and they would probably get married and have a family...Now, Joey kept his feelings buried so deep, Finn couldn't imagine getting to the core of them.

'Because of what?' Joey said.

'Nothing. Forget it. Believe me if you want or don't.' He almost said *my conscience is clear*... but the words stuck in his throat. His conscience was clear with Rose, just about, but as for Lauren? He remembered another summer evening, another moment alone with a woman who Joey was close to. Much closer than Rose.

Finn had played a part in destroying their relationship. However much he'd tried not to shatter it, simply by staying in Falford when he could have left, he'd played his part.

He'd put his work, his own passion for the yard, the life he had and even the boat before Joey.

Joey downed the rest of his pint. 'I'm going to bed. Busy day tomorrow,' he said, then moments later he ducked under the door lintel and into the night.

Not wanting to draw attention to their row, Finn stayed in his seat, sipping his pint and pretending to look at his phone.

★ ★ ★

Finn didn't need to wait long to test his reaction to seeing Rose again. She was in the general stores the following morning, queueing up at the post office counter. He'd gone in to get fresh supplies of coffee and chocolate to keep spirits up at the yard. With the arrival of the yawl, everyone was going to have to put in overtime. He tried to wait patiently in line, joining

243

in the banter about the regatta, and who might win various competitions.

Rose was served before him and left the shop with a brief 'hi', but when he walked out, she was still outside.

'Hello,' he said, surprised.

'Hi. Stocking up on supplies?' She nodded at the bag in his arms.

'Yeah. We've a new restoration project come in. I need to keep morale up.'

'Those will help . . . I've just posted a birthday card to Maddie. She's coming to stay with me this weekend for a belated celebration.'

'Sounds good. What will she make of Falford?' He didn't know why he'd asked it, but he had a compulsion to make the conversation last. Despite his determination not to cross the line with her again, he was more attracted to her than ever. She was a magnet, drawing him in the moment he was close.

'I don't know,' she started, but Kev approached them as he left the store before she could finish.

'Hi, Rose. Hello, mate,' he said to Finn before focusing on Rose, and who wouldn't? 'I hear you're judging the sandcastle contest?'

'Afraid so. Oriel told the committee I'd do it.'

Kev gave a sharp intake of breath. 'They probably wanted a neutral. Hope you've got a thick skin. That contest ended in fisticuffs a few years back. The Patels, McKinnons and Bannons all thought their creation was best. Bannon Senior swiped at McKinnon with a plastic spade and the Patels threatened to sue. The RNLI crew had to separate them.'

'Oh my God. Not really?'

Kev grinned. 'Don't worry. I think drink had been

consumed. They've moved the contest back to the morning now before anyone can get lairy. I'm sure you'll be fine. See ya,' he said, then walked off, humming.

'I think I might have bitten off more than I can chew.' Rose had gone pale.

'Ignore Kev. He's prone to exaggerate.' Finn smiled at her. 'Pick the one you like and leave. After all, you won't have to be here forever.'

She met his eye and he almost — almost — added: '*I wish you'd stay longer.*' 'No. Of course not . . . but I am here until September and I'd rather not cause a diplomatic incident.'

'You won't. The regatta's only a bit of fun,' he said. 'Apart from the sandcastle contest of course, which is deadly serious.'

'Oh, stop making it worse!' Rose dissolved into giggles.

What a joy to make her laugh again . . . Finn fought the urge to sweep her into his arms and kiss her outside the post office, but contented himself with a grin. 'Are you doing anything else at the regatta besides judging the sandcastles?'

Colour rose in her cheeks. 'I'm afraid Oriel's asked me to be part of the water pageant.'

'Really? That'll be a laugh. What's the theme of your boat?'

'I could tell you but then I'd have to kill you.' She pushed a strand of her hair off her face. 'I'm sworn to secrecy by Oriel and Naomi, but I wouldn't get too excited, if I were you.'

It was way too late for that, thought Finn, fighting the impulse to tell her that he wished he hadn't backed away from her and that he wished he'd taken

245

that kiss much further and let her know exactly how he felt.

Then he remembered Joey's angry words in the pub. It looked to him as if Joey felt more for Rose than perhaps she did for him. Otherwise why would Joey be so touchy? And why would Rose have made a move on *him?*

'Better go,' he said.

'Oh. Yes. Me too.'

Finn watched her make her way down the cobbled lane, her dress blowing in the breeze off the estuary. Why did he have to fall for Joey's girl again?

28

On Saturday morning, Maddie swept into the flat on a waft of Chanel-scented air, bearing an 'up-for-it' attitude and several bags. She'd arrived ten minutes before, leaving her car in a reserved space on the village car park. Rose had lugged her suitcase while Maddie carried her overnight bag and a large suit carrier. She could hardly believe Maddie needed so much stuff for a four-day stay.

After dropping the bags on the floor to hug Rose, she waved her hands excitedly.

'I've brought you a present!' She thrust the bag into Rose's hands. 'Hope you like it. I got it from Seasalt during my lunch break. I thought you could keep it here as a treat then take it back when you come home.'

'Oh, this is lovely. Very appropriate,' Rose said, examining the pale blue duvet and pillowcase set, with its discreet pattern of sailing boats. 'Oriel gave me a spare set of hers, but I don't think she'll mind.' Rose smiled, thinking of the duvet cover printed with meerkats. Mind you, she had been looking forward to seeing Maddie's face when she'd made up the sofa bed.

'You're welcome.' Maddie hugged her again. 'Now, let's check out this famous view I've heard so much about.'

Rose let Maddie go to the window, and hung back, awaiting the verdict. Had she exaggerated how wonderful it was? Had her love of Falford been coloured by the people who lived here and the emotions associated with them?

Maddie's silence gave no clue but then she turned around and let out a breath.

'Wow. Just wow. This is . . . truly breathtaking. I can see exactly why you wanted to rent the place.' Maddie turned away from the window, a look of wonder in her eyes. Rose puffed up with happiness. It took a lot to impress her friend who had travelled to many beautiful places in the world.

Maddie breathed in. 'Smell that?' She wrinkled her nose. 'Actually, what is that? There's a bit of a pong.'

Rose laughed. 'It's seaweed and the mudflats. They can niff at low tide.'

'Nowhere is perfect I suppose, but it is a stunning location. No wonder you've fallen in love with Falford.'

'I had to take the flat once I saw the view. Mind you, you haven't seen the bathroom yet.'

'It could have an avocado suite with gold taps and I wouldn't mind, with that view,' Maddie declared. 'Talking of which, I could do with a wee.'

Rose smiled to herself. 'You must be psychic. It's that blue door on the right.'

After Maddie had settled in, Rose made some tea and they both tucked into scones with jam and clotted cream from the Falford Stores. Maddie pulled her legs under her on the sofa and seemed very much at home.

'Well, you haven't exaggerated about how gorgeous Falford is,' she said.

'Do I ever?'

'Not really. This place could be amazing, you know.'

'I've already grown to love it. Even the avocado bathroom suite.'

'Avocado. Hmm, that's an interesting colour. Why

did people think avocado was a great colour for a bathroom? Why not turnip or satsuma?'

After catching up with the gossip, Maddie's latest case and Geraint's job, the conversation turned close to home. Maddie was eager to grill Rose on 'the locals' and to meet them as soon as possible.

'Before we meet anyone, you need to know that I haven't told anyone here about the transplant. Apart from Oriel and her girlfriend Naomi, and they're sworn to secrecy.'

'Is it such a secret?'

'No, it's more that it's so much simpler and it's great to be able to make a fresh start. Everyone at home and work knows how ill I was and they try to be kind, but for a change, I'd really like people's first question not to be: 'Oh, you're still alive, then?''

Maddie laughed. 'Oh, Rose, they don't all do that!'

'Some do — or some version of it like 'How are you?' 'Still doing OK?' 'You look well. I can't believe how lucky you were.'' Rose thought of Oriel, asking if she might have a serial killer's DNA in her. She smiled. At least it was original.

'Asking how someone is, is a perfectly acceptable way to greet them,' Maddie said.

'But not a fun topic of conversation for a whole evening. I don't want to be treated as a freak show. Coming here is a chance to start again. I'm just Rose, the archaeologist. The woman who lives above the pisky shop. Rose, the emmet.'

Maddie screwed up her nose. 'The *what*?'

'Emmet'. It means tourist. It's from the Old English word for ant.'

Maddie laughed. 'I guess I'm an emmet too.'

'Don't forget you're also a criminal lawyer.'

'Oh God. You haven't told them . . .'

Rose laughed at Maddie's horrified expression. 'Why not? They're lovely, honestly, but I can't save you from an interrogation. It'll make a change.'

'Is there anyone interesting down here?'

'Hmm. No one in particular.'

'Now, you hesitated that bit too long. That means there must be. Maybe I'll be lucky enough to meet this 'no one in particular'.'

'Maybe.' Rose hid a smile, not sure whether she wanted her mate to meet the Morvahs or not.

She decided to introduce Maddie to Falford life by taking a stroll past the pub and gallery to the end of the headland where the ferry took passengers across to the other side of the estuary. The tide had come in and on this warm July evening, the water was busy with craft floating, rowing or puttering by.

Maddie was in French indigo jeans, a white jersey T-shirt and Jigsaw pointed loafers, and had draped a tailored blazer around her shoulders. It was her casual look, because she had to wear sombre suits all day in her job. Then again, thought Rose, a defendant might be a bit alarmed to be represented by someone wearing Doc Martens and a maxi dress. She just hoped Maddie had brought a pair of trainers and by the look of her perfectly coiffed bob, a pair of hair straighteners.

For the first time, Rose felt that she looked more at home in Falford than the person next to her. Not that she minded how Maddie was dressed, only that she was here and appeared more than ready to launch into local life. Maddie looked a little tired from her long journey down, but still didn't have a hair out of place.

They might have chosen very different paths in life, but they'd developed a strong bond, made stronger by recent experience. They'd both been to state schools, they'd worked hard and been lucky to have supportive teachers and friends. Maddie's dad was still working as an engineer for a water company and her mum as a speech therapist. They had ordinary backgrounds, but Rose was well aware that she and Maddie were more fortunate than many people.

They stopped by a bench on a favourite viewpoint above the passenger ferry jetty. Raindrops still sparkled on the leaves after an earlier shower, and honeysuckle scent filled the air.

Maddie leaned on the back of the bench and sniffed. 'This is beautiful. The estuary is much bigger than I expected, and so green and wooded. I can well imagine smugglers and pirates hiding here.'

'The whole river is littered with tiny coves and beaches. You can only get into some of them with a kayak or paddleboard.'

Maddie's eyes lit up. 'I have *always* wanted to try paddleboarding. Someone at work invited me to have a trial session on a reservoir but I didn't fancy gliding serenely along to the sound of the M25 rumbling past.'

'I've wanted to try it,' Rose admitted. 'But it would be so much more fun with you. Oh and by the way, I ought to tell you that I've taken up sailing.'

Maddie's gasp of amazement could surely be heard all over Falford. 'You? Sailing?'

Rose grinned. 'Yes, and I know the people at the hire centre so if you want to have a go, let's not wait. Let's go down to the hire centre first thing and book a session.'

251

Rose spent the next twenty minutes talking about her sailing lessons and how she'd gone from nothing to being able to take her small training dinghy up and down the estuary under the supervision of the safety boat. She decided not to mention Joey or Finn or her adventure on board Siren, no matter how tempting. Maddie would most definitely have asked a thousand questions and Rose couldn't face explaining feelings she wasn't sure about herself.

Luckily, there were many other exciting new topics to stick to, with Falford being all new to Maddie.

'I hope you don't mind but I do need to work while you're here and I promised to meet Oriel and Naomi to talk about our plans for the regatta. You can come if you want to — I know they're dying to meet you.'

'I'd love to and at least you don't have to make a costume. I've got it all sorted and I'll bring it when I come back for the regatta. My client says she's pulling out all the stops to get a good one.'

'Oh goodie,' Rose said. 'I can't wait.'

★   ★   ★

The next day, Rose and Maddie presented themselves at the sailing centre where an instructor kitted them out in shortie wetsuits and buoyancy aids and gave them a basic intro to paddleboarding. It was nothing like sailing, that was for sure, and Rose's experience counted for zero.

She fell off once, but the water was only waist deep. Even though it was July, the shock of being dumped suddenly into cold water made her shriek before she dissolved into laughter.

Maddie stayed upright, and quickly got the hang

of it, wanting to paddle off to the far end of the creek that led on to the main inlet. Rose wasn't so sure, having seen for herself how conditions could change very quickly out of the shelter of the creek. She managed to persuade Maddie to confine herself to pootling around in the creek, exploring little beaches and tranquil offshoots where thatched cottages were tucked away.

After an hour of paddling, they decided to return to the centre, having allowed plenty of time. However, Maddie soon realised that the wind and tide weren't helping.

'I'm paddling like mad, but we don't seem to be making much progress!' she complained to Rose.

'The tide's against us, I think. We'll just have to paddle harder.'

'I'm knackered. I'll have arms like Nicola Adams at this rate.'

'You should be so lucky,' Rose called back. Her own arms and shoulders were burning, and they weren't even in sight of the sailing centre yet. 'We've no choice but to carry on.'

'It looks so gentle from land,' Maddie said, sweeping her paddle into the water.

'You wanted to explore the end of the creek.'

'Why didn't you talk me out of it? I wish we'd brought some G&Ts with us.'

Amused, Rose decided to save all her energy for paddling rather than replying.

They soldiered on and were making some progress. The centre came into view, but it looked a long way off, and there were swirls and currents all around, as the tide flowed out and they battled against it.

'Remind. Me. Never. To. Do. This. Again,' Maddie

said between huffs, then: 'Whoa!' She toppled, in almost-comic slow-motion before falling sideways off the board with a splash.

'Maddie!' Rose tried to paddle over, but at the same time that took her back towards the mouth of the estuary. Worse still, Maddie had parted company with the board and was trying to swim after it. However, it was floating slowly but very surely towards the mouth of the creek.

'Oh bugger,' she said and swam towards Rose. She trod water. 'I think you'd better give me a tow to the shore. I hope the hire centre won't be too angry at me for losing their board.'

Thanks to her regular visits to the local lido, Maddie was a decent swimmer, yet Rose was glad when she reached the board. Even though she was soaked, she giggled. 'This hasn't ended how I expected.'

Rose laughed too but was slightly worried Maddie might try to do a *Titanic* and climb on the board and they'd both end up in the drink.

'I'll be glad to get out of the water,' Maddie said as Rose started to paddle for the bank. 'It's bloody cold in here.'

'Hey there!'

The board wobbled and Rose almost fell off again. She was filled with a mixture of relief and dismay at the sight of Joey motoring towards them in the RIB from his yacht.

Maddie had no such qualms about being rescued. 'Hurrah!' Maddie called from the rear of the board. 'The cavalry are here!'

'Need a hand?' Joey called.

'Um . . .' Rose started.

'Yes, wouldn't mind!' Maddie shouted.

'Hang on,' Joey said.

The RIB was suddenly much closer, much to Rose's alarm. She was worried the wake might capsize her but then it slowed. Joey took Maddie's hand and helped her into the boat.

'Thank you. My board's probably halfway to France by now,' she wailed.

'Don't worry about the board. You're OK, which is all that matters.'

Maddie threw a dazzling smile at Joey. 'Oh, yes, I think I'm going to be fine.'

Rose held on to the RIB, keeping herself alongside it.

Joey smiled. 'You look cold. Do you want a lift to the hire centre?'

'Would you mind?' Maddie said sweetly.

There was no way Rose wanted that kind of humiliation, but she had to admit she didn't relish the prospect of battling the tide now they were cold and tired. 'Maybe to somewhere nearby? Though I'd rather not go back without the board.'

'I can retrieve the board for you, and then meet you at Finn's jetty and you can launch from there? You'll be back at the hire centre as if nothing had happened.'

Maddie snorted. 'Apart from being dripping wet, of course.'

'Oh, they'll expect that,' said Joey with a chuckle.

Rose nodded, but had misgivings about being dropped off under Finn's nose. 'I don't want to put you to any trouble.'

'It isn't. It's much closer to the centre, but they probably won't see us. Then I can go and retrieve the board and bring it to you so you can carry on as if nothing had happened.'

'As long as you don't tell anyone,' Rose said.

'Would I?' Joey feigned innocence while, Rose had to admit, managing to look wickedly sexy.

'That would be absolutely brilliant.' Maddie had turned on the charm to full volume. She was obviously amazed by this handsome local coming to the rescue, even though neither of them really needed it.

'Thanks,' said Rose as they motored back towards Finn's, with her sitting on the board, being towed alongside. She hoped they weren't being watched.

Joey dropped them off and they climbed out, tying the board up temporarily. Rose hoped that Finn was out and luckily there was no sign of him. Joey then zoomed off to get the board. In a couple of minutes, he was back.

'You're a star. Um — we haven't actually been introduced,' Maddie said, shooting a look at Rose.

'This is Joey,' Rose said. 'He and Finn work at the boatbuilders opposite the flat. This is Maddie, my best friend. Sometimes,' Rose said laughing.

'Hiya,' said Joey.

'Pleased to meet you, Joey. This is lovely,' Maddie said, eyeing the white-painted boathouse over the water.

'Yeah,' Joey glanced up at it. 'Finn fell on his feet when he landed this place. There he is now.'

Joey waved but Rose had mixed feelings. Chatting to Finn alone outside the store was one thing but being in his presence under Maddie's — and Joey's — scrutiny was quite another.

She could tell Finn was puzzled to see them. He frowned as he walked towards them. 'Everything OK?' he said, striding onto the wooden jetty.

'Rose and Maddie needed a lift back,' Joey said.

'Luckily I was passing.'

'What happened?'

'I fell off and the board decided it wanted to go to France for the day,' Maddie said, her eyes on stalks at the sight of Finn, coming on top of her first encounter with Joey. 'I hope you don't mind us landing at your — um — property.'

'If I did, it wouldn't stop Joey,' Finn said wryly.

Joey burst out laughing. 'What a warm welcome.'

'Of course I don't mind,' Finn said, raising a smile.

Rose cut in. 'Finn and Joey are brothers, Maddie,' she said, trying to explain the edge to the banter.

'*Brothers*.' Maddie had her smile in place, but her eyes betrayed her assessment of the situation. Had Maddie worked out that the Morvahs were much more than 'no one in particular?' 'Pleased to meet you, Finn.' Maddie held out her wet hand.

Finn took it and smiled. 'Do you need to come inside? Dry off?'

Maddie smiled. 'Well — '

'No!' Rose said. 'Maddie, we *have* to get these boards back to the hire centre.'

'I thought we had ages? Joey said it's only a few minutes back to the centre from here.'

'OK, but we don't have time for afternoon tea,' Rose said sarcastically, eager to be back on their way and sensing tensions between the Morvahs might rise if they stayed any longer though she had no idea why.

'That's OK. Finn's all out of scones but I'm sure he'd be only too eager to ask you inside if he had any . . .' Joey slid a look his brother's way. 'Isn't that right?'

'I haven't made a scone since school, and I do believe they ended up as ballast under the boatyard

257

jetty.' He turned to Rose. 'I do have towels, though.'

'That's only any use if we don't plan on getting wet again.'

'They'll keep you warm if you plan to stay. Hold on.' He nipped onto *Siren*, down the ladder and returning with two towels.

Maddie wrapped hers around her tightly and Rose took one with a thank you. Finn also handed over a bottle of water each.

'Thank you. Much needed,' Maddie said, clearly unable to take her eyes off him. Rose didn't blame her. She'd have a hell of a lot of explaining to do later. Thank goodness she hadn't told her friend about spending the night on board a boat with Finn.

'How's the pageant going?' Finn asked Rose.

'OK. I hadn't realised how seriously people take it. I was up two nights until after midnight making bunting for the boat.'

Joey sucked in a breath. 'Oh, it's deadly serious.'

Maddie made an 'o' with her mouth.

'Mum's joining in with Bo's boat,' he said.

'Yes, I saw her making costumes at the cricket match,' Rose said, still finding it hard to imagine Dorinda in rockabilly gear.

'Then you'll know how keen everyone is to win.'

'Wow,' Maddie said.

'Oriel's desperate to get one over on Nigel and win first prize,' Rose said. 'He and his mates are con-structing a battleship, apparently. We can't compete with that.'

Joey rolled his eyes. 'That sounds like Nige. Always has to go ten better than anyone else. He won last year with a *Titanic* theme. It even had an iceberg. He's a complete tool to be honest. Even Finn will agree with me on that.'

Maddie laughed but Finn stayed silent. Rose could feel the undercurrent of tension between the brothers.

'Look, if you and Oriel need a hand with your boat, then you only have to ask,' Joey said. 'Can we help?'

'Not unless you can make a life-size model of a mermaid's grotto or Tintagel. Our efforts with corrugated cardboard and poster paint aren't really cutting it and Oriel has big ambitions.'

'A grotto or castle. Hmm. Might be a bit of a stretch in four weeks.' Joey rubbed his chin. 'On the other hand, I'm sure we can help with something: props, a backdrop? You could paint a castle or knock up a grotto. We've plenty of offcuts at the yard and all the equipment. I'm happy to have a look at your design and see if we can come up with anything.'

Rose snorted. ''Design' is pushing it.' She thought of Oriel's sketch in the back of Rose's notebook and Naomi's airy 'don't worry, we'll wing it'.

'I'm sure Finn will lend a hand too, if we ask him nicely.' Joey turned pointedly towards him.

Rose caught Finn's startled expression.

'See, he's really enthusiastic.'

Rose cringed. 'I'm sure you're *both* far too busy with the cutter,' she said firmly.

'Actually, we've been busting a gut to get on with her lately. Finn's had our noses to the grindstone and she's back on schedule so I think we can make time to help our friends. We can all get together after work if you like.'

'Naomi's on late shifts for the next two weeks . . . Are you sure you're not too busy?' She added this to try and get Finn's opinion.

'All work and no play, et cetera,' Joey said. 'We all

need some fun.'

'Yes, absolutely.' Finn suddenly spoke up. 'We're never too busy to help defeat Nige. I haven't forgotten him giving me out for LBW when I'd definitely got an edge on that ball.' Finn's eyes had lit up with amusement.

Rose stared at him. Joey seemed momentarily dumbfounded.

'Many hands make light work, Rose,' Maddie said, then squeezed her friend's arm significantly. Rose guessed she was in for the cross-examination of the year as soon as she and Maddie were alone.

'That would be . . . great. I just need to ask Oriel.'

'There you go, then.' Joey sounded delighted. 'Shall we get you on your way back to the hire centre?'

Finn helped Rose and Maddie launch. Maddie made sure she'd secured the leash before wobbling off with Rose in the direction of the hire centre. It took all Maddie's concentration to reach the centre without another soaking, but once she was safely on dry land, the Maddie mask of confidence was back.

'Did you have a good paddle?' the owner asked.

'Lovely, thank you.'

'No problems.'

'Not at all. Piece of cake,' Maddie declared.

Rose almost choked. 'Thanks.'

'You're obviously naturals,' she said but Rose detected more than a hint of irony. 'I've got a great deal on the double sea kayaks this week, if you fancy trying those,' she said. 'Or you could join the coasteering trip tomorrow morning? Lots of fun jumping off rocks, scrambling down cliffs. You'd love it.'

'We'll certainly give it serious consideration,' Maddie muttered, tugging Rose's arm. 'Come on,

Rose. I've a Zoom meeting with the head of chambers.'

They got changed in the hut and walked home in the cool of the early evening. 'Well, that was an adventure!' Maddie declared. 'And my, what an end to it. You never mentioned that those two lived in Falford.'

'Who do you mean?'

'Finn and Joey! You know very well.' Maddie fanned herself. 'I've never warmed up so fast in my life.'

'You are married, Maddie. Have you forgotten?'

'No, and I love Geraint to bits but he's not here and I can still look, can't I? They don't inject you with an immunity-to-fancying-other-people serum when you sign the register, you know.'

'Finn's a *friend*. He works at the yard. It's run by him and his mother. Joey too.'

Maddie peered over her sunglasses. 'They seemed very keen to help you out with this boat.'

'Everyone helps each other in Falford. There's a lot of community spirit and Finn and Joey aren't Nige's biggest fans either.'

'Nothing to do with them being fans of you, of course?'

'They know Oriel and Naomi. It isn't only me they want to help.'

Maddie raised an eyebrow. 'I take it both of these Morgans will be at the regatta?'

'Everyone will be there. And it's Mor-vah, not Morgan.'

'Morvah. How exotic.'

'Not really. It's a hamlet in West Cornwall. I expect their ancestors came from there. There's a pierced stone nearby called Men-an-Tol, which—'

'Fascinating . . .' Maddie was already staring off

261

into the distance.

'No need for sarcasm,' Rose muttered, wondering if she should have been quite so enthusiastic about Joey and Finn's offer of help with the boat design. It might mean them spending far too much time together. However, by the time she'd returned to the flat, she'd convinced herself that she'd have to deal with it for the sake of Team Oriel.

Finn, on the other hand, hadn't seemed too keen at first, until he'd suddenly changed tack, taking Rose by surprise.

A not *totally* unpleasant surprise . . . though how they'd all get on working side by side for the next few weeks, she had no idea.

29

Maddie went home on the Tuesday, with a promise to return for the regatta weekend in August. Although still a few weeks away, the bunting was already going up all over Falford. The yacht club, pub terraces, gallery and sailing centre were festooned in jaunty-coloured pennants and there was a buzz around the post office and village store.

Finn, Joey and Oriel hadn't exaggerated when they'd said that the competitions were taken seriously. The waters of the estuary were already markedly busier with yachts and a fresh influx of summer visitors hiring or taking out their own craft.

'I'm so glad I learned to drive your boat while it was quiet,' Rose said to Oriel one evening at the Ferryman. It was only her quick thinking that had avoided a collision with a hired speedboat on her way back from a lesson at the sailing centre that afternoon. 'Some of the people on the water think they're Lewis Hamilton! Did you hear about that guy in the Fairline who ran into the cardinal buoy by Falstaff Creek? Ripped a hole in the hull and when the RNLI arrived, he told them to do one! And some woman in a speedboat almost mowed us down during our lesson earlier.'

Oriel sighed and nodded sagely. 'Half those big gin palaces never leave the moorings and when they do, the skippers haven't got a clue or are half cut. They should be forced to pass their RYA before they can set sail. Fuckwits, the lot of 'em!'

Rose and Oriel indulged in half an hour of juicy

gossip about useless emmets and the latest regatta rumours before motoring across to the boatyard, where they showed their 'design' to Joey and discussed what he thought could be achieved in the limited time they had.

Wood, tools and skills would be no problem and there was no shortage of enthusiasm on any side. Finn wasn't at the first session, but he was there the next evening, working on the cutter. Naomi had also promised to drop by as and when she could.

Joey offered to help Oriel create an Excalibur sword and provide the basis for a wooden 'castle' backdrop. Rose wondered how much 'modification' the little motor launch could take but Joey seemed confident that the lightweight 'props and scenery' wouldn't make it unsafe.

'Finn and I are on marshalling duty anyway, so we can always fish you out if it goes wrong.' His eyes twinkled and Rose had to laugh at Oriel's disgusted face.

'I can handle my own boat!' she declared.

Joey mimed reeling in a fishing line.

'Ha-ha. Very funny. Not.' Oriel rolled her eyes. 'Now, what about Rose's grotto?'

Now that was a phrase Rose never thought she'd hear. Hiding a sigh, she reminded herself once again that she was doing this for Oriel and Naomi's sake.

'I've no problem with the Lady of the Lake costume. I was thinking a Goth look would do. Black and purple medieval dress, green wig, covered in slime. Auntie Lynne has offered to help with the dress as long as I don't tell Nigel.'

Rose again wondered what kind of hold Nigel had over Auntie Lynne or if she even realised what a bully he was.

'Don't you think that the Mermaid of Zennor is a bit . . . random?' Rose said. 'It doesn't really fit in with the King Arthur narrative.'

'Oh, no one will care,' Oriel declared. 'It's all about creating an impact and you'll look amazing as the mermaid. Everyone will know what you are and we *are* meant to be about Cornish myths and legends. It'll be brilliant publicity for Cornish Magick and even Auntie Lynne agrees with *that*. Especially if we win!'

Over the next week, Rose, Oriel and Naomi spent all their spare time at Morvah Marine after work, hammering, sawing and painting until dark. It was a welcome distraction to all of them, especially as Oriel was nervous about her first tour, which was coming up in just a week's time. Along with the dig and her research, plus the boat construction, Rose was steeling herself to 'mind the shop' for a morning while Oriel did her stuff.

The phrase 'bitten off more than she could chew' rang in her ears every night as she collapsed into bed, not that she lay awake for long.

They worked hard, making the battlements for their 'Tintagel' castle with Joey's help. Having done A-level art, Naomi was going to paint them to look like real stone.

Finn was 'knocking up' a grotto for Rose, which consisted of a hardboard frame with a net over it, which would be decorated with shells and dried seaweed. Oriel wanted it to be littered with plastic bags and old flips-flops to show the pollution of the seas, but it was decided after a long and heated argument that although that was accurate for the twenty-first century, it probably wasn't such an issue in medieval Cornwall.

'Not that mermaids were an issue ever . . .' Rose said one evening.

'Don't spoil things,' Joey said, giving her one of his twinkly-eyed looks, making Rose laugh. Rose wondered why it didn't have the effect on her that it was meant to. It certainly seemed to affect Finn, however. He went even quieter than before although his hammering definitely grew louder.

After initially offering to make the mermaid's chair, Finn had said nothing since and Rose didn't want to push it. However, with the pageant only a few weeks away, and Oriel asking about it, Rose felt she could no longer put off the question.

Taking her cue, she followed him outside into the evening sun and found him at the woodpile, moving planks and offcuts.

'Finn. I know you've already done loads for us and you're absolutely rushed off your feet with the business . . . and I really don't expect you to spend all your time making scenery for our amusement.'

'It's not a waste of time. In fact, I came out here to find a piece of oak. I know it's here somewhere.'

'Oak? Real oak?'

'Yes. No point making it of hardboard.'

'You don't think we're going to sink under the weight of all this?'

He laughed. 'No. I was going to carve the end piece and fix that behind you, not a whole chair.'

'OK. I'm glad to hear it. Actually, I was planning to call in at Zennor church next week on my way back from visiting an Iron Age village with a colleague. Thought I'd take some photos of the pew and measure

266

it. I know you have photos from the Internet but if it's any help . . . plus I wanted to see it myself and I'll be in the vicinity.'

'That sounds like a great idea,' Finn said.

'I'm sure you're too busy to come with me . . .' She laughed. 'Of course you are but I thought I'd mention it in case there was anything you particularly wanted me to get photos of or check out. Not that I'm expecting a replica of the actual mermaid! I didn't mean anything like that.'

'Anything you can get would be a help,' he said, clearly trying to inject some pleasure into his voice. 'Measurements and photos are perfect.'

'OK.' Rose gave herself a reality check. He was actually working. It was ridiculous to expect him to bunk off on a jolly and anyway she had a meeting first herself.

They finally stopped work at half past ten. Oriel picked up her car and drove home to her flat while Rose lingered a while, watching the lights shimmering in the water. The evening was still and warm and water lapped gently on the sides of the boats. The boatyard was dark but the lamps were lit in Curlew Studio and birds called in the dusk. She thought back to her conversation with Oriel about tourists . . . She was no longer considered an emmet; she'd slowly but surely become part of the community.

It would be so easy to be lulled into staying.

30

The upcoming visit to Zennor church wasn't the only significant event on Rose's mind a few days later as she stood behind the counter, trying to get to grips with a cash register that wouldn't look out of place in the university archaeology museum.

Oriel was in the loo — again before her first Myths and Legends Tour. Rose had been trying to calm her down for the past hour.

A flush was followed by a spurt of water and Oriel emerged with a pale face.

'I can't do this! I'm so nervous, I keep needing a wee.'

Rose sympathised, having been there herself, but firmness was required. 'Don't worry, they'll love you! You're a real Cornish expert. They'll lap it up.'

'I wish you'd come with me.'

'I'm minding the shop, remember? Hopefully when the tour party arrives, they'll buy loads of stuff.'

'Nige says it won't work. He thinks it's a 'barmy' idea.'

'Nige thinks the Pyramids were built by aliens. I wouldn't trust his judgement.'

'Naomi says I can do it.' Her phone went off. 'Oh shit. That's Mr Simpson. The tour party bus is in the car park. I have to go.'

'Don't forget your notes! You don't need them though.'

Oriel snatched up her bag with a clipboard and various props that, conveniently, you could buy from

Cornish Magick.

Mr Simpson and his daughter had agreed to manage the admin and bookings while Oriel did the Myths and Legends Tours. Professor Ziegler had called a colleague in the English Literature department and had no trouble finding a PhD student to take on the du Maurier stuff. The student was writing her thesis on *Rebecca* so was delighted to talk about her subject — and be paid for it.

Rose didn't dare confess to Oriel that she was almost as nervous about serving in the shop on her own. It would take all her powers of tact and diplomacy to pretend she thought the crystals and other 'healing' bits and bobs had any benefit as she didn't want to upset anyone — or lose any sales. She wasn't expecting a rush, but it was peak season and she wondered if she'd get any chance to get any work done on her paper while waiting for the bell to ding.

Less than two minutes later she had her first customer. One who made her pulse beat that little bit faster.

'Hello, sir. Can I interest you in a geode?' she said, thrusting a rather lovely amethyst-coloured crystal in front of Finn's nose.

'Will it make sure this cutter gets finished?'

'They're meant to bring calm to your home so . . . it can't do any harm.'

'Actually, we're getting on really well with it at the moment.'

'Good job because we've created extra work for you!'

'Ah, but I count the pageant as pleasure, not work.' He took the geode. 'This is actually very pretty. I'll buy it for my place, for Oriel's sake.'

'You don't have to.'

'I don't have to do a lot of things but if it helps . . . I thought I might find you here after Oriel told me about the tour today. How's it going?'

Rose found some bubble wrap while chatting to him. 'She was very nervous but I'm sure she'll be fine once she gets this first one over with. I'm not sure if it will be enough to prevent her auntie from selling this place, but it's a start.'

'Anything you can do to stop Nige is a community service in my opinion.'

'I agree, but I think Oriel's set a lot of hope on beating him in the pageant, and even winning the whole thing. There are some great boats entering as well as Nigel's.'

'We can only do our best.'

Was that why he'd come into the shop? To see how Oriel's tour was going and talk about the pageant? Rose was puzzled, but she took his money, finally getting to grips with the till.

She handed over the geode in a paper bag. 'There you are. All your troubles are over now.'

A flicker of amusement crossed his face. 'In my dreams . . . Actually, I came over to see if you were still planning on going to Zennor later this week to look at the mermaid?'

'Yes. I've arranged to meet a colleague at the Iron Age site near Penzance on Thursday and I thought I'd drive over the moor to the village from there.'

'Good. Good . . . I've got to go to St Ives too . . . There's a rowing club needs a new pilot gig . . . and I could arrange so that we could meet up later in the afternoon and take a look at it. If it's convenient.'

'That would be good. My meeting's after lunch so I'd have time to get to Zennor afterwards. That was my plan.' Secretly, Rose heartily wished she could skip the meeting altogether and spend all afternoon with Finn at Zennor.

The bell dinged and a middle-aged couple came in, wearing matching kaftans and sandals.

'I'll leave you to it,' Finn said, with an amused glint in his eye.

Rose served the couple who were actually very sweet and bought some joss sticks and a large rose-coloured crystal. She handed them a leaflet about the new folk-lore tour schedule and they promised to check out the website. She didn't get much work done in between helping customers and was starting to grow anxious for Oriel when the door was flung open so hard, the bell almost rang off its mounting.

'Rose!' Oriel flew to Rose and hugged her. 'Thank you!'

'It went well, then?' Rose said, while Oriel regained her breath.

'Yes. Oh, I almost wet myself I was so terrified to start with. I wanted to be sick when I saw all those faces staring at me, waiting for me to entertain them.' She closed her eyes then burst out, 'But once I got going, it was OK. I forgot some of the stuff we rehearsed, but I kept thinking: they don't know what I've left out. They can't read my mind. Naomi also told me to imagine them naked but I don't think that was a good idea.' She shuddered and Rose laughed.

'You are a superstar. It takes a lot of guts to face your first audience, but I knew you'd be wonderful.'

'I wasn't wonderful. I did um and ah a bit and one woman — she said she was a history teacher —

271

did say I'd got my Arthurian history wrong.' Oriel smirked. 'But I said that as he was a mythical figure and there's no real evidence for his existence, dates were academic anyway.'

Rose smiled at Oriel's cheek.

'I remembered the stuff about the phallic stone and I told them all about your dig. They seemed well impressed that I had an actual expert working in the shop. I think it added to my credibility.'

She beamed. Rose squashed down any mixed feelings about endorsing a 'pisky shop'. She was only delighted that Oriel had smashed it.

'I knew you'd be brilliant.'

'I have to go! They're all using the public loos, but I said I'd be back to escort them to the shop.'

Oriel flew out of the door, leaving Rose almost as excited as she was. She was so proud of her friend. Yet, happy as she was for Oriel, all she could think about was Finn and his invitation to see the mermaid together. As an archaeologist, Rose had received countless requests to look at unusual objects but she had to admit, none had ever been quite as tempting as this one.

31

Finn didn't exactly see the sun come up on his way to the boatyard on the Thursday morning but it was very early. Far too early to get any caffeine from Bo's. There was barely a soul stirring when he unlocked the door and got to work, preparing the oak he'd found for the mermaid's chair.

He'd been at it for a couple of hours when his mother walked down the steps from the office with two mugs of coffee. He hadn't even noticed her come into the shed.

'Still at this regatta stuff?' she asked, seeing Finn pulling offcuts of wood from the 'scrap' pile at the rear of the boatshed.

'We're making some bits and pieces for Oriel's boat at the pageant,' he said, adding, 'Thanks,' as she handed him a mug.

'You'll be telling me you're both joining those girls in fancy dress next.'

'I'll be too busy marshalling,' Finn said. 'As you well know, Mum. And they're women, not girls.'

Dorinda tutted. 'I don't need a lecture on feminism, thanks. Have you forgotten who runs this place?' She spoke more warmly but Finn knew she was joking. 'That's a beautiful piece of oak. Is it for the regatta?'

'Yes. It's going to be a chair.'

'Some chair.' Dorinda ran her hand over the oak which still had bark on it. 'Came from Tregothnan woods, did it?'

'Yes.' Most of the oak they used did. 'How's Bo's

273

boat coming along? Do you need any help with it?'

'No, we're fine. There's not a huge amount of wood-work required, most of it is costumes and decoration and I can't see you running up a net petticoat as well as making a chair.' Dorinda sipped her own coffee. 'Good luck with the meeting this afternoon. It would be good to get the commission for the boat.'

'They seem keen for us to build it, but I'm not counting on it. I'll do my best.'

'I know you will.' She touched his arm. 'Off to work for me.'

Finn returned to preparing the wood, knowing he'd have to stop soon and start on his real work. He had a long day ahead, but he was in a good mood, and knew it had very little to do with the prospect of winning a new commission for the yard.

It was late afternoon when he left St Ives behind on his way west towards Zennor. It wasn't his territory, but he knew most of the lanes that led over the high moors that even in the height of the summer were almost deserted. Anyone waking up and finding them-selves on the lonely moorland might be forgiven for thinking they were in Scotland until they noticed the ruined engine houses standing sentinel on the coast.

He left his pick-up in the village car park and got out, feeling the heat against his skin. There were plenty of other cars there, but not one he recognised. His heart sank. Had Rose changed her mind about meeting him? He locked up but hadn't gone more than a few paces when Rose strolled through a gap in the wall, an ice cream in her hand.

Her face lit up, and made him blossom inside with renewed hope.

'Finn. Hello!' She let out a little 'oh' of shock and

274

Finn saw why. 'Damn.' Ice cream dripped onto her bare legs. They were long and tanned golden by the Cornish sun. Finn's heart lurched. He shouldn't have come but he was so glad he had.

'I was a bit early. How did your meeting in St Ives go?'

Finn had — truthfully — told her he needed to call in to discuss a new project. What he hadn't added was that he'd deliberately pulled the meeting forward by a day so he'd have an excuse to make a detour to Zennor.

'The client wanted to commission us to build a new pilot gig, but while I was there, one of the club officials also asked if we'd be interested in restoring an old herring boat. Obviously, I told him we were.' He smiled. 'The gig's our next job when the cutter's finished and the herring boat will be a fantastic project.'

'Sounds promising and at least it's meant we can see the mermaid together now.'

He smiled. 'Better finish your ice cream first.'

'Oh, yes!' She licked the bottom of the cone. 'I got it from the café. They make them here in the village, which I must admit is an added attraction. I couldn't resist.'

'Don't blame you.'

They walked slowly up past the pub and cottages towards the church to give Rose time to finish her ice cream. Finn thought she looked good enough to eat herself in her T-shirt and cut-offs, a smear of ice cream still on her knee despite her attempts to wipe it off. He decided not to mention it and simply enjoy the sight of her, the afternoon sun shining through her hair.

He was dazzled by her, almost awkward in her

presence though he knew she'd probably be horrified and astonished if he told her. Yet she *had* tried to kiss him after the storm . . . Or had he, without realising it, made the first move? Had he made her feel that he might reciprocate?

They hung around at the bottom of the church steps while Rose crunched the bottom of the cone. 'Have you been here before?' she asked once she'd finished.

'To Zennor, yes. I've been in the pub a few times when I was younger with some of my sailing mates. Not into the church, though. No reason. Me being a heathen.'

She laughed. 'Join the club. I've always wanted to see the mermaid though. I've read so much about it.'

'Me too, and especially now I'm trying to make a chair of my own.'

'I'm not expecting a copy.'

'It'll help if I actually see it.'

'Come on, then,' she said, and they went inside, speaking in hushed tones although they were the only people in the church. It took a few minutes to find the chair. It was one of the treasures of Cornwall, the source of the county's most famous legends yet it was simply standing in the church for everyone to see and admire.

The oak was stained a dark brown, with an almost black patina. What struck Finn most was how simple it was, yet also how beautiful in its simplicity. He knew it was made from old pew ends, quite roughly put together and burnished by thousands of bodies that had sat on it over the five hundred years since it had been made.

Rose knelt down on the tiled floor next to the chair.

276

'Wow. There she is. With her mirror and comb,' she said, pointing to the carving of a mermaid.

Finn looked closer. It seemed an unusual figure to find in a church. The mermaid, with her flowing hair, a looking glass in one hand and a comb in the other. It was even more unusual when you knew the idea behind it: that the mermaid had fallen for a young man from the choir and lured him away to sea.

'It doesn't seem like the kind of image you usually find in a church,' he said.

'No, she's pretty curvaceous, isn't she, and I think she must have been cool though I think she hid her tail under a cloak in the legends.'

Finn laughed. 'It's beautiful. Humble but grand if you know what I mean.'

'I do.'

He crouched down for a better look. He knew he probably shouldn't touch the pew but he was drawn to it. His fingers rested lightly on the smooth oak, and he felt privileged to see it in person and a strange kind of connection to the ancient craftsman who'd carved it. 'I wonder which came first, the story or the pew.'

'From what I can find out, no one really knows. That's part of the appeal of these sites and legends — they're wreathed in mystery. I don't know much about this legend; it's not my field.'

'But what's your instinct about the story behind the chair?'

She laughed out loud, the sound echoing in the church, then reverted to a low voice. 'You must know it.'

'Why?'

'You're Cornish.'

He chuckled. 'I heard it once at school, but I wasn't

277

interested in stories about love and mermaids. I've seen plenty of pictures of the pew though. As a crafts-man, it fascinates me.'

Finn knew he had no chance of replicating the original created by the medieval carver, and obviously could not recreate the patina and age. He found him-self lost in the work, eager to hear the tale.

'I do remember the photos of the carving the teacher showed us. Most of my mates weren't interested but I was, secretly. Must have been around seven or eight but I was spending hours in the workshop at the boat-shed with my grandad Billy by then. He let me help him work on oars and poles and even on wooden row-ing boats. He taught me to sail too, because Mum was too busy keeping a roof over our heads.'

'My grandad sparked my interest in history too,' Rose told him. 'I was only tiny but he loved the ancient world. After he passed away, my grandmother encour-aged me. She read a lot of those Usborne myths and legends stories to me. Apparently I once asked for the same picture book story about Hercules fifteen nights in a row. I've never grown up . . .'

Finn took some photos on his phone. 'How did she get here, then?' he asked.

'The pew?'

'The mermaid.'

'Well, some say . . .' Rose laughed. 'I sound like Oriel but it's true. All stories and legends begin with 'some say' because that's how legends were mostly passed down: orally. Although the first written record was in Victorian times. There are a lot of versions but here's one: There was a handsome young man from this parish called Matty Trewhella, who had the most beautiful tenor voice and sang in the choir here in this very church.'

'Wow. Here in this very church?' Finn pointed to the spot, amused.

'Yes. You can tell I've been practising my tour guide skills.'

He laughed.

Rose sat down in a pew opposite the chair and he joined her. 'Anyway, one day, a beautiful young woman was seen at the rear of the church, and she seemed to be enraptured by his singing. No one knew where she was from, but everyone agreed she was ethereally beautiful. She wore a long cloak and a hood, but Matty could see glimpses of her long red hair. He became transfixed by her too, and she returned again and again to hear him sing. When he tried to find her after the service, she was always nowhere to be seen.'

'So, why isn't she wearing the cloak in the carving?' he asked, as transfixed by Rose as Matty had been by the mermaid.

'Patience, all will be revealed . . .' Rose smiled and walked a little way down the aisle. 'One summer evening, after Evensong according to some stories, the mystery woman vanished as usual but Matty fled after her and was never seen again.' Rose stopped at the back of the church, gazing at the altar.

'Wow.' Finn walked closer to her. 'So erm . . . how did they know he'd gone off with a mermaid?'

'Because many years later a ship's captain dropped anchor and reported seeing a mermaid who popped up and asked him to haul up his anchor because it was blocking the door of her undersea home and she couldn't get inside to her Matty and her children.'

'That sounds completely plausible. I see mermaids all the time when I take *Siren* out.'

279

'There you go, then. One of them might be the Mermaid of Zennor.'

'I must ask the next one I see.' He folded his arms. 'And that is *the* pew where the actual mermaid sat?'

'Of course. Although some say that the legend of the mermaid came long after the chair was carved. The chair inspired the story, not vice versa.'

'Now you've ruined the whole thing for me,' he said, shaking his head solemnly. 'I was hoping it might be one miracle tale that actually had some foundation in it.'

Rose hesitated. 'I'd like to think that too but I'm afraid the idea that someone did the carving then the story was built around it is more likely to be true. You can believe the mermaid and Matty were real, if you like, especially if you're used to seeing mermaids all the time.'

Rose's eyes danced with mischief. He wanted to kiss her — again.

'Maybe I will.'

'And there are real-life miracles, I suppose,' she said. 'If you look hard enough . . .'

There was a whimsical edge to her voice that didn't quite fit with the Rose he'd grown to know.

'I'm not sure I believe in miracles,' he said. 'But I'll need one to make a decent job of this chair in time for the regatta, so perhaps I should.'

'Don't put yourself under pressure. I'm honestly not expecting it. *We're* not expecting it.' She corrected herself quickly, too quickly for Finn's liking. 'Oriel will understand and I'm sure the boat's going to look amazing anyway.'

'I'd still like to try it though. It's a beautiful object and I'm glad I came to see it in the flesh.'

The church clock struck, the chimes echoing loudly.

'Oh, wow. It can't be six already?' She exhaled in surprise. 'I said I'd get back to the boatshed for half past. Oriel and Naomi are coming over. Joey wants us to help put the finishing touches to the battlements. He's missing cricket practice specially to do it.'

'There's no way you can make it to Falford by then; it'll take at least an hour, even if you follow me on the back roads.'

'I'll have to tell Joey I'll be late. I hope he'll forgive me.'

'I'm sure he will,' said Finn, his buoyant mood vanishing in an instant. 'I'd bet my life on it.'

★ ★ ★

Finn set to work that evening. Three weeks to replicate a medieval work of art was pushing it and carving wasn't his speciality but he was determined to give it everything he'd got. He had to make the wooden panel as light as possible because Rose's fears about the weight of the boat had been valid to an extent. He'd already discussed it with Joey and they'd decided to rein in some of their more ambitious plans, while still making the Cornish Magick boat look as exciting and fun as possible.

He'd decided to work on the chair in a corner at the rear of the workshop, claiming he'd be making a lot of dust and noise but really so that he could have a little privacy. Perhaps the others sensed this because they kept their distance over the next week. Finn liked to work on it early, and in the evenings. Rose, Oriel, Naomi and Joey were busy with other parts of the boat, finishing and painting the battlements, modifications to Oriel's boat, their costumes and other decorations.

His visit to St Ives had also been a success, and the rowing club confirmed Morvah Marine had the commission for the new pilot gig, wanting work to start as soon as possible, meaning Finn had to make another visit to discuss timelines and view the older boat to consider the work that might be involved. Added to meetings about the marshalling and safety for the regatta, the days flew by and soon it was regatta week itself.

By the Thursday evening before the regatta, Finn had almost finished the chair, which was just as well with them having to fix everything to the boat the following afternoon ready for Saturday's festivities.

'You're burning the midnight oil.'

Finn started. Joey stood in the doorway. 'Is this the chair? Is it finished?'

'Almost. It'll have to be.'

'Can I take a look?'

'Sure.'

Finn had carved the oak piece, stained and varnished it, and fixed it to a lightweight metal frame, which he'd covered in hardboard stained to look like the real chair. Luckily, its simple design had kept the weight down.

Joey came over and Finn stood back from his creation. 'Don't touch it. It's just had a final coat of varnish.'

Joey let out a whistle. 'It's good. Very good.'

Finn shot him a glance.

'I'm not being sarcastic. It's great. Rose will love it.'

'It's for Oriel and Naomi too.'

'Yeah . . . course it is. Have they seen it yet?'

'Not yet. They'll see it tomorrow when we fix up

Oriel's boat.'

Joey nodded. 'Better get an early night, then. I've a feeling the next two days are going to be long ones.'

After helping Finn cover the rest of the props with a tarpaulin, Joey left him alone in the shed.

Finn watched his brother walk round to the annexe, shoulders hunched and head down. He was definitely subdued. Finn wasn't sure if that had anything to do with Rose — whether Joey was in deeper and wasn't sure how Rose felt. There had certainly been no more mention of further dates or sailing lessons on *Spindrift*.

Of course, Joey might simply be knackered after all the hours they'd both been putting in. He'd enjoyed working on the chair, which had given him a focus and reminded him why he loved working with wood so much. It felt like it had been too long since he'd done something for the pure pleasure of it, rather than being on a work deadline. While the carving could never live up to the original, Finn was anxiously waiting for Rose's reaction.

★ ★ ★

Rose and Oriel turned up as planned at five o'clock the following evening, tying up the boat at the boat-yard pontoon. It was a dry if overcast evening with no rain forecast, which was a huge help. They'd have had to store the boat under Curlew Studio if rain had been on the cards, and it would have put a real damp-ener on the regatta.

The chair was now dry and waiting with the other creations in the boatshed. Finn felt a rush of excitement and trepidation as he and Joey uncovered everything. In contrast to his mood of the previous evening, Joey seemed buoyant again.

'On my God, that looks amazing,' Oriel said. 'I can't believe we made all that. The castle, the grotto and the mermaid's chair.'

'It was a joint effort,' he said. 'Naomi's artwork made all the difference.'

'That chair is incredible,' Oriel said. 'Rose, you'll look amazing in that with your costume. You should see it. Rose's friend Maddie brought it this afternoon. It's a professional film costume!'

'I can't wait,' Joey said.

Finn saw Rose's cheeks colour. 'I wouldn't get too excited,' she murmured, looking at the chair. She still hadn't said anything.

'What do you think, Rose?' Oriel said. 'Isn't it fantastic?'

Either she was speechless or disappointed or . . .

'I don't know what to say. It's beautiful. A work of art. I didn't think it was possible,' she said eventually.

It was a good job she couldn't hear his inward sigh of relief. 'You wanted a miracle.'

She laughed. He'd no idea how much her approval meant to him. Over a piece of wood. What was he like?

He laughed at himself, and with the sheer pleasure of seeing Rose happy.

Oriel and Joey were moving the grotto and battlements.

'Thank you . . .' Rose hugged Joey but she kept back from Finn, as if she was wary of him. It was just as well. If she touched him, he couldn't bear it. Everyone would know how he felt. Couldn't they see it now?

284

'You're welcome,' Joey said.

'No need to thank me. I enjoyed the chance to make something different,' Finn said.

'I can't wait to see Nige's face,' Oriel chirped.

'Nor me. Come on,' Finn said briskly, getting a grip of himself. 'Let's get everything onto the boat and covered up before it goes dark. We've got a big day tomorrow.'

32

The creature that stared back at Rose from the bedroom mirror was not one that she recognised. It was wearing a silver bra top, and its hair was decorated with dried seaweed and shells.

'I can't go out like this.' She swung round, and almost tripped over her tail. 'I look ridiculous!'

Maddie took her shoulders. 'Rose Vernon. You look beautiful and also remember, you're doing this for Oriel, and for the community. Now, take that tail off for the time being and let's get going. I've already had a text from Oriel to say they're waiting for you at the jetty. Here's your robe.' Maddie held out a large fluffy dressing gown.

'Why did I ever agree to letting you find a costume? Where did you say your client got it from?'

'Liquidation sale at a theatrical costumier. She bought a job lot.'

'What film was this for? I bet it wasn't *Pirates of the Caribbean*!'

'I'm not sure. Some low-budget thing. Probably went straight onto rental.'

'It had better not have been anything dodgy,' Rose cried in dismay.

'Like what? *Red Hot Mermaids*? I'm not sure they bother with costumes for that kind of film. Now come on, and be careful of that net. We don't want you snagging on the furniture.'

Rose took off the tail and wrapped the 'net' attached to her top around her. The costume was in two parts.

Her 'top' was no more than a bra made of netting and silver scallops and the tail was an elaborate padded affair shimmering with silvery blue scales that was virtually impossible to walk in despite the hole at the bottom for her feet.

Maddie helped her into the robe and scooped up a bag and the flat keys. It was ten a.m. and they'd been up at six with Oriel, helping to make sure the boat was finally fixed with its scenery and props. Naomi had been having a lie-in after her late shift but planned to join them at the jetty with Oriel who'd gone home to change. Joey and Finn had had to leave for a briefing with the regatta organisers.

It was time to face the music.

Rose took a final look in the mirror before locking up and following Maddie down the stairs and into the village street. She was dreading being seen, but within half a minute, her fears were calmed somewhat by the sight of the pub landlord walking past in a Long John Silver outfit and the postmistress dressed as a lobster.

'This is delicious!' Maddie said, snapping away with her phone.

'Don't you dare put those on Facebook,' Rose warned.

'Chill out. It won't do your street cred any harm for people to see a new side to you.'

'I've never had any street cred,' Rose said. 'And I don't want this getting round the archaeology department.'

'Why on earth would that happen?' Maddie rolled her eyes. 'Come on, I can see your boat.'

They caught their first glimpse of the little day boat waiting by the pub jetty in all its glory. Rose had a lump in her throat and stopped to look at it.

'What's the matter?' Maddie said.

'Nothing . . . it's beautiful, but I can't help thinking of Gran. She'd have loved all of this.'

'And been amazed to see you dressed as a mer-maid!'

This brought a smile to Rose's face. 'She'd have adored it, to be honest. Make sure you take some photos just for Mum, won't you? She won't be able to believe it either and I can't wait to hear her reaction.'

Maddie took a few there and then and promised to take more when Rose was in her grotto. With that, they hurried towards the jetty. Oriel was already on board, with Naomi, when they arrived.

'Wow! You've knocked it out the park with this,' Maddie said, referring to the boat. 'It's so sweet!'

'It is rather lovely,' Rose said.

Her 'grotto', made of old fishing net fixed to a wooden frame and covered in buoys, seaweed, drift-wood and shells had been fixed where the boat's canvas canopy was normally in place. Oriel sat in the bow while Naomi was standing behind the wheel, brandishing the sword.

A wooden sign, hand-painted by one of the Morvah apprentices, had been fixed over the name.

Cornish Magick
Myths and Legends

She had to admit it looked beautiful and all the hard graft had been worth it. She'd thoroughly enjoyed working on it with her friends, and Joey and Finn.

'Actually, this *is* rather magical,' Maddie said. 'Your throne is especially beautiful. Where was that from?'

'It's a pew, actually, or a copy of the famous one in Zennor church. Finn made it.'

'The dark one made it for you? You kept that quiet.'

Avoiding a reply, Rose waved at the jetty and hurried forward. 'Oh, look. Oriel's seen us. Hello! Hello!'

Oriel's eyes were like saucers the moment she clapped eyes on Rose. 'You look bloody amazing.'

'Just wait until she gets the tail on,' Maddie said proudly.

'Better get in the boat first,' Naomi said, splendid in a Lycra crusader costume and silver helmet.

'So do you.'

While Maddie remained on the jetty, Rose climbed aboard and positioned herself in her 'grotto'. In the confined space it wasn't easy to put the tail on but with Naomi's help, she was finally ready. Her feet poked out of the bottom, concealed by the fin.

'See, I told you you'd be a wonderful mermaid!' Maddie called down to her.

'You do look amazin',' Oriel said in awe.

'Thanks,' Rose, said. 'I feel a bit of an idiot, to be honest but you both look fantastic.'

The green hair and Goth dress really suited Oriel. 'Who did your make-up?' Rose asked her, admiring the eerie watery effect.

'Naomi's friend. He's an orthopaedic surgeon but he likes to relax by glamming up and going to drag clubs. He also helped us alter our costumes.'

'Well, he's done a brilliant job,' Maddie said.

'Have you seen Excalibur?' Oriel asked.

Naomi held out the sword. 'Joey made it out of wood.'

'Naomi painted it, though. It looks like real steel.'

'I can't believe how great it looks. Has anyone seen the other boats yet?'

'I think Nige is launching from the yacht club so he'll be behind us,' Oriel said. 'Bo's Diner looked good from a distance and there's a couple of vessels from the yacht club that were done up as pirate ships. I don't think our little boat can beat any of those, no matter how hard we've worked.'

'It doesn't matter,' Maddie said firmly. 'You've given it your all.'

Rose was amused. Maddie was fond of telling her that only winning counted in her profession.

'*All craft in the water pageant. Fifteen minutes to go. Prepare to join the parade!*' speakers fixed at the pub and yacht club blared out.

'Why am I doing this?' Rose said through gritted teeth.

'To whip Nige's sorry ass?' Maddie crouched down on the jetty next to her. 'It'll be worth it and you are fabulous. Gorgeous. I can well believe you might lure away the young men of the parish.'

'I just want to beat Nige!' Rose declared, horrified at someone overhearing. 'And hope I don't need a wee before the judging.'

'Cross your fins!' Maddie ordered.

Music blared out of the speakers of the Ferryman.

'Ah the whole gamut of seaside-themed pop,' she said as The Beatles 'Octopus's Garden' tinkled out. A few teens nearby exchanged 'WTF' glances. 'Granny Marge loved The Beatles,' she said.

'Hi there!'

Finn and Joey jogged down the jetty towards them. Rose wanted to sink beneath the waves. *Of course* they would see her in her costume. That was the general idea but to be confronted with Finn in particular, while wearing all her finery, made her cringe. What would he think? Why did she care so much what he thought?

Her cheeks glowed as the two Morvahs stood by the boat. All she could do was sit on her chair, trying to look as casual as you can in a giant tail with seaweed dangling from your hair.

'Wow. Just wow.' Joey stood with his hands on his hips. 'It looks brilliant, if I say so myself. What a team effort!'

Oriel and Naomi high-fived him, but Rose stayed where she was.

'It looks great,' Finn said. He exchanged a glance with Rose and she thought he mouthed the words: '*You look beautiful.*' Or was that wishful thinking? She didn't trust her instincts or any reaction where he was concerned. She'd been so wrong on board *Siren* after the storm.

'Time to go!' Naomi ordered, raising her wooden sword.

'We'll untie you,' Joey said and Finn helped him.

'I'm so nervous,' Oriel murmured. 'What if Nige wins?'

'Then it'll be a fix,' Naomi said.

'If Nige wins, I promise I will sue,' Maddie declared.

'On what basis?'

'Gross Arrogance? Offensive Mansplaining? I'll make something up. Now, off you go, me hearties, and knock 'em dead!'

'Good luck and fair winds!' Joey called and Finn stood behind him, waving before turning away.

Naomi steered Cornish Magick away from the jetty.

Maddie was a smiling figure who grew smaller as Cornish Magick Myths and Legends puttered into the estuary to join the pageant. It was too late to escape so she had to make the most of it. The moment of truth had come. Would all their efforts be worth it?

291

They joined the flotilla and forgot about Nige while they admired a succession of ingenious craft. Bo's Fifties Diner Boat was amazing — a Fifties cabin cruiser decked up like a diner with a bar serving milkshakes and people with quiffs and sticky-out skirts. Rock 'n' roll played from the speakers.

'Look at Dorinda!' Oriel shouted and waved at Bo's boat.

'Where?' Rose asked.

'Pink spotty dress!' Oriel cried and sure enough, Rose finally recognised the woman with the ponytail and sticky-out skirt bopping with the man from the dairy who delivered the milk to the café.

It was a joyous floating riot of noise and colour. Kev's Seafood Shack had a giant lobster on it, and a couple of his mates were playing a Calypso beat on the steel drums while he cooked seafood on a grill on the deck. The smell was divine. The cricket club yacht was crewed by men in whites and blasting out the Test Match Special music, and the local sea cadets had gone for an Olympic theme. There were at least twenty craft in total, from fishing boats to yachts and even a double kayak with people in fancy dress.

Rose forgot about her outfit and threw herself into enjoying the whole quirky madness of it. Oriel and Naomi were beaming too, and so Rose started waving at the crowds lining the bank. Children waved at her and she threw herself into the spirit of it, pretending to comb her hair and gaze into her mirror.

They were enjoying themselves when their little boat was eclipsed by a huge dark shadow.

33

Rose glanced up. Nige's 'battleship' loomed alongside, a metre higher than their deck, blotting out the
sun. Whatever craft was underneath was obscured
by wood panels painted in camouflage. Nige was
decked out like Admiral Nelson, standing on the bow
with a telescope to the eye that wasn't covered by a
patch. Another man was dressed as Captain Hook
and shouting 'Pieces of eight!' while a third, wearing
a naval uniform and captain's cap, bellowed over the
side at Cornish Magick.

'Hello, ladies. Make way for the head of the fleet or
prepare to be boarded!' he shouted.

Oriel waved Excalibur at him. 'Prepare to have an
oar shoved up your —'

Boom!

''Kin hell, what was that?' Naomi called.

'They have a cannon. An actual cannon!'

'No! That's anachronistic! Aircraft carriers don't
have cannons,' Rose cried. 'It's cheating!'

'When did that ever stop Nige? Maybe he couldn't
get a heat-seeking missile in time for the regatta?'

Boom!

The Cornish Magick boat actually shuddered.
Rose's ears rang. Oriel swore loudly and Naomi muttered about doing something to his crew that sounded
incredibly painful.

Another explosion blotted out Oriel's shout and
they ducked as red smoke billowed from the back
of the battleship. Cornish Magick wobbled again,

causing Rose to grip her throne tighter. Nige's ship was already steaming ahead, leaving a wake that caused some of the smaller craft to bob up and down. A child almost fell off a kayak and the father shook his fist.

'He'll win, won't he?' Oriel said, as Naomi managed to steer their boat back on course and the wake from Nige's battleship dissipated.

'Not if there's any justice,' Rose said.

The course marshals ordered everyone back into position and they made it out to the end of the creek where there was room for everyone to wait while the judging took place. However, Nige's battleship had broken ranks and seemed to be heading off course.

People started shouting as it made for the middle of the estuary.

'What the hell is Nige doing?' Oriel cried.

'I don't know — oh . . .' Rose held on to the arms of her chair. 'I'm no expert but the battleship seems, very low in the water.'

Naomi stood on the bow for a better book. 'Bloody hell. I think it might be sinking!'

A moment later, the orange RNLI lifeboat zoomed past the pageant flotilla towards the battleship. It was definitely listing at the bow and Nige and his two mates were waving frantically from the deck. Finn and Joey followed the RNLI in their own RIBs, accompanied by a couple of other speedboats.

In her short time in Falford, Rose had heard enough horror stories about how fast a boat could sink, but nothing could have prepared her for the alarming speed at which the battleship bow was vanishing below the waves like the *Titanic*. Everyone was watching through binoculars, from windows, pontoons and from the shore in horrified fascination. Nigel and his two mates were at the stern, ripping off their costumes and screaming. The RNLI were close but not close enough because the crew had started to climb over the rails. 'Oh my God, they're going to abandon ship!' Naomi exclaimed.

Seconds later, the three men plummeted into the waves.

'Auntie Lynne will have a heart attack,' Oriel wailed.

Rose was more worried that the three overweight middle-aged men would have one but, fortunately, the two crew members were scooped up immediately by the RNLI. Nige was still splashing around and seconds later, Finn's boat zoomed after him and hauled him from the water into the RIB.

From the angry gestures, Rose guessed he was giving Nige a piece of his mind.

'If I could get off this boat, I could help. They might need me,' Naomi said. 'Oriel!'

* * *

Oriel steered the boat alongside the nearest pontoon, and Naomi jumped out. Rose would never forget the sight of Naomi haring down the quayside in her King Arthur outfit towards Finn's RIB, which had gone alongside the yacht club pontoon.

'Let's go and see if he's OK. Auntie Lynne will be beside herself,' Oriel said, bringing the boat closer to the yacht club where all the action was happening.

Two women helped Nige out so Naomi could tend to him with the RNLI. But judging by the language being used by Nige and his crew, it was clear they'd suffered nothing more than bruised pride. Nige was actually batting Naomi away and seemed more interested in berating his mates than being helped.

But while they didn't seem to have come to any harm, their boat was no more than a pile of floating wood and patches of oil on the surface of the water.

'That'll be a bloody hazard for weeks,' Rose heard the yacht commodore complaining. 'What an absolute tit that man is.'

'At least someone's realised,' Oriel said. 'There's Auntie Lynne. I ought to go and see how she is. Will you be OK tying up?'

'Of course,' Rose said, wondering how she'd secure the boat with her tail on.

Luckily Maddie arrived and under Rose's instructions, helped to tie up the boat. 'Oh my God. What drama. I never expected this,' her friend said, taking charge of Rose's tail. 'Poetic justice if you ask me. Serves them right.'

Privately Rose agreed and with Cornish Magick safely alongside the pub jetty, Rose got out.

As Rose and Maddie approached Oriel and her aunt, it was clear that Auntie Lynne was more angry than worried.

'I knew this would happen! I told him not to put those flares on, or the cannon thing. He wouldn't listen! He never does. Always has to be better than everyone else! Wait till I get hold of him.'

Lynne stormed off towards the yacht club.

All the boats were now tied up, out of harm's way, while the floating wreckage of Nige's battleship was being guarded by boats.

Maddie heaved an amused sigh. 'Well, I think we can say that went off with a bang. What happens next?'

Finn happened next, or at least Rose could see him

walking towards her. Close behind him, she spotted a grey-haired woman in hiking shorts, staring at her in nothing short of amazed horror.

'Oh God, no.'

'What's up?' Maddie took the tail from Rose.

'It's Professor Ziegler. The head of department at the local university. She's the one who's been deciding whether to support my grant application.'

Maddie stared back at the prof, who appeared to be taking a photo of Rose on her phone, and talking to a reedy, bald man next to her who Rose suspected was her husband.

'He looks like he swallowed a bottle of vinegar.'

'He's a professor too. And vice chancellor.' Rose groaned. 'Why did they have to be here just when I look like Ariel? Why did you have to get such a . . . a . . . flashy tail?'

'My client says that tail is worth five hundred quid. Those are Swarovski crystals on it, you know.'

Rose bit back a retort because Professor Ziegler had caught her eye. She smiled and the professor inclined her head and gave the briefest of smiles in return. Her husband still looked like he was about to announce the end of the world was nigh.

Maddie whispered in Rose's ear. 'Um. You have seaweed down your bra.'

'Ew.' Rose fished the bladderwrack from her cleavage, not that she had much.

The professor stared and her husband's long face was punctuated by an 'oh' of fascination. Rose turned her back and swore.

Maddie giggled. 'Stop worrying. It's all good clean fun.'

Despite her embarrassment, Rose had to admit that

Maddie was right. During the pageant, Rose had been having enormous fun, and been transported back to her undergraduate days before she'd first fallen ill. Everything had seemed rosy, her future stretching before her then. Now Nige and his scurvy crew were safe, she was still glowing from the natural justice of seeing his bombastic boat go up in smoke. However, she'd still rather not have been seen prancing around in a silver shell bra and sparkly mermaid tail.

She shouldn't be worried about what people thought. It was just . . .

'Ah. Rosy! Found you at last!'

The committee chair, a woman in a cowgirl outfit, bore down on Rose and Maddie. 'I think we need a distraction after that disaster with bloody Nigel. The sandcastles are ready for judging if you can come down to the beach.' She lowered her voice. 'We've made everyone wait behind a rope this year while you do the judging. Less chance of you being intimidated by the entrants.'

'You don't think that would really happen?'

'Well, I'd hope not but Seth Treblecock's taking part and he can be a bit lairy if he's been at the Rattler. Mind you, the Patels and Bannons are here again too. They'd smile in your face while aiming a carving knife between your shoulder blades, if you know what I mean.'

The chair dashed away, talking into her radio.

'What fresh hell is this?' Maddie whispered, taking care of Rose's tail and handing her a hoodie to put on over the crop top.

'I dread to think. Let's get it over with.'

★ ★ ★

298

In her shorts and hoodie, but still with shells and seaweed in her hair, Rose must have looked a strange sight to the families gathered on the beach below the pub.

Bracing herself, she put on a smile and went between the twenty or so sandcastles, studying each one and marking the score on a clipboard provided by the committee chair. Their creators twitched behind a rope at the side of the beach, jostling each other for a better view. Rose tried not to glance in their direction but couldn't miss a few of the comments, some delivered in stage whispers, others blatantly loud.

'Of course, Tarquin, last year's contest was judged by a chartered surveyor.'

'Mummy! If we don't win, Livia Collingford from pony club says it'll prove I'm a total loos-ah.'

'Who is that woman, anyway? She looks barely old enough to build a decent sandcastle, let alone judge one.'

Rose reminded herself she had survived departmental meetings, lectures, interviews and a PhD viva — not to mention an actual brush with death. She was determined to choose the most appealing castle, no matter how high others' battlements or how expertly their portcullis had been crafted. Just like when she was interviewing students, she tried to look beyond the polish for the candidate who showed genuine passion for their subject.

There were several contenders with straight walls, regimented fortifications and elaborate moats. Their perfect angles must have been created with tools and rulers. Rose lingered by one that reminded her of a miniature Tower of London, complete with model Beefeaters and a plastic raven and — in a macabre twist — a little executioners' block and axe. Shuddering at the mindset behind such a creation, Rose crossed it off her shortlist.

There were some perfectly executed pyramids too, but time and time again, she kept being drawn by a ruined castle, which had Tintagel etched in the sand next to it in wobbly writing. It wasn't the neatest effort but that added to the authenticity, especially as one side of the walls had already collapsed. Rose thought that great effort — and more importantly, passion — had been lavished on its construction.

She decided that was her winner. Making a mark on her clipboard, and ignoring the hostile and anxious faces pressing in on her, Rose moved to leave, feeling massively relieved. At least she didn't have to give her verdict in front of everyone, thereby crushing dreams and inciting a mini-riot.

Even so, the pleas and complaints followed her.

'Who's won? Let us know!'

'Who is it?'

'All the winners will be announced at the end of the regatta,' the chair said.

'It's outrageous!'

'Patience, ladies and gentlemen,' the chair pleaded, ushering Rose through the mob. 'Come on, clear a path for our judge!'

An hour later, Rose had managed to calm down, change into a T-shirt, and remove most of the shells and weed from her hair. Oriel and Naomi had joined her and Maddie at the pub barbecue. Most of the pageant competitors were there, and most of the talk was about the sinking of Nigel's boat. Nigel himself was nowhere to be seen. Oriel was on tenterhooks about the results even though Rose tried to manage her expectations by telling her they'd done their best and could do no more. By four, the competitive programme was winding up and the loudspeakers started blaring that they would soon announce the results.

Joey and Finn sauntered up, pints in hand now their duties were done. They'd barely had time to say hello, when the chair of the regatta announced the winners, starting with the swimming races, then the children's dinghy race and . . .

'*The sandcastle competition.*'

Rose pulled a face.

'*This year was won by Harry and Una Ziegler.*'

'Ziegler?' Rose mouthed.

'Is that your professor's kids?' Oriel asked.

'Grandkids I should think, but how embarrassing. I didn't know they'd entered.'

'I'd keep that quiet if I were you,' Naomi said.

'You know the winners?' Joey asked, laughing.

'Not personally. Oh, bugger.'

'Don't worry about it,' Finn said. 'It would be hard not to know one of the entrants in Falford.'

'But I was chosen to be judge precisely because I didn't know anyone. So, shh . . .'

'Yes. Shh. Discretion is the better part of valour,' Maddie said.

'*Now to the results you've all been waiting for. The water pageant!*'

The loudspeaker announcement saved Rose from further comment.

'*Firstly, you'll be relieved to know that the crew of* HMS Battleship *are all safe and sound thanks to the RNLI and the marshals.*'

'That's a mixed reaction if ever I heard one,' Maddie whispered in Rose's ear as the faintest of applause petered out in seconds.

301

'*However, their entry has been disqualified for endangering other competitors. In future, the committee will be inspecting all craft before they take part, in the interests of safety.*'

A loud collective cheer rang out.

'*So, to the winners — first prize in the Annual Falford Regatta fancy-dress water pageant is . . . Bo's Diner!*'

Rose joined in the even louder round of applause, Finn cheered and Joey let out a whistle.

'Never mind,' Rose said seeing Oriel's downcast face.

'I knew it would win. I like Bo. It was the best boat, but I'm still gutted. I wanted to get the extra publicity for Cornish Magick and show my auntie I could be the best at something.'

They all cheered warmly while Bo and her vintage dance group friends went to collect their prize from the chair.

'*And the runners-up prize goes to . . . Cornish Magick with their Myths and Legends theme.*'

'There you go! Congratulations!' Maddie said.

'Runners-up . . .' Oriel murmured.

Naomi hugged her, saying, 'Well done!'

'*Please come up and collect your prize,*' the announcer declared.

'You go,' Rose urged Oriel. 'You deserve the limelight.'

'OK, but you all have to come too.' Oriel tugged her arm.

Rose protested, but had no choice but to allow herself to be dragged up to the stage with Naomi while Maddie waited on the sidelines. Oriel was awarded a voucher for a meal for four at the Ferryman and a plastic silver boat on a wooden plinth. Someone took a pile of photos for the regatta webpage of the local online newspaper.

Naomi and Oriel were giving an interview to the reporter.

'I'm going back to the flat to change for this evening party,' Maddie said, referring to the post-regatta party at the pub.

'I'll do the same myself when I've spoken to Naomi and Oriel,' Rose said.

'Well done, by the way,' Maddie added, with a smile. 'You really have thrown yourself into the community spirit. It suits you, Rose. Very much. You're glowing.'

Leaving Rose to ponder what exactly 'glowing' meant, Maddie walked off. It was true Rose had enjoyed the pageant and its preparations far more than she'd expected and she'd been drawn into the heart of the community. Maddie could have no idea, however, of Rose's mission to track down her donor, or that she'd ended up falling for the man who might be him.

She waited for Oriel and Naomi's interview to finish before arranging to meet them later at the pub party. The crowds were thinning as the day visitors went home, and Rose took her time about returning to the flat, reflecting on the day, and her feelings for Finn. She paused in a quiet spot by the hedgerow looking down on the estuary. A boat was fishing some of the debris from Nige's battleship from the water.

She felt a tap on her shoulder. Not Maddie, but Joey, who gave her a quick kiss on the cheek. 'Congratulations, Mermaid. You beat Nige and his crew.'

'Thanks, but Oriel and Naomi had the original idea and you and Finn helped massively. I don't think my mermaid outfit contributed much!'

'I don't know, it suits you.'

'Now I know you're winding me up.'

He laughed. 'You did look great. You still do, of course.' His smile faded.. He was staring further up the lane to the wall of a thatched cottage where a woman was standing. She was about Rose's age and clutching an overnight bag in both hands. As they watched, she put the bag on the ground, reached up, took Finn's face in her hands and kissed him. It was only a brush of the lips, but moments later, Finn had picked up her bag and followed her round the corner of the cottage, vanishing out of sight behind the pub.

Joey's jaw dropped.

'Lauren . . .' he murmured.

34

Lauren was back.

Finn hurried her towards Curlew Studio, insisting on carrying her bag and taking her somewhere 'private to talk'.

'Fine,' she'd said, seeming bemused but going with him anyway.

Hurrying with her along the creekside path, he felt overwhelmed with memories, regrets and fears. He remembered so clearly that night, the previous year, when Lauren had turned up at his place, upset and the worse for wear. She'd told Finn that she and Joey had had an almighty row and broken up.

She'd turned to Finn for comfort and he'd done what he could: listened, made her coffee and tried to persuade her to make it up with Joey. She'd turned to Finn for comfort and he'd almost crossed a line with her; he *had* crossed it if holding her counted.

He'd comforted her as she cried and then she'd tried to kiss him and for a brief moment he'd kissed her back. He shouldn't have even let things get that far. He'd regretted it and her greeting at the regatta — the kiss — had brought back guilty memories.

Just like Rose's kiss on board *Siren* after the storm. Twice Finn felt he'd kissed a woman Joey was involved with.

Finn and Lauren had been friends even before she and Joey became an item. He'd met her at a yacht club party a few years previously and introduced her to his brother. Finn even thought he was in love with her at one point, though he never told her. He'd since realised that he wasn't and that Joey and Lauren were meant to be together.

Now he wondered if Lauren had realised what his feelings were — or once had been?

He opened the door of the studio and ushered her inside.

She walked into the middle of the room but he lingered a few paces away.

'I'm sorry for that kiss, Finn. I only meant it as a friend, but I can tell it embarrassed you. You know I'd never want to do that . . . not after you've been such a good friend to me over the years.'

'I'm not embarrassed,' he said though in truth he was reeling. She was the very last person he'd expected to turn up at the regatta. She'd tapped him on the shoulder and before he could even speak, she'd greeted him with that kiss. It was a good friend's kiss but given their history, it had a resonance that troubled him. His first instinct had been getting her out of there, where Joey couldn't see her. Or Rose. Luckily, he didn't think anyone had, and he'd quickly persuaded her to come with him somewhere private. Now, he could see he might have overreacted in the heat of the moment.

'I'm not embarrassed just surprised to see you.' He handed her a glass of iced water. 'I'd no idea you were coming. What brings you back here?'

'It's a free country,' she said lightly. 'It's not as if I've emigrated.' She wandered to the window where laughter and music drifted up from the waterside. Finn joined her.

'I know that.'

The party was ramping up in the village. People

306

would be wondering where he was. Joey would be wondering.

'So,' he began as calmly as he could. 'Joey doesn't know you're here?'

'Not yet.' Lauren sank into the sofa, no doubt exhausted after her journey from London. 'I'm sorry for overreacting too. Of course I've a reason for coming back. In fact, I've thought about it every day since I walked out last year. I love my job, but I miss what I left behind so much. It was precious. I think I made a huge mistake.'

'With Joey?' Finn couldn't help his shock.

'Yes. I've realised what I threw away with Joey and I want to put that right.'

Finn suppressed a groan. While he suspected Joey was still in love with Lauren, he wasn't sure his brother would want to start all over again after he'd been so badly hurt. Joey had changed . . . but Finn had no control over that.

'Have you ever told Joey why you left in the first place?' he said softly.

'Why would I do that? He'd be gutted.'

'I — I wrestled with myself a long time about whether to tell him, but nothing happened between us.'

'You wanted it to, Finn. Don't deny it.'

'No. Yes. I like you and yes, of course I was attracted to you, but you were virtually engaged to Joey.' He couldn't disguise his frustration or his shock that Lauren was back, and once again in his flat behind his brother's back. 'Joey and I don't see eye to eye over a lot of things, but I'd never have betrayed him like that. The kiss we had . . .' He remembered the charged atmosphere when Lauren had come round to the studio, in tears after the fight with Joey.

'You know I'd had a bad shift at work. Lots of bad shifts. I was exhausted and Joey and I had a row. He — you may as well know — he proposed to me that evening, but I said it wasn't the right time.'

Finn closed his eyes in dismay. '*He proposed?*'

'Yes. He was upset when I didn't say yes and I tried to make him understand that I couldn't think about marriage yet, kids and all that. He blew up and walked out. I told him that if he wasn't prepared to wait and give me some breathing space then maybe we weren't right for each other.'

'Don't say that. You loved Joey.'

'I know that *now* but that night, I wanted you. I wanted you so badly and that kiss . . .'

'When you were upset and exhausted and needed comfort,' Finn repeated.

'Yes. All those things. I realise that now, but it sowed the seeds of doubt in my mind. I thought if I'd kissed his brother, and I wasn't sure I wanted to marry him, then we *really* did need some space. I'd been headhunted for the London job and I'd been stalling. When I left here that morning . . .'

Finn swallowed hard. He'd let Lauren sleep at his place. In his bed, while he took the sofa. He couldn't say he'd slept because he'd not had a wink.

'When I left, I went back to my parents. You know the rest.'

Finn knew only too well. Dorinda had called to say that Joey's boat had gone out but he hadn't told anyone where he was. She'd said she couldn't raise Lauren either and wondered if she might have gone to work. Finn had said he didn't know anything because he didn't, but he'd been sick with worry and guilt.

What if Joey had done something . . .

In the end, Joey *had* come back. Albeit a different version of Joey: bitter, cocksure, declaring Lauren could do what she wanted and he didn't care. He was going to have a good time, not get serious again.

Yet Rose had come onto his radar . . . a bigger challenge than most of the women he'd dated since, but perhaps only that, as Finn had suspected at the start, a challenge . . .

'Why don't you sit down?' Lauren asked. 'Pacing about like this won't do you any good . . .'

'I don't want to sit down.'

'If you're afraid I'll jump on you, you're wrong.' She smiled at him. 'I came back to see Joey.'

Finn perched on the sofa, as tense as a coiled spring. 'Are you really serious about getting back with Joey? It'll finish him if you're not.'

'Yes, I'm serious about trying to make a go of it again. Can I stay here for a moment? Just while I get myself together to face Joey? It's been a long journey and I came straight to Falford in a taxi. I haven't even been to see my folks.'

'Yes.' Finn softened. 'But you will *have* to talk to him. I'm not sure who might have seen us come back here.'

'I think I should go to Joey now. Where will he be?'

'He might still be in the Ferryman. There's a band and disco. Or the yacht club.'

Lauren smiled. 'I miss the Ferryman and all the old gang.' She sighed before adding wistfully, 'I miss Falford, even though I thought it was stifling me. The big city isn't all it's cracked up to be.'

'You're a doctor. What you've done is incredible.'

'Yes, but it's been a hell of a year as you can imagine.

I'm knackered and I've had a lot of long dark nights of the soul to think about what I left behind.' She stood up. 'I'm going to find Joey. I'll message him and arrange to meet. Do you think he'll mind being dragged away from the party?'

'Mind?' Finn gave an intake of breath. 'No, he won't mind but he's going to be shocked. He'll need time to adjust.'

'I do know I'll have to rebuild his trust. If I even can.' She embraced Finn again, briefly, as a brother. 'Thank you for being here again. For trying to pick up the pieces of me and of Joey. I'll leave you now.' She searched his face and laughed. 'You seem relieved.'

He smiled. 'I'm only a bit knackered; I've been burning the candle at both ends. I shouldn't have said that to an A&E doctor,' Finn said.

She patted his arm. 'Now I've settled in and have the headspace, I've realised what I should have valued before. Take care you don't do the same, lovely Finn. Work is important but don't forget the people as you're racing by. You mustn't lose sight of them in the rush.'

He pictured her walking down the hill towards the boatyard. He also pictured Joey, lifting a pint at the Ferryman, oblivious to the fact that the woman who'd broken his heart was about to walk into his life — and shatter it again. Or put it back together.

He thought of Rose, perhaps she was at the Ferryman too — oh God, let Lauren not crash into them both.

How would Rose feel when she knew Lauren was back? Would Joey cause a scene with Lauren? Blank her? Have another row? As soon as Lauren had gone, he had to find Rose and make sure she was OK.

35

Rose stepped back into the shadow of the trees at the top of the lane above Curlew Studio. After she'd recovered from the shock of seeing Finn and Lauren kissing, she'd thought of going straight back to the flat but the impulse to warn Finn that Joey had seen him eclipsed that. She texted Maddie to say she'd be back at the flat in a little while.

She'd made her way through the crowds, past the food stalls set up outside the shop and gallery, past the pub and the beach barbecue. There were so many people, it was hard to make progress. Locals and some holidaymakers were enjoying the late afternoon sun, drinks in hand, listening to music coming from the yacht club and pub. It was a joyful, chaotic throng, but Rose had only one thing on her mind: Lauren kissing Finn. Joey charging after them.

She had known for months that she and Joey were only meant to be friends, but Finn was different — she was in love with him. She couldn't deny it. So why were he and Lauren so close? Had they been having an affair while Joey and Lauren were still together?

Was that why Lauren had left?

She felt sick. No wonder Finn was so reluctant to reciprocate her own kiss if he was secretly in love with Lauren.

Her gut instinct was that Finn would go to Curlew Studio. The question was, had Joey got there first?

When she arrived, all was silent and she waited in the shadow of the trees. Was anyone even in? She got her breath back, adrenaline surging after making her way past the crowds and up the hill to Curlew.

While she composed herself, she saw Joey march up the side of the cottage. He must have arrived by water and had made his way from the jetty below. Rose shrank back into the shadow of the trees. Joey was clearly on a mission, oblivious to anything else. He almost jogged to the front door, banged on it and shouted. 'Finn! I know she's with you. Open the door!'

'Joey!'

Finn appeared.

'Lauren's here, isn't she?'

'Yes, but — '

'I saw you kissing her. I went home first, I thought you might have gone there, but then I thought: no. They want to be secret. They've something to hide so I decided to come here. I was right.'

Joey stepped forward as if he might push his way past Finn, but Finn barred the way. 'It's not what it looked like.'

Joey laughed. 'I expected better from you than that, bro. How can it be anything else?'

Lauren stepped past Finn and outside. 'Finn, let me sort this out. It's my life. Mine and Joey's. Come inside. Let's talk it over out of view.'

Joey hesitated. 'You know, now I'm here, I'm not sure I want to hear it.'

'You *do*. That's why you came over here. I was just on my way to find you. Finn's right. Nothing has happened. I came back for you, Joey, but we need to get some things straight. They're long overdue.'

Joey hesitated a moment longer before going inside. The door closed, shutting Rose out.

36

Finn's stomach clenched. He'd been fairly sure he and Lauren hadn't been seen by anyone. Now Joey was here, and his face held not anger but sheer desolation.

Joey shook his head. 'My God, I've been blind. What a complete idiot you must think I am,' he said, his tone bitter and hard. 'That's why you left, isn't it? Because you and Finn were having an affair.'

'No, you couldn't be more wrong,' Lauren said gently. 'Finn and I are just friends. Close friends. That embrace you saw was only an impulse, relief at being home again, being back in Falford after a shitty time. I didn't even think. I just threw my arms around him. Finn was as shocked as you.'

'You can't expect me to believe that.' Joey switched focus to Finn. 'Bro? Can you?'

'It's true. I came home for you. I came to see if we can make a go of things again. I was on my way to see you when you turned up at the door. I didn't want things to start like this.'

Joey shook his head. 'I can't believe that's why you're here. I won't believe it.'

'You'd better try,' Finn said firmly. 'It's the only answer you're going to get. The truth.'

The wind taken from his sails, Joey looked from Finn to Lauren and back again. His face was agonised. 'I want to be wrong. I just can't handle being let down again. I love you, Lauren, I always have. I

313

still do and I can't deal with you being here if it's only to say goodbye again.'

'I can't guarantee anything — who can? But I promise you this: I came here to see if it was worth picking up the pieces.'

'I still don't get why you left in the first place. I was convinced there had to be someone else.'

'No.' Finn caught her glance at him. 'There never has been. No one but you — not then or now, Joey, but I want to tell you exactly what happened the night I decided to leave.'

Finn stood aside. 'I think this is something you two should sort out.'

'Thanks, Finn,' Lauren said with a grateful look. Joey was more reluctant but nodded.

'I think we should go back to my place to talk about it,' Joey said.

Lauren nodded.

'OK,' Finn replied, hoping they could talk things over calmly.

Before they left, Joey paused by the door. 'I just remembered. Rose was with me when I saw you and Lauren. I hared off to find you, but I wondered if she might have got the wrong idea too.'

'Rose saw *us*?' Finn grew cold with dismay.

'Yes, and I'd hate her to get the wrong idea too. I think she likes you, Finn. A lot more than you realise.'

'I have to find her.'

Without another word, Finn strode out of the studio. He was pleased his brother and Lauren were trying to sort out their differences and make a go of things again. It was clear now that Joey had never been serious about Rose; he had always been in love with Lauren.

Which was all fine for Joey but the question that was now gnawing at Finn, was if Rose had misconstrued the kiss between him and Lauren too. He had to find her and put everything right.

37

Finn sent Rose a message although he wasn't sure she'd answer it. He could head over to Cornish Magick of course, but she might be with her friends . . . He had to explain without an audience.

'Hello.'

Rose stepped out of the shadows by the top of his drive. She was still wearing shorts and a hoodie, a shell headband on her head, a strand of green weed in her hair. She looked beautiful and bizarre all at the same time, and his stomach flipped.

'Rose. Thank God. I was coming to find you.'

'Same here,' she said. 'Although it was a mistake. I came to find out. Or rather . . . I didn't know what to do. I saw Joey go inside and Lauren at the door-way with you. I shouldn't have eavesdropped, but I couldn't *not* hear some of the conversation even though it's none of my business.'

Finn caught her hand. 'Don't go. Please don't go. I need to tell you what happened.' As he spoke, Joey and Lauren walked out of the studio and in the oppo-site direction to the lane that led to the village. They were too intent on each other to notice Finn and Rose by the trees.

'I need to say this first. After Joey saw you — and Lauren — on the path behind Cornish Magick, I didn't know what to do. I didn't want to interfere but I wanted to warn you so I hung around for a while, then I took a chance that you'd both come back here . . .'

Finn cut her off. 'I know. He — um — misconstrued

316

the situation.'

'OK . . .' She seemed unconvinced.

'It was a kiss between friends. Nothing more. We were close — we are close — but as nothing more than good mates. She and Joey love each other. Lauren's back in Falford to try and make a go of it with Joey.'

'Oh, I'm sorry I got things wrong. When you walked off with Lauren and Joey followed you, I assumed . . . things I shouldn't have.'

'I've got things completely wrong too, I thought — I thought that you and Joey were keen on each other, especially he . . . liked you.'

'*Like.* Yes.' Rose frowned. 'That's where it ends.'

'I — I don't understand.'

'Has Joey led you to believe there was more?' she asked.

'Not openly, but he hasn't said there wasn't. You've spent time together, when you've been sailing.'

'And that is all it's ever been about: the sailing. I'm sorry if you had the wrong idea. If you'd asked me, I'd have told you as much.' She sounded frustrated but not as frustrated as Finn himself.

'I *couldn't* ask you. Not while I thought my brother was serious about you. I'd never step in and ruin another relationship.'

'I don't understand?'

'Things became complicated between Lauren and me for a while but that kiss you saw earlier was an impulse, a greeting. I'll tell you about it if you'll let me but first, are you *sure* you're not upset by my brother getting back with Lauren? He's not behaved how he should have towards you or other women. He's never gotten over Lauren but that's no excuse for hurting *you*.'

317

'Finn.' Rose put her hand on his arm. 'Let me put this straight. I'm not upset that Lauren is back. In fact, I'd be delighted if she and Joey could make a go of their relationship. I've long sensed that he was probably still not over her and that he and I would never be more than friends.' She smiled. 'To be honest, I don't even fancy him.'

He let out a breath of pure relief. 'Really?'

'Yes.' She hesitated. 'His brother, now that's a different matter, but of course, you're not interested in me that way, are you?'

'What? Oh, Rose, you have no idea . . .' He laughed in amazement at her confession. 'The truth is, I didn't dare hope you were interested in me or make a move on you. Not while I thought Joey had feelings for you.'

Rose's mouth opened. 'Was *that* why you were so hesitant on board *Siren* after the storm?'

'Rose, I don't think I've ever found it so hard to resist doing something in my entire life.'

Her eyes lit up with surprise and happiness. 'I've wanted to replay that moment every day since. In my fantasies, it had a different outcome. I've tried to keep away from you, and failed miserably every time,' she said.

The sunlight streamed in behind her, lighting up her beautiful hair. He wanted to hold her, kiss her, tell her how much he felt for her — that he was in love with her and had been for many weeks. He didn't dare yet, but he was aware of a weight having been lifted from his shoulders. A few minutes before, he'd thought disaster might strike, that he'd hurt Joey, Lauren and Rose and now every possibility lay before him if he would only grasp it.

'Did you know you have seaweed in your hair?'

'Do I?' She touched her head and laughed awkwardly. 'I thought I'd pulled most of it out.'

'No, there's still a piece left.' Carefully, he teased a strand of green weed from a lock of hair. 'Here you go.'

'Thanks.'

The air was warm. Very warm and snatches of laughter and music drifted in through the open doors.

Rose turned her head towards the sound before looking back at him. 'We're missing the party.'

'I don't care.'

'Good. So,' she said very softly. 'If it happened again, would you feel the need to be noble?'

'I'm afraid not, but I'd need to put myself in the way of temptation, just to make sure.'

With a gleam of happiness in her eyes he'd never seen before, she stood on tiptoes and kissed him on the lips. Once again, he pulled her closer, savouring the sweetness of her body against his without the sting of guilt. There would be no regrets this time.

'There's nothing to hold us back any more,' he said.

'Apart from the fact everyone will wonder where we are . . .' Rose said.

'Let them. I don't care.'

'Neither do I, but I have to let Maddie know I may be even longer than I'd said.'

Rose sent her friend a message, then put her phone away.

'Joey and Lauren are gone,' he said. 'There's nothing to stop us now.'

'No . . .' Rose hesitated and Finn's heart thumped. He sensed a slight hesitancy in her that terrified him. Was she going to change her mind? Instead, she smiled and reached for his hand and together they walked into the studio. 'You're right. There is absolutely nothing to stop us now.'

She helped him off with his T-shirt and they sank down onto his bed. The music from across the water grew louder, along with laughter and singing. She pressed her body against his and he heard the shell headband roll off the bed and land on the floorboards.

★ ★ ★

As twilight fell, she lay in the crook of his arm, stroking his chest. All the tension had gone from his body and he realised he was smiling up at the open eaves of the studio, filled with a sense of happiness deeper than he'd ever known.

I think I might be in love with you. He wanted to say the words, but was worried it was still too much too soon. He and Rose had a lot of time to catch up on, though he still wasn't sure how long he could hold back from telling her how he felt. All he knew was that for the first time in his life, he had everything that truly mattered to him and he was never letting it go.

38

Rose arrived back at Cornish Magick later that evening, excited, exhilarated but with an unease she couldn't quite shake off now that she'd left Finn's bed.

She'd come to Falford intending to find out who her donor was, but not to tell him, despite her Gran's letter. Now, she still didn't know who he was and she'd ended up falling in love. None of it had been in the plan — and what of the future? There were other things she'd need to say to him, if things went further, but they could wait.

There was Maddie to face first and the interrogation began the moment she stepped through the door.

Maddie assessed her in a sweeping glance. 'Finn borrowed your headband, did he?'

Rose touched her hair and her cheeks glowed. 'I must have left it there.'

'Your hair's damp too.' Maddie's eyes bored into her.

'I had a shower. 'Am I in the dock? I'm sorry I've been so long.'

'Of course not.' Chastened, Maddie bit her lip. 'I want you to have a good time and be happy but I do care about you too. Or don't I want to know? I saw the blond one — Joey — thump off. You seemed to be getting on fine with him until then.'

'We were. We are getting on. Joey and I are friends and he's gorgeous, but it's nothing more and we're both happy with that.'

'It's the other one I'm worried about. Finn. It's not

321

just friends with him, is it?'

'No. It's not.' She broke into a huge smile, remembering the past few hours of sheer bliss. 'Finn and I are together. At least, I think we are . . .'

'How does Joey come into this?'

'He doesn't. Not in a serious way. Finn thought that Joey and I were closer than we are and was holding back. We never have been more than friends — yes, we've flirted and we've spent a lot of time together. That's as far as it went, though Finn got the wrong impression. He cares about Joey, even though they row, and he didn't want to wreck things for his brother.'

Maddie let out a breath. 'Wow. Very noble.'

'Don't laugh. I think there's real history between them.'

'Hmm. I'd worked that one out from the snippy remarks between them.'

'Look, all of this — everything I've told you about me, Finn, Joey and Lauren — stays between us.'

'I'm a lawyer, Lauren. I can keep a secret.' Maddie hugged her briefly. 'You've really fallen for this man, haven't you?'

It was frustration not amusement that made Rose laugh. 'Fallen? You sound like Gran used to. As if I'm about to crash.'

'Only because I care. Be careful, Rose, you're at a . . . difficult time.'

''Difficult?' For a moment I was wondering if you were about to use the 'V' word.'

'If you mean, vulnerable, then no, I wasn't.'

'Good, because I'm not.' Rose threw her bag on the sofa.

'No, of course not.' Maddie softened her tone. 'I'm only trying — badly — to say that the experience you've been through must have taken an emotional toll. You know the doctors said that. Then losing your gran. You and she had a special bond. She worshipped you.'

Rose found it hard to keep the exasperation out of her voice. 'The experience hasn't regressed me to teenage years. I'm not going to get a crush on some bloke just because he might have saved my life.'

Maddie's brow wrinkled. 'What do you mean? ''Might have saved your life?''

Rose swore silently at her faux pas. The last thing she wanted was for Maddie to seize on her unguarded words. 'Nothing. It's just a figure of speech. I only meant that he makes me happy.'

'Rose . . .' Maddie peered at her. 'Is there more to this than you're telling me?'

'No. I mean. Oh God, Maddie. I— Look before I tell you this, please don't judge me and please don't think I deliberately came here looking for him.'

'Looking for who? What exactly are you trying to say?'

'That Finn — or Joey — one of them is very likely the man who donated my stem cells!'

Maddie's eyebrows shot up her forehead. She exhaled. It wasn't often Rose saw her lost for words.

'That's one hell of a coincidence . . .' Maddie said gently. 'And I rarely believe in coincidences.'

'It's not a coincidence,' Rose said, wishing she'd never mentioned it but almost relieved to have finally told someone her secret.

'You mean you came here to hunt this guy down?'

'Not 'hunt' exactly. Gran left me a letter urging me to find my donor and thank him. I did write via the donor charity, and you know I had a card back from

323

him, and I wrote again but heard nothing so I did a little Internet research. Cutting a long story short, I narrowed him down to one of the Morvah brothers. When the opportunity to work in Cornwall came up, I decided to visit Falford and ended up basing myself here. It's serendipity not coincidence.'

'Sounds more like stalking to me.'

'No. Oh God, I hope not. Please don't say a word about this. I haven't told Finn or Joey why I'm here.'

'I thought you said tracking them down is *not* why you're here?'

'Maddie, don't torment me. I've questioned myself about it every day and wondered whether to say anything to Joey and Finn but I couldn't make up my mind, then I kind of got embroiled in their world and now it seems much too late to come clean.'

'I've heard similar stories before . . .' Maddie said archly.

Rose opened her mouth to protest but saw the glint in Maddie's eye. 'I wouldn't know what to say, if I could and anyway, I still don't know which one of them it is. I don't want Finn to think I've only got together with him because he saved me. That would seem weird and I'm not sure he'd understand. *If* it's him.'

'What a tangled web we do weave,' Maddie said. 'I think this calls for a drink, while you tell me exactly how you decided that the Morvahs were your saviours. Alleged saviours,' she added. 'Come on, sit down. I'll open the wine and you can tell me *everything* you know.'

39

The next day, Joey messaged Finn early, inviting him for an early morning sail. They hadn't had much chance to get out on the water with all the business of the regatta preparations. Finn agreed and for his part of the deal, he offered to take *Siren*.

The wind was brisk and conditions challenging and for the first hour, they were completely absorbed in sailing the boat up to the limit of its abilities. Finn was reminded of their youth and the days when Grandad Billy or their mother had taken them out, teaching them new skills and instilling a love of sailing these waters that he knew would never leave them

Finally, they anchored in a sheltered bay and Finn brought two coffees up from the galley. The wind dropped and the gulls cried. Finn felt at peace, but he knew there was more to be said before they could completely lay the past to rest.

Joey kicked off. 'Lauren's told me what happened the night we split up.'

'And?' Finn asked, still wary but relieved that Lauren had given her side of the story.

'That she came over to yours after we'd had a massive row. That she . . .' Joey paused. 'That she needed someone to talk to — needed comfort — but you weren't interested in providing it.'

'I'm sorry.'

'Why? You'd only need to be sorry if you had slept with her and you didn't, did you?' He looked directly at Finn. Finn saw the desperate need in his eyes for confirmation of what Lauren had told him. The trust between them couldn't be rebuilt overnight, but at least this was a start.

'No, I didn't. There was a kiss, that was it, but I did — do — feel partly responsible for her leaving at all. If I hadn't opened the door to her, or let her stay the night, I have often wondered if things might have been different. Maybe I should have tried harder to persuade her to go back to you and sort things out.'

'They wouldn't have been different. Not then. She's told me that she needed a break from — us. She'd been pushed to the edge by work. She was exhausted and we were arguing a lot. I hadn't realised how bad things had become between us, or how much pressure she was under. I thought she just needed a holiday. When I asked her to marry me, that was the last straw.'

'You didn't know how bad she was feeling.'

'No . . . but I ought to have listened more, looked for the signs and not pushed her. The thing is . . .' Joey glanced at his hands, a sure sign he was about to say something of which his big brother might not approve. 'We want to move in together again.'

'And will you?'

'Probably. Yes. She's got a week's leave, but she has to go back to the hospital and I don't know how we're going to deal with the distance. All that matters is that she says she still loves me and I still love her, but you've realised that all along.'

Finn nodded. 'I knew you were hurting pretty badly.'

'I didn't want to admit that.' He sighed. 'I ought to speak to Rose . . . I'm sorry I let you think there was more between us than there was. I — we haven't got on well for a long time and I'm to blame for that. I

326

took my hurt at Lauren leaving out on everyone else, including you, bro.

'I wanted to live up to my reputation, except I couldn't. I can't fall for anyone else. Every time I've tried, I've never felt more than physical attraction — not since her. It's not enough. It's not the same. You're right. I still love Lauren and I can't get over her — not even with someone as lovely as Rose.'

'Luckily for you, she's never fallen for the charm,' Finn shot back, still annoyed that Joey had wound him up and caused him a lot of dark nights of the soul.

'I realised that. I could have told you, but I bloody-mindedly let you go on thinking there might be more. I can't forgive myself for that.'

No matter how angry Finn had been with Joey, he couldn't stop the hint of a smile. 'There's no need. Rose told me herself she doesn't fancy you and never has.'

'Great. Thanks for that.' Joey sipped his coffee. 'Though I suppose I deserve it and worse.'

'I said she didn't fancy *you*,' Finn added.

Joey's mouth opened. 'You and Rose. You're together, aren't you? You and she — you . . .'

'Yes. We are.' Finn found it impossible not to grin.

'Wow. I can see what she means to you. OK. So, all's well that ends well, then.'

'It hasn't ended,' Finn said firmly. 'This is only a beginning, for both of us and, bro, we'd better not blow it again.'

40

August brought some of the hottest days of the year. Not as hot as Cambridge of course, where Rose had heard from her tenants that the thermometer in the garden had nudged past thirty-seven in the shade. In Cornwall, the excesses were tempered by the sea breezes, but it was still sweltering work on the dig while awaiting the result of her grant application with Professor Ziegler.

Rose made sure her team of students took plenty of breaks and when work was over, they headed off to the local beaches to swim and surf. The long, hot days had made Rose even happier that she'd learned to sail and she'd begun to long for the moments when she could take the sailing school dinghy out on the estuary, though still as part of a flotilla. Finn had taken over her schooling, with *Siren* as the classroom.

After the regatta weekend, Maddie had gone home to London. After all the excitement of the past few weeks, life settled down and might have been an anti-climax, but Rose relished the stability and the constant steady joy of knowing she and Finn were now together. She still hadn't found the courage to tell Finn about her illness yet and felt the chance was slipping through her fingers as the time passed.

She stayed over with him several nights a week, and threw herself into the life of the village. Her spare time was spent with her friends at the pub, the cricket and yacht clubs or simply sharing a glass of wine with Finn on the balcony of Curlew Studio.

On the bright side, Nigel's name was still mud around Falford; it had taken a week to clear the wreck of his battleship.

'Surely Lynne must see what a prat he is now?' Rose told Oriel while helping her plan a new autumn tour that stopped at Zennor. Oriel had had the bright idea of striking a deal with the café in the village to do an afternoon tea.

'Well, she's still pissed off with him for creating a scene at the regatta. She reckons everyone at Zumba is secretly laughing at her,' Oriel said. 'It's not her fault that he's an idiot. Now he keeps on at her to sell the shop because his mate Wayne's boat wasn't properly insured and he's demanding Nige pay for it . . .' Her face fell. 'There was a bloke in here the other day. He kept saying what a lovely space it was, eyeing it up and asking questions about the flat above. I took a sneaky picture of him on my phone and showed it to Naomi because I was sure I recognised him. I was right. It's Sophie Crean's friend. He's a commercial property agent.'

'Oh no. Does Lynne know about this?'

'She hasn't mentioned it but I wouldn't put it past Nige to send him round anyway.'

'Hmm . . .' Rose said. 'Finn told me the authorities might make Wayne and Nigel pay for the cost of recovering the wreck too. Apparently, Nige and Wayne aren't the respected members of the local community they thought they were so he might be short of money.'

'I hope Auntie Lynne doesn't bail him out. She can't afford it and selfishly, I want to stay here! I love doing the tours and working in the shop.'

'All you can do is keep on doing your best. Let's hope your auntie finally sees the light about Nigel and maybe you mention this agent came round?'

'I'll think about it. We *are* making more money but I'd love something really big to present to my auntie before I tell her about this agent. Something that would be the final nail in Nigel's coffin and get him off my back for good. If you know what I mean.'

'I'll try to help in any way I can,' Rose said, hoping inspiration might come fast enough to help Oriel — and before it was time for her to leave. *If* she left . .

Oriel turned the conversation to Rose, whose own life was going swimmingly. She didn't think she'd ever been happier. She and Finn were now 'official'. There had been no point in hiding their relationship and for a few days, according to Oriel, they'd been the talk of the village, although Lauren's return had eclipsed it.

'Falford can't cope with so much juicy gossip, what with Lauren coming home and you and Finn getting together,' Oriel said.

'They'll soon find something else to talk about,' Rose replied. A delivery had arrived so they took a break from the tour planning to unpack some books about local folklore.

Oriel added them to the display carousel. 'These have been going well with the tour parties. I had to reorder.'

'That's brilliant.' Rose wanted to hug Oriel, she was so relieved for her.

'Have you heard anything from the university about your grant thingy?'

'Not yet.'

'If you do . . . will you be staying?' Oriel asked, tentatively.

'I doubt it. I can't. The money is to go towards a community exhibition, rather than me personally. It means I would be more involved but I'd have to do most of the research remotely from Cambridge and I'm committed to next term at my own uni.'

'That's a shame. I thought you might want to keep the flat. Or you might move in with Finn.'

'It's a bit soon for that.'

'Why? If you like him, why wait? Especially if you finally found someone you really like. If he's 'The One'.'

Rose answered with a nod. Oriel was right, wasn't she? Finn was 'The One'. She didn't have to have had scores of lovers or relationships to know that, deep in her soul. Yet how could they be together, when he was rooted here in Cornwall, the water of the estuary flowing through his veins?

If she could get the grant, she might be able to spend a bit more time in Falford but she still couldn't move here without a permanent academic post. However, that issue paled in comparison to not having told Finn about the transplant. Each day that passed made it harder to confess and added to her worry about how he might react.

'I'll really miss you,' Oriel said, heaving a sigh. 'I'm really glad I took the plunge and did the tours and I've loved finding out more about all the sites. You should see all those faces looking up at me, waiting for me to tell them all about the ghosts and legends. I never thought I'd say this, but I bloody love it!'

All those faces looking at her expectantly . . . Rose thought of her students, the hush, the initial enthusiasm at the start of term, when they thought she did have all the answers. Except she didn't. A moment was coming when she had to make decisions because time was running out fast. Tell Finn who she was or not? Stay or go?

'I'll miss you too,' she said, sensing a chill in the air. 'Look, how do you fancy coming up to the dig site with me on Sunday? It'll be quiet and if you want to, we can do some digging. We might turn up a fragment of pot. You never know.'

★ ★ ★

As the end of August approached, Rose was invited by Dorinda to a weekend barbecue at the Seafood Shack with Finn, Joey and Lauren who was taking a week's leave.

It was the first formal 'family' occasion she'd been asked to and she was looking forward to it with a mix of excitement and nerves.

Conditions were calm and Rose had taken on the role of skipper under Finn's supervision, managing to sail *Siren* to within a few hundred yards of the Seafood Shack jetty before Finn had taken over. They tied up at the jetty to find Joey and Lauren were already there and talking to Dorinda, having anchored a little way off and taken the RIB to the shore.

After a chat with Dorinda, Rose found herself with Lauren while the brothers admired Kev's new fishing boat and Dorinda helped Kev in the kitchen.

Dorinda had been polite during their conversation, but Rose sensed that everyone was feeling their way around the new situation.

'Two women coming into her boys' lives,' Lauren said quietly. 'I can understand why she's nervous. One new one; one an old flame. She must be wondering what happens next.'

Lauren was right but Rose had perhaps more sympathy for Dorinda — because there was little history between them.

'The business and the boys were her life . . . perhaps she's anxious that everything she loves might disappear?' Rose suggested.

'I'm sure she is.' Lauren checked to make sure Dorinda was still out of sight. 'Joey and I have talked about making a new start elsewhere, but I don't think I could do that to him. It's easier for me to find a job here than for him to start all over again even if it might be a good idea. The important thing is, if we're going to start afresh, we need our own place away from the boatyard.'

'That sounds like a good compromise,' Rose said.

'I've already started looking for new jobs down here, and Joey's promised to check out if we can afford to buy something. It can't be in Falford that's for sure. Way out of our budget, not that it's a bad thing,' Lauren said. 'What about you and Finn? Will you move in together eventually?'

'I hadn't really thought about it,' Rose lied. 'I have to go back to my job in Cambridge at some point.'

She raised her eyebrows. 'Joey told me you were getting a grant so you could stay here?'

'It's not a job for me personally. It's a grant to do more research and hopefully set up an exhibition that could travel round schools and communities. I'd do most of the analysis and liaison from Cambridge.'

'Oh, sorry, he must have got the wrong end of the stick.'

'It's OK. No one really understands the ways of academia and funding.' She laughed. 'If I wanted to stay I'd have to apply for something with Penryn Uni and I hadn't thought that far ahead.' Rose felt guilty because she'd been thinking along these exact lines, but she didn't want to mention it to Lauren before she'd even discussed it with Finn. It was far too soon.

'We talk of nothing else but the future,' Lauren said with a wry smile. 'I suspect Dorinda would secretly love me to move here and for us to settle down. She's probably already dreaming of what boat to buy for her grandchildren. A new Morvah dynasty . . . Can the world cope?'

Rose laughed.

'Unless you and Finn get there first, of course.'

'We've only been together a few weeks!' Rose exclaimed.

'I know. I'm joking, sorry. Mind you, Finn is totally smitten. Joey says he's fallen for you hook line and sinker.'

'Oh, I don't know . . .' The fact that it could be very difficult for her to conceive was another issue she might one day have to discuss with Finn if they were to have any long-term future. There seemed so many barriers in the way, including the one she'd thrown up herself by not telling him about her transplant. Yet she had fallen for him, and the idea that he felt the same thrilled her. She was deeper in love with him every day and if, as she hoped, they did have a longer-term future, the question of how it could ever work with them four hundred miles apart had to be faced up to sooner or later. September was around the corner.

'Grub's up!'

Dorinda and Kev came out to the decking area with plates of lobster and bowls of salad.

'About time!' Joey joked, hurrying towards them at the sound and smell of food.

334

Finn joined Rose and put his arm around her. 'OK?' he murmured in her ear. 'Not too much of an ordeal.'

'Not an ordeal at all. I'm enjoying myself,' Rose said.

Yet as they sat down to the lunch, laughing and joining in the banter, Lauren's words stuck in her mind.

She would have to be honest with Finn one day soon. About their plans, about the future and if they were to have a future, about children . . . About why she might not be able to have any, or that it could be very difficult. She didn't think she could tell him why without revealing everything, and the longer she held it back, the harder it was going to be — and the bigger the fallout when he found out.

41

The sun returned to Falford with a vengeance for the first days of September. Even though summer was drawing to a close, there were plenty of people eager to flock to Cornwall now that the children had had to return to school, and Oriel's Zennor tour had plenty of interest. She still seemed down and worried about the visit from the agent so Rose took her to the dig site to take her mind off things and give her some inspiration.

They arrived at the pool, armed with hats, sunscreen and gallons of water.

'It'll be hot work today,' Rose said as they tramped up to the site.

There were a few hikers from time to time, but the vast majority of people would have headed for the beach.

'The roads'll be packed with the 'gin 'n' Jag' brigade,' Oriel said with a curl of her lip. 'You won't be able to park or get an inch of space on the beach.'

'All the better for us,' Rose giggled, imagining hordes of middle-aged couples from 'up country', crates of artisan gin rattling in the boot as they bumped down a lane to a secret cove that wasn't secret any more thanks to Instagram. She really was becoming a local now . . .

'Have you asked your auntie about that agent?' she said.

'Yes, and she looked upset but she said it was probably a coincidence and he just popped in on a 'whim'.

336

Whim, my arse.'

'It can be very hard to face up to the fact your partner might not be what they seem,' Rose said. Immediately she thought about her own reluctance to tell Finn the truth. It wasn't the same situation as Nigel and Lynne and yet . . .

Leaving their drinks in the shade of the tent, they set to work while it was still relatively early. Rose showed Oriel how to check the trenches and carefully scrape at the earth. Soon she slipped into the intense concentration required to work on a tiny square of earth.

It needed patience, focus. In an ideal world, nothing should be done in haste, but in reality, projects were always time-limited — limited by money, which was the same thing. Developers needed to start work, or perhaps a site was in danger of being flooded by the tide or eroded by the wind.

'Look, there's a fragment of a pot here by the look of it.'

She helped Oriel to work delicately on the soil, gently uncovering the piece of earthenware until it could be lifted out. They added it to the dig.

The sun climbed higher in the sky and by one o'clock it was almost thirty degrees. Rose and Oriel retreated into the shade of the tent for lunch then tried to start work again. The heat beat down on their backs and sweat trickled down Rose's neck. Her eyes were gritty with dust and her thighs and knees were aching.

Oriel stood up and wiped her forehead. 'I'm not sure I want to do any more digging.'

Rose thought her friend looked overheated and she'd had enough herself. 'It's hard going in this weather. I think it's worse toiling away in the heat

337

than on a cold day.'

'I've had enough. I'm sweating buckets . . . I might go for a swim in the pool.'

'That's not a bad idea, but I haven't brought my swimsuit.'

'Neither have I but I don't care.' Oriel smirked. 'I'm usually happy to go skinny-dipping, but there's too many dog walkers about, so it'll be underwear for me.'

Rose laughed. 'Go ahead. I'll stick to paddling.'

They wandered up to the pool whose dark surface reflected the blue sky above. Rose thought of poor lost 'Dozy Mary,' the unfortunate girl who was reputed to have drowned there, and wondered if there was any truth at all to any of the stories surrounding the site. Despite the heat, she shivered.

Oriel stripped down to her bra and knickers and waded into the pool. Rose took her Vans off.

'It's cold. Oh. Ow. And the rocks are a bit slimy.'

With a shriek, Oriel pushed off and began to swim a frantic breaststroke. Rose pootled around at the edge, savouring the cool water around her ankles. As she became used to the initial chill, she went in further. The shallower water now felt deliciously warm in comparison.

Oriel was now floating on her back, sculling. 'This is amazin'.'

Shading her eyes with her hand, Rose watched her friend. Ripples spread around her to the edge of the pool. The moorland was bright with purple ling, and harebells nodded in the sun. In the hazy distance, the sea was the deepest of blues. Rose thought of her moment with Finn at the Maidens back in the spring, and her powerful reaction to him. It hadn't been anything to do with magic and everything to do with sex. She smiled then a pang of regret seized her.

It was so beautiful here. The place, Cornwall — and Finn. How could she leave him at the end of the month? How could she stay?

It felt impossible.

'Woo!'

Oriel splashed water over Rose, laughing and taunting her, calling her a wimp for not swimming. Cold droplets spattered her face and she laughed. The next moment Oriel had vanished under the surface, only to pop up again spluttering. 'There's fish!' she cried, sounding horrified. 'And weed. Ew.'

Rose grinned as Oriel went under again. This time she didn't pop up so fast and when she did, she let out a scream. 'Oh my God. There's something down here!'

Rose burst out laughing. 'A fish? Cornwall's own Loch Ness Monster?'

'No. It's not an animal. It's hard. I stepped right on it and thought it was a rock. Hang on.' She did a duck dive. Rose waited, watching splashes on the surface but Oriel didn't come up. Rose waded in deeper, wetting the bottom of her shorts.

When Oriel did come up, she was standing up to her neck in water, gasping for breath and in her hand she held a sword.

Rose gasped herself. She waded towards Oriel, not caring that she was soaking wet. 'What have you got there? Oh my God.'

Oriel handed her the sword. It was heavy, rusting but largely intact. Her heart started to thump. It couldn't be . . .

They waded out, Rose carrying the sword until

they were at the side of the pool. Rose balanced the sword across her hands. Water glinted on the blade and dripped onto her feet.

'It was in the mud at the bottom. It's Arthur's, isn't it? I just found bloody Excalibur!'

Mesmerised, Rose stared at the sword, which was about two feet long, brown with mud and rust, the handle badly decayed, the blade already being eaten away. 'No, I don't think so.'

'It has to be. It must be!'

'It's not Excalibur. It's something just as wonderful though.' She smiled at Oriel. 'I think it's a gladius. A Roman sword.'

'Roman?' Oriel cried in disbelief. 'How can a Roman sword end up in Cornwall?'

'Because Iron Age people here traded tin with the Romans. Of course, I can't be certain until it's been researched so don't get your hopes up . . .'

It was too late for that. Oriel was bouncing around with delight. 'But what if it *is* Roman?'

Rose grinned like an idiot, breathless with wonder. 'Then it's very, very exciting indeed.'

42

'Don't tell anyone about this yet. No one,' Rose warned Oriel, carefully wrapping the sword in bubble wrap from a box in the tent. It sent a thrill of excitement through her to put the two-thousand-year-old object in such modern packaging.

'I have to tell Naomi. I'll burst if I don't tell her!'

Oriel did look about to go pop.

'OK, but *no one* else because this will be all over the news,' Rose relented. 'Nothing like this has ever been found in Cornwall and with the King Arthur connection, it's bound to attract a lot of attention.' Which was an understatement, Rose knew, but didn't want to raise Oriel's hopes even higher than they already were. She was almost certain it was a gladius, but she wasn't infallible.

'Not a word on social media. Don't tell your auntie and for God's sake, don't let Nigel get a whiff of this.'

'I won't say a word until you say so. Promise.' Oriel zipped her lips, but literally skipped back to the cars. 'But I cannot wait to see his face when he finds out!'

'Before we go, I need to take lots of photos of where it was found. Obviously, we can't go into the water, but we need to do our best to pinpoint the site and all the conditions we found it in. I can geocache it . . . and I need to make some notes now while everything is fresh in my mind.'

Oriel was still punching the air and doing a happy dance at intervals, and Rose felt trembly with anticipation, but she forced herself to go through the ritual of making her notes, taking the pictures before placing the bubble-wrapped sword in a cardboard box from her boot.

★   ★   ★

With it being Sunday, and with no way of returning the sword to its original site, Rose had no choice but to keep it at Cornish Magick in its bubble wrap and box. She laid it on the little dining table, hoping she wasn't doing it any further damage and wondering if she should have called Professor Ziegler or the local antiquities officer anyway. Deciding she couldn't possibly leave it, she fired off an email to the prof.

The reply was peppered with exclamation marks and superlatives in a most un-prof-like way.

Bring it to the dig site TOMORROW and I'll meet you there first thing. This is VERY exciting!!!! ☺

The smiley said everything.

After calling Oriel and inviting her to join them at the dig, Rose went to share the news with Finn. She felt slightly guilty after warning Oriel to be discreet, but of all people in Falford, she knew she could trust him. He was working on *Siren* when she came alongside in Oriel's boat. He helped her tie up and kissed her.

'You look happy,' Finn said. 'You feel happy.'

'What do you mean? I feel happy?'

'You're buzzing.'

She burst out laughing. 'You make me sound like a

342

hive of angry bees.'

'I meant buzzing in a good way,' he said with a glint of amusement in his eyes. 'You seem very excited and that smile — what's happened?'

'I *am* excited. Hold on.' She handed over a bottle of champagne that Maddie had brought on her last visit.

'Wow.' He looked at the label. 'Nice. What are we celebrating?'

'Finding Excalibur.'

He frowned. 'Excalibur? OK, now I really am confused.'

'All will be revealed,' Rose said. 'Shall we take this up onto the balcony and I'll explain?'

He stopped work and found two glasses, and they sat on the balcony drinking champagne while Rose told him about the sword and what it might mean for Oriel in terms of money and, more importantly, publicity for Cornish Magick.

'I'm really happy for her, especially if it sticks one up Nigel, but what will it mean for *you*? It's your dig.'

'Not really my dig. It's the professor's, but I am excited to be part of such a find.' She laughed. 'I'm a geek, I know.'

'Never apologise for being you. I'm a boatbuilding geek, remember?'

Rose wanted to tell him that he was the least geeky geek she'd ever seen but contented herself with a happy grin. 'I'll forgive you. As for the sword, it's bound to attract attention. I'm meeting the professor and the people who are the local authority on finds tomorrow at the dig.'

Finn poured a second glass of fizz, but it didn't get drunk.

Afterwards she lay in his arms, wishing she didn't

have to go back to the flat, or go back at all.

'I'd love to stay here for the night, but I have to leave really early for the university.'

'I have a very reliable alarm clock.'

She thought for all of two seconds. 'OK. I trust you.'

★ ★ ★

A few days later, Professor Ziegler had confirmed the sword was Roman and the county antiquities officer had agreed. For the time being, it was being kept in the university archaeology department before it was decided what to do with it. Rose knew it could be weeks before anyone announced the find to the press but a phone call from Oriel soon blew any prospect of secrecy out of the water.

'I'm sorry! Don't be mad at me. I did tell Naomi and she let it slip to Sophie Crean and her friend works for the *South-West News*. They want to meet us at the dig tomorrow!'

Rose groaned inwardly, but couldn't be cross for long. It was Oriel's find.

She had to break the news to the professor, who seemed resigned to it getting out and offered to come along. Rose told Finn about it when she went round to the studio. She stayed the night again. She'd stayed every night lately.

There weren't many days left and she still had no idea how often or if she would be back again. If she didn't get the grant, she'd have no excuse for even visiting in Falford, apart from seeing Finn. Somehow, they'd have to try and manage a long-distance relationship and Rose only had to look at her students, many of whom had partners in other parts

344

of the country or abroad, to see how difficult that could be.

The alternative was to try and find a job in Cornwall, but Finn hadn't asked her about staying . . . Was that because he didn't want to pressure her? It was early days between them, yet Rose knew in her heart that she'd found the person she wanted to be with. Some things could never be explained by science; some things defied all logic and practicality.

Finn opened the balcony window. It was high tide and a soft mist rose from the water. He came back in, rubbing his hands. 'There's a chill in the air. You can tell autumn's coming.'

'Yes.' For a moment, Rose expected him to mention what might come next — she was about to raise the subject herself but again, she was too cowardly. No conversation about the future could end well, no matter how many times she rehearsed it.

Over a hasty coffee and a pastry, they talked about anything else. 'What are you doing today?' he asked.

'The local TV news are coming to interview me and Oriel at the dig site.'

'Are you nervous?'

'A bit. Oriel's bouncing off the walls.'

He smiled.

'What about you?' she asked. 'Are you nervous about your client coming today? Or just relieved the boat's nearly finished?'

'Not nervous now we're almost there. She's only a couple of weeks off completion and then we can get her off our hands.'

'You sound sad about that?'

'It's mixed feelings.' He smiled. 'Always hard to see something you've given so much of your time and care leave. She's become part of our lives and it's hard to let her go.'

He looked at Rose. She had a lump in her throat. 'I'll probably feel that way about the dig, and the sword . . .'

He laughed. 'It's crazy to get so attached . . .'

'It is.'

Finn broke off to answer a call. 'It's Mum. The client wants to bring the visit forward by an hour. I'll have to run, I'm afraid.'

'Talk later,' she said, half in farewell, half questioning.

Finn kissed her on the lips, and his gaze lingered. 'I think that might be a good idea.'

He was gone so Rose cleared away hastily and sent a calming text to Oriel who she'd arranged to meet at the shop; the TV crew wanted to get a few shots there before they set off for the dig site.

The morning was chilly and Rose had arrived in sunlight in only a T-shirt. With a mile walk around the creek, she needed something warmer, so opened the drawer under the wardrobe where Finn kept some sweaters.

Finn had made the wardrobe himself and the drawer slid out with buttery smoothness. Rose smiled at the neatness of it; the unshowy but expert craftsmanship that summed up the man himself. The dark navy sweater she found in the drawer, neatly folded, was peak Finn too and made Rose smile as she took it out. He wouldn't mind her borrowing it.

'Oh.'

Her fingers found a piece of paper. A blue envelope.

Under any other circumstances she wouldn't have dreamed of opening letters addressed to anyone else

— except this one was addressed in her own handwriting to:

'My Donor'

43

Rose let out a cry of shock. She rocked back on her haunches and collapsed onto the floorboards, holding the envelope. She pulled out the sheet of blue writing paper. It trembled in her fingers.

Even though every word was already imprinted on her heart, she began to read it.

Dear donor,

I hope it's OK to write to you though I suppose it's a bit late for that now! :) I've written a hundred versions of this letter in my mind but finally I've put my thoughts on paper. No words could ever live up to what I want — need — to say, but I have to send one of them before I chicken out.

So this may not be the perfect letter but believe me, I've learned to be happy with way less than perfect. My life, my health, is enough and you have given me that precious gift — and the gift of knowing just what it means to be alive.

I may never get to meet you, but quite simply, you have given me my life back. You've given me a future and I can never ever thank you enough for that.

You may not realise, fully, what your gift means. I understand if that's overwhelming for you: it's not every day we get the chance to save a life. I'm trying not to go over the top here, but it's almost impossible.

Thanks to you, I got the chance to achieve my

dreams and my family had the chance to see me start the career I love. One day, I hope to start my own family and they will also have you to thank, as will my descendants.

I don't know why you volunteered to go on the donors' register but I'm so happy and thankful that you did.

I wish you everything you want in life and much more.

Best wishes,
Your Grateful Recipient
X

'Oh, God. Oh my God . . .'

Her cheeks were wet and a tear had splashed onto the edge of the letter. Cursing, she scrambled to her feet, and laid the letter on the bed while she found some tissues to wipe her eyes.

Hairdryer . . . she needed a hairdryer to dry the edge of the paper, but Finn wouldn't have such a thing. Of course he wouldn't!

Instead she laid the paper on a chair in the sunlight coming through the balcony window . . . But she didn't have time to wait for it to dry. She'd have to put it back, where she found it, this ticking time bomb she'd found hidden in Finn's house. Perhaps he wouldn't notice. Likely he never looked at the letter these days — maybe not from the moment he'd read it and sent his reply.

Carefully, Rose folded up the sweater in the way all of the others were folded. She inserted the envelope inside the folds and laid it in the drawer.

It was Finn who had saved her. No doubt . . . unless . . .

349

She found the wastepaper basket and turned it out onto the boards. Finn kept a tidy ship, but it still held a few odd scraps of paper, the champagne wire and cork from a few days before, an envelope from an electric bill. She found what she wanted, put the litter back in the bin and went home in her T-shirt, the autumn chill forgotten.

Oriel pulled open the shop door. 'Rose! You're late. I am wetting myself!'

'Sorry, I was at Finn's.'

'Yeah, I worked that one out. Oh my God, I can see the telly people in the car park. Arghh.'

Rose couldn't have cared less about the telly people or the sword. The knowledge that it was Finn who'd saved her life swept away anything else. All she wanted to do was fly upstairs and do one thing that would make her one hundred per cent certain, but it would have to wait.

★ ★ ★

Many hours later, Rose locked the door on the world. She'd answered dozens of questions, been interviewed by the regional TV, Radio Cornwall and correspondents from several national newspapers.

Her inbox and Twitter feed were swamped with requests from historical journals, bloggers and podcasters worldwide, all dying to know the story of the 'girls' who'd pulled the Roman sword from the lake. Rose could have directed them all to Oriel, but she was even more inundated. She had turned off her phone and was hiding at home, half-wishing she'd 'never found the bloody thing at all'.

Rose knew it wasn't true, but she didn't blame Oriel

for being overwhelmed. It had taken every ounce of concentration to get through the day, but now, no one was going to stop her from doing the one thing that really mattered to her.

She took the card from the drawer in her bedroom and laid it out on the bed next to the list she'd found in the wastepaper basket at Finn's.

The words were mundane enough. Boatbuilding stuff, biscuits, milk, Mum's dry-cleaning . . . She smiled briefly. The bottom line brought a lump to her throat.

Nice wine for R.

Like all lists, it was hastily written and yet, when laid side by side with the card, no one could deny that they were both written by the same person. The hand sloping backwards, which when the card had first arrived, Maddie had said meant the writer was reticent, cautious . . .

She could have compared the writing in her card with Finn's weeks ago . . . if she could have got hold of some . . . but it hadn't occurred to her. It was a step too far even for her.

Only the discovery of her own letter in Finn's drawer had changed everything.

She took out her card and read it again.

Glad you're feeling better.
Good luck in the future,
Wishing you a fair wind and calm seas.

It was *so* Finn. She'd always known it was. How could it be anyone else but Finn?

351

The genie was out of the bottle and she had no way of putting it back in.

'Everything OK?'

Rose glanced up at Finn over the dining table at Curlew Studio. He'd invited her for dinner and cooked sea bass that he'd caught himself, with potatoes and samphire. It was simple and delicious and Rose did her best to eat it but ended up pushing her food around her plate.

'It's great but I'm not very hungry. Sorry. It's been a hell of a day.'

'I bet. Sounds exciting but it would be my worst nightmare having to give all those interviews. I'm sure you were great, though.'

His sexy grin would have normally been the prelude to whisking him straight off to bed, but Rose's dread only grew. She had to tell him the truth, no matter what his reaction might be.

She placed her knife and fork side by side across her plate. 'You know this morning, you said we'd speak later?'

'We did.'

'Well, I think now's the time. There's something important that I need to tell you.'

He raised an eyebrow and she could tell he still wasn't expecting her to share anything too momentous. That made her even more jittery.

'Wow. Should I brace myself?'

'Actually, yes, it might be a good idea.'

A tiny frown appeared. 'Is it a bad thing?'

'No. Not *bad*.' She smiled fleetingly, wondering if he suspected she was going to say she was pregnant, though there'd hardly been time for that — and anyway, it wasn't likely, given the treatment she'd been through. 'Actually, just the opposite but it might come as a shock.'

'OK. Hit me.' He folded his arms. 'I'm braced.'

'I . . . Oh God, this is so difficult. It's weird and you have to hear me out before you react. You need to hear the context, the background . . . It's complicated . . .'

'Rose. Rose.' He took her hands and frowned. 'You're cold . . .'

'Probably because I'm nervous.'

'Don't be. Slow down a little, take a breath.'

'OK. Here goes. I think — I know — you're the man who saved my life.'

44

Finn leaned back in his seat and let out a breath. 'It's safe to say I wasn't expecting that.'

'Why would you? There was no easy way to break it to you but . . . you *did* join a bone marrow register a few years ago?'

'Yes . . . Yes, I did.'

'Then it *is* you! I knew it was either you or Joey. I just wasn't sure . . .' Rose hesitated. 'Until very recently.'

'I see . . .' Finn felt as if he was picking himself up from the ground after a massive explosion. He was still disorientated; his brain couldn't process what she'd told him. 'Is that why you're here?'

'It's why I came to Falford in the first place. It's not why I'm here with you — now. I've thought about my donor every day since I received the transplant, who he was and where he might be. I only knew it was a man and that he would have been under thirty when he gave the stem cells.' Rose seemed to be racing through the words, piling one shock on top of another. She'd obviously had years to prepare for this moment; he'd had seconds.

He'd fully expected her to say she was leaving Falford for Cambridge and that they were over. In fact, he'd been bracing himself for that unwelcome news for weeks. He'd harboured a faint hope she might say she was staying, or at least wanted to continue the relationship but now, he felt completely blindsided.

'I — is the donation the only thing that made you decide to come here?'

354

'Not only that. I was offered the study grant in Cornwall and I knew — had worked out it was one of you — it's a long story but I had a very good idea. I couldn't help myself. Your card had a painting of the estuary by Nash. You haven't been in this situation or you might have done the same. I wanted to — to thank you and tell you what you've done for me. How your gift of life has transformed me.' She smiled. 'But you know that because you replied to my letter.'

None of this made much sense to Finn but his whole world had been turned upside down. 'Yes . . . but I still can't believe it was you.'

'It sounds *so* embarrassing. Now that I know you. It's . . . a bit weird.'

'I don't think it's *weird*.' He didn't have a word to describe what had happened. 'Rose, did you want to get close to us — to me and Joey — because you were convinced that one of us saved your life?'

'Yes. I suppose so . . . initially, but that's absolutely *not* why I've stayed friends. Why I've enjoyed getting closer to you.' She seemed on the edge of tears. 'Much closer.'

'If you hadn't thought it was us, you wouldn't have come to Falford at all though.'

'No. Finn, I can see this is a massive shock, but I don't want it to make a difference to me and you *now*. I should have been honest from the start, but I liked you — I knew I wanted to be with you from before I knew it was you.' She groaned. 'I wish I'd told you who I was before I found my letter in your drawer.'

'You were *looking* for the letter?'

'No. I promise you! That was an accident. I needed a sweater this morning so I thought you wouldn't mind if I borrowed one and my letter was in the drawer.

355

Then I went home and to make sure I wasn't going mad, I checked the handwriting on the card you sent me against a . . .' She glanced away, chewing her bottom lip. 'Against a shopping list in the bin . . . It is your writing, isn't it?'

'Yes, it is.' Finn felt sick.

'I was so worried that you might not believe I genuinely like you because you're the donor, but it's not true. Falling for your rescuer. The man who saved your life. It's a cliché. Psychologically it's a terrible idea but I can't *help* it.' She let out a huge breath. 'Phew. I feel better for telling you even if it has been a shock. I know you'll have loads of questions. Ask me anything.'

The relief was clear in her eyes. He had a hundred questions but still could hardly frame his thoughts.

'I — I — so when did you first become ill?'

'Looking back, I was probably developing the condition towards the start of my master's degree but I assumed it was only tiredness and stress because I'd been off to do a year as a field archaeologist and learn my trade . . .' She laughed, probably because she was so relieved to have told him.

Finn wasn't relieved, he was stunned, overwhelmed that the woman he loved had sought him out so very deliberately.

'I'd worked in the UK and on a necropolis in Malta and for a year after my finals and then started the master's. Gradually I felt more and more run-down and exhausted. I wondered if I'd picked up a bug or glandular fever somewhere. Somehow I managed to get through the next few terms and got my degree, but I had a sense I was on borrowed time.'

He saw the fear in her eyes. It was the memory of

356

terrible times. He wanted to hold her but couldn't. 'Go on . . .'

'I got my master's and started my PhD, but I knew I'd have to stop. I started feeling light-headed. I thought it was stress, but when I fainted while I was out with my friends, I decided to go to the doctor. They ordered tests and eventually I was diagnosed with aplastic anaemia.'

She must have seen his puzzled look. He'd heard of people having anaemia but not of anyone dying because of it.

'It means your bone marrow doesn't make enough blood cells to move the oxygen around your body. Gradually the fatigue and headaches were so severe, I couldn't even concentrate on a newspaper let alone study and research.'

'Do you . . . have any idea why you got so sick in the first place?'

'It might have been caused by a viral infection that triggered an autoimmune reaction and caused my immune system to turn against my own cells.'

He was too stunned to reply. He couldn't believe what Rose had been through, or that she hadn't told him that she'd come to Falford to find her donor.

'I can see you're pretty overwhelmed. I hope this doesn't change things?' There was hope — and doubt — in her voice, but Finn was still too floored to know how to respond.

'No . . . I . . . I just need time to take it in.'

'I'm not sure how much the transplant charity will have told you about me? Probably not a lot. Did you even know a woman was receiving the stem cells?'

'No . . . they didn't say that.'

She nodded, smiling. 'I thought not. They did tell

357

me a man had donated, however. You have no idea what it felt like, that moment when I was told they'd found a match and the hope — it nearly finished me, wondering if the tests would show we could go ahead. I was in agony, wondering if you might change your mind, but I tried not to show it to my gran.'

Finn nodded, too full of emotion to answer coherently. He might embarrass himself. He'd never fully realised what going on the register meant. He'd tried not to imagine too much about the people waiting . . . hoping . . . He'd gone on that list because of the drive for donors in the village when a local lad had become sick and because, although Nash hadn't died from a blood disorder, Finn had wanted to try and prevent someone else from losing a loved one to cancer.

Sadly, no one had turned out to be a match and, horrifyingly, the boy had passed away. It had been a devastating blow to the family and community so Finn had pushed the fact he'd signed up to the back of his mind. Secretly, in his dark moments after the boy had died, he'd convinced himself that he'd begun to think joining it was a waste of time until the phone at the boatyard had rung one morning.

That call had resulted in Rose being in front of him now.

'I don't need to tell you about the transplant day. I expect it's imprinted on your memory but while you got to go home after a day giving your blood, I was in hospital for a month. I'd had chemo to destroy my old immune system and my hair fell out.'

'But it's so beautiful now . . .'

She smiled. 'Thanks, but I feel I've cheated. My old hair was darker and straighter. It's hard to believe because it grew back like this.' She held up a curl. 'Lighter and curlier. I'm too scared to have more than a trim now. I thought it might never come back.

'I was home for a couple of weeks, thinking everything was slowly getting to be more normal when I had an infection and had to go back in for another two weeks. That wasn't much fun but . . .' She heaved a sigh. 'After that setback, I really was on the road out of it all. Slowly I got stronger, finished my PhD part-time and got a job as a researcher and lecturer in the archaeology department. In fact, I've even stopped the immuno-suppressants. I just take the antibiotics now.'

'It must have been terrifying.'

'It was. One day I was enjoying being a student, the next I was a patient, and my life depended on a stranger and on chance. Having control over my very existence taken from me was the worst part. But there's another side to it. I knew the cure was out there. It wasn't as if I'd been told there was nothing that could be done, like so many people. I was incredibly lucky that this amazing treatment is available. And even luckier I found a match that was a good one. Better than that: the best kind. I was young and my body had accepted the bone marrow.'

Finn's throat dried, confronted with the possibility that Rose might have died — would have died without the transplant, and the possibility that she might get sick again. 'And you're fully recovered now?' he said, fearing the answer.

'Yes, as much as anyone ever can be. It's been four and a half years since the transplant and the risk of me relapsing is now pretty low. Of course, it could come back, but that's very unusual. They look after

359

me—' she rolled her eyes '—I have regular check-ups, blood tests and scans but so far I've been OK. I don't worry about it as much. Some days I don't even think about it and I just get on with living my life like a normal person.' She laughed. 'If you can call it normal to travel three hundred miles to find the man who saved your life and end up—' she smiled and looked awkward '—here with him.'

'I'm glad you're here.' It was all Finn could say.

'And this — you knowing it was you — does it change things between us?'

'No . . . of course not.' How could he say anything else, even though her revelation had knocked his world from its axis and the whole basis for their relationship had been turned on its head?

She reached for his hand and held it. He wanted to hold her and kiss her, but he didn't dare.

'Thank God I've got it off my chest. I knew you'd have loads of questions. Ask anything you want whenever, but first . . .'

She kissed him and Finn allowed himself to forget. Holding her was infinitely more precious, and after they'd made love, he lay with her in his arms, stroking her hair and wondering over and over at the miracle that she was here at all.

She propped herself up on one elbow and looked into his face. 'I've got some other good news too.'

'What's that?'

'I've — me and the local uni — have been awarded a grant from the Foundation for Antiquities to put the sword on display here in an exhibition. The sword stays in Falford and it will help Cornish Magick.'

He smiled because he couldn't help being caught up in the excitement and pleased for the community but it evaporated instantly.

In her happiness, Rose hadn't noticed and rushed on. 'And — and — the other piece of good news. I hope it's good news . . .' She faltered. 'I have to tell you. I've been offered a job!' Her eyes gleamed with joy, which made Finn's misery even greater. 'I've been offered a fellowship at Penryn.'

'Penryn?'

'Yes. If I take it, it would mean I would be based here in Cornwall after Christmas for the spring term and summer term next year. It's partly because of Oriel finding the sword, which helped to finally swing the grant application our way,' she said, her eyes shining. 'But that's not all. Professor Ziegler has offered me an academic position at Penryn. It's a promotion. I'd be head of department.'

'Congratulations. That's brilliant.'

'Isn't it? I can't believe it. Not only will I be researching and teaching students, but they also want me to do public engagement work, going out to schools as well as setting up an exhibition about the sword and other ancient sites. Professor Ziegler was at the regatta. I was dressed as a mermaid and I awarded her grandkids the sandcastle prize — I thought any credibility I had was blown out of the water, but she said that my passion for the community shone through, that I wasn't 'simply paying lip service' and so the university was happy to offer me the job.'

'That's wonderful . . .' Finn found he was grinning and yet dying inside.

'It means you won't be getting rid of me after all. If I take the job, of course.' She laughed, seemingly unaware of the turmoil in his heart. 'You know I don't believe in magic or any of that stuff and there's

361

a perfectly logical reason why I came here to Falford. It was my decision entirely but . . . us getting together and the way we feel about each other . . .' She laughed. 'Don't quote me on this but I can't help thinking it might be fate.'

45

Rose trudged home. A few hours ago, her decision had seemed so simple. She'd been so nervous of telling him and yet he'd acted calmly and accepted it.

Had she sensed a chill in his embrace or was she being silly? Had she delivered too much at once: the news he was the donor and she'd been offered the job? Should she have saved a piece of it and drip-fed it until he'd had time to come to terms with it?

Or not have told him at all?

She'd been so sure of her plans.

She would leave Falford for Cambridge in a week's time to meet her teaching commitments for the autumn term, while working on research into the sword and setting up the exhibition centre. She'd be back for Christmas — Christmas in Falford with Finn — the idea had made her so excited. Then, from late January she would base herself at Cornish Magick ready to start her new temporary job.

Finn said he was happy for her but . . . at no point had he actually *suggested* she should accept the permanent position and stay.

She didn't need his approval, of course, and he was probably being neutral because he didn't want to pressure her, yet Rose had left the studio with a sense of foreboding she couldn't quite put her finger on.

It hadn't gone away the following morning when she headed over to the boatyard to see how preparations were going for the cutter launch. She hoped that she'd get some clue as to Finn's mood, a reassurance that her fears were unfounded.

She turned up the collar of her coat and made her way around the creek, noticing leaves floating in the shallows and stuck in the mud. It wasn't much past eight and there was a distinct chilly edge to the air, and a light mist rising off the water.

The doors of the Morvah boatshed were wide open and the lights were on. She had a feeling that Finn had been working there since before it was light, ready for the big day. From yards away the cutter consumed the space, casting deep shadows on the floor.

She walked in cautiously and announced her presence with a 'Morning!'

The cutter loomed above her, magnificent and dominating.

'Wow. Just wow,' she breathed. 'I can't believe the day has come. It looks incredible. You should be proud of it.'

Finn wiped his hands on a rag and joined her by the stern. 'Thank you. Like I said, in one way we'll be sad to see her go but sometimes you have to.' There was a poignancy in his voice that made her shiver inwardly.

Was he giving her a veiled hint that he wasn't as happy for her to stay as she'd hoped?

It was clear they needed to have another conversation, but this wasn't the moment. The sound of approaching voices caused them both to turn. Joey, Dorinda and the man who Rose assumed was the client, walked from the sunlight into the boatshed.

'We can talk later. Your client is here.'

He nodded. 'Rose . . .'

'Yes?'

'You'll be here for the launch itself this afternoon?'

His plea lifted her spirits. Perhaps all wasn't lost yet.

364

'I said I would after I've been to my meeting at the university. Later. Enjoy this day — you've all earned it. I'll be back.'

★ ★ ★

It was mid-afternoon when she returned to the flat after her meeting. She changed out of her skirt and top into old jeans and a sweatshirt more suitable for hanging around a dusty boatshed.

She arrived to find the boatshed — the whole yard in fact — a hive of activity. A wheeled trailer was parked at the entrance to the shed and, judging by the shouts and people milling around, the cutter was ready to be loaded onto it before it was transferred to the water.

She wandered over, snapping some photos of the boat, even before she reached the yard. There had to be at least a dozen people involved in the launch, with a dozen more onlookers, including Bo. There was an air of tension, and a few swearwords.

She stopped, taking in the scene. She should have been excited at the prospect of now being a part of the life of the yard, of the community, invited to witness the Morvahs' big moment — such a contrast to a few months previously when she'd been a stranger . . . an intruder.

Yet, even now, Rose had the same feeling: that she was on the outside looking in on a world that she would never be fully part of. No matter how much she tried to deny it, that feeling of otherness had originated from the moment she'd told Finn he was her donor. Instead of bringing her closer to him, she'd driven him further away.

'Hi there!' Bo met her. 'Big moment, eh?'

'Yes. Huge. It looks a tricky manoeuvre,' Rose said, hiding her worries.

'It is. Everyone will be glad when she's finally on the water. She'll be off the Morvahs' hands then and they'll be mightily relieved.'

'Absolutely. I know. I'm almost as excited as Finn is about their new project. I can't wait to see them working on her in the shed.'

'Oh?' Bo sounded very surprised. 'You changed your mind then?'

'Changed it?' Rose was confused. 'What makes you say that?'

'Only that Finn said he wasn't sure you'd decided to stay.' Bo smiled. 'I'm really happy. We'd have missed you.'

'Yes, at least until next year. We got a grant to tour the sword and our other finds around the county.' Rose wondered exactly how much Bo knew about her grant and the job offer. 'When did you speak to Finn?' she asked.

Bo frowned. 'We were chatting earlier and he said you hadn't decided whether to stay yet . . . that he wasn't sure of your plans?'

'Oh?' Unease stirred in Rose's mind, like the muddy bottom of the pool, swirling up in a dark cloud. Rose had made it clear to Finn that she wanted to come back to Falford — so why had he been cagey about it to Bo? Was he simply trying to keep their private life private or was her instinct that he was backing off from the idea, true?

She hid her worries with a smile. 'I'm definitely coming back. I couldn't keep away from Falford.'

'Sorry, I must have got the wrong end of the stick.' Bo looked embarrassed. 'I didn't realise it was all settled, but it was only a quick conversation and I was in a rush serving breakfast at the time. I'm sure Finn's really pleased you're staying on,' Bo added hurriedly. 'Oh look! They're ready to move the boat! Shall we get a bit closer?'

Rose tried to focus on the hustle and bustle of the launch. There was a lot of to-ing and fro-ing with the trailer vehicle as various ways of getting it into the exact position were tried out. Reversing beeps, engines running, shouts and arm waving. She took more photos. The trailer drove out again and Finn went inside.

Dorinda was outside, standing by the client, a tall man in a panama hat.

'Will they ever get there?' Bo asked her, shaking her head.

Rose's reply was swallowed up by a huge bang and a flash of flame that lit up the door of the boathouse.

46

'Oh my God! What the hell was that?'

Bo's shout reached Rose as she was already starting to run towards the boathouse. Flames were visible inside, engulfing the rear of the shed. Other people were running too and there were yells and the sound of a fire alarm going off.

'Where's Finn? I saw him go inside!'

'I don't know . . .' Dorinda stammered back, rooted to the spot.

Rose dashed towards the door of the boathouse, where scarlet flames were visible deep inside.

'Rose! No!'

An arm reached for her. She brushed it off. She knew it was Joey's, but his warning cry was just a blur of sound. All she could think of was the last thing she'd seen before the explosion: Finn silhouetted in the boatshed doorway.

She managed to get a couple of steps inside, shielding her face with her arm. The far end of the space was ablaze and tongues of fire licked at the stern of the cutter. Smoke had already filled half the shed, making her gag. There had been cans of paint and varnish and God knows what in there. It could go up again at any moment.

Where was Finn?

What if he was lying behind the boat, injured, unable to escape the smoke and flames? The thought was too horrific to contemplate but drove her on. Shielding her face with her hand, she forced herself to step deeper inside, towards the blaze and choking clouds.

The heat was staggering, and she could barely see the other end of the workshop, let alone Finn. She tried to call his name but only swallowed smoke.

The fire already had seized a hold of one end of the cutter. It was as if Rose were standing at the door of a furnace.

'F-finn!' she spluttered.

There was no answer just the roar and crackle of fire, the pop and hiss of wood consumed by flames. Rose shrank down, hunched and beaten back by the heat. She thought she could feel the hairs on her bare arms singeing but she couldn't leave Finn, not hurt and alone, helpless in that inferno.

'Rose!'

Arms encircled her.

'No!' she shouted, coughed and tried to push the person away. He was stopping her from getting to Finn but then she was dragged backwards.

'It's me!' He pulled her by the arm and towards the door. 'Come away now!'

Her first thought was relief, so great that her legs buckled. 'We have to move further back. The whole place could go up.'

A loud bang shook the air. Rose staggered, fell to the floor just outside the entrance to the boatshed. Smoke billowed up from the shed. She pushed herself onto her feet, but Finn seized her hand and hurried her away from the smoke and into fresher air, both of them coughing and gasping for breath.

'Your b-boat!' she said, tears streaming down her face. 'All that w-work. It means everything to you! We have to try and save it.'

Finn reached for her. 'It doesn't matter.'

'But I want to give you back what you gave me. That boat, the business, it's your life.'

'Rose, I didn't give anything to you! I didn't save you.'

'What?'

'It was Joey. Joey is your donor. And even if it had been me, nothing on the earth means anything to me without you.' Finn looked around. 'Where is he? I can't see him.'

47

Finn let Rose go. Her heart pounded. The bombshell Finn had dropped was eclipsed by the fact that Joey was nowhere to be seen.

She wiped tears from her eyes and then, a few yards away, saw Dorinda with Joey clamped to her tightly. They spotted Finn and broke apart and Finn and Rose ran over to them.

Finn coughed while Rose hauled in some breaths.

'What were you thinking of?' Dorinda bawled at them. 'You bloody lunatics.'

'Rose thought I was inside and then she wanted to save the cutter,' Finn said.

'Screw the cutter. You could both have been killed.'

'I'm sorry.'

'Thank you for going after Finn, but as for the boat. It's only a lump of wood.' Even so, Dorinda looked at the burning boatshed and covered her face with her hands.

Finn patted her back then said, 'I must make sure no one tries to get back inside and double-check everyone's accounted for.'

Turning to Rose, he murmured, 'Swear to me you'll never try anything like that again.'

'I won't.' A shiver racked her despite the heat, yet she'd have done anything to help Finn. His words came back to her — it was Joey. Had she heard him right or lost his meaning in the literal heat of the moment?

Finn went to speak, but they were engulfed by

people swarming around them from the boatyard with water and hoses. There were other boat owners, the yard manager, people from the yacht club and even staff from the Ferryman in aprons and chef's whites. .

'You'll have to move much further back, guys. *Now.*'

One of the local volunteer firefighters from the village herded them all onto the slipway. Sirens wailed, heralding the arrival of a fire engine and a few minutes later an ambulance stopped near Rose, its blue light flashing.

Naomi jumped out and made straight for Rose. 'Rose! What happened? Are you injured? Is anyone else hurt?'

'No. I'm fine. I don't think anyone's inside, thank God. Finn will tell you.'

'You should get checked over if you inhaled any smoke.'

Rose nodded, having no intention of doing such a thing.

Finn was talking to the fire chief. Joey had his arm around one of the apprentices who'd arrived to find his place of work going up in smoke.

'You go,' Rose said to Naomi. 'Someone else might need you more.'

Amid the chaos of locals and the emergency services hurrying back and forth, hoses being unreeled and another fire engine arriving, Rose saw Dorinda sitting on a mooring post, her head in her hands. Her shoulders shook and she heaved in sobs. Rose crouched down and put her arm around her. She half-expected Dorinda to shrink away but she let Rose soothe her.

'I thought I'd lost everything. When you and Finn went into the shed and I couldn't see Joey, it was the worst moment of my life. I don't care about the boat or the business. I'd have given it all up for everyone to be safe.'

'I know how you feel.' Rose stared at the scene. The flames had diminished though smoke still billowed from the shed and rose high into the blue sky above the estuary. She shuddered. 'But everyone's OK,' she said gently.

One of the fire crew came up. 'Mrs Morvah? We need to find out exactly what substances were kept in the boatshed.'

Dorinda got to her feet, shaking off her fears. 'I can tell you that. It's my business. I'm responsible.'

Rose admired her more than ever. She was a hell of a woman.

She moved away from the scene while Dorinda, Finn and Joey spoke to the fire crew.

She saw Bo standing by the café. 'I'd like to help,' she said.

'This lot will need feeding and watering soon enough,' Bo said. 'I've asked if we can keep the café open, and the fire officer said they'll let me know.'

An hour later, the fire officer gave Bo and Rose the all-clear to open the café. Rose's only experience of catering was helping out with a stint on a student bar at a college ball but she was eager to help. Kev arrived and soon, they were handing out water, tea and coffee to the emergency services as they damped down the fire and helped to salvage what they could. Lauren had turned up and gone straight to support Joey. Rose was too busy to speak to Finn, and glad to be busy.

She turned Finn's words over and over. Even in the heat and smoke, the danger, she knew she hadn't misheard.

He wasn't her donor. Joey was.

The questions licked at her like flames, tormenting her. Why had Finn lied and let her think it was him? Why did he have her letter and send her the card? No matter how badly she wanted answers, they'd have to wait until this immediate crisis was over.

Joey came up to the café. His face was blackened by soot, his hair grey with ash. In the distance, Finn was still part of a group helping to remove wood from the front of the shed to a safer distance.

'I've come to get some drinks,' he said.

Rose handed him a bottle of water. 'I'll give you a pack of bottles for everyone,' she said. He'd no idea that she knew. She still hadn't accepted it herself.

'How bad is it?' she asked.

'Bad enough. There's extensive damage to the rear of the sheds. We'll have to rebuild some of it. Looks like an electrical fault with the fridge in the staff room. Can you believe it? All that wood, all that varnish and paint and a bloody fridge caused it. The cutter's got off lightly.'

'So, it can be saved?'

'It'll take a while and we don't have a functioning shed at the moment but yes. Thank God Finn was religious about having top-notch insurance. Mum used to complain we were paying over the odds for cover we'd never need, but Finn insisted. Cautious as ever.' Joey grinned, his smile bright against his soot-stained skin.

'What a relief. It's a terrible thing to happen, but I'm so pleased the cutter can be saved.'

'Finn's talking to the owner now,' Joey said, his gaze travelling to Finn in animated conversation with the panama-hatted man.

Dorinda was nearby and Rose could see she was sobbing. Poor woman, no matter how strong she was, seeing your life's work almost destroyed must be devastating. The adrenaline had probably gone and this was the aftermath.

'Look after your mum,' Rose said to Joey.

'I will. Thank you for trying to save Finn and the boat. It was very brave.' He shook his head and smiled. 'Even if it was the stupidest idea you've ever had.'

Rose just laughed; she tended to agree now that everyone was safe.

Evening was falling by the time the last of the fire engines left. The house itself was mercifully untouched. Rose helped Bo clear up and shut the café kiosk. She'd had no time to think about what Finn had told her when he came over. He looked totally spent, grey with exhaustion and like Joey, covered in ash and soot.

'Don't come too close,' he said gruffly. 'I'm filthy.'

On any other occasion, Rose would have been tempted to a smart reply to this.

'You need to get some rest and a proper meal.'

'I've had enough tea and coffee to fill me up. Thanks for helping, by the way. Everyone appreciated it.'

'It was the least I could do and Bo organised it all.'

He nodded. 'I need a shower.'

'That's true. Joey told me the boat can be saved.'

'Yes. I suppose we should count our blessings.'

'He said you'd paid over the odds for decent insurance and that would help.'

'Did he?' Finn gave a bitter laugh. 'I've done something right, then.' He looked anguished. 'Rose, I want to tell you why I lied.' He glanced at his dirty hands, encrusted with black soot. 'Can you come over after

375

I've had a shower? If you still can bear to be in my company.'

Rose needed a shower too; she was dirty and stank of smoke. Her jeans and top were probably beyond saving. When she saw herself in the mirror, she was shocked at the dishevelled, exhausted face that stared back at her, reminding her of the way she had often looked during her illness.

Soap and water helped to wash away the smoke and grime, but nothing could chase away the confusion and shock that Finn had lied about being her donor. Birds called as they returned to their roosts and the stink of charred wood and chemicals hung in the air. The sun had set by the time she reached Curlew, passing the boatshed, now dark with a tarpaulin covering the side. The cutter was on a trailer outside, also shrouded in tarpaulin.

To the Morvahs, it must feel as if a living breathing thing they'd nurtured had been wounded, almost fatally.

Finn was waiting for her in the doorway to the studio. 'Rose.'

He was clean, but his hair was still damp. He didn't try to kiss her, yet his scent filled her senses: the sharp tang of citrus. She walked into the room and he gestured to her to sit down. A glass, a bottle of whisky and a jug of water were on the coffee table.

'Join me?' he said.

'A small one.'

He poured her a measure, adding water, and topped up his own, leaving it neat. Cradling the glass in both hands, he seemed to look for answers in the amber liquid. 'I must be getting old, drinking whisky. This was Nash's,' he said. 'He was a bit of a connoisseur

376

and gave it to me before he died. He said I should drink it now and not save it for special occasions in case they never came. I only opened it tonight.'

Rose sipped it. 'It's very smooth, but I know nothing about whisky.'

'I think it's a rare year or something.' He put the glass down. 'He shouldn't have wasted it on me. I've fucked up again, haven't I?'

'You?'

'I lied about me being your donor. I could have told you straightaway that it was Joey but I didn't.'

'Was it really a lie?' Rose said carefully. 'Did you want it to be true?'

'You have no idea . . .' He leaned forward. '*Of course* I wanted it to be true. I'd have given almost anything to be the one.'

'Why didn't you trust me and tell the truth?'

'I wanted to; I should have and I was on the verge of telling you many times but you said it was fate, that we were destined to be together.'

'I didn't mean it.'

'No, but I was too scared to gamble that if you knew it wasn't me, it might change your feelings.'

'Finn, how could you have thought that? Give me more credit.'

'It was stupid. I can see that now . . . Rose, this is all my fault, but I also thought . . . that *you* wanted it to be me.'

Rose caught her breath. Momentarily, she was shocked. Indignant that he'd even tried to pass the responsibility to her, but then her anger was punctured. It was true. She had bought into that fantasy: that she'd come here, found her saviour and fallen in love with him.

'It doesn't matter. You tried, that's all I care about. In fact, if it hadn't been either of you — if you'd never even gone on that register — it wouldn't make the slightest difference to how I feel about you.'

'Do you mean that?'

'Of course I do.' She got up and sat on the sofa next to him. He pulled her into his arms and she kissed him. 'I was excited, high I suppose, when I found the letter, and I wanted it to be you ... but I still don't understand why you had my letter or why you wrote the card. It is your writing, isn't it?'

'I sent the card and kept the letter because Joey couldn't handle the whole donation business. Oh, he didn't hesitate to volunteer for the register and he was over the moon when he was a match for you — for the unknown recipient.' Finn smiled. 'I was envious of him, even then.'

'Yet he didn't want to reply?'

'He said he was still too upset by his break-up with Lauren to deal with any more 'emotional pressure'. I'm sorry, Rose.'

'No. Don't be. I was warned by the transplant coordinators that some donors don't want any thanks, or even to know what happened to their recipient. It doesn't always go as well as it has for me ...' She paused. 'That's tough for anyone to handle.'

'Not as tough as for you.' Finn held her. 'I don't even want to think of the alternative.'

They kissed again then Rose said, 'So why did you write back to me?'

'I didn't think it was right to ignore you. It seemed callous even though I understood Joey's feelings. He was so cut up after the split with Lauren. I tried to change his mind, which was probably wrong of me,

378

but if I hadn't, you wouldn't be here so I'm glad I did.'

Rose imagined the conversation. She understood and didn't blame Joey but also thanked every lucky star that Finn had written anyway.

'He said he was happy — privileged — to help this person — you — but he didn't want anything else to do with it.'

'I can understand that.'

'Even so, I didn't think it was enough after what you might have gone through and after you'd bothered to write to him. I told him you deserved a reply and it wouldn't hurt him so he said: "If you're that bothered, you send something, but don't mention me."'

Rose felt tears choking her. She didn't blame Joey for not wanting to answer but it was so typical of Finn to care enough.

'So I sent the card,' he said.

'Did you realise it gave a clue to where you lived?'

'No . . . I dunno. I just grabbed it and wrote a quick message before I could change my mind. I'm no wordsmith, but I wanted you to know — whoever you were — that we wished you well.'

'You saved me as much as Joey.'

'How?'

'You were willing to do it. You wanted to help and you replied to my letter. It meant so much to me, especially when I'd just lost my gran. She was the one who'd encouraged me to find the donor and thank him so I really needed the connection to the person — the people — who'd helped me. Everyone who went on the register saved my life. Every person everywhere who signs up to donate, or supports someone else to do it. You all helped me be here now.'

Rose bit back tears. Finn held her and she held him. She'd found him. She was at peace, no matter what the future held.

48

Two days later, Oriel was waiting for Rose when she went downstairs to the shop. They'd already gone over every detail of the fire half a dozen times, and it was still the talk of the village. This morning Oriel was jigging around the moment she saw Rose.

'You are not going to believe what's happened!'

'I might after the past couple of weeks.'

'It's about Nige,' Oriel declared.

'Has he been beamed up by the same aliens who built the Pyramids?'

Oriel sniggered. 'No. It's better than that. It's miraculous. Auntie Lynne has kicked him out!'

'What? That's fantastic!'

Oriel hugged her. 'I know.'

'Why? What's he done now?'

'Well, I went round to see her because she's been so down, despite me finding the sword and all the people coming to the shop. She was crying and I felt so sorry for her because she's really been like a mum to me. I hugged her and then she told me that Nigel had used some of her savings to try and pay his friend back for the boat they blew up.'

'Oh, your poor auntie. Was it a lot of money?'

'A couple of grand. She'd let him have the password to one of her savings accounts, but his mate's wife found out and made him pay it all back. She's changed all her passwords, got a locksmith in and thrown him out. She said she was sorry she'd let him take over both our lives.'

'I have to say that's great news, even though I feel sorry for your auntie.'

'I don't like to see her upset but it's the best thing that could have happened. She told me 'the scales had fallen from her eyes' whatever the hell that means. Now she's got rid of him, all of her friends from the cricket club catering committee have said they couldn't stand him. I'm going round to see her again later.'

'Give her a hug from me,' Rose said, hating the idea of Lynne being upset but hugely relieved.

After listening to more about the final comeuppance of Nigel, Rose left, leaving Oriel to serve a bunch of people who all wanted to know about the Roman sword.

She walked around the estuary, which was mirror-still and serene. The sounds of hammering and planing drifted over the water. Temporary repairs had been carried out to the rear of the shed, but Finn had told her that Morvah Marine was going to be rebuilt once the cutter had been finished. The boat was back inside and he and Joey were working on it all the hours to get it ready for launching again, hopefully by early October.

Rose passed Bo's and saw Joey outside, laughing while he waited for his order. He collected a foil-wrapped parcel and a coffee and turned away.

Rose jogged after him, her heart pounding.

'Joey!'

He smiled and joined her. 'Rose. I'm glad I saw you. Finn says you have to go back to Cambridge?'

'Yes. For now, but it's only for this term. I'll be back for Christmas in Falford and I can start my new project with Penryn Uni in the new year.'

'I'm really pleased. We'll miss you.' He rolled his eyes. 'Finn will be climbing the walls until you come back.'

'I'm sure he'll cope.'

'Trust me, he'll be like a bear with a sore head.'

She laughed. 'How about you? How are you doing?'

He rested the food and coffee on a mooring post. 'You mean without Lauren? I'll have to manage. She's gone back to her job. I couldn't take her away from what she loves so we're going to find a way of making things work long-distance.' He sighed. 'Or one of us will have to move. Probably me. Maybe it's time I fled the nest.'

Rose smiled. 'Maybe.'

'I've already started looking at yards I could join that are closer to Lauren. She's also checking out some senior positions down here. That's life but the most important thing is that we want to be with each other. We'll work it out.'

Rose believed they would.

'And I'm sorry if we got off to a bad start.'

She laughed. 'I wouldn't call it that.'

He raised an eyebrow. 'No?'

'No. I'm glad we got to know each other. I hope we'll always stay friends.'

'The way things are going, you'll be part of the family. I've never seen Finn smitten before.'

She laughed and her face warmed. 'I doubt it.'

'Oh, he is — and no one is happier than me to see him happy. The day you breezed in here was a good one, Rose.'

She nodded, almost too full of emotion to reply.

'I have to get back to work and I guess you want to see Finn.'

'Yes, I do.'

'Then I'll say goodbye for now.' He kissed her cheek. 'Thanks for being a friend to us all, and saving Finn's miserable life.'

Her stomach fluttered. She and Finn had agreed that it was better if Joey didn't know the truth about her but it was still very tempting. 'Thank you,' she said, teetering on the very edge of blurting it out — of shouting it to the world: 'Do you have *any* idea of what you've done?'

She hugged him, trying not to hold him too tightly. 'Thank you, Joey. Thank you so much.'

He laughed, but there was pleasure in his eyes and a little embarrassment. 'God knows, why. Most people think I've been a pain in the arse.' He pecked her cheek and picked up his food. 'See ya, then.'

'Fair winds,' Rose said quietly but he was already walking away, oblivious to the fact that without him, she would only be a memory to her family and friends, and nothing at all to him, to Finn or anyone who'd never known her.

It was a lot to deal with. Too much for some.

She let him go, unmarred by the burden of knowing he'd saved her life, and carried on to Curlew where Finn was waiting for her.

Epilogue

Valentine's Day, the following year

'You look gorgeous.'

Finn's comment made Rose glow inwardly, but also provoked a wry smile. A 'normal' night out at the Ferryman was always a casual affair, with people arriving in anything from damp board shorts to salty oilskins. However, this was not a normal night out and such a celebration deserved a special effort.

Her mum had treated her to the dress, which Rose had chosen for formal dinners at Cambridge but had never yet worn. It was deep blue velvet with three-quarter sleeves. It felt fitting to give it a debut here in Cornwall as a fresh spring dawned.

Using the new mirror in the bedroom, she fixed some gold earrings in her ears. They were shaped like tiny scallop shells and had been a gift from Finn at Christmas. Rose opened the drawer under the wardrobe and fished out a purple cashmere scarf from Maddie, 'to keep out the cold Cornish wind'.

Truth be told, it was very mild out compared to the clear and biting cold of Cambridge. Spring had been around the corner in the city when she'd visited her old university the previous weekend, but it had already taken up residence in Cornwall. Camellias and magnolias were bursting out in the gardens, and some of the flower farmers' fields were packed with yellow daffodils nodding in the breeze.

Finn held out her new teddy coat — a present to herself — and put it on. She still thought it was a miracle he'd managed to find room for her clothes in the studio. On the other hand, his own hadn't taken up a lot of space. Most of Rose's other possessions were packed away and stored in the cottage in Cambridge.

Rose took the helm of the RIB Finn kept under the boathouse and they motored up the creek to the pub, where music was playing and lights glittered in the dark surface of the water. People were out on the terraces, a few in shirt sleeves, laughing and enjoying a drink.

Laughter greeted them the moment they walked into the bar, where a *Congratulations* banner had been hung from the rafters. A table was already piled high with gifts and within a few moments they were chattering away, while more guests arrived behind them.

It seemed as if everyone from Falford was there, including Bo and her dance club friends and half the cricket club.

'Joey and Lauren here yet?' Rose asked Bo, while Finn fetched some drinks.

'No sign yet, but you know what he's like, always late. Lauren will make sure he turns up.'

'I heard they were busy moving into the new flat,' Rose said. 'I'm glad she decided to move here.'

Lauren had been promoted and had taken up a post at Treliske Hospital. It was a fair journey every day but they both seemed blissfully happy.

'Dorinda will miss them, even though they're only half an hour away,' Bo said. 'But they had to find somewhere between Truro and here.'

'She will, but I think it will be good for them all to have their own space.'

'Besides, Kev seems to be filling the gap quite well,' Rose said. Bo's gaze rested on Dorinda, chatting to

Kev by the fire. He rested his hand in the small of her back and Dorinda gave him a peck on the cheek.

'Yes.'

Rose and Bo had become closer since she'd moved to Falford. They chatted a while longer, but then Bo moved away to talk to a man with impressive rock 'n' roll style sideburns. Rose recognised him from the cricket match and thought he'd been playing for the Lizards. She didn't know much about him, but it wasn't long before he had his arm around her, so they were definitely more than friends. Mmm. Now that was something she looked forward to hearing about over the next few weeks.

A ripple went around the room and Joey and Lauren walked in.

'Late as usual,' someone shouted.

'Blame Lauren,' Joey said good-naturedly. 'She was driving.'

'Blame Joey. He couldn't find his new shirt in all the moving chaos. He's *such* a peacock. Vain.' Lauren shook her head and they moved away to admire the presents table.

Finn returned to Rose's side.

'Talking of which, I wonder where they are?' Finn checked his watch.

'I hope nothing's happened,' Rose said.

'I doubt it . . . as long as they haven't changed their minds after all this planning,' Finn said.

'Shh! I've had the nod that they're on their way!' the landlord called, holding up his phone. People fiddled with party poppers and nudged each other, some trying not to giggle with excitement. A minute later, a couple walked in.

'Surprise!' The poppers exploded and the pub rang

to whoops and whistles.

'What? What's going on?' Oriel and Naomi froze halfway into the bar.

Oriel's jaw almost dropped onto the flagstones.

'It's an engagement party for you.' Rose hugged her. 'Well done, Naomi!'

'What do you mean?' Oriel shot a glance at Naomi, who was grinning fit to burst. 'You knew about this?'

'I might have had an inkling. Someone had to get you here safely but I didn't organise it. Bo and Rose planned it all.'

Oriel let out a shriek. 'I hope you won't be keeping secrets from me when we're married.'

Naomi kissed her. 'What secrets could I possibly have?'

'I had no idea! I thought we were coming for a romantic meal out. I must admit I thought the Ferryman looked packed but it is Valentine's night.'

Someone handed the happy couple glasses of fizz. Oriel was buzzing with excitement. She held up her left hand and a blue opal ring sparkled on her finger. 'You *like*?'

'Oh my God. I love it! When did you get that?'

Naomi laughed and showed her own finger. 'I got one too. We went to Falmouth to choose them last week.'

'We decided to wear them for the first time tonight.' Oriel glanced around her. 'Is Auntie Lynne here?'

'I think she's in the kitchen,' Rose said. 'She's been supervising the catering for the landlord.'

'I wouldn't have missed it for the world.' Lynne tapped her on the shoulder and hugged her, before hugging Naomi too. 'Who do you think made the cake?'

'What cake?' Oriel's eyes widened.

Right on cue, to the sound of 'Happy' by Pharrell, Kev emerged from the bar with a large iced cake. It was covered in blue royal icing and on top had a woman's arm emerging from a lake in the middle with a knight in armour at the edge.

'It's my sword!' Oriel cried in delight.

'With Naomi as the knight,' Lynne said. 'Most unusual engagement cake I've ever made but Rose said you'd love it.'

Oriel's eyes filled with tears. 'It's fantastic.'

'Thanks, Auntie Lynne,' Naomi said.

Lynne beamed. 'I quite like gaining an extra niece,' she said. 'And I'm so proud of you, Oriel, for working so hard to make Cornish Magick a success.'

'We're fully booked with tours for the spring already!' Oriel said. 'And I've been invited to do a folklore spot on Radio Cornwall!'

'Oh, you'll be famous next,' said Lynne, hugging her tighter.

Rose had a lump in her throat. She was proud of Oriel too, for facing up to her fears, getting the tours going and never giving up. Even without the sword discovery, she suspected Oriel would have succeeded, but that had added the extra bit of magic to take it to a new level.

The music was turned up and the chatter grew in volume, as champagne corks popped.

As the party continued, Dorinda found Rose for a chat.

'It's a happy night, isn't it? Who'd have thought it after that dark day at the boatyard?'

'I know . . .'

'It's an ill wind,' she said, sliding a glance at Kev

who was chatting to Joey and Lauren. 'Kev's been a rock to me, since the fire. He was a good friend before but after that day, we've grown into something much more.'

'I'm really happy for you.'

'I'm glad to welcome you to the family. You were brave going in for Finn. I'll never forget that.'

Rose was so touched; she could barely speak so she just smiled and accepted a hug from Dorinda, something she wouldn't have believed possible many months ago.

'You're good for Finn. You've brought him back to life.'

'And he's done the same for me. You all have,' Rose said, aware that Dorinda had no idea of the full import of her words.

Finn joined them. 'Are you talking about me? I hope not.'

Rose and Dorinda exchanged a glance and they both burst out laughing.

★　★　★

It was past midnight and bitterly cold when they tied up at the studio jetty and finally shut the door on the world. Yet it seemed too momentous a night to go to bed, and Rose had one more thing to get off her chest. She took Finn onto the balcony and they gazed at the stars twinkling in the Cornish sky and the lights shimmering in the estuary. Rose thought of her gran, and thanked her silently for bringing her to Falford to find the man who'd given her a second chance at life — and the one she wanted to spend the rest of it with.

'I have something to tell you. It'll come as a surprise.

A shock. You could say it's magical. Remember I told you that I might not be able to have any children?'

Finn slid his arm around her. 'And I said I don't mind. I'll support you; whatever life throws at us.'

'I love you for that.' Rose filled up. 'But, Finn, I saw my consultant in Cambridge. Things have changed in the past few months. She says I might be able to get pregnant after all with some help.'

His eyes lit up in delight. 'That's wonderful news, but does it mean we'll have to be careful from now on? Until you're ready? I know I am, but it has to be a joint decision.'

'The thing is . . .' Rose said, bracing herself, but feeling as if she was about to take off with happiness. 'It's my experience that you shouldn't wait until you're ready, if you really want something badly enough. You should go after it with all your heart because the perfect time may never come.'

Finn kissed her. 'In that case,' he said, leading her back into the warmth. 'I don't think we should waste another minute.'

Acknowledgements

First of all, I want to say that this book required a lot of research, which was fascinating, fun and time-consuming in the best way — exactly the distraction I needed in these strange, unsettling times.

While I love the *idea* of being out on the open ocean, boats and me don't mix. Having been sick on a cross channel ferry and on a seal snorkelling trip, I'd decided my sailing days were over . . . or so I thought . . .

However, it became clear I couldn't possibly write this book without actually going on a sailing yacht, so I decided, with much trepidation, to book a day trip with Bowman Yacht Charters around Falmouth bay and the Helford estuary.

Not only did I not feel the slightest bit seasick, I loved it and even took the helm for a short while. The stories I heard and the information I gleaned on my trip were invaluable, so I want to thank our skipper Adam and Cyprian from Bowman for their patience, insight and advice. A special thanks goes to Andy Aston who crewed the boat and has answered my many questions since our sail. I also want to thank Ben Harris, who builds beautiful traditional wooden boats at Gweek in Cornwall, and took the time to show me around his workshop and answer my questions.

On the archaeology side, a big thanks goes to Dave Hamilton, whose excellent and fun guide, *Wild Ruins BC*, inspired my interest in ancient sites. You can find him @DaveWildish on Twitter.